THE PREDATOR & THE PREY

THE PREDATOR AND THE PREY

Ashley Godschild

FHK

This book is a work of fiction. Names, characters, businesses, organizations, places, events and incidents either are the product of the author's imagination or are used fictitiously. Any resemblance to actual persons, living or dead, events, or locales is entirely coincidental.

The Predator and The Prey

First Edition: August 2025

The text of this book is set in 11-point FreeSerif. The chapters are 20-point and their numbers are 72-point Casanova Serif Display. The chapter titles are 26-point Chiller.

Paperback ISBN: 978-1-0689345-4-4
E-Book ISBN: 978-1-0689345-5-1

Cover design by Jessica Cvilo
Editing by Eden Editorial

10 9 8 7 6 5 4 3 2 1

TW

Trichotillomania (self-harm), suicidal ideation, mention of suicide, suicide recounted, mention of rape, rape recounted (graphic, on page, *marks chapter, **marks beginning and end of section), mention of abortion, mention of forced sterilization, murder, racism (between Otherworlders, not based off skin colour), alcoholism, vomit

Recap

Our FMC, Delilah Christos, was hunting Otherworlders for pleasure (and let's be honest a little bit of revenge) when she discovered a serial killer loose in the town her little sister—Athena—called home. She returned to Witchhill, the place she fled after her parent's death, to find her sister in more danger than she thought, because Athena was dating a werewolf.

Not just any werewolf either: Ibrahim Salama was the Gamma and a cousin to Killian Garity, an Alpha who displayed a special interest in Delilah. They formed an unlikely alliance when a member of the Imperium (the governing body of hunters) arrived in Witchhill intent on finding the killer before them.

This member of the Imperium, Nattalius Kartal, was Delilah's ex-boyfriend and though he abandoned her to die before they broke up, she suspected his appearance was more than a coincidence. Nattalius, a descendant of the Hunter Queen, had been obsessed with her Sacraments since his childhood.

The Sacraments of the Hunter Queen were magically imbued objects created by her to subdue and defeat the legions of hell (the Otherworlders) once and for all. However, the objects were considered too powerful and were scattered across the globe and hidden from all.

Except the magic in them called to Otherworlders and Witchhill was swarming with them. It was soon revealed that the Crown—an object granting control over the mind/will—was hidden in the Witch's Hill. A scramble for power, and the revelation of Delilah's darkest secret, resulted in her taking the Crown.

After this battle and Athena's graduation from high school, Delilah told her sister about the family business: hunting Otherworlders. They thought this might create a rift between Athena and her werewolf boyfriend, but her love for him never wavered, and the young couple got engaged with tears and a whole lot of snot.

It seemed everything worked out in the end—the killer who was revealed to be Nattalius was sent back to Imperio to answer for his crimes, the werewolves protected their pack, and Athena got her man. However, Delilah was warned that one of the Imperium's oldest enemies, the werewolf king Hozeir, was alive and actively seeking the Sacraments in an attempt to destroy the hunters and possibly, the whole of humanity.

Last Line

Reaching into the drawer of my desk, I pull out the Crown. It picks up the office light as I hear Paisley's excited congratulations. *First, I need to deal with this.*

To Mrs. Plaum, my fourth-grade teacher who read my not-so-short short story and asked me if I'd ever thought of being an author… thank you for giving me this dream

TABLE OF CONTENTS

Are all Others evil? I suppose the answer to that question depends on whom you ask. If you ask my aunt, the queen, the answer is yes. I remember the first time I heard about the beginning of our creation—the slaughter of Great Uncle Eadgar's family—and thought my aunt the strongest woman alive. She was the first child to receive the blood that binds us. In a way, she was an experiment of our newfound strength—the paradigm of hunters. Her experience blinds her to the truth as it stands now.

Otherworlders are not what they once were. Far be it from me to commend witches, but they have domesticated their hell spawn. Otherworlders with humanoid appearances could arguably blend into society and lead a normal life. The firstfolk, the Fathers of Hunters, do not want to listen to what my peers and I have to say, but I worry this war they wage will end with more human lives lost because of our actions than those of the Others.

My concern that my aunt will find and read this is outweighed by my horror at what we are becoming. We were meant to subdue the monsters, not become them. These so-called "Sacraments" the queen has created are an abomination to God, to humans, to us. I do not yet have proof, but I know she experiments with magic—the very transgression we condemn and burn witches for.

Do not mistake me, reader, and think me a lover of Other. Those creatures are undoubtedly sired in the depths of Hades and pose a threat to all that lives: human, hunter, animal, nature. They are soulless but not brainless. They are slaves to their desires as much as we are. What is blood to a vampire, if not food? What are groves to a centaur, if not a home?

I do not fault these creatures for what they are. I do not fault them for where they have been brought. I do, however, recognize that they must be controlled. As the witches domesticated and mothered them, we must now *be* the control they do not possess. Why kill them when we can govern them?

The Imperium Begins, an excerpt from the diary of Elke, niece of the Hunter Queen, Mother of the Imperium

** translated from the original German into English

Prologue

It is a truth universally acknowledged that a fine-tailored suit on a handsome man is naughtier than the skimpiest lingerie on any woman. The kind of fine where you ask God why He didn't make a three-piece suit the default for all men. Killian Joseph Garity fills out a suit like no man. He is no man.

He's a werewolf.

That used to deter me. The mere thought of a wolf would boil my blood. Now I watch his lips as they form the word 'kiss', and my blood heats for a different reason. What might kissing him be like? A list of questions forms in my mind, given I've never kissed a werewolf before. Dogs like licking things… is he going to try to lick me? How long is his tongue? Does he pant after kissing?

He's got nice, wide lips that remain full even when he smiles, and he doesn't have those gross beard hairs that grow too long and curl over them. Killian's one of the most dedicated manscapers I've met and that's including my narcissistic ex.

I shouldn't be thinking about Nattalius right now. Hell, I shouldn't be thinking about Killian right now.

But he's handsome, and it's about that time in my cycle. The time when I notice the broadness of his shoulders in a sports jacket and how his cheeks become waves when he laughs and the wrinkles that crease the skin around his sparkling eyes when he smiles. Who knew wrinkles would be it? I want to bite them—delicately

Like a lady.

Shouts erupt around me and shatter my reverie. My world sways from side to side for a moment before a hand touches my back. Four months ago, I would've killed a werewolf for touching me. Now, Paisley Mitchell, Gamma of the Garity Pack, considers herself my friend... a friend who's preventing me from fainting.

Don't lock your knees!

"That's not a kiss!" One of the he-wolves shouts from the crowd. Athena and Ibrahim part, both blushing, like they're not getting married in front of the largest group of people and creatures I've ever seen. "Really lay it on her, Iba!"

I should throw my bouquet at his head. That's what a good maid of honour would do, right? Killian's touch, a brush of his knuckle against my elbow, successfully tears any ideas of revenge from my head, along with the rest of my sense. The heckler sits down and frowns as his Alpha scolds him through the pack link.

Athena kisses Ibrahim again. She wraps both arms around his neck and makes a loud, obnoxious noise for everyone to hear. Ibrahim, laughing, dips her. A human photographer snaps picture after picture, and I refrain from flinching at each *click* and *whir.* There's a videographer too, somewhere on the pack's impeccably decorated land. I've been avoiding him.

"Ladies and gentlemen, please rise for Mr. and Mrs. Ibrahim and Athena Salama." Killian tucks his speech and Bible beneath his armpit and starts the next round of cheers and clapping. The orphans shower Athena and Ibrahim with petals as they scurry down the aisle.

"Milady," Mona drawls sarcastically, offering her arm. I barely contained my laughter this morning when she walked out of the groom's suite in a frilly suit. Somewhere between me delivering a secret letter from Athena to Ibrahim, and our walk down the aisle, she removed her ascot, unbuttoned the jacket, and cinched the vest tight enough to accentuate her cleavage. Most women couldn't rock the faux 1700s look, but I've yet to see a male pass Mona without a purposeful double-take. Unfortunately for them, she and Scarface have something going on. "If you smile, I will trip you."

"Not very gentlemanly of you," I taunt, stepping over her outstretched leg. Athena chose killer heels for Paisley and me to wear—ones I already struggle to walk in. While they might make my legs look great, the skirt of our bridesmaid dresses are too long for that to matter. Plus, a neck brace would kind of ruin the princessy vibe. "You should be grateful you aren't required to wear these shoes."

We plaster fake smiles on our faces as the photographer's assistant jumps out with a camera. This entire wedding is a jump scare. People continue clapping until Graham and Paisley finish their walk down the aisle behind us. At the front, Killian informs everyone about refreshments and advises them to check their programs if they have questions about the schedule or when dinner will be.

I shake off Mona as soon as we're out of sight. She snarls while brushing her sleeves and takes a step away from me. "This perfume is worse than your last."

"I chose it just for you."

A little hand slips into mine, preventing me from punching the snarl off Mona's face. "You look like a princess."

"And you look like a queen," I whisper, crouching to fix Sloane's bangs. Guests pour out of the ceremony. Most head towards the bar, where I so desperately want to go. Unfortunately, I promised Athena I would be on my best behaviour, which doesn't include drinking—for now. "You did well."

Sloane got robbed. My sister and her 'husband', instead of picking two orphans for the ring bearer and flower girl, chose all of them. The boys formed an assembly line in their little embroidered suits, and the girls showered the forest in hundreds of petals. Sloane deserved to be *the* flower girl: she's the prettiest and best-behaved girl of them all. Her dress is the only clean one after the kids got roped into a game before the ceremony. It's a bastardized version of the bridesmaid's dress with an atrocious amount of tulle and a waistband of silk. I made sure to curl and braid her hair in a special way, so she'd stand out from the others.

Tugging on my hand, Sloane drags me away from the bar and bridal party. The further we get from people, the looser the band around my lungs. Athena insisted on having the wedding on pack territory to honour their traditions. I offered to pay for a literal castle—any castle, anywhere not belonging to Otherworlders—but I lost out to a literal backyard. Chandeliers and ropes of crystal hang from the trees, and shimmering chimes dance in the wind. It's magical and mystical and makes my skin chafe. "Where are we going, Sloane?"

"I think Athena looked like the queen. She's so pretty." Athena chose a white dress inspired by the recent remake. I've never seen a skirt so poufy before. She looked the part of a forest queen, with embroidered flowers and vines coating her skin, and her hair twisted around a diadem.

Dad would've cried.

Sloane sighs dreamily, carrying me forward despite the sudden weight in my chest. "I can't wait to get married."

"Oh yes, you can. You're too young for that." She giggles at my half-hearted growl. When I look at her, I see Athena as she used to be. My baby sister with her heart of gold and head filled with fairytales, convinced of God and His people's goodness and sure of a fair and just world. Thea hasn't changed much, but I have. Somehow, she's as naïve as the day she was born. A werewolf convinced her to get married a month after she turned eighteen, and now she's going to live with the pack.

I know Ibrahim and Athena are Mates. I know Sloane is a werewolf. I know God takes care of His children… but I also know aside from my sister, the rest of those I listed—including myself—are not His.

"It's you and me against the world," I whisper to Sloane, the way I used to with Athena. Making promises to Sloane and continuing to build on the foundation of our relationship is another strike against me, but I cannot seem to help it. Maybe I want to be naïve too. "You know that saying about lone wolves."

"No wolf is lonely. We cannot survive without one another."

Sloane frowns, as if I should know that. Maybe I should. Lone wolves, homeless wolves, packless wolves, die. Ibrahim and Mona's dad died from Pack Sickness when they immigrated here. He was one of hundreds of wolves unable to bond and paid the ultimate price. Fortunately, I'm not a wolf.

Not completely.

"Are you lonely?"

I flick the end of her nose kindly and don my happiest smile. "I'm with you."

"Mona said you seem like a lonely bi—"

I cover her mouth and shake my head as she laughs against my palm. She runs her manicured nails over mine. "You need to stop listening to Mona."

"Ibrahim and Paisley say we need to respect and obey our elders."

"Well, I'm older than them, so there." It feels nice to laugh with her. Her laughter chases away the demons lurking in the shadows of my mind. "You didn't answer my question. Where are we going?"

"Oh. Nowhere. You looked uncomfortable with all the people walking around you."

Staggering, I stare down at her. She's maybe 4'2 and 50 pounds soaking wet, but she knows how to gut me faster than any opponent I've faced. "Has anyone told you you're too smart?"

"Ian says you can't be too much of a good thing."

Of course he does. Bending, I snap off the ankle strap on my heels. Sloane takes them from my hands and tries, unsuccessfully, to stand in them. I should head back to take pictures with the bridal party, but Thea said she wanted half an hour alone with Ibrahim so they could 'live in the moment'. Half an hour is more than enough time for a run.

"What about too fast?" I inquire, pulling the clips from my hair until it tumbles over my shoulders, wild and free, just like I'm meant to be. Sloane flashes me a grin and kicks off her flats. "Last one to Mona has to call her 'sir'."

"Why are you sitting alone in the dark?" Athena questions, hands on her hips. She looks so much like our mother; I briefly consider tearing up.

"Del?"

"Mom and Dad are so proud of you," I state, swallowing past the burn in my throat. The first glass of wine provided a nice cushion for the pain. A bottle of that and some clear, unlabelled drink from Killian's stores later, and I'm sitting on a cloud. It won't last, but Athena's outrage might if she figures out how much I've had to drink since the reception started. *Keep it together.* "How does it feel knowing you've ruined weddings for every other girl here? No bride could be half as beautiful, graceful, or elegant as you."

Her eyes mist. Whoever did her makeup must've added cement to her mascara. Athena's cried more times than any woman should at her wedding. She reaches for me with a shaky hand. All I can see is the new tattoo on her wedding finger.

Accessories tend to break on Werewolves. Multiple rips pattern Paisley's ears from where her earrings snagged when she shifted. She's the one who suggested they get their ring fingers tattooed. She's also the one currently bent over a drunk human, trying to tattoo a little heart on their bare hip, and cursing at a volume only Otherworlders can hear.

"Paisley did a good job," I mutter, playing with the edge of the second skin. The Celtic knot's lines are precise and intricate—no easy feat on a finger, and I should know as someone with multiple finger tattoos. The 'I' in the center looks precisely like the one Ibrahim practiced for the last two months.

I advised against it, seeing as Athena's time at Seminary could change her mind, but she's confident her love for Ibrahim cannot be changed or broken. She hasn't experienced the xenophobia and racism embedded in the hunter's culture. If Requisite doesn't change her, war will.

It's been brewing between Otherworlders and hunters since the Imperium took power 300 years ago. While her heart longs for her werewolf, her blood wants him dead. She cannot escape her biology or our dad's legacy, try as she might. I do not like the Imperium, but I will play my part when the time comes. I must. War makes patriots out of everyone.

"Are you okay?"

"Of course," I laugh, forcing enthusiasm into my voice. This is her wedding. My only family's wedding. It's the eye of my storm… perhaps my last taste of life. She's giving me that look, the 'you're not telling me something' look, but it melts away when I press a kiss on her knuckles. "Go enjoy your husband, Thea. You'll be too sore to for the next three months."

"Delilah Phillipa Anne—"

"Because of Requisite training," I finish, shaking my head. Her face flushes as she glances at the surrounding tables. The orphans and everyone under the age of 16 were required to go to bed at 10:30 PM. Now, half the dancers are holding flasks, and there's a bunch of teenagers, probably my sister's age, grinding on one another. *I'm too old to be here.* "Get your mind out of the gutter." She nods, taking a deep breath. I recognize the slight panic in her eyes. It's the same look she got when she injured her knee and ended her snowboarding career. "Thea, it's not a requirement to consummate the marriage on the first night—or ever. Don't stress about it."

Run in the other direction.

With me.

Brushing a loose strand of hair from her brow, she musters a smile. "You love parties. I know you have a thing about Otherworlders seeing you have fun, but please? For me? One dance."

A weird taste fills my mouth when I look at the grinding teenagers. That was me. Three years ago, before Mom and Dad killed themselves, before they told me about my father, before I recognized the depths of my darkness. Athena's right. I love parties—the music and heartbeats all pumping to the bass. My favourite part, though, is the sweaty mass of bodies absorbing me into the crowd until I become another faceless person claimed by the neon lights.

This isn't a party, and I am not a faceless person. Paisley, Mona and I hung chandeliers up on pillars in a pack field, and the Deltas laid the marble slabs for the dance floor. Everyone here knows each other's names, their scents, and their alliances.

I crave anonymity.

I crave to be forgotten.

Besides, there's only one male I'd choose for my one dance, and he's occupied. I find him, like a moth to a flame. Killian's head drops back when he laughs, exposing the columns of his throat and his fluttering pulse. A she-wolf, who clearly craves death, touches his arm—his *bare* forearm. He must have taken off his jacket and vest after the photos. With rolled-up sleeves, a dropped collar, and tailored slacks, he resembles a rake more than a prince, which only makes him ten times more appetizing.

"He's a good man. No matter what you've been taught." She doesn't understand that's half of the problem. Athena tugs on my hand, trying to bring me to my feet. When she fails, she sighs in that dramatic way she knows will get a rise out of me. "I know he'd love to dance."

"Sloane tired me out."

Thea frowns again, pulling on the bodice of her golden reception dress, like she's done all evening. The dress came right out of our wedding notebook, but if I'd known she'd spend three hours trying to stop her sweetheart neckline from being a sweetheart neckline, I'd have insisted on the tailor adding straps. Her dresses were the only thing no one else got an opinion on. It was just me and her. "I know you don't like *Beauty and the Beast*."

"Thea, it's beautiful. You're beautiful. Everything is okay. I'm just tired."

She doesn't know yet.

Whose fault is that?

"Are you sure?"

The depth of my self-hatred expands. Athena's at her wedding, having married her Mate, and yet she's standing in a dark corner, checking on me. I have so much to tell her still and not enough time for any of it. She thinks the *Beauty and the Beast* is a fairytale. She doesn't know about our mother's captivity. She doesn't know I'm the beast in this story.

PART 1: THE BEAUTY

CHAPTER

1

A Tale as Old as Time

Airports are terrifying. People rushing everywhere, random stores vying for traveller's attention, but worst of all are the security guards waiting to call out the knives hidden in young women's bags.

Athena shifts self-consciously, brushing the zipper on the front of her suitcase. She hadn't expected to find a neatly wrapped package on the front steps of her Seminary dorm, but she should've expected it to be something dangerous when she saw Delilah's name on the sender line. The knife set complements the suit of armour all Requisite graduates receive at their certification ceremony.

Most graduates receive their first hunting knife from the matriarch or patriarch of their family in front of the graduates and professors.

Delilah should've hand delivered it.

"Sorry I took so long. Someone was having card trouble." Ibrahim, Athena's husband, sits in one of the stiff airport chairs, and leans in to press a light kiss on her cheek. The heavy smell of his cologne stings her nose. Delilah put the fear of God into him about smelling bad, and now he douses himself in it three times a day. He's a sweetheart like that, even if the heavy ginger smell burns her eyes and nostrils. "I offered to pay for them. I assumed that was okay—?"

"I love you," Athena whispers, kissing him. Her stomach growls when he produces a meaty croissant. Twenty minutes ago, he asked if she wanted something from the coffee shop, and twenty minutes ago, she didn't. She wanted to study the flashcards in her lap, so she could 'talk shop' with Delilah when they stopped by Witches Alcove on the way home. Now, she chews her lips to avoid asking for a bite. "How did I get so lucky to have a husband like you?"

He grins, exposing the cheese caught between his teeth. After three and a half months of marriage, she's more in love than ever. When she brushes a thumb over his mayo-covered cheek and brings it to her mouth, he offers something wrapped in crinkle paper. "It's a BELT bagel."

"I am going to marry you again."

"You want a bite?" He offers the crushed sandwich with a knowing smile. Delilah made a list of the things she wished she knew prior to beginning her hunter training, and though it was comprehensive and insightful, she forgot to mention how much their metabolism increases. Athena was a gold snowboarder. Before the accident, she worked out six times a week, only resting on Sabbat. That hunger and thirst cannot compete with the sensations her body experiences after the three-month Requisite program. "I got two."

Luckily, Ibrahim eats a lot too. Well, all werewolves eat a lot—it says so on her flash cards. "You're so smart."

"Thank you, *ya amar.*"

She swings her legs with each bite, unable to sit still after five months of chaos. Five months ago, Delilah told her the truth about their 'family business'. As children, Delilah and Athena traded ridiculous stories about their parents being mafia bosses, and only when Athena turned thirteen did she decide she was too old to believe her mom and dad were part of a clandestine organization. Little did she know how outlandish the truth was.

Werewolves? Vampires? Leprechauns? Unicorns? They all exist. Unicorns aren't the creatures little girls are taught to worship. Based on the information she gathered from Delilah, Catarina, and the Senate Library, Unicorns are the deadliest Otherworlders out there. All creatures have a proven kill method, *except* for them; no one's gotten close enough and lived to tell the tale.

Her husband is a werewolf. By blood, she should want to hunt and kill him. Every hunter in her basics class shared their story about the first-time bloodlust hit. When it was Athena's turn to speak, she proudly declared she'd married a werewolf, her Mate, and had yet to experience a desire for violence. The entire room fell silent. When she texted Delilah about it, she replied with a face palm emoji. That was the last time Athena heard from her.

Athena involuntarily pulls out her phone. She feels Iba's eyes on it when she scrolls through her texts with her sister. Everything he wants to say, but doesn't, slips into her mind as his hand brushes her legging-covered knee. He doesn't understand Delilah. Few do. She hates winter. Witchhill's icy roads prevent her joy rides, which she needs to stay sane.

Driving, running, *escaping*—it's only then Athena sees her joyful sister again.

"Nothing." Of course, Iba knows that—he can see her phone. He also knows she's been checking it dozens of times a day after sending a text last month that never got read. "She's probably busy."

Busy is Delilah's norm. She's not someone who relaxes or rests. Mom and Del got into it on Sabbat more than once because she'd wake up early, before Mom, to run and burn some of her energy.

Disappearing for weeks at a time is also her norm. Normally, she employs a proxy, like Ingrid or Archie or even Iman, if the other two take too long. Ingrid and Iman checked on Athena regularly in Imperio, but they didn't mention Delilah once, despite Athena asking about her on several occasions. She called the staff at least once a week to see how Delilah, the house, and the animals were doing. They avoided mentioning Del and focused entirely on the animals.

Ibrahim thinks it might be that Delilah plans to sell Witches Alcove. Unlike Athena, who inherited their dad's tender-heartedness, her sister isn't very sentimental. If she had it her way, the house would be gone, possibly burned to the ground, and the staff would follow Athena to her small house on the pack lands. Nevertheless, Delilah's soft spot is Athena, who occasionally takes advantage of that. Athena asked for three months in the hopes she'd have enough time to come up with a convincing reason for Delilah to keep their childhood home.

Unfortunately, she's returning home empty-handed.

"It's weird none of them have mentioned her." It's her twentieth time implying the same thing, except it's more of a statement now than a question. Her confidence grew when her poor husband finally agreed for the seventh time. It *is* weird. The staff have varying opinions on Delilah and often avoid mentioning her—much to Athena's chagrin and against her instructions—but this is different. It's not just the staff.

The wolves haven't said a thing either. Athena selfishly hoped Killian would keep tabs on Delilah. He likes her. She… well, she doesn't hate him… it's hard to get a read on how Delilah feels sometimes. Two weeks after that last emoji, Athena asked Killian to check on her. He went to the house, but the gates were closed, and everyone was gone. Unbeknownst to her, the staff were given the entire month of October off by none other than Delilah. Killian said the scents in the house were stale and had no other clues for Athena.

Every visit after from him or Paisley ended with the same news: the gates were locked, there were no new scents, and Delilah couldn't be seen from any of the windows. It might be a coincidence. She *really* doesn't like werewolves; after spending eleven hours with them at Ibrahim and Athena's wedding, maybe she needed a break. She fled the wedding like Satan himself was on her heels.

Catarina, Delilah's Companion and Athena's gracious tour guide, offered little insight. She kept implying that Delilah's hate for the wolves was justified. The way she said it, the way she looked at Athena, made her feel almost *guilty* for not hating them too. Like she should—like she should know why Delilah does.

"There's a piano," Ibrahim whispers eagerly, wiping the corner of his lips with a napkin. He offers one to her after she inhales the last of her sandwich. They first connected over their shared love of music. Most do not appreciate the French tuba, but Ibrahim kept complimenting her in choir and eventually convinced her to play with him alone in the music room at lunchtime. They kept playing together for weeks until he built up the courage to ask her out on a date. He knew they were Mates… she knew he was the cutest boy in the world. "Like old times?"

"Archie might be here soon." She grazes the mark on her neck without realizing it. It's her newest habit; one she tried to stop when she noticed how disgusted the hunters looked when seeing the permanent bite on her skin. The bite mark partially covers the scars left by the animal that attacked her when she was two years old. Touching the scars used to be how she self-soothed. "I don't want to keep him waiting."

"That's okay. Our house has a piano."

Their house. Athena smiles, sliding her hand into his, and banishes the cloud gathering over her head. Living with the pack will be an adjustment, but it's the change she's been most excited about since getting married. The wolves take care of one another; they communicate, they understand one another… they're a family. Unlike the one she grew up with.

"We're still stopping at the house first, right?" He rubs her knee, undoubtedly sensing her unrest through their Mate bond. Feeling her feelings and hearing her thoughts is second nature to Ibrahim. Athena, on the rare occasions he feels something intensely, gets indigestion. "I think everything will be okay."

"I think studying is making me paranoid," Athena laughs, planting a kiss on his jaw. He offers to hold up the flash cards and quiz her, but before he can finish his sentence, a man in a full-denim outfit walks into the airport. A beaver toque rests on his balding head, obscuring some of her favourite tattoos. Athena used to be obsessed with them and spent hours bent over her little sketchbook with crayons trying to replicate some of the intricate designs around his skull and down his spine. The drawings still hang in the garage over his workbench. "Archie!"

He laughs, spreading his arms for her. The hug smells like home. A little bit like Delilah with the gasoline, and a lot like him with the aftershave. Tears spring to her eyes when he squeezes her to his barrel chest. She missed home more than she realized. "You've lost weight."

"No one makes food like Chef," Athena jokes, wiping her eyes. He reaches forward, brushing them away with a calloused thumb. "I'm sorry. I missed you guys."

"And we missed you. The house feels like a gravey—it's not the same without you."

In a lot of ways, it is a graveyard. The candles they lit for her parents sit on the dining table, though they've been cold for years. Her staff fill the rooms with laughter, but it's not the place she immortalized as a kid. It hasn't been since her parents died.

"Let me grab your bags," Archie demands, pausing to shake Ibrahim's hand. He straps her carry-on over his chest and hauls her suitcase into his arms to avoid the snow when they step outside. Ibrahim allows him to take one of his bags but keeps the others in his arms. "Mathéo planned a roast."

And just like that, her stomach growls again. She blushes when the men laugh and bashfully follows them to the back of Archie's truck. "I've really missed his food."

"There's a lot of it. He says we simpletons don't appreciate his 'art'." Rolling his eyes, Archie opens the back door for Athena and throws the bags into the back with Ibrahim. He slides into the driver's seat with a low curse. A gust of heat hits her the next moment.

"I just had the best idea," Athena announces with a pleased smile when Ibrahim gets into the truck. "We should go to the hot springs."

"That is the best idea." The hot springs are her favourite part of the mountains, considering she cannot take part in snow sports… or couldn't.

After intensive physio and healing with a trainer in Imperio, her range of motion has drastically improved. Her knee doesn't hurt as much when bad weather comes around. A fellow 'crip', Daniel (who coined the term for all hunters needing physio), told her about a witch-made injection that breaks up scar tissue. She texted Delilah about it, but she didn't respond. "Is that a you and me thing, or can Paisley come too?"

"I miss her. She definitely needs to come." They were close before the wedding, but prepping for it added a new layer to their friendship. Paisley and Delilah spent hours with her DIYing half of the decorations. "Do you think we should invite Mona, too?"

"If we invite Mona, Delilah won't come."

"How is Delilah?" Athena leans over the console, desperate to see Archie's face. It's easy for the staff to hide their reactions behind texts or change the subject on the phone, but he cannot hide with her right beside him. "She left, didn't she?"

The muscles in his shoulders bunch. Despite her resolve not to be disappointed or surprised, Athena's stomach twists. After all this time—after training to be a hunter like Delilah wanted—she thought she'd be 'in the know', but she's just like the rest of them: completely clueless about her sister's life or what she's doing.

"The day after your wedding," Archie says, pulling onto the highway. He drums his fingers to the radio blaring country music but glances at Athena in the rearview mirror almost as much as he checks the road. "It took us a while to notice. You know how quiet she is."

"How much did she pack?"

"Ingrid wants to talk to you about that… you know how she gets."

Ingrid. Also, a hunter. Something Athena never would've guessed. "She knows where Delilah is?"

"She might be slipping in and out," he offers, eyes softening. He and Delilah connect in a way no one understands. He's the only person Athena feels comfortable talking about Delilah with, because his love for her may rival, or even surpass, her own. After Del left three and a half years ago, Athena would often sit in the garage for hours, crying, and he would hand her the clean end of a grease-covered rag without a word. Mourning her parents and Delilah took a lot of life out of her; it took a lot out of him. "She's stealthy."

Athena musters a smile, though her lips quiver around her teeth, and her brain calls her a liar.

CHAPTER 2

Gone Girl

"Look at what the cat dragged in!" Archie stamps his feet on the front mat to announce his entrance. A beat of silence passes and then the staff of Witches Alcove swarms the front hall. Mathéo, otherwise known as Chef, reaches Athena first, lifting her off her feet.

"They're all animals," he whispers in French before letting her go. Tutting, she hugs Chun. After so many years, he still seems surprised by the affection but returns her hug with a squeeze. "I made your favourite."

"It's been too long." She rubs her flat stomach, eagerly hugging Iman. They hold on to one another the longest, simply breathing the other in. Iman's neither an emotional person nor an effusive one, so the intensity with which she squeezes Athena speaks volumes. "I missed you."

"And I you." Her eyes subtly drop to Athena's stomach when she holds her at arm's length. Athena's lungs constrict, wringing the oxygen out of her, but despite the ache building in her chest, she forces a smile. Years ago, Athena promised to share her children with the nanny because Iman lost the ability to conceive after an assault in her adolescence. With Iman and the rest of the staff at her side, she imagined raising her family in Witchhill, because no other town would do. She cannot picture her life without them: the staff *and* her children.

"Give the girl some room," Ingrid commands, stamping her cane on the ground like an old-fashioned herald. Chun and Mathéo depart to the kitchen while Iman reaches for her bags. "They're not staying, Iman."

Iman opens her mouth but shuts it before nodding. Being in the house, eating dinner, knowing she'll have to leave… it ruins Athena's appetite. Offering a sympathetic smile to Iman, she steps into Ingrid's embrace. Her husband, being the incredible man he is, distracts Iman by asking where to hang their coats. "Delilah?"

"You look good." Ingrid's a master at avoiding uncomfortable conversations, just like Delilah. They are more alike than they care to admit. "You're a natural."

"I am a Christos."

No longer by name, but by blood. When Delilah shared the importance of their family line, she thought it was an over exaggeration. After meeting her class and introducing herself as a Christos, she realized how serious her sister was. The Christos' rule the Greek division of the Imperium, and their name seems to carry the weight of the world with it. She avoided using it after people from her class started opening doors and promising her favours in return for one of hers.

"You look it too. I remember the way Seminary changed your dad.

You've got his looks and confidence now."

Athena blushes. She watches Ibrahim share some of the human-friendly moments from their trip with her old nanny. The confidence might be the training. It might also be married life. She's learned a lot about herself—about her body—in the last few months. "Thanks, Ingrid. Is Delilah in her office?"

The housekeeper sighs. Whenever Athena brings up her big sister, it evokes the same look on Ingrid's face. It used to make her sad. Now, she straightens her spine and channels her inner hunter.

"She's not. She left when you did."

"Has she checked in with you?" Ingrid walks away, a rare response for Athena, one she's not quite sure how to handle. When she finds Ingrid, she's in her bedroom, phone in hand. Confident in Ibrahim's ability to keep the staff entertained, Athena closes the door and rests her back against it. "Ingrid."

"No. I've sent her multiple messages, and she hasn't responded to any of them." She's got a bad feeling about this. A terrible one. Delilah disappears, but she knows better than to make Athena worry, especially after their parents died. "Don't make yourself sick. She does this."

"Not like this."

"She packed a bag."

"Do you think it's because I got married? To Iba?" Running her finger over the tattoo she got in place of a wedding ring, Athena swallows back bile. Delilah hates *Beauty and the Beast.* Always has. She hates werewolves. As for weddings, affection, happiness… it all makes her uncomfortable. She wanted Del to be her maid of honour desperately enough to ask, but a part of Athena knew her older sister would never refuse. Gosh, she practically forced her into it… "I should've thought about how that would—"

"Athena Tassos Eliana Chri-Salama. Your sister has and will forever be consumed in her own world."

"You're being unfair."

"I am not trying to be." Ingrid sighs, adjusting her grip on the head of a wooden cane. "Your sister wouldn't want you to worry about her. She's too bull-headed to think about how her actions impact those who love her, but I know she's okay."

"How?"

Ingrid's mouth snaps shut, but her eyes speak. For two women who dislike each another so greatly, Ingrid and Delilah share a lot of secrets. "Delilah has an emergency plan if anything goes wrong. You, Ibrahim, and I will go to Imperio and meet with Catarina. She has a safe house, far away from the Imperium and the Otherworlders."

"If anything goes wrong?" Delilah mentioned a war, but nobody in Imperio seemed to know about it or the missing Sacraments. According to the professors, the Sacraments were under Imperium control—three hidden, four kept—but Athena wasn't brave enough to ask if they knew that for sure. Navigating the world of the hunters felt a lot more dangerous than spending time with the pack. There were hidden messages in every conversation and threats no one dared to speak, but all knew. Athena wouldn't have survived without Delilah's advice. "Wait. You said me, Ibrahim, and you… what about Del?"

"It's time for dinner."

"Ingrid."

"If you wish to understand your sister, I am the last person to seek, dear." Ingrid reaches for the doorknob and waits until Athena steps aside to open it. "She finished her case—she got the killer, she got her money, and she left. Chances are she's chasing her next high."

"It's not like her," Athena insists for the umpteenth time, leaning over the bathroom sink. She fights back the urge to gag when she scrubs her tongue too hard with the toothbrush. "I know I sound like a broken record."

"Dark, brooding, and mysterious is Delilah's thing," Ibrahim offers gently while seated on the edge of their bathtub. He stops brushing his teeth when she gives him an unimpressed look. Dark, brooding, and mysterious *is* Delilah's thing, but it seems rude for people to keep saying it. Especially when Delilah's not around to defend herself.

"This isn't like her."

"*Ya amar.*" He finishes brushing his teeth and wraps an arm around her. It's silly to fight over this, but no one's listening. Don't they get it? Delilah's her sister. Her family. Yes, Iba's hers too, and she inherited Mona and Killian through him, but Delilah's… Delilah. She's the closest thing to an idol Athena keeps. Her best friend. Her confidant. "She disappeared for three years."

"No. She checked in. She told me where she was going. She sent pictures." Delilah might push everyone away with her words, but she loves through action. Texts. Pictures. Occasional deposits into Athena's bank account with the suggestion to get herself a treat or something special. "It's been a month and nothing. She hasn't read my texts. She hasn't opened my email with our honeymoon pictures or listened to my voicemails. She knows I worry; she wouldn't do this to me."

"Okay. I hear you. What do you need from me?" Ibrahim steps

back, giving her the room she didn't think to crave. The Mate bond gets stronger the closer he comes, consuming her thoughts with warmth and affection. Right now, she needs a clear mind. "I can get Killian. He'll know how to help."

"It's late," Athena murmurs, glancing at the clock in their bedroom. It's weird to call it theirs. It's weird to have a house that belongs to them. Killian hired someone to build it using blueprints Delilah must've provided, because Athena recognized it the moment they drove up in a car Archie gave them—provided again by Delilah. Athena drew the house at ten years old. Her miniature fairytale cottage hidden in the garden Chun planted. There's nothing miniature about it now. Ibrahim stands easily in the house without worrying about hitting his head. It's everything she dreamed and fantasized about for years, down to the flower planters on the windows, and the pictures of her loved ones in different antique frames. "What time is it?"

"11:30 PM."

"It would be rude to wake him up."

"Killer doesn't sleep," Ibrahim jokes, eyes crinkling. His smile melts when she takes out her phone again. She texted Delilah to say they were back in town. If Delilah were anywhere near Witchhill, she'd come to see them. "I'll go right now."

"No. No. I-I'll check out her office tomorrow and her room. Maybe I'll see what she brought with her. Who knows? Maybe she left a note for me in there." He returns to her side, nuzzling the Mark on her neck. It's hard not to smile when he does it. "I need to go to the bathroom."

He presses a kiss on it and steps back. With goosebumps on her arms, she watches him go. They've been naked together more times than she can count, but the intimacy of using the bathroom with him so close… she cannot imagine ever being comfortable with it. Especially with her period starting.

As she drops onto the toilet, Athena reaches for her phone again. Guilt tugs on her when she scrolls through the unanswered texts. She has a surefire way to get a response, but she doesn't want to invade Delilah's space. If she needs it, she needs it.

You, Ibrahim, and I. Ingrid's voice grows louder and louder in her head with each moment she stares at the blank text box. How long has Delilah known about a war brewing, and why did she create a contingency plan without including herself? The sick feeling sweeps back in when Athena starts typing. Delilah might think she's expendable, but she hasn't seen the changes in Athena like Ingrid has. They can conquer this together, just like they used to.

Athena sends the **SOS** text, swallowing back her guilt. If Delilah left to get some space, she's going to respond. No matter what. Eyes on her phone, Athena inserts her menstrual cup, praying for those three little dots to appear.

CHAPTER 3

Taken

"You guys need a new code word," Paisley suggests, scrolling through Athena's phone. She offers a dry laugh, unable to cry after spending the whole of last night—and this morning—in Ibrahim's arms, sobbing. They've never used their code word before. Athena briefly considered it when Delilah first left because she knew it would bring her back home, but she didn't want to betray their sistership. 'SOS' supersedes fights or work or even spouses. Had Delilah been able, she would've responded the minute Athena sent the text, not left it unanswered for over ten hours now. "SOS is too obvious."

"You think someone has her?" Athena asks worriedly, torn between her duty to watch the road and her desire to check Paisley's reaction. She shouldn't be driving. Driving is already anxiety-inducing as it is. Her parents died in the winter on icy roads like these. Maybe this exact road. Athena's eyes drift to the ditch, and she shudders. "Why would anyone take Delilah?"

"I don't know about taking… I just know if I saw that, it would be obvious you're important to her. If she got into a sticky situation and they have her phone and need leverage, they'll know to go after you."

"Heavens forbid."

"Foot in my mouth." Paisley winces and slips the phone into the cup holders when they enter the town of Witchhill. Snow blankets the town, laying it to rest for the winter. Frost coats every treetop; every branch is silent and devoid of critters, and the road is clear of travellers—mostly. "Next time, I'll cover for Ibrahim, and he can come."

"I appreciate you. Foot and all." Paisley's aura far outshines her worst qualities. She is sunshine and glitter bombs. When they first met, Athena couldn't believe Ibrahim would choose her over Paisley. She listens. She makes everyone laugh. Her injection of fun into every activity is almost intoxicating and makes it hard not to be impulsive. Athena and Ibrahim appreciate her endless drive for adventure, even if the subsequent recklessness occasionally takes a year off their lives. She's the person Delilah would be were it not for Atlas' burden. "Do you think I'm being silly?"

No doubt the wolves would step in if she asked. Athena thought about the possibility of a cooling whiskey glass waiting on the desk in her parent's office, or finding Delilah passed out in her room, and asked Ibrahim to wait. Del moves like a wraith wherever and whenever she goes, and it wouldn't be the first time she left without a word. Why risk wasting their time without further investigation?

Athena intended to conduct her 'investigation' alone, but Paisley saw right through her as soon as she got in the truck. "I don't have any sisters, but if Iba went missing, I'd raise heaven and hell to find him."

"But Delilah's not Iba."

Pais opens her mouth and shuts it. The underlying current and implication tighten the knots in Athena's stomach. Pulling into the driveway, Athena cuts the engine and sighs in such a way that her body melts into the seat. They made it. Step one complete.

Gentle music plays in the shed-turned-home where the male staff sleep. The other staff left Chun in charge of upkeep until they return from their adventure across the mountain. Snow and ice sculptures decorate the yard in the absence of bright colours, each more extravagant than the last. Witches Alcove looks like it belongs in a fairytale, like it's frozen in time.

"There are no footprints." Paisley kicks her booted foot over the driveway and ventures further into the yard to peer into the office window. "No evidence of her sneaking in or out."

As a hunter, Athena should notice these things. Footsteps in the snow. Scent on the air. Athena takes a whiff and coughs against the cold invasion. "You make it look so effortless."

"Been a wolf my whole life, babe. You've been a hunter for five months." Her Scottish accent alters the endearment. Kelsey Dyck, a bully, and someone who was killed months ago, used to call her that. Babe. Pumpkin. Darling. It was belittling, but Paisley says it affectionately, like a mother to their child. "And you're married and Mated to a wolf. I heard it's the equivalent of stuffing your brain with cotton balls."

"Who told you that?"

"I don't remember," Paisley confesses, drawing her eyebrows

together. "It might have been your sister. We drank a lot together at the wedding. She's not bad, ya know? A little surly, but I like surly. She knows how to hold her liquor."

"You talked to her at the wedding?"

"A bunch," Paisley confirms, waiting for Athena to unlock the door. She steps with shaky legs into the front hall. "I invited her on a camping trip."

"You did?"

Paisley laughs, tilting her head back. That's Paisley. She makes friends out of everyone and yet refuses to change herself to please them. Most people couldn't file their teeth into little daggers without frightening people, but their schoolmates used to compliment her modification. She effortlessly mixes the bohemian and edgy aesthetics, with her dyed hair, ripped ears, and gentle makeup. Her go-to outfit consists of a leather jacket, loose joggers, and a t-shirt adorned with lace or spray paint or both.

Her tattoos are Athena's particular favourite, though. Paisley wants to cover her body like Archie did, and she's halfway there with one leg completely sleeved. Once she fully recovers, she intends to get the other covered in ink too.

"Yeah. I thought we'd have fun hunting together." Werewolves no longer hunt out of necessity. Some old pack leaders require their wolves to hunt to keep their senses primed. Killian permits hunting where the government allows, but he doesn't hold hunts himself or force anyone to partake in the old traditions. Five months ago, if someone told Athena her friends were going hunting, she'd assume that meant with rifles and gilly suits, not with claws and teeth. Athena tries to picture Paisley as a wolf, with her dyed hair and tattooed skin, but the picture in her mind looks more like a garbled child's drawing than a magnificent beast. "What?"

"What colour is your wolf?"

"Rusty. I think your sister called me an overgrown fox."

Sounds like something she'd say. Affection tugs at Athena when she enters the office. It smells like Delilah. Cinnamon, baked goods, and a hint of coffee. Like Dad, like Delilah, a bit like Ibrahim. "It's faded."

"What is?"

"Her scent." She smiles at being useful, but the knowledge settles and takes her smile with it. Delilah hasn't been here for at least a month. If not longer. There's no evidence she ever even touched this office. It looks the same as when their parents used it. Books on shelves. Chair tucked into the desk. Curtains closed. Where's her giant blackboard? "She cleaned up."

"What are the chances she finished up her case, got her money, and found her next one? Someone needs to pay for this house."

"She put me as a secondary on her bank account, and while I think it's bad taste to boast… she can afford four of these houses." Athena pushes aside the desk chair to get a better look at the glass case between the bookshelves. It's locked by key, not by code, which makes breaking in that much easier. "Do you think you can pick this lock?"

"Got a hair grip?"

"In my room."

Paisley heads out of the office, leaving Athena in the empty office. Forcing herself to stay calm, Athena goes through every unlocked drawer. There's a handful of papers, a few candy wrappers, and a disturbing amount of small liquor bottles. Athena flips through each of the books and checks the back of the picture frames, just in case. A slight obsession with mystery books prepared her for this moment. There's a hidden door behind the bookshelves that connects to Iman and Ingrid's room, but it doesn't go anywhere besides their bedroom. After eighteen years of living here, Athena knows this house like the back of her hand. If there was a secret room, she'd know about it.

Paisley returns with the bobby pin raised triumphantly like a sword. "You think she put something in this glass case?"

"I hope so," Athena whispers, praying again for wisdom and direction. She'd lowered onto her knees in the moments between her bouts of crying, pleading with God to bring Delilah back or show Athena how to find her. "It's the only secretive thing I can find in here."

"Do you reckon she put the Crown in here?"

"The Crown." She smacks a hand against her forehead. This could have something to do with the Sacraments! Delilah refused to tell the wolves—or Athena—about what she did with the Sacrament. 'Better not to know', she'd said. With a click and a grin, Paisley opens the small door to the case. "I bet that's it. Paisley, you're a genius."

"All in a day's work," Paisley drawls, peering into the safe. Their excitement perishes in the same breath as papers, not a magically imbued crown, wait within. "That would've been too lucky."

"These have nothing to do with the Sacraments," Athena whispers, flipping through the deeds in her hand. Investments, the house, financial paperwork. No mention of the Hunter Queen or her quest for domination. "What do we do now?"

"Does she have a laptop? Maybe she backs it up to the Cloud—"

"I don't know, but she has a Companion who works in the Senate Library. Cat sent her all the information she had about the Sacraments." Athena digs out her cellphone and calls Catarina through a video app.

The line rings and rings, and, with each passing moment, Athena watches the eagerness drain from her own face. "Catarina's part of Delilah's emergency plan, so she probably knows the code, eh?"

"I think everyone knows what SOS means, El."

Athena sends the three little letters with a hammering heart, tasting the sweat slicked along her upper lip. Paisley continues talking as if war and her sister's disappearance are nothing to worry about. Focusing on Delilah's disappearance is better than considering the meaning behind why she didn't include herself in said emergency plans.

"It's kind of slimy not to include *me*. Mona, I get. Graham too. Killian is his own thing, but we shared two shots. Some of the best shots of my life. She's a loyal member of the daddy issues club."

"Our dad was an incredible man."

Paisley sucks her teeth, cocking her head to the side. "Right."

"She struggled with them," Athena admits, watching the **read** appear underneath her message. A full second doesn't even go by before a shrill ring breaks up the tension. "Hey Cat."

"What's wrong?"

"Delilah's missing."

She slumps on video, running her hands over her unnaturally sleek black hair. The video becomes grainy for a second before it buffers and shows Catarina Guerrero in full colour, seated at her desk in her office in the Great Library. "I thought you were dying."

"Cat, I need you to be concerned about Delilah. Because *I'm* concerned about Delilah. Because no one else is concerned about Del—"

"Deep breaths. Deeeeeeeeeep breaths. You're working me up." Athena drops into her dad's office chair and groans at the full weight of her distress. She takes two deep breaths, as advised, before propping her phone against a pen holder. “Who’s there with you?”

“Hi. Paisley. Best friend. Big fan. Delilah told me you’d probably join the daddy issues club, too. We’ve got tattoos.”

Catarina blinks before her eyes slide towards Athena. After a brief pause, she laughs. “It’s good to finally meet you.”

“Delilah talked about me?”

“I did.” Athena offers Paisley her most sympathetic smile to ease the disappointment. “When was the last time you heard from Delilah?”

“I texted her on her birthday. She sent me the middle finger.” Delilah considers being born on Halloween as a ‘sign’... Athena never quite understood what kind of sign, but Del refuses to celebrate it. She wouldn’t even pick up when Athena called to wish her a happy birthday. After four attempts, Del answered with a warning not to even mention the word ‘birth’, or she’d hang up. “When did she last contact you?”

“November second. You might remember that I told my ‘Nature vs Nurture’ class about being married to Ibrahim and they were....”

“Unimpressed.” Catarina finished with a nod. “Did Del chew you out?”

“No, she just sent an emoji.”

Delilah’s Companion pauses, eyebrows drawn together. Weight pistons against Athena’s stomach lining when she pulls back. “That’s not like her.”

“Thank you.” Gratitude replaces the weight. Someone gets it. “Where does that leave us?”

“She wouldn’t tell me her plans for the Crown.” Cat crosses one leg over the other, her bangles *clinking* together with the movement. “That’s not unusual for Del.”

“Has she alluded to anything?”

"Nothing. We do not talk to each other constantly… we went months without talking until the murders." Cat picks at her nails. Silence stretches between them as Athena takes time to process what that means. Yet with each passing second, she's left with fewer answers and more questions. Where is Delilah? What is she doing? Is she safe? Why didn't she stay in contact with Catarina? Did Delilah get into contact with anyone else before disappearing? "She thinks protecting people means keeping up her walls, but they just isolate her inside of them—anyone who needs to know about the Sacraments would go to He Who Doesn't Deserve a Name."

Paisley's face blanks. "Isn't that douche in prison?"

"He should be." Catarina sighs, brushing hair out of her eyes. It's rare for Athena not to like someone, but the reference to Nattalius makes her teeth grind. While Delilah didn't share the specifics about what he did, she knows he hurt her. That man broke Delilah's heart—a heart she's been protecting with barbs and claws and teeth since the moment she realized it beats in her chest. "I swore him off. We both were supposed to."

"Do you think she would go to him?" Paisley directs the question to Catarina, but Athena knows the answer. People assume Delilah doesn't have feelings—an odd assumption, considering she wears them on her sleeves—but she's forgiving and pathologically understanding. As complicated as her relationship with the Lord might be, Delilah admires Him and His ceaseless grace. "I'm taking it from the weird quiet thing happening that she would. Why?"

"If anyone knows how to destroy it, it's him. His family descends from the original Hunter Queen."

"What are the chances she was taken?" Athena forces herself to ask, despite the bile coating her tongue when she does. With bated breath, she waits for Catarina's response, the silence stretching until holding it becomes painful. Cat's face blanches. The corner of her top lip twitches. "Please tell me that's a good twitch. Tell me it's a 'I'm laughing at you because that's a ridiculous idea bred from your sister's paranoia' twitch."

"Some people would cheat, lie, steal, kill... do anything for a Sacrament. Especially one as powerful as the Crown." Catarina shakes her head, hair moving like water. She taps something on her keyboard and ducks her head when someone walks into the room. Chatter fills the background for a minute. "There's a slight chance she brought it to the Senate or the Imperium."

"She doesn't trust the Imperium."

"She doesn't trust anyone. That's part of the problem."

"Ingrid mentioned an emergency plan. You, me, Ibrahim, and her." Catarina's silence increases the pressure building up behind Athena's eyes. She needs a nap. She needs a snack. She needs her sister. "Why did she have an emergency plan in place?"

"You know about the possibility of war. We talked about it."

"A war that would include you, me, and Ingrid. It would involve all of us. It would involve her." Athena stands when Catarina inspects her nails. There it is. The twitch again! "You were thinking about someone specific when I said taken, Cat. Who would want to take Delilah?"

She sighs. "How much did she tell you about your parents?"

Alarm bells ring. She glances at Paisley, who mouths something along the lines of 'oh shoot'. Her parents kept secrets their entire lives. Delilah seemed to inherit them upon their deaths, but now Ingrid and Cat appear to hold keys to this secret place Athena's never been permitted to enter. What could possibly be kept there? "What do you mean?"

"That answers that." She drops her chin into her palm and shuffles again before reorganizing her hands. Catarina, having worked most of her life in an academic setting, dons the cloth of diplomacy well. "I will not betray her trust by telling you. She deserves to share that story—I'll know by tomorrow whether she came to Imperio or if anyone has heard about the Crown. Wait for my call before you do anything."

She hangs up without another word. Paisley and Athena stare at one another, twins in their perplexion. What 'story'? Athena's suspicions about her parents' deaths started the moment the police told her and Delilah their overly cautious mother and doting father were speeding in a blizzard and grew when her hunter classmates laughed at her proclamation that her dad, a Christos, died by car crash. They thought she was joking and kept trying to prompt her into sharing 'the rest of the story'... clearly, she doesn't know what that is.

"That was vaguely ominous. Now, I want to find Delilah for the tea." Paisley's voice penetrates the fog falling over Athena's mind. She stares transfixed at her own reflection cast by her dark phone screen. Bushy eyebrows. Wide nose. Pinched eyes. She's staring into her parents' faces, the bits of them knit together by God's hand to form a new creation, and yet she almost doesn't recognize them anymore. "What do you think she meant?"

"I have no idea."

CHAPTER 4

Show Me the Money

Bzzzt bzzzt bzzzt. Five months ago, her phone vibrating with a text message wouldn't have ripped her from sleep. Now, Athena flies halfway off the bed to grab it from her nightstand. Ibrahim's hand slips over her bare leg, and his lips smack adorably. By the steady rhythm of his heart, beating as audibly as her own, he's still sleeping.

Athena opens the text with one hand and uses the other to hold his.

I've reached out to my friends in the Senate.

They haven't gotten back to me yet.

Another text appears before she can respond.

Can you take pictures of everything in her office?

And ask Ingrid if there's anywhere else she might keep her research.

Athena told Cat she tried that already… but a distraction, however obvious, is welcome in place of her new hobby—worrying. Her husband hears every worried thought, and though he is too much of a gentleman to complain, it must be a hindrance during his workday. The further apart they are, the less he hears, and the more she can focus on being upset about Delilah without upsetting anyone else.

She slides the phone back onto the nightstand and twists to stare at the husband in question. Unable to help herself, she traces a line down Ibrahim's spine, watching goosebumps erupt on his dark skin. Every morning since their wedding, they've woken up together and begun their day side-by-side. It's earlier than usual, but he'll be upset if she breaks their new tradition.

"*Heure de se réveiller, mon loup*." He loves when she speaks French, so much so he uses the hand around her leg to pull her closer. With pink cheeks, she presses a hand to his chest and a soft kiss on his shoulder. "I need to go."

"Go?" he mumbles into the pillow, ears perking. Athena cannot resist the temptation to give him another kiss before she pulls the blankets off her body. "Nooo, don't go."

He pulls her right back into the bed, and she giggles, burrowing her face into his chest. The silk ends of his durag brush her forehead. "Catarina wants me to check the house again."

"What time is it?"

She strains to check the clock and winces. "5:02 AM."

"It's too early to go to the house."

"Chun is the only one there, and he doesn't even sleep in the house. Maybe my senses are sharper in the morning after a good sleep—I might notice something."

He grunts and lifts a fist, rubbing the sleep from his eyes. Tiptoeing to her dresser, she pulls out a pair of jeans and a thick embroidered sweater. "I'll come with yo—"

"No, no, no. Don't worry about it. I'll be back in time to help you and Paisley set up the snowball fight." Part of Paisley and Ibrahim's Gamma duties are coming up with after-school activities, like sports, dance parties, flinging paint at stretched out canvases—anything to give the kids a chance to burn off their energy after sitting for most of the day. "Sleep. I'll pick something up for breakfast? Donuts?"

This time, he hums. Smiling, she pads her way to the en-suite bathroom. With the door closed, she removes her menstrual cup and cleans it with special soap. Her period's lighter than normal and early enough to surprise her. Delilah warned Athena that sex might change her cycle, but she didn't expect the sporadicity to kick in after three months. After washing her hands, she forces herself to start her morning routine, despite the lump growing in her throat.

Between Delilah's warning to her, and Killian's to Ibrahim, they've been careful. Vasectomy. Barriers. Athena bites her tongue and tries to breathe through the swell of grief winding through her defenses, and the tears burning her eyes and throat. As a kid, she dreamed about being pregnant and all the beautiful moments that come with it: surprising everyone with the news, gender reveals, themed baby showers, nurseries with a different aesthetic for each child, and most of all, watching Delilah meet her baby, and meeting Delilah's.

Ibrahim's presence chases away the anguish. When he wraps his arms around her though, and his hands brush her empty stomach, she chokes back a sob. "I'm sorry, *ya amar.*"

"It's not your fault." After brushing away her tears, she rinses her mouth out. "I choose you. In sickness and in health. In good times and in bad times. Forsaking all others, even those who don't exist."

"I wanted to see our babies," he admits, his voice cracking. She turns and wraps her arms around him. It's these moments where she thanks God for a Mate. In the good and the bad, he is here; he understands her in a way no one other than the Lord could. "I imagined a little girl with your peach chin."

She laughs, or sobs, while shaking in his arms. "I wanted her to have your crooked teeth."

"We'd be getting her braces," Ibrahim argues darkly, planting a kiss between her brows. The tension melts away the longer he stays there. Squeezing her sides one last time, he pulls away. "Better go. I'm about to stink up the place."

Laughing, she runs out of the room.

"Lord, open my eyes, please." After tearing apart her older sister's bedroom, Athena returned to the office. Books litter the floor. One chair is upside down. She tugged on all the different items lining the bookshelves behind the desk in case there was another secret entrance, like the one leading to Iman and Ingrid's room, yet she found nothing. Nada. Zilch. "There must be something."

Even if Delilah shredded all her notes, the scraps of them exist somewhere. In this house or another one… when she wasn't in Witchhill, she had to stay *somewhere*. Athena stares down at her phone, thumb hovering over the banking app. It's a bit invasive to go into Delilah's account, but she insisted on giving Athena full access. Maybe she knew a moment like this would come where Athena would need to check her bank records.

Decision made, Athena logs into their shared bank account. Their chequing and savings accounts appear first as the mortgages and investments are kept on a different tab. She opens the mortgages before returning to the main page. Right there, under purchases—a POS transaction from Munich on November 1st.

The previous purchase took place in an unspecified location. Athena would bet every dollar in their account that Del was in Imperio before November 1st. If she ended up in Munich, it was probably so she could use the airport or train. Yet based on her bank statement, she didn't pay for a ticket, which meant she either went to Munich for a day trip, returned to Imperio, and is still there now, or someone else paid for her to leave.

Athena scrolls through the last four months of statements and screenshots every purchase. Days after their wedding, Delilah bought tickets to New York City and made a purchase there at an unspecified store. Two weeks later, she purchased a ticket to Munich. She was in Imperio at the same time as Athena and didn't say a word about it.

Sending the bundle of screenshots to Cat, she types out a message.

Munich means Imperio, right?

The trail ends with that purchase in Munich. Either she's using cash, someone's footing the bill, or she's… Athena swallows the lump in her throat.

The likelihood of her sister being kidnapped seemed low until Catarina reacted like she did yesterday. There's a chance someone took Delilah, but who would do that, and *why*? Did they want the Crown? Did they want Delilah?

It seems likely. She's got a place in Rhode Island.

I know she picks up 90% of her assignments in the greater NY area.

Why do you think she was in New York for two weeks and then went to Imperio?

I don't know.

Okay… what do you think?

Three little dots bounce and dance on Athena's screen in time with her erratic heartbeat. Unable to hold back a wave of vertigo, she closes her eyes and falls straight into a memory. Pale sunlight glints off the foiled letters of her parents' tombstones. The tissue, damp with tears, burns against her raw skin. Instead of standing with Delilah at her side, she stares at her sister's name lined up beside her parents'.

"I can't bury someone else," she whispers aloud to God. Acid burns the back of her throat. "Please Tzevaot, protect her. Surround her with Your angels so she does not scuff her feet."

Knowing Delilah? She thought she could get rid of the Crown by herself and realized she couldn't. She came to Imperio for Nattalius or the Imperium.

If it's the Imperium, she left the Crown behind.

At your house, or the one in Rhode Island.

Do you know where the house is?

Athena stands, light-headed, and scrambles for the front door. Her lungs beg for fresh air and its chill to chase away all her worries. Before she opens the front door, she smells it. Fresh air. Cold air. It competes with the staleness of a winterized house. No one in their right mind would open a window in this weather, let alone leave it open the entire weekend.

The phone buzzes in her hand, but she ignores it and chases the smell with a twitching nose. A shiver claims her skin when she reaches the basement door. Athena has hated the basement since the age of four. It's dark, wet, and unfinished—a total eyesore. Mom and Dad added it after buying the house, and though they never expressed a purpose for it, she hoped for years it would house a younger sibling.

Foreboding washes over her as she turns on the light. An exposed lightbulb swings in the empty space, both casting and peeling shadows. Oddly, it is Delilah's voice in her head that warns her to turn around. The basement stairs creak with each step. Her socked feet hit the rough cement, and the fresh smell grows stronger amidst the dust and dirt.

It's coming from the storage room. A howl rattles from within. With a prayer on her tongue, and fear in her heart, Athena pulls out her phone.

I think we need to stop looking. I know she's your sister, but it's obvious she wants to stay hidden.

Hold that thought, I might have found where she's hiding everything. If I don't respond in ten minutes, send Iba to the basement.

I do not like the sound of that.

Slipping her phone into her back pocket, Athena inches forward. In the darkest part of the storage room, backed into a corner, one of the shelves wiggles. It smacks against the wall with a powerful *bang*.

The sight of a familiar yellow box is a welcome one. Athena reaches into her dad's old toolbox and pulls out a hammer. It's useless, especially because she cannot stomach the idea of using it on a person, but maybe it will scare them.

Another howl comes.

The shelf shudders.

With a little shove, the entire wall flies back. A mud tunnel with wooden joists greets her. It's dark inside but since being Awakened, the pitch of shadows appear more grey than obsidian.

Her phone buzzes loud enough to make her jump. She continues forward, despite the pang of guilt burning in her stomach for ignoring Catarina. The air gets colder and colder until her breath mists. Mom and Dad used to complain about the cost of heating 'old houses', but clearly this isn't any old house.

A secret cabin.

That's what her parents' secret tunnel led to. A long trek and a trapdoor, and she ended up somewhere deep in the forests of Witchhill. It smells like her parents in here, and the grief overwhelms her enough to pause in place.

The sight of her old school backpack breaks the ice from around her feet. Athena crouches beside it, opening the flap with shaky fingers. The clothes inside are hers, and when she digs deeper, her fingers meet the hard edge of a passport. While it's not her name inside, it has her ID picture, with a few edits made to modify her identity. She doesn't need to look into the other two bags to know who they belong to. One smells like Ingrid, and the other has a man's coat hanging out of it. The price tag flutters in the winter wind snaking through the wooden slats of the old cottage. This is Delilah's emergency plan.

Pushing the bags aside, Athena forces herself to breathe and braces for the torrent of emotion waiting behind the dam in her mind. It's sweet her sister cares enough to take care of them. Delilah's always taken care of Athena.

However, Athena and Ibrahim must think of the pack. If war is coming, there may be more orphans to care for. It was different a couple months ago when she was Unawakened; when she was ignorant of all the happenings in Imperio.

She's Awake now. They all are.

A quick search of the cottage reveals keys to a vehicle. Athena steps outside and finds the truck tucked underneath a snow-laden tarp. She wrestles with the tarp under the rising sun, trying not to disturb the peace of the sleeping forest with the sounds of her grunts and groans.

With the tarp vanquished, and sweat coating her brow, Athena climbs into the front seat. She half expects the truck not to start, but it roars to life under her. The interior's been kept clean and empty, except for a single air freshener hanging from the rearview. Narrowing her eyes, Athena adjusts the rearview mirror… the cabin looks bigger than it should.

The snow soaks her socks with every step she takes towards the cabin. Racing against the pain in her feet, Athena counts every window and wall. There *must* be another room. Athena storms into the house and tears into every kitchen cupboard. She moves the beds, kicks aside the rug, and tears down the curtains. There's only one place left to hide: the bathroom. Athena meets her red-rimmed eyes in the grimy mirror and draws closer with a tired sigh.

"Mirror, mirror, on the wall, where's the secret room… that comes at my call?" She shakes her head when nothing happens. It was worth a shot. Athena's nose scrunches, and she glances at the toilet. They wouldn't do that, right? She fights back a gag at the idea. "If I were a secret room, where would I be?"

She opens the mirror to reveal the cabinet within but seeing her parent's toothbrushes sends her reeling in a different direction. The tiles in the shower and on the floor line up perfectly, with no signs of grout being disturbed or moved. Cleaning products and extra toilet paper line the cabinet beneath the sink… which leaves the toilet. Athena chokes back a whimper. There's a ring inside it, and she cannot—

Her foot catches when she tries to flee the bathroom. Falling to one knee, she grabs onto the doorframe to steady herself. Pain shoots up her hip and keeps her on the ground for a breath. The door to the vanity sink swings open and reveals the rows of cleaning products again. At this angle, she can see the plumbing and how it goes into the *side* of the cabinet instead of the back.

Athena climbs to her feet and inches towards the medicine cabinet again. This time, she ignores her parents' toothbrushes and shoves the wall between the shelves. Fluorescent lights flicker within the room, revealing an entire wall of screens that flare to life with footage of the forest outside.

"What the—"

Weapons line an entire wall. Two mannequins, the size of her parents, stand in the corner beside those. Delilah's black board waits on the far wall, perpendicular to the screen. There are two desks and two office chairs here, unlike the office at home. Of course! Why didn't she think about the one desk in their at-home office?

Athena crawls through the hole and pulls out her phone. She snaps photo after photo and backs up to take a picture of the entire room when something brushes against her neck.

The secret truck works, but the sounds it makes when Athena tries to turn into Pack Territory sets her teeth on edge. She cranks the stick into park and releases the breath she'd been holding since leaving the cottage. A russet-coloured wolf runs past her opening door and barks in greeting, followed by a pack of pups. That must be Paisley.

Athena swallows back her desire to call Paisley and instead focuses on emptying the truck. She loads the front porch of the packhouse with boxes, brushing aside any offer of assistance from the Deltas training on the nets. It took two painstaking hours to empty the cottage, and her arms shake under the weight of the box in her hands when she steps into the house.

"I understand that." Killian's voice beckons Athena towards the kitchen. He'll know what to do. "You're not understanding me. Athena is a grown woman."

She pauses outside the kitchen. For a naïve moment, she hopes Delilah is on the other end of the phone. A woman's voice drifts towards her, deep and accented, and entirely different from Delilah's.

"They are sisters," he continues, dishing up pancakes on a plate. The smell of food—the thought of food—threatens her tight control over her curdling stomach. "You think Delilah's the only stubborn one? Athena's stronger than you two give her credit f—"

His mouth snaps shut as his eyes lock onto hers, poorly hidden behind the doorframe. He caught her. She caught him.

They stare at one another from opposite sides of the same island. Athena pours the contents of the box onto the granite surface and pushes a piece of paper towards him. Someone, likely Delilah, wrote out a list of the Sacraments in black ink and crossed half of them off with red. A sticky note with the same red ink protrudes from one corner of the sheet. **We need to find him. We need to end him.**

"You're the one without understanding, Killian," Catarina says on the phone. "If we can find her, so can someone else."

"I'll call you back."

Athena pulls the sticky note off the paper and thrusts it towards him with all the bravado left in her. "Do you know who 'him' is?"

CHAPTER 5

I am a He

"No." Killian tosses his phone onto the counter and rakes his hands through his hair. "I have been trying to figure out what she's been running from ever since we met."

"Cat hasn't told you?"

He pushes a plate towards her with a heavy sigh and circles the island between them. The stool groans under his weight when he takes a seat. Killian pulls a stool out for her, scanning the photos and notes spread out on the island. "She, like your sister, uses words like a shield. I don't think she trusts me."

"Delilah does," Athena promises, squeezing his arm. He continues moving the pictures around with a knit between his eyebrows. It's hard not meddling sometimes. God knows how happy Killian could make her sister if she'd just give him a chance. "Or she wouldn't have left me here."

"Catarina wanted me to dissuade you from finding her." He holds the ominous sticky note in one hand, flattening the crumbled edges with his thumb. End 'him', not them. Delilah and an unnamed accomplice want to find one man, one person, and end *him.* Who is him and who is we? "I don't know why she thinks I have that power, or why I'd use it to stop you from finding Del."

"She's scared," Athena whispers. A man who scares someone as fierce as Catarina is not a man Athena wants to meet, and yet she'd march against the principalities and powers of the fallen world for her sister. "I am going to find her, Killian."

He nods, his Adam's apple bobbing. "Have these pictures given you an idea of where she is?"

"I know she was last in Munich. She put me as a secondary on her bank account so I can access all her statements." A blush colours her face, but he says nothing about it. Killian's a provider by nature. It's one of the reasons he and Delilah would be so good together. Givers need to be with givers. "She has a place in Rhode Island, but I think I'm going to go to Imperio."

"Why?"

There's nothing in Rhode Island. Athena can't explain why she knows that, but she knows it intrinsically. Delilah went to New York City for a specific reason—the note on Athena's knife set said it came from Delilah's favourite utility shop, maybe that shop is in the city. "I just feel like New York was a pit stop, not the destination."

"Do you know why she would go to Imperio?"

"I didn't find any clues, but this isn't all of it."

Paisley sits cross-legged on the roof of the truck, mumbling to herself as they approach. She lifts two pictures to the sun and speaks over her shoulder when she says, "Is this what an actual mermaid looks like? I thought they were supposed to be beautiful."

"She's… nice-looking," Ibrahim supplies from the side of the truck. He jumps to attention at their approach and offers a sheepish smile to his Alpha. "I couldn't stop her."

"We were concerned," Paisley declares, flipping the picture around. "Do we think mermaids have Delilah?"

"*We* do not think anything at the moment. Bring the boxes inside." Killian's voice draws the two silent partakers, Mona and Graham, out from behind the truck. After stacking boxes in their arms, they shuffle silently into the house. "Get off the roof, please."

Pictures of the rarest creatures known to hunters——mermaids, unicorns, leprechauns, dragons—were pinned underneath the list of crossed-out Sacraments. Delilah made flash cards, like Athena's, with the best kill methods for each creature, and the weaknesses known to hunters. 'Horn??' and 'run' were the only two words written under the picture of a unicorn.

"I'd kill to fight a unicorn," Paisley confesses, allowing Killian to help her off the truck. With her bare feet on the snow, she approaches Athena and slings an arm around her shoulders. "I'm sure she was just doing research."

"She's looking for the other Sacraments," Mona argues from the front porch, arms still full of boxes. "I said this would happen. She got a taste of power, and she wants more."

"We're not having this conversation out in the open," Killian says, voice rich with authority. The wolves bow to it, following his unsaid directions to bring the boxes to his office. Athena rushes ahead of them to clear the strategy table from the diagram of Witchhill, which they made to track the movement of the serial killer who took so many lives in spring. Memories flood back when she looks at the tiny figurines meant to represent Delilah, the wolves, and the killer who ended up being Delilah's ex. "You can put that on my desk, Athena."

She nods, sliding it onto the C-shaped desk where Killian does most of his work. The others bring the rest of the boxes in while she opens the curtains behind his desk and cracks a window. It may be winter, and freezing outside, but 'heated argument' is more than metaphorical when the Garity Pack's governing body meets.

"Have some class," Paisley mutters the moment the double doors at the end of the long room close. She points a finger at Mona, stepping between her and Athena. "Maybe the Sacraments are crossed out because they've been destroyed."

"Or maybe it's because she's found them."

"Or someone else has," Killian adds, gripping the edge of the thick table. He and Graham stare at one another over the varnished surface. There's something there again—an involuntary reaction to a dark secret, like Ingrid's sighs and Cat's twitches. "There have been whispers for the last two years that King Hozeir still lives."

The room falls silent. Athena lumbers to Ibrahim's side, wrapping her hand around his. She clears her throat in the silence and asks, "As in the evil Werewolf King?"

She did a test on him during Requisite. His experiments and actions led to one of the Imperium's most successful raids. Every man and woman who declared their loyalty to the Hielanders were killed. Children were relocated between the packs—the Garity Pack included. Werewolves were dragged out of their beds at night. Packs were visited by hunters, and hundreds were killed when they could not give a clear answer on their involvement or feelings about the king.

A king who they said died alongside his people.

"He was killed." Goosebumps blaze a trail of pure fire down Athena's arm to her hand, intertwined with Ibrahim's. She glances at each wolf, looking for someone to agree with her, but no one does. They found his body. They *documented* his body. "He was killed, right?"

He tried to create hybrids through magic and force. Dozens, if not hundreds, of Otherworlders were taken by him and forced to procreate. The Imperium put an end to that, or at least they claimed they did.

"King Hozeir claimed to be one of the original Lycanthropes from Hell. He spent years trying to make the humans worship him as the Underlord before the war began." Graham says the words like they are poisonous. His skin pulls taut around his clenched jaw, stretching the thick pink scar Athena has never been brave enough to ask about. She knows it has something to do with the uprising against King Hozeir; Paisley told her that much. Wolves across Europe stood up to his tyranny—something none of the hunter history classes mentioned—and often paid for it with their lives. "When the Hunter Queen started using the Sacraments, he became obsessed. He wanted that power for his people. He hated the laws and governance of the Imperium."

"He tried to collect them," Athena states. Graham's revelation gives the pictures new meaning; crossed out doesn't mean destroyed or accounted for, it might mean taken by *him*. King Hozeir could be alive, ready to wage the war he'd threatened… the war Delilah kept warning her about. "He might have all those items already."

Mona growls, crumpling a picture of a man who *must* be the king. "He might not be alive."

"Now is not the time for hopeful thinking. Whether King Hozeir is alive or not, there are players making moves for the Sacraments. If the Crown was the first revealed, which I doubt, that leaves six other pieces." Killian rubs a hand over his beard, scanning the clues laid out before him. He pauses on the same thing Athena did before packing everything up: a world map. Scribble marks cover a couple of the cities, and she counts thirteen holes where push pins had been. One in Witchhill, three in the UK, one in Mexico, two in South America, one in Australia, one in Asia, one in Africa, and three in Europe. Six Sacraments, twelve possible locations. "An Alpha might have claimed kingship and took up his predecessor's torch."

"The only person who would dare is Uncle Sean," Mona says, smacking both palms onto the table. It's no secret Killian's dad wanted to take the empty throne, or at least Ibrahim said it's not. After the raids, most Alphas were too scared to expose their packs to the Imperium's eyes, but Sean Garity welcomed their scrutiny. "Everyone's been waiting for you."

Athena chokes on her shock and slaps a hand over her mouth when they all look at her. "Sorry, I didn't mean… I d-didn't think—didn't know."

"I am not interested." Killian smiles at her, even though she basically just laughed at him. His soft expression melts the second he looks at Mona. "They can keep waiting."

"Killian's the strongest werewolf that's been born in… centuries?

Millenia?" Mona cocks her head to the side, appraising him. No one contradicts her, because why would they? He's a giant—six-foot-five, broad-chested, and covered in layers of muscle. Everyone in the pack has seen him in scraps of clothing, either training the Deltas or leading the morning run. *They*, the people under his protection, know better than to challenge him. "Uncle Sean descended from a Hielander."

"I am not meant to be king." Killian's conviction rattles Athena enough for her to look at Ibrahim. He squeezes her hand, silencing the whirlwind of his thoughts and desires for his Alpha. Ibrahim wants him to be king. All of them do. After the death of King Hozeir, the wolves were divided. Those who wanted better for their species were vilified, and those who suggested submission to the hunters were called traitors. Young wolves were raised without pack pride—and without their parents—and were expected to stay silent in the face of the Imperium's injustice. The Imperium made it impossible to recover, but there are those, like Iba and Pais, who believe a strong, *good* King could fix everything. "Drop it, Mona."

"Who cares about being king? The Sacraments are being unearthed, and that didn't go so well for our kind last time." Paisley trembles like a leaf. Without hesitation, Athena rushes to her side and wraps her arms around her. "So, what do we do? Do we send a report to the Imperium? Do we hide the pups and prepare the Deltas?"

"We find Delilah," Ibrahim murmurs, stepping up to the table. It's rare for him to speak in these meetings, but he doesn't back down when they all look his way. Pride burns through Athena, and she prays he feels it through their link. "It's obvious she's trying to stop someone from getting the Sacraments. It could be the king, or her ex, or it could be some random—it doesn't matter who it is, it matters that she's trying, and she cannot do it alone."

"And how are you planning to find her?" Mona questions, rolling her eyes. "She obviously doesn't want help."

Athena pipes up. "We'll go to Imperio."

"Oh yeah? What're you going to do when you get there?"

"Ask questions," Athena sputters, raising her hands and dropping them. Imperio is the last known place Delilah had been to. There's an Imperium task force charged with overseeing Sacrament infractions; she probably went there to make her case. "She's a Christos. I know that may not mean a lot here, but it means a lot there. Someone must know where she is."

"I think the questions we'd need to ask are the kinds that get people like us in trouble," Killian states with a pained smile. The blood drains from her face at the implication. Werewolves are not hunters. If they walk the streets of Imperio, they'll draw attention and depending on the hunter, or time of day, they might be in danger.

"I'm so sorry. I didn't think." Athena clumsily pulls out her phone and taps the screen to life. "Let me text Cat. I-I know she wants to help Delilah stay hidden, but I think she'll help when she knows we're not backing down."

Ibrahim wraps an arm around Athena's waist. Puffing out his chest, he stares down at the others. "We're going back to Imperio with or without your approval… Mona and Graham. Killian?"

"I am coming too."

That pulls Athena's eyes right off her phone. A pin could drop and result in a nuclear level boom. Everyone in the room stares at him with mixed expressions of surprise and, in Mona's case, horror. Alphas don't leave their packs if they do not have a Luna. Ibrahim and Paisley emphasized that point when they educated Athena on the way of wolves.

"War is on our front step." Graham's voice gets louder and louder as Killian walks past Ibrahim, Paisley, and Athena. He rifles noisily through his desk without a second glance at his Beta. "If King Hozeir is alive—"

"I might be the only one who can kill him," Killian declares, straightening. The light from outside highlights every curve of his muscles. He may not want to be king, but the sunlight wrapping around his head like a crown certainly makes him look like one. "He lived because hunters tried to kill him."

Wounds inflicted by another werewolf take longer to heal. The silver used by hunters may cut and kill, but clean wounds heal faster. Athena clears her throat and squeezes Ibrahim's hand. "Let's hope it doesn't come to that. Maybe Delilah found a way to destroy the Crown."

"We need a day to get ready and get our flights." The rhythmic whir of a printer coming to life flares from one side of the room. It squeaks and cries around the paper inching through it. "Graham will serve as Alpha in my stead. Paisley, you will be Bet—"

"Please let me come." Paisley clasps her hands together, bouncing towards him. He glances between her and Mona. The eagerness in Mona's eyes hurts Athena's heart as much as Ibrahim's. "Please, please, please. I love travelling. I am good in a fight AND I've gone camping more than any of you. I can hunt and scavenge and make any tent my bi—"

"Mona. Are you willing to step in as Beta?"

Mona's hands fall from her hips. For the first time in Athena's memory, Mona looks happy. Ibrahim rushes to her side to clap her on the back. "Of course."

A thunderous expression crosses Killian's face, brought on by words

Athena cannot hear. She searches the wolves' faces, finding Graham's eyes expressing what his lips do not. The tension ratchets to a suffocating degree when Mona inserts herself telepathically. “I am going to tell Cat.”

“It might be better to show up unannounced,” Paisley suggests, skipping beside Athena. She and Ibrahim high five one another on their way out. “That way, she can't hide the bodies, ya know?”

“She's Delilah's Companion, though.” Athena sends her a quick heads up and grins at her two best friends. “Besides, you haven't seen her place. If she wanted to hide something in there, you'd never find it.”

CHAPTER 6

On the Hunt

Athena wakes from a dead sleep for the second morning in a row. She rubs the sleep from her eyes and sits up, despite the lure of her warm bed. The darkness is so oppressive it makes her think it's way too early to get up and yet she's wide awake.

She reaches for her phone out of habit, not because it's buzzing like it did yesterday. After sending the text to Catarina about continuing the search for Delilah and requesting her help, Athena expected a response—whether a dismissal or a warning or a concession. But her sister's Companion read the message and didn't reply.

Athena types out another text and deletes it after a breath. Maybe the message came off as too aggressive. Catarina's been nothing but kind and considerate. She opened up her home to them in Imperio and offered advice about what stretches to do when Athena could barely walk after gruelling training session after gruelling training session. She types another response but deletes that too.

For once, she's 100% sure this is what she should do. Going to Imperio feels right. Following Delilah feels right. It's a God thing, it must be, because she cannot depend on her instincts nine times out of ten.

"It's too early."

She apologizes by sliding along Ibrahim's arm and pressing a kiss on the thin skin behind his ear. Goosebumps erupt down his neck, towards the Mark she left on his skin. "I'll let you get back to sl—"

He growls playfully and pulls her right back under the blanket. Giggles pour out, despite the recent tension. His touch and kisses dissolve all rational thought, leaving only instinct and sense behind. The same instinct that woke her in the first place. The same sense that tried to warn her the moment she opened her eyes.

"El?" Ibrahim pauses, his lips hovering over the skin of her collarbone. She sees the outline of Ibrahim's body, and the dim light underneath the door coming from the oven range in the kitchen. Silk and skin meet her touch, and she tastes sweat on her tongue. The house smells of last night's pasta and the earth, beyond the thin walls, smells like snow and pine. Beyond even that, she smells every wolf who lives on pack territory, and the animals sleeping and stalking in the forest beyond. Heartbeats pulse in a subtle rhythm beneath the sound of the fridge kicking in and the river outside. "What is it?"

"I-I—" It's her hunter sense. It must be. There's something… or a lack of something out there. The more she focuses on it, the surer she is. She tastes and smells nothing new, but she hears something—the faint heartbeat of a creature she cannot smell. "There's a hunter here."

Their eyes bleed into each other for one second, and then Ibrahim gets up. She knows he's speaking to Killian when his eyes dart back and forth. This is the day every Otherworlder dreads. Having a single hunter approach them, especially in the dead of night, is how the Imperium conducts a raid.

Otherworlders don't survive raids.

Athena runs out of the room before Ibrahim can stop her. She pulls a jacket over her nightie and, with one foot in a boot, hops onto the front deck. The hunter wears a hood over their head and a long, black woollen jacket. With their hands tucked in their pockets, and their back to her, it's impossible to know what weapons they might be hiding.

Channeling her inner Delilah, Athena stomps into the snow. "Can I help you?"

"Yes," a familiar voice responds. Puffs of white air come out of Catarina's painted lips as she laughs. "You can get me somewhere warm."

"Is entertaining hunters becoming our thing?" demands Mona, voice nothing more than a hiss. When Paisley opens her mouth, Mona continues speaking. "The pack might have moved to Canada, but we are not Canadian. This hospitality and self-sacrificing altruism needs to stop."

"You're not Beta yet," Graham snaps, glaring at her over his shoulder. The two Gammas and Athena uncomfortably shuffle to one side to avoid Mona's retaliation. Five grown adults spying on someone through a tiny crack in the door is proving increasingly ridiculous.

"And you're not Alpha."

Paisley and Athena share a look. If Killian is leaving the pack with these two, he must be pretty worried about King Hozeir.

Or pretty attached to Delilah.

"Why are you all standing out here like children?" Killian appears behind the bunch of them, quirking his eyebrow. He divides their small group like the Red Sea and walks into the office with his normal confident air. "Catarina, it's nice to finally meet you in person."

The hunter straightens, all five-foot-four inches of her, and stares at him, wide-eyed. Her reaction brings Athena back to her own. She had also been intimidated by his size, and of course by his relationship to Ibrahim. This was before they became officially exclusive, and Athena spent the entire dinner with Ibrahim's family thinking about how much she wanted Delilah to be there… that old wound smarts.

"You are a giant," Catarina remarks, stretching her dark red lips into a grin. She whistles through the gap between her two front teeth and twirls a finger in the air. "Do a turn for me, *gato.*"

She says something else in Portuguese underneath her breath when he follows her instructions and spins in place. The comment includes Delilah's name and, based on the feminine appreciation lighting up Catarina's hazel-green eyes, must have something to do with how attractive Killian is.

"*Você me lisonjeia.*"

Her eyebrows raise at Killian's response. Athena was shocked when he responded the first time she spoke in French. She soon learned that while she enjoys languages, he loves them. Ukrainian is his current obsession—the twelfth language in his repertoire. "Are you fluent?"

"Yes."

Her cheeks might be red from the violent winter wind or because he understood what the rest of them cannot. Ever the composed woman, Catarina brushes her bangs aside and waves a hand. "It's all true. These are all from Delilah?"

Athena chimes in. "I found her hiding place."

She nods, arranging pictures together on the wolf's table. There's an elegance and grace to her that Athena lacks. All properly trained hunters have it. Catarina grew up in Imperio and attended Primary before completing the standard four years at Seminary. Every movement, every expression, every glance serves a purpose. Athena can only hope that the purpose Catarina wants to serve is finding Delilah.

"She met with someone. I asked a friend that works in the Administration Office who, but she had no idea. It must be someone from the Fifteen, or the Chancellor." The wolves and Athena stand back as she rearranges the papers and pictures. Catarina moves like she knows exactly how Delilah displayed them, bringing fragments together to form a completed picture. The colours of the X's on the Sacraments match scribbles on the map. "Does that say 'we'?"

"'We need to find him. We need to end him.'" Athena frowns at the twitch in Cat's lip. "You know who the 'we' is, don't you?"

"Delilah's devil got out."

Mona swears. Loud enough to make Catarina jump. She turns to her with a raised eyebrow, holding two pieces of text-filled paper in her hands. "Classic. He probably got a slap on the wrist."

"I said he *got* out… he escaped. One second, he was in prison, the next he was not." Catarina glares at a picture of Nattalius beside the uncrumpled image of King Hozeir. There were pictures of other people too, like the mermaid or the woman with no eyes, but Nattalius and King Hozeir were the only two anyone recognized. "If someone wanted to know about the Sacraments, or find them, he would be the one to ask."

"What if King Hozeir grabbed him?" Athena whispers, wringing her hands. No matter what Nattalius did to Delilah, she'd go after him. She'd even risk her life to save him from the Werewolf King, which sickens Athena to her core. Ibrahim comes to her aid, pulling her back into his chest.

"If King Hozeir is alive as you all seem to believe, he won't need the help of N—the traitor to find anything. Hozeir lived when the objects were created. He knows them better than any of us." She sighs, slapping her hands onto the table. "It's more likely Delilah and Nattalius were tasked with destroying the Crown or finding the other Sacraments by a member of the Senate. It's very hush hush."

If Delilah and Nattalius were sanctioned by the Senate, wouldn't they need the entire legion? Companions are stronger together. Athena inches closer to Catarina and lowers her voice. "And they didn't include you?"

"Delilah knows I would take the Crown and use her little loophole to make that piece of shit break his own legs."

"What loophole?"

"What actually happened between them?" Paisley flashes an apologetic smile at Athena but continues forward without pause. "It's not my place, I know, but come on. I can't be the only one who's dying to know."

"He betrayed her. That is all that matters." With her hunter gear on, Catarina's got no bracelets to play with, but what she lacks in jewellery, she makes up for in the glitter on her sunset eyes. Though, the glitter doesn't help with her self-soothing habit. Athena reaches for her floundering hands and squeezes them. "It means she cannot trust him. If they get into a fight, he will not watch her back. He will throw her to the dogs—no offense."

"It wasn't offensive until you said that," Paisley murmurs, shrugging when Graham and Killian give her a look. "If I didn't say it Mona would, and she'd be meaner."

"I know you think we should leave her," Athena begins, watching the conflict play out on Catarina's face. They can do this without her, but Cat knows Imperio and their world better than any of them. If Delilah met with the Senate, there's politics involved. Politics Athena didn't take the chance to learn, because she was too preoccupied with the creatures wanting to kill her, and those she should supposedly want to kill. "But I'm worried. Something's wrong. I feel nauseous every time I think about her."

Catarina's eyes narrow infinitesimally on her stomach. The glance is worse than a stake to the heart. Iba comes protectively closer but that only makes it worse. "I said that before I thought about that *filho da mãe* with her. We are going to find them, and I'm going to drag him back to prison myself."

Killian sits at his desk, booting up his computer. "I'll see if I can find another seat on our flight."

"And what flight is that?"

"To Munich."

"We need to start in Imperio. It was the last place she was seen." Athena offers a tentative smile when Cat tuts. "We can find out who Del spoke to."

"Why did I come here then?" she laughs, dropping into one of the armchairs next to Killian's desk. The pit in Athena's stomach disappears without Catarina's scrutiny. She's here, and she's going to help. They're going to find Delilah. "What is the opposite of Hell? Is there a really cold place where the souls of sinners suffer?"

Graham's the one who offers, "Russia."

"He's funny," Catarina murmurs, missing—or ignoring—Mona's menacing growl. She settles her eyes back on Athena and Ibrahim where they cling to one another. "Unless you made powerful friends during your visit, I do not think it will be easy to figure out who she visited."

"I'm a Christos." Athena tries to channel some of their confidence into her smile.

CHAPTER 7

Daniel in the Senate's Den

Only one name came to mind when Catarina mentioned powerful friends. After declaring her husband was a wolf, Athena lost the opportunity to build relationships with her classmates or professors, but she met a few like-minded individuals in physio. Daniel, the one who suggested that witch-made injection to break up scar tissue, shared Athena's distaste for the Imperium's system, and they spent many mornings whispering their ideas for a better world.

She knew he worked at Seminary, but she didn't know his exact role. If anyone had asked her a week ago who Daniel from physio was, she'd tell them he was a successful vegan who inspired her to try again; she'd tell them he rivalled Archie's skin-to-tattoo ratio, and that he told Athena to leave Imperio and never look back. She never would've guessed he moved like a shadow avoiding the light and struck with the ferocity of a lightning bolt in the name of killing as many Otherworlders as possible in as little time as possible.

"You should've mentioned your friend was Daniel *Blau.*"

Had she'd known he was Daniel Blau, head of the fourth-year combat training—not Daniel, friendly holistic anarchist—she would've been more careful with how she spoke about the Imperium. Athena sucks as much air into her lungs as possible to stave off the vertigo and twists to face Catarina. "I—is that a name I should recognize?"

"Delilah really didn't tell you anything about your family?"

"She told me about the Christos'."

"And what's your mom's maiden name?"

Athena opens her mouth, then shuts it. "I don't know."

"It's Blau, Athena." Catarina shields her eyes with her hands and hisses when Daniel slams three of his students into the dirt. "Daniel's dad and your mom were cousins. Your great uncle, Levi, raised them together in a house not far from here."

"Really?" Unlike Delilah and Athena, Daniel has thick black hair, with perpetually wet-looking curls. His nose is petite and rounded, his cheekbones high, and he has a thin face, thinner than theirs. She wishes they shared his cherub lips, but those must be from his mother's side. Tattoos cover most of his visible skin, except for where his Companion marks will one day go, so she cannot see if they share freckles or birth marks or skin tones. "Are you sure?"

"Levi's the one who enrolled Delilah in Seminary. I don't think she met Daniel, or his twin Diza, but she knows they exist."

"What are the chances?"

"Imperio's small." Catarina doesn't seem convinced of her own words. There's no way it is purely coincidental. God knew. He must've known Athena would need a connection to the Senate and Imperium, and who better than the man who trains their children and best fighters? "He is incredible."

"Do you think he knows?" Athena briefly averts her eyes from Daniel to check Cat's expression. By the time she looks back, he is motionless on the field, staring at them. He shouts something over his shoulder at his trainees before heading towards the girls. "Why isn't he, you know, hunting? He's incredible, ankle injury or not."

"No idea. He is…." Catarina trails off, staring at him in a way that makes Athena blush. The trainers and trainees alike wear an all-black ensemble of shorts and tanks. The outfit exposes many of Daniel's tattoos, from the words spread across his knuckles to the almost completed sleeves on his arms and the wings curled around both sides of his neck. The tattoo on his right leg grabbed Athena's attention the first time she met him, and it has the same effect on Catarina. A saint with his arms spread overshadows the widow with two coins and the offering plate. "I'm not even sure I believe in God, but I'm thanking Him right now."

Well, perhaps it was not the tattoo on his thigh that caught Catarina's attention, but the sculpted muscle underneath it.

Daniel pauses ten feet away and rests his hands on his hips, expression darker than his clothing. Athena smiles with all of her teeth exposed and nervously steps closer. "Physio seems to be paying off."

"Not enough," Daniel jokes, the tension melting off his body. He swaggers closer, sparing a quick glance at Catarina before smiling at Athena like he did every morning whenever their paths crossed. "I thought you were getting out of here, kid."

"I wanted to," Athena confesses, wrapping her arms around herself. How does one respond to meeting a family member they never knew existed? The other kids in her elementary class had family trees with branches so long they went off the colouring page. When she made hers, she had four names on it. "Did you know we're cousins?"

He steps back, narrowing his eyes. "David?"

Who's David? A million questions flood her head and none have anything to do with who Delilah and Nattalius met with. "Eliana."

"Grandpa said she had two girls." He uses the bottom of his shirt to wipe his brow, stunning Catarina, who makes a strangled noise. Trying not to expire on the spot, Athena's smile widens. "David's her older brother. He's still human as far as I know, but he has dormant children."

"Mom has a brother?"

"She had two, but Isaac died. They think that's the reason she... how much do you know about your mom?"

"Not as much as I thought," Athena murmurs, focusing on the shaved line through one of his eyebrows. Thoughts fly through her mind, bouncing from one side of her skull to the other, so quick she's unable to collect them. "I want to know—I have so many questions, but we came here for something else and it's more important."

Cocking one eyebrow, he glances back at his class. "Okay."

"My sister Delilah is missing. We know she went to meet someone from the Senate, but no one will tell us who."

"I try to keep myself out of politics," he laughs, dropping his hands from his hips. The amusement falls off his face when he stares at the townhouses surrounding the Seminary. Everyone but the inner circle of the Imperium live in townhouses, each building a carbon copy of the one before it. Every tree, plant, rock, sidewalk, and road serve the purpose of the Imperium. Even the weather is controlled by a spell, so it's never too hot or too cold. "I meant what I said, Athena. Get as far away from here as possible. David made the smart choice—"

"Your grandpa works directly with the Imperium, and I know he keeps an eye on Delilah." Catarina puts her hands on her hips, feet firmly planted. Being more of the begging type, Athena searches for a sob story to convince him, yet she ends up caught in the crosswind of her thoughts. Her mind, capable of memory, imagination, and sin, repeats the words 'I have a family' until the cry reaches a fever pitch. "I can figure out where he lives myself and tell him you refused to help us, or you can just text him right now and get an answer."

Scoffing, Daniel pulls out his phone. "You sure she wants to be found?"

"I don't care what she wants," Athena mumbles, her stomach twisting with the admission. It's selfish to drag Delilah back, but if there's a war coming, they should face it together. They are family… they have family. "Thank you for helping."

"Didn't have much choice. Grandpa's not someone you mess with." He smiles at Athena and levels Catarina with a look a lesser woman might crumble from. "Can I know the name of my extortionist?"

"We've passed each other at work." Athena fights back the urge to leave them alone together, especially when Daniel wets his lip. "Did he respond yet?"

"Maybe. What's your name?"

"Figure it out, pretty boy."

Daniel grins, and in that grin, Athena finally sees his resemblance to Delilah. His lip tilts, like Delilah's, when mischief calls his name. His phone buzzes before he can say anything else. "Chancellor

Montgomery."

"That means the Imperium and Senate might not know," Catarina whispers, low enough for all three of them to hear, but no one else. "Chancellor Montgomery is the king of pissing contests. It should be easy to get answers out of him if we flutter our eyelashes a little."

"I don't think you need to do much fluttering." Daniel drags his eyes up and down Catarina, driving the point home. Athena blushes for her, but Cat's face remains as blank as ever. Twisting on her heel, Cat grabs Athena's hand. "Wait." They both pause, one eager for his interruption, the other pinning him with a dry glare. "I haven't met Delilah, but she's family. If you need something, let me know.... I'm not much good in a fight, but I can make a mean sandwich."

"What're you talking about? You're the best fighter I've ever seen." Athena frowns at his smile, which looks more like a grimace. Instead of explaining the weird contradiction, he jogs back to his students without another word—and without a hint of his limp. "I like him."

"He knew Delilah was here. The whole family did. Just like the Christos'." Cat's tone adopts a cool edge like nothing Athena's heard before. Chills crawl up her arms and she chases them with the warmth of her palms. "They made no attempt to invite her for 'sandwiches' or for family dinner. Levi may have enrolled her and paid for her, but he's far from uncle of the year."

"Knowing Delilah, she probably kept them at arm's length."

"And they did nothing to shorten that distance." Catarina hooks her elbow around Athena's arm, and they leave the overly green fields for the cobblestone streets of Imperio. "You might want to consider if there's a reason for that."

Chancellor Montgomery's home breaks up the monotony of Imperio. The brickwork mansion sits outside Imperium Circle, where the Five live, but it's every bit the picture of grandeur. Oddly shaped shrubbery fills the front yard: one pairing of trees and bushes depict the war, and another shows a man towering over a dog—or a wolf—with his boot planted firmly between the creature's shoulder blades.

They waited for nightfall before approaching the Chancellor, hoping most hunters would be in bed, to avoid a confrontation with the three werewolves, but it was beginning to seem like conflict was unavoidable. For some reason, she expected the governing body of hunters to be unbiased. They exist to protect humans and Otherworlders alike, right? Athena draws closer to Iba and tightens her grip on his arm.

"Stop looking at it." Ibrahim's eyes soften at the tears filling hers. It's been an emotional day. Ibrahim was excited for Athena at the revelation of a cousin—*cousins*—and a great uncle, but she cried as soon as she crawled into his arms. Catarina shared her chocolate after dinner, and she cried about that too. As they complained about the scruples of being a woman, and Paisley explained going into heat, she cried again. Ovulation sucks for the best of women, often making them strangers to their own impulses, but she-wolves can *die* if they go into heat without their Mates too many times. She panicked thinking about Paisley dying, which led to another bout of crying. The sound of Cat knocking on the Chairman's door shocks Athena out of her stupor. "Cat said he regards himself too highly."

"Do not let him hear you say that," Catarina suggests, tugging on her tight shirt. She exchanged her pantsuit for a tight long-sleeve with cut-outs and leggings. Paired with thigh high boots, she looks like a vigilante from an old comic book. “He has thirty seconds to open this door.”

She uses the brass knocker again, her nostrils flaring. There’s a small glass peephole above it that Catarina covers with one finger, as if blocking the Chairman’s view of the wolves might somehow stop him from smelling them. Cat knocks again, successfully shocking Athena for a second time. If she gets much louder, neighbours will start to wake up.

“I can feel you sweating,” Ibrahim whispers, pressing his lips to Athena’s ear. If Delilah were here, she’d feel safe. Until now, under the German moon, on the front steps of a man who has enough power to imprison and execute innocent people, Athena took her older sister for granted. It takes this moment, watching the light flicker under the door, for her to realize it. Even with Delilah in a different country, she felt safe… but that feeling went missing along with her. “Here he comes.”

Chancellor Shaun Montgomery opens the door with a huff. A smog of mint and balsam pour off the twitchy-eyed man; his smell strikes so keenly that everyone takes a step back. Short straw-coloured hair hangs across his wrinkling brow and, despite his natural height and practiced pride, he looks like a toddler compared to Killian and Ibrahim. Athena expected… more.

He speaks in German first. Despite speaking the language fluently, Athena and Catarina stay silent. The Chancellor reaches beneath his fur house coat, into the pocket of his silk pajama top, and produces a chained pocket watch. Tutting, he shoves it back into his breast pocket. “English?”

“You met with Deli—”

He cuts Catarina off with a swipe of his hand and a little noise. Swinging the door open, he gestures them all inside. When she steps over the threshold, followed by Athena and three werewolves, the peculiar man curses. “Into my office. Now.”

Their footsteps echo down the marble halls, but Catarina grabs Athena and prevents her from exploring the grand foyer. Killian enters last and closes the door for the glaring Chancellor. He opens his mouth to speak when a woman calls for him from the second floor. With a scoff, the German man ushers them out of sight. The house is too dark to discern the decorations or the different rooms, but his office becomes obvious when the door drifts open. It smells like him. Athena holds her breath when Paisley enters first. She and Catarina watch the Otherworlders’ backs as Chancellor Montgomery stands beside the open doors before shutting them, uncaring of the other people sleeping inside the house.

“You must be the sister,” he spits at Athena. The Chancellor retrieves a glass from his desk and dutifully fills it to the brim. “You actually look like a Christos.”

Does looking like a Christos mean she looks like their dad? His appearance mirrored the demigods from the stories he told Delilah and Athena as kids—golden skin, golden hair that burned like fire in the sunlight, and eyes like the Greek sea. Delilah inherited most of his characteristics, while Athena got his looks. “Del takes after our mother.”

Chancellor Montgomery harrumphs, holding the glass from the mouth. His dull hazel eyes scan her from head to toe and then move to Ibrahim. They step away from each other when his eyes rest on their hands. “Mated?”

“And married,” Athena confirms quietly, glancing at Catarina. They had to register under the Senate as such. Unregistered cross-race Mates end up in prison too often to risk it. "And registered."

"Your sister is sneaky. She failed to mention the werewolf who saved your life was your Mate—he is the one who saved you, is he not?"

A muscle flexes in Killian's jaw. Athena notices it, and then she notices Ibrahim's hand clenching. Refusing to speak, she reaches for him. A squeeze and a smile dissipate some of the foreign resentment in his eyes. "I am."

The Chancellor seems less interested in Ibrahim's response and more interested in the way they hold onto one another. "Mates are my strangest curiosity. Had I not set my aspirations for the Five, I would've made a dutiful researcher."

"Chancellor Montgomery, we need your help." Cat puts enough desperation in her tone to capture the man's attention. Without his probing eyes on Athena, she releases her breath and kisses Ibrahim's shoulder. "You were the last person to see Delilah before she went missing. You must know where she went? A man like you knows everything that happens in this world."

"You are good," he says. His shoulders shake with silent laughter. The others take a seat when he turns his back on them for a sip of his drink. With nerves as raw as a live wire, Athena gravitates towards the door. "Ms. Christos was supposed to be quiet. Three werewolves and a Christos showing up at my door in the middle of the night is not quiet."

"We would be happy to leave out the back." Catarina lowers her voice, eyes demurely narrowed. The Chancellor's expression reminds Athena of Archie when he spots an old sports car. "If you tell us where she went and what she's doing."

"You expect me to know? I meet with dozens of people every day,

Ms. Engel." Her lip twitches. The only sign his words struck a nerve. The Chancellor adjusts his honour roll certificate from Seminary, and by doing so, draws their eyes to the wall of achievements behind his desk. Trophies take up every inch of the shelves; where there are not trophies, there are certificates and wall ornaments depicting his life of success. "Perhaps I do not remember what we were meeting about."

"Given your relationship with Philip Christos the seventh, I expect you'd remember his granddaughter seeking your help."

He flops into an office chair and spreads out his legs. He dips one finger into his half-full glass. The way Cat sashays forward, like a lioness, and the way the Chancellor smiles, like a hyena, rivals the tension-filled clips of a documentary and compels Athena to watch in growing horror. She and the wolves aren't needed in this room—that much is clear—and yet Athena inches closer before settling on the couch armrest beside her husband. Should she be taking notes?

"You. Not the Fifteen. Not the Five. Chancellor Shaun Montgomery, the man who will run Imperio one day." Catarina flattens her palms on his desk and tilts her head to one side, displaying the lines of her body. A strange urge to start making flashcards hits, and Ibrahim bites back his laugh beside her. "You want power? You want men on their knees for you? You recognize the man behind me. Killian Garity is the most powerful Alpha on this earth. You know they want to make him king."

Everyone, most especially Killian, freeze on the spot. Paisley, mouth forming an 'o', swings her eyes from Killian to Catarina and back again. The Witchillers didn't have much of a strategy before coming to the Chancellor's office, but clearly Catarina did.

"Imagine he owes you a favour. The King of Wolves."

"She came to me in September, claiming that someone has been stealing Sacraments. Based on her intel, the Cloak, the Book, and the Breastplate have gone missing in the last ten years." Chancellor Montgomery gestures to the couches and rises from his seat. When Catarina sits beside Killian, she chances an apologetic look. "I was aware of the Breastplate. Seeing as it was taken from right under my nose… she said she wanted my permission and resources to see if the others were taken as well."

"Are the Imperium aware?"

"I thought it best to wait and see how many pieces were missing." He approaches a throne-shaped armchair across from them and drains the rest of his glass before sitting. "Many are eager for a new war, allowing old fears to control them—we must never forget the power of fear."

He regards them, tilting his glass from one side to the other. Paisley follows the movement, and his eyes follow hers. When he looks at Athena, she offers a pained half-smile.

"Ms. Christos left the next day—I believe to England—but she wouldn't give me exact details. Last we spoke, on November 2nd, if I am correct, she said there were no more places to search. They'd found nothing."

"You said they."

He shifts in his seat. "Did I?"

"Nattalius is with her," Catarina mutters, cussing under her breath. She throws her head back with a sigh. "They are back together."

The Chancellor nods, drawing his eyebrows together. "It is rare to see Companions working together after the line's been struck out."

"Not back together, back together," Catarina whispers, resting a hand on Killian's bicep. He pretends not to notice as Chancellor

Montgomery eyes them. God forbid this power-hungry man, or the Imperium, discovers his affection for Delilah. "What does 'they found nothing' mean? Have the Sacraments all been taken?"

"That, or they were unable to locate those left unclaimed." He places the glass on the end table beside his armchair and sighs with the grandness of a man in politics. "I wish I could tell you more, but Ms. Christos kept her cards close to her chest. She wouldn't confirm whether she had the Cro—"

"And because you kept this secret from the Imperium, you couldn't detain her and command answers." Catarina stands, her former charm gone. He grinds his teeth but offers a slight nod. If everything he says is true, Delilah really was in Imperio the day Athena texted her. There were only three streets between them. "Do you know where they went?"

"No. I know they left Imperio again. Mr. Kartal missed an important dinner, and Ayça was furious."

Maybe they left Imperio. Maybe they're in prison, detained by the Imperium or Senate. Maybe King Hozeir is alive and took them. The monster from children's nightmares might have the Crown of the Hunter Queen and the Book of Other. If he does, he has the power to control and create every creature under the sun. The Cloak makes it impossible to track or see him, and the Breastplate makes him invincible.

"Oh, Delilah," Athena whispers, dropping her face into her hands. Now is not the time for a full-on spiral, but all she can picture is Delilah standing alone against the forces of hell. The power of God has no equal, but Delilah's too stubborn to even accept *His* help. Her Creator. Her Abba.

"Thank you for meeting with us," Catarina sings, pulling Athena off the couch. She flashes a megawatt smile at the Chancellor while shooing them towards the door. "Knowing Nattalius, they're probably neck-deep in the library looking for any clues he missed."

"Ms. Engel."

Catarina pauses at the door, forcing Paisley through it before turning to face him. "Chancellor?"

"You will keep me informed of your findings?"

Athena swallows against the knot growing in her throat and clenches her hands into fists. Deception and politics are dangerous games to play, whether there are werewolves beside her or not. "You will be the first to know."

Catarina rushes out of the office, forcing them ahead of her. A servant stands beside the door now, narrowing his eyes on Killian who towers over them. Paisley tries to speak but snaps her mouth shut after one look from Catarina. It isn't until they march past the weird shrubs and into the street that Cat's shoulders drop.

"That was badass," Paisley hisses, punching Catarina's shoulder. She rubs it, a grateful smile on her coloured lips. "I felt seduced. I feel a little *dirty*."

"WWDD: 'What would Delilah do'. Some of the librarians share more gossip than the columns, and they all say Chancellor Montgomery loves to be the centre of attention." Catarina straightens her shirt with shaking hands and pauses at the street corner. "We could start with England. It's a pretty big place but the fairie community is well-connected. They'd listen to me."

Killian inches closer to her, his eyebrows raised. "Or?"

"We know Nattalius and Delilah are together." She offers a secretive smile and pulls a blade out of her sleeve. Athena glances nervously at the others, but the wolves come alive underneath the bright light of the moon. "How do we feel about breaking and entering?"

CHAPTER 8

The Devil's Doorstep

"Are we going to TP this while we're at it?" Paisley whispers, leaning over Catarina who messes with the front door of a Tudor-style mansion. The house smells like magic, rendering her lock-picking attempts useless, but she refuses to give up. "This is the douche's house, right? I'll pee all over the floor. Just say the word."

Catarina chortles, angling her head into her task. "No peeing necessary, but we can move everything a centimetre. It will drive him nuts."

"Isn't the door enchanted?" Athena hisses, wrapping her arms around herself. The two huge men standing so close to the household of an affluent member of Imperio is suspicious enough; the fact they are werewolves gives citizens the right to detain them—with excessive force, if needed. Athena should've offered to be their lookout. "If we get caught by the Imperium—"

"Imperium hunters don't work in city limits. We do not have a police force because there are no crimes in Imperio." Catarina sighs and slips the knife back into her sleeve. There may not be a police force, but Nattalius' house shares a backyard with Herzog's Manor, and the man who lives in that house, Nattalius' grandfather Eren, is the closest thing to a king the hunters have. If he catches them… she shakes the thought from her head. "I know the witch who enchanted his house, but it will take a day to get her here."

Paisley leans closer to the door and glances around conspiratorially. "Abracadabra," she whispers. When nothing happens, she sighs and backs off the front steps. "I really thought that would work."

"There's enough ivy to climb the house," suggests Ibrahim, abandoning his post. He tests the strength of the stems by dropping like a potato. "Are the windows enchanted, too?"

"The whole house is under a protection spell. He collects art and secrets." Catarina glowers at the front door and cusses too loudly for the quiet street. She steps under the brick portico and whispers, "I am Seneca."

The door swings open. A warm yellow light flickers on, illuminating the long rich hall in front of them. Nattalius' house is as swanky as he is with its dark, mosaic-patterned wood floors, candelabra-lined beige walls, and obscure art. A big metal chandelier with little dagger-shaped gems hangs over the front foyer and casts shadows along the wide staircase, practically accusing Athena of being too plebeian to walk the halls in her worn ankle boots.

"Who is Seneca?" Athena stoops to remove her shoes, but then

Catarina steps into the house and purposefully kicks the mud off her boots in the direction of Nattalius' living room. She leaves them on and rushes to catch up with her sister's Companion on the stairs.

"One of Nero's advisors. The emperor uncovered a supposed plot on his life and condemned his childhood tutor and closest confidant to death. Seneca didn't argue, despite his innocence. He cut himself. When that didn't work fast enough, he ingested hemlock. When *that* didn't work fast enough, he took a warm bath to hasten the poison." Catarina stoops to grab the floor runner and drapes it over the banister. "I knew that walking advertisement for therapy said, 'I am Nero' to enter. I assumed he wouldn't let anyone else say the same."

As awful as Nattalius is, Athena admires his taste. Wiggling her eyebrows at her husband, she runs her hands over the intricate woodwork of the grand staircase.

"Is this guy serious?" Paisley stabs a finger at an oil painting of Nattalius hung on the wall across the stairs. "Talk about overinflated sense of self."

Cat laughs, and the sound echoes down both sides of the upper hall. She leads them towards the left branch and pauses at a closed door there. "Blame his family. They think sharing blood with the Hunter Queen gives them a right to rule. Those people eager for a new war? Half of them are Kartals. They're supremacists who believe returning to a monarchy would 'be beneficial to Otherworlders'. The only people who would benefit are them—blind obedience and 'loyalty' is their expectation."

"And Delilah was into this guy? Enough to be *sad* about dumping him?"

"He's very charismatic."

Light bursts out of the room Catarina enters. A scribble-free, tack-free version of Delilah's map takes up an entire wall where the bed must've been. The bed has been shoved against the far wall, covered with the dresser and a white sheet. In the room's centre, they pushed two nightstands together to form a makeshift table, which hosts a single blank notebook.

"If Delilah's laptop is here, I can get on it," Athena whispers, channelling the disappointment into motivation. Her friends leave the room to go search for it while she runs her fingers over the holes in the map. "Why would they need to hide their research if Nattalius' house is so well-guarded?"

Killian shrugs, lifting the sheet off the furniture. "We got in here using three words."

"Which were very difficult to say," Catarina declares with a scoff.

"She left a bag here," Ibrahim reports, helping Paisley haul the bag in. They lift it onto the nightstands and step away to let Athena rifle through it. "What does that mean for us?"

"It means they were planning to come back." Catarina meets Athena's eyes across the bag for a moment before returning her attention to the map. *Were*. Focusing on the task at hand, Athena unearths the laptop from her sister's clothes.

Tears spring in Athena's eyes when she comes face-to-face with herself. She invited Delilah to the digital wedding album, thinking she'd refuse. Her screensaver is one of Athena's favourite pictures, featuring the bridal party 'pretending' to be disgusted by Ibrahim and Athena kissing. It's the only one where everyone looks happy to be there.

"And it's been a month since they planned to come back?" Paisley asks, sucking her bottom lip. She averts her eyes from Athena and throws her arms out at her sides, as if breaking free from invisible chains. "Okay, I know this is going to make matters worse, but that bag was *definitely* in the master bedroom—don't give me that look, Iba! I couldn't not say it!"

"The bed was made," Iba mutters, staring at Athena. She purposefully avoids looking at anyone as she opens the app containing Delilah's documents. If anyone in the room will be upset or hurt by that, it's Killian, and she cannot bear to see that. "It smelled too much like him to mean anything."

"What does 'line struck out' mean?" Paisley directs the question at Catarina, her eyebrows drawn together. Most of Delilah's documents were created in high school; those created afterwards offer no insight on their search. Athena opens the internet browser, but given Delilah's bank statements, the information on where they went will be on Nattalius' devices. What are the chances his bank password is 'I am Nero'? "That's what the Chancellor said, right?"

Catarina pulls off her long sleeve shirt, displaying her tattooed arms. The bands cover her bicep, five or so inches in height. Thick lines on the bottom and top sandwich the designs within. Swirls burst out of anointing vase and rain down on the flowers surrounding it. Snakes peek around the petals, one with their fangs bared, another with their forked tongue exposed, and the other too hidden to describe. A puma stalks towards the vase from the interior of the arm, leaving a trail of bloody footprints behind it. That blood is the only colour of the tattoo. Instead of eyes, the puma has roses and their thorns swirl within the pits of its face. Paisley, the tattoo artist of the group, steps forward, her eyes shining. She compliments the linework reverentially while moving around Catarina's arm.

The tattoo on her wrist mimics the design, except this time, a snake winds around the vase and forms the handle. The top of its head rests on the rim. A single rose wilts away from the snake's mouth. Nattalius' intricate designs were slashed in half by a thick black line.

"You know what Companions are?"

"Athena explained what she learned in class," Ibrahim remarks, massaging Athena's ankle. Requisite provides scraps of the deep history and knowledge of the Imperium. If their way of life wasn't driven by hate, she might've stayed for all four years of Seminary.

Most human systems were built with racism and prejudice at the root, but there's something about Imperio. The way it's written clearly in their laws and proudly displayed with their art. Maybe it's more personal with Ibrahim at her side. Especially given how often the hunters' stories contradict the wolves. If she were braver, she'd seek one of the first witches and strip the stories and mythologies down to the truth.

"The Imperium believes Companions are the result of diluted Werewolf blood. It's not about romance: it's about who makes you a better hunter. The more time you spend with your Companion, the more engrained these changes become in your DNA." Catarina stares at the vase on her wrist, lips tugging downwards. "They call it the *vitazeil.* Lifeline. Some say if you get close enough—intimate enough—you hear each other's thoughts and feel each other's pains… the tattoos are identifiers. Companions form legions. The tattoos mark who belongs to which legion.

"Striking it out doesn't sever *vitazeil.* Nothing does, as far as we know. It's protected under the spell that binds hunter blood." She pulls her shirt back on and paces the room thrice. There's a familiarity in how she walks around the house and regards the room. Athena, so focused on

Delilah's hurt, never thought to check in on the other woman betrayed by Nattalius' actions. "It's a sign to other hunters the person cannot be trusted. So, you see, we're all tethered to one another. He betrayed us, and we're stuck with him until death do us part… hopefully."

"Sometimes people have personalities only a Mate can love."

Catarina offers a small laugh. "It doesn't force affection—I never liked Nattalius. We didn't like each other. Can you two see if he has a laptop or phone here? Something I can use to access his emails."

"You know his passwords?" Killian asks after they leave the room.

"No, but the room was getting a little crowded." She clears her throat, staring at the map. "The holes above Brazil and the UK are wider than the others. It could mean they ran out of tacks, or they narrowed down their search to these two locations. Two locations, two Sacraments unclaimed."

Athena wraps her arms around herself and asks the Lord for wisdom. "We know she probably went to England… should we start there or go right to Brazil?"

"My co-worker Albert thinks the Sword in the Stone is about the Hunter Queen's Sword. King Arthur was British, right?"

"Retracing their steps is the likely the quickest way to find them. If I catch Delilah's scent, I may be able to find her without this map." Killian adds, rubbing his lip. "Do you think if they found one, or both, of the Sacraments they would tell the Chancellor?"

"Nattalius would want to bring them home," Catarina murmurs, sitting on the floor beside Athena. She draws her knees in, shaking her head at Killian. "Delilah wouldn't let him try."

"The Chancellor claimed they didn't find anything, which makes me think they've already gone to UK, Brazil, and everywhere else marked on the map. If Del found the Sword and the Uterus before other interested parties—and needed a place to hide—where would they go?" Killian's questions hang between the three of them. He stares at the map as though it will answer back. "She might seek out the Dejma Coven if she's br—well, we know she is brave enough. Is Nattalius?"

"I don't know the Dejma Coven," Catarina confesses. "What are you thinking?"

"You don't—" Killian crosses his arms and narrows his eyes at Catarina. Caught in the crosshairs of their strange stare-off, Athena hides behind the laptop. "The First Mothers. You must know them."

"You mean the First Coven," Catarina states, raising her eyebrows. Information on the First Coven flies through Athena's head. She makes a mental note to add the contradiction to her flashcards later. Maybe it should be embarrassing she brought them with her, but they were Delilah's, and the only way they'll find Delilah is if they get into her head.

"Hunters call it the First Coven?" Both of them nod to answer Killian's question. The First Coven, or Dejma as Killian called it, created the Otherworlders. Well, some of them. It was the Crystal Coven who made it their mission to let loose as many creatures as possible. They tried to make hybrids, too. As the world expanded, the First Coven splintered, with the original members settling in Haiti and removing themselves from society. The Imperium monitors them closely though. "That aside, if anyone knows how to destroy the Sacraments, it's them. Nattalius wouldn't go though, would he?"

"He'd rather die than ask or accept help from a witch." Catarina bites the inside of her cheek, holding Athena's eye. Surely Killian knows why that plan wouldn't work. "The Dejma, as you call them, killed the

Blind Witch for creating the Sacraments. Only she, the one who cast the spell, can undo it."

Killian clears his throat. "Or someone of her blood."

Another tidbit of knowledge not included in the Imperium curriculum. Based on Catarina stiffening at her side, it's not knowledge written in the Book of Other either. Athena stashes it in the back of her mind to add to her flashcards later. "Delilah might have found that out."

"If the Blind Witch had a child with her hunter, they would've been killed, either by the Coven or the Queen's Legion," Killian says. Hybrids do not live long under the Imperium's eye, but it was not the Imperium who separated them. Witches killed the hunter; witches clawed their sister's eyes out; witches brought the Otherworlders to life… if there was a child, would they view it as one of their own or as a hunter's? "Would she leave Nattalius and go to them alone?"

"Del wouldn't bring the Sacraments into a coven. While she likes witches the most, she doesn't trust them. She suspects most Otherworlders want King Hozeir in power… There's a chance she went to my house in Ponte de Lima, but the devil knows he isn't welcome there."

Killian moves to speak when a crash sounds from within the house. The three of them jump, but Paisley shouts 'sorry!' a moment later. Her words are quickly followed by giddy, childish laughter. Athena desperately considers joining them, until something shatters and steals the amusement from Killian's eyes.

"Excuse me."

His footsteps pound on the hardwood floors, announcing his departure from the top floor.

"I hope they broke something." Catarina flops onto the ground and crosses her ankles while Paisley loudly apologizes for the broken vase below them. "I hope it was the one his mother gave him."

Spreading out on the floor beside her, Athena tries to figure out a way to broach the subject of Nattalius with Cat. The question escapes in a jumble. "Are you upset she didn't bring you?"

"No. She knew I would drag him back to prison." Cat kicks her feet against the wall, encouraging Athena to do the same. "After growing up with parents like mine, I thought I understood two-faced people. I knew he was a pompous prick, but I never would've guessed… I should have protected her from him."

"Delilah sees the best and worst in people and she goes into every relationship braced for impact."

"She expects to get hit by the shrapnel," mutters Catarina, glancing sneakily at the door. She turns to face Athena with a new gleam in her eye. "Are you a betting woman?"

"Not usually," she answers with the same enthusiasm. Another noise sounds, and their eyes flicker to the door again before returning to one another. "What are we betting on?"

"How long it takes Killian to sweep Delilah off her feet."

Hope swells in Athena's chest. "You think she'll fall in love with him?"

"How can she not?" Catarina questions, her eyes wide enough to explode. She glances back at the door in case he's close enough to hear. "He's well-read, emotionally intelligent, and his accent… the sexy lumberjack thing? Forget about it. It doesn't matter how bad he smells; she'll get over it."

Athena laughs for her sake, but in the recesses of her brain, something wriggles. Didn't Delilah once say he had no right to smell so good?

CHAPTER

9

Set in Stone

"I've always wanted to storm the castle." Paisley's voice drips excitement all over the sidewalk. Sleeves rolled up and teeth bared, she points at the flag mounted atop Buckingham Palace. "One word, and I'll do it."

"Now is not the time," Killian murmurs, though his eyes spark with the same hint of hunger. A strange energy pulses between the wolves, and the red-coated guard staring dead-eyed at the street. Athena naturally gravitates towards Catarina, scanning the green spaces surrounding the castle instead of the walls. "What do you think Cat? Do we need to find a way inside?"

"I am not feeling a pull," she admits, cocking her head. The little braids in her hair thwack Athena's shoulders when she twists. "If Del was here, she left weeks ago."

"I lost her scent," Killian agrees, hands on his hips. He leaves the guards and crowd of tourists behind, heading for a greenspace east of Buckingham Palace. A duck quacks obnoxiously at them from its throne on the glittering lake. Paisley, her nose twitching, prowls towards the edge of the water and waits there, growling. "Now is not the time to chase birds either."

"It's taunting me."

"Where'd you lose her?" Catarina asks, covering her brow with her hands. Sunlight warms Athena's face, but a chill spreads beneath her skin towards her fingertips. She adjusts the baseball cap they bought from a souvenir kiosk and tries to hide her probing gaze. "Why are you acting strange?"

"Do you guys feel like we're being watched?" Athena lowers her voice to the pitch of the wind and wraps her arms around herself. It could be Killian and Ibrahim with the way they draw attention from the humans. Some of them gawk like children in a candy store, forgetting all manners and etiquette. "Maybe I'm being paranoid—"

"Don't undermine yourself." Catarina breathes in slowly enough to make Athena's lungs uncomfortable. A gentle breeze caresses the lake's surface, casting crystals of light onto the plants and trees surrounding the water. With the sounds of humans chattering, and the fountain further down the water, it's difficult to hear much of anything. It smells like dirt and water—and a bit like hot dogs, thanks to the food vendor a couple feet away. Hunger and adrenaline flood Athena's veins in the same breath. "You're right. There's something here."

Ibrahim reaches for Athena, wrapping a protective arm around Athena's shoulders, and the other around her stomach. He's naturally protective, all werewolves are, but for the first time, she doesn't appreciate it. The hunter within her awakens with fire and burns her wherever he touches, propelling her away from him and towards the water. "A Sacrament?"

"Or its protector. The Imperium put safeguards in place to prevent the Sacraments from being taken. Magic, traps, guardians…."

"Delilah's scent ends there," Killian mutters, jerking his head at the bench behind them, where two older women are chatting while staring appreciatively at his backside. "Are we going cave diving?"

"It's definitely in or on the water," Paisley supplies with a groan. She throws an arm around Athena and points at one of the geese on the bank. Two men pass, staring at them. "I heard that geese are bigger in Canada, would ya believe it?"

The men aren't the only ones monitoring the park. Athena noticed the undercover guards the second they stepped off the street into the green space. Although they blend into the crowd, her enhanced senses catalogued their measured steps, and the whispers in their earpieces. Those same senses tell her the Sacrament isn't in the water, but across it.

"There," Athena whispers, pointing at the island less than twenty feet away. From the brochure they borrowed, the island is off limits to the public. A perfect cover for a Sacrament. "I think it's there. I don't know why."

"That would explain why Delilah's scent ends," Catarina remarks, covering her eyes again.

"We aren't allowed over there," Paisley points out, raising her eyebrow. She tightens her ponytail and grins in a way that chases the heat from Athena's body. "Permission to distract?"

Killian takes a deep breath, assessing the packed sidewalks around them. There's a park and café to the right, and the sidewalk to the street above to the left. With hundreds, if not thousands, of tourists, and dozens of guards, the chance of distracting everyone is low. It's a short swim, though. They need thirty seconds at most. "Do your worst."

Smirking, Paisley marches towards the park, shoving into a group of people. When they shout after her, she lifts both middle fingers and peels off her shirt. Athena's jaw drops. Shirtless and screaming, Paisley takes off at a full sprint towards the children's play area. The guards monitoring the park run after her, and by the time she shimmies out of her pants, she's got a dedicated audience.

"Stand guard," Killian commands, clasping Ibrahim's shoulder to silence his argument. His thoughts pierce through Athena's newfound confidence, worry and desire to shelter Athena warring with his duty to obey his Alpha. "I'll protect her with my life."

Shouting interrupts them. Paisley at a full sprint, with no shoes on, dives into the water. Tourists run past their small group with excited whispers and raise their phones, recording. Uniformed officers arrive on the scene, swarming from above, clutching their walkie talkies.

"Wait." Killian holds one hand out while removing his shoes with the other. They leave what they can with Ibrahim and wait by the bench for the right moment.

Paisley disappears into the water, pursued by a handful of officers. A man stands on a bridge over the lake, holding a megaphone which he uses to command her to leave the water. He sends men to head her off on the other side of the lake.

Everything stills.

Then terrified screams erupt from the park. Children and parents flee. Someone shouts 'monster', and that's enough. Killian leads the charge into the lake until they're knee-deep in mud and filthy lake water.

Paisley, in wolf form, chases a squad of police into the street and doubles back around to keep humans from heading towards them. The waterfowl squawk and fly off, away from the park. Walkie talkies crackle, amplifying the sounds of crying children.

Killian pulls himself onto the island first, offering an arm to Catarina and Athena. The force of his yank sends them flying onto land. Athena props herself up on one elbow, trying to catch her breath, when two glowing eyes appear in the trees.

"Cat." Athena desperately searches the forest floor for a weapon. The eyes disappear when Catarina curses in Portuguese. Branches snap. The darkness cackles and grows, like a living organism. "What is it?"

"It's a leprechaun," Cat whispers, pulling her back. Killian jumps over them, shifting mid-air; he unleashes a growl so menacing the hairs on Athena's arms stand on end. The hackles on his back rise in response to the echoing cackle of the demonic creature. "We might need him alive."

The wolf nods, waiting for them to get up behind him, before stalking into the trees. Flashcards swirl around Athena's head. Violent. Fast. Bounce around like a ball. Most leprechauns live in the Giant's Causeway. Small pots of them exist across the UK and Europe. The Imperium dealt with an invasion of them in America during the colonization and Gold Rush. Years ago, Killian and his pack chased out a lone leprechaun, who claimed Witchhill as his own. Kill Method: kill them as fast as you can with whatever you can.

"We could go back," Athena says, hunched over Killian's flank. "I have some gold ri—"

"Gold?"

Athena winces, catching her mistake before the horror sets on Catarina's face. She opens her mouth to apologize when Killian knocks her back. He barks and stands over her, baring his teeth at a little creature in a tree. She peeks out from under him, staring at the little, beady-eyed gremlin.

The corners of his lips are split, revealing all twenty-six of his jagged, sharp teeth, and the froth dripping out from both sides of his mouth. Hunger flashes in his eyes when Athena plays with one of her gold earrings. He's gone in a blink.

Catarina grabs a rock from the ground, breaking it in half. She uses one piece to sharpen the other to a point. A twig snaps—a purposeful distraction because leprechauns are light on their feet. In a blur of green, the creature flies over Killian's back, bounces across the forest floor, and launches itself into the trees.

"Take us to the Sacrament, and I will give you one of my earrings," Athena offers, wetting her lips. All movement stops. Shouts sound beyond the island, but she is pinned by the weight of the leprechaun's stare. "It's real gold."

A gift from her parents, years ago, because other metals irritated her skin. Her parents gave her many things, including other pairs of earrings, though these have been her favourite. Putting on and taking off her jewellery is part of her daily ritual, akin to donning her armour and removing it. She swallows back the swell of sentimentality. They need to get off the island alive, no matter the cost.

"We can take him," Catarina whispers, glaring into the forest. Athena follows her gaze and finds the leprechaun standing on a stone. He runs his tongue over one tooth and winks when he realizes she's staring. "It's one leprechaun."

"He doesn't deserve to be killed." Killing a leprechaun would undoubtedly earn her some street cred, but she'd rather keep her soul. "We can barter."

"He's an Otherworlder, Athena."

"So is Killian. So is Ibrahim. So are we." Dragging herself out from underneath Killian, she removes one earring. The Otherworlders are not human. There's no getting around that. Athena had a crisis of faith when Delilah first explained their existence. She's known about demons and angels since she was a child, but it's different to face creatures of hell head-on. Especially when her own husband is, supposedly, the descendent of one.

Nonetheless, God looked at all creation and called it good. Things came from the Fall. Pain, death, disease, demons… but He's omniscient. He knows these creatures. In some way, they belong to Him as much as humans—as much as her. Whether they have redeemable souls or not, God's people were tasked with being good stewards of His Creation and caring for those who cannot care for themselves.

Athena doesn't know how deep a leprechaun's craving for gold is, and while greed may be a deadly sin, these creatures don't know better. Why would she fault them for that? Why kill them for it? The drive might be as natural to them as hunger for a human.

"I'd like you to take us to the Sacrament first," Athena begins, holding out the earring in her palm. As the leprechaun comes closer, she closes her fist around it. "Then I will give you the gold."

"Gold first."

"No offense, sir, but we outnumber you. I don't doubt your strength and ferocity, but I know the odds of who would walk out of this battle unscathed, and it's not you."

"Did the little missy just call me sir?" He laughs, though it's no longer a cackle; it sounds like someone hammering a bell. Marching forward with broad steps, he offers a real smile. "First time that's happened."

Athena blushes and follows him with sweaty palms and a dry mouth. She's not naïve enough to think there's any promise of safety in his sudden amusement. Leprechauns are dangerous. The man bounced around faster than her eyes could move.

However, it's nice to think of him as civilized, and capable of common decency. She pushes her shoulders back a little and proudly smiles back at Cat and Killian. Her 'Nature vs Nurture' Professor would be appalled.

The island dips in the centre, drawing them towards a small stone circle. A moss-covered rock sits in its heart. There's nothing particularly remarkable about it. It's a normal shape, half the height of Athena, and shines under a sliver of sunlight.

The leprechaun extends his little hand, eyes trained on the gold. She drops the ring into his palm, ashamed at how much her skin crawls when they accidentally touch. He puts the earring to his mouth and bites it. With a proud hum, he dances away, and hops onto one of the megaliths.

"It's hexed," the leprechaun warns as Athena goes to touch it. "Give me the other one, and I'll tell you how."

Killian growls. Fur gives way to flesh. He draws back onto two legs, growing up instead of out. When he reaches his human form, the leprechaun whistles. "Ignore the imp."

"I'm happy to go for round two," the leprechaun spits, his heavy accent slurring his words. When Killian says something back, in a language Athena doesn't recognize, the leprechaun hops up. Catarina steps in front of Athena and brandishes her knife. "You've never fought the likes of me. I smell your fear."

"That's the lake water," Killian assures him casually, peering over the top of the rock. "There's an opening."

"I've seen this before, and I didn't like it then." A movie plays behind Athena's eyes. Sure, the man was pretending his hand got stuck in there, but what happens if one of theirs *actually* does? Are they supposed to do a field amputation? Do hunter/werewolf limbs grow back? "We should not stick our hand into that hole."

"The Sacrament's in there," Killian murmurs, rubbing a hand over his face. Catarina warily inches closer, squinting at the hole. She's the resident Sacrament aficionado. "I'm going to stick my hand in."

Catarina nods, pulling Athena back with her. "I have no other ideas."

"Is the Sacrament still in there?" Athena asks, trying to unclasp her other earring. In the time it takes to do so, Killian plunges his hand into the rock. Heart pounding, she waits for him to shout in pain or slip his hand back out, but a minute of silence passes and ends with Killian grunting. "You're stuck, aren't you?"

The leprechaun laughs, grabbing his small stomach. "Not so big now, are ya, wolfy?"

Growling, Killian kicks both feet onto the rock and pulls. The rock doesn't give an inch. Catarina grabs his arm, attempting to help him, while the leprechaun watches gleefully from above.

"How do we get him out?" Athena offers the gold earring with shaky hands. For all Killian's struggling and Catarina's gentle murmuring, she's out of her depth. The hunters don't know a lot about magic. They understand what terms mean—hexes, blessings, curses, spells, potions… They know magic can only be undone by the one who cast it. This hex might kill Killian. It could be injecting poison into his veins or crushing his arm. Who knows how long he might be trapped? He might become stone! "Please."

The leprechaun snatches the earring away with a gleaming smile, chewing on both when he says, "It'll release him in five minutes."

"Don't panic." Athena whirls to face Killian with a gentle smile on her face. "It'll release you in five minutes."

"I'm not panicking," Killian assures her, dropping his head against the stone. "Those are important to you. If he hadn't already ruined them, I would take them back."

"We made a deal," Athena argues, resting her hands on her hips. The leprechaun peers at her, froth now surrounding the earrings as he smacks his lips together. "Now we wait."

"The other girl was smart enough to ask me first."

Athena tries to hide her excitement when she glances at Catarina. She's got nothing left to give the leprechaun. She left most of her gold rings behind at home, despite normally wearing them every day, because she didn't want to lose anything precious. "Smart enough to ask what?"

"Whether the Sword was still in the stone."

The Sword. Crafted by the Hunter Queen's own hands, despite the unwritten law of hunters not practicing magic. The sword itself, in material and shape, is nothing special, but she enchanted the blade. It becomes exactly what the wielder needs. Fire for vampires. Silver for werewolves. A net for pixies. It moves itself for leprechauns, like a moth to a flame.

"She sounds smart." Timidly taking a seat beside the little man, Athena crosses her legs. He's too busy munching on her gold hoops to care about her proximity. Catarina clutches her rock stake, keeping her eyes on the ground, but her body angled towards the leprechaun. "What did you tell her?"

"You got more gold for me?"

Killian growls, snapping his teeth together. "It better be in this stone."

After spending so many years getting to know him, she knows the flash of his temper is a ruse. Killian's a mirror. He becomes a reflection of anyone he spends time with. For the airy, he becomes earth. For those chill like water, he becomes a cistern. For people like Delilah, those who burn too bright, he becomes a log house. Paisley made the joke he's the pants from the Sisterhood books. It doesn't matter who he comes across—he fits them.

He's smart. A revolving door of relentless force. Athena's eyes prick with gratitude, because he's laughing. The leprechaun, not Killian. Cackling like he did before. Shoulders shaking. Teeth flashing.

"It's been gone a long time. You wasted your breath."

"Aren't you here to protect it?" Athena inquires, smiling at Killian. His flash of anger melts away, replaced by his usual neutrality. "You must get lonely on this island."

"I have ducks."

"Do they make good company?" She swings her legs on their rock, trying to peer at the sky though the canopies. Finally, the shouting outside the island dwindles. Sirens blare further in the city. "How many questions did she get?"

"Her friend brought many gold coins."

Athena nods, trying to figure out a sneaky way to figure out what questions Delilah asked. "You must be pretty hungry, though. Since it's been so long."

"I eat duck."

"And had many coins."

He grumbles, wrenching the earrings apart. "Measly two."

Two questions. Delilah and Nattalius got all the answers they needed with two coins. She glances at Catarina and Killian to see if they are measuring their performance like she is. Based on the way Catarina mutters and kicks a mushroom over, she is. They asked whether the Sacrament was still in the stone… and who took it.

"You won't tell us who took it, will you?" Athena stares at him, wide-eyed. She mastered the puppy dog look years ago.

The leprechaun scoffs, spittle coming from his lips, and hops right off the rock. Perhaps he is less susceptible than Delilah and her dad. He pats Killian on the shoulder and jumps away before Killian can kick him. Dangling off the tree, he offers a devilish smile. "I give you my luck. You'll need it."

CHAPTER 10

A Little Horny

"I take you no further," declares Gabriel, the Amazonian guide, when Paisley steps off the boat. He tuts his tongue at the trees and then at Catarina, who extends the final payment for their passage. One of his leathery hands wraps around her delicate wrist, pulling her towards him. "Quem entra não sai."

The man nods at Catarina before looking at Athena with so much intensity she shivers. He snatches the money from her friend's hand and pushes his boat off the bank without another glance.

"What did he say?" Athena asks, adjusting her hat over her brow. Beads of sweat roll down her forehead and into the neckline of her thin tank. The weight of the humid air makes it difficult to draw a full breath. All the air she'd been fighting so desperately to get into her lungs gushes out when something brushes her elbow. Yelping, she jumps back.

Ibrahim surges forward and yanks her away from the slippery bank. "Watch out!"

"He said 'people who enter do not leave'," Killian states, hands on his hips. The forest comes alive as if to emphasize the guide's warning. Bugs chirp, monkeys howl, and the river itself churns ferociously along the shoreline.

"Oh, lovely." Paisley scoffs into her canteen and takes a hearty sip. After days of travel, the water tastes more like canteen than water. Was it just yesterday they arrived in Ecuador?

"We are not people," Catarina remarks, clapping loud enough to make Athena jump again. "Compass please."

Nattalius and Delilah's pin left a rather wide radius to search, so the group decided to ask a guide to take them to the heart of the jungle, where the land seemed most lush and the animals most active. Based on the volume, which is loud enough to drown Athena's thoughts, the guide knew exactly where to bring them. Killian hands Cat the compass and pulls out his own paper map.

It droops with every step they take from the bank.

"Well, let's get to it, shall we?" Paisley adjusts the straps of her backpack and plunges into the forest with bravado. Her enthusiasm gives Athena the boost she needs to follow.

The light and openness of the river fades into a distant memory. Oppressive green trees gather in tight-knit groups around them. Tiny critters skitter back and forth in the underbrush. A gaping, hollow sound comes off from one side, followed by grunts and quieter whimpers. Athena presses into Ibrahim's side without realizing it, hand in his.

"Scared?" Ibrahim inquires, gazing up at the thick canopies above them. He squeezes her palm and points to a monkey crouched on a branch. Its round mouth opens and quivers, and the deep, haunting sound bounces from its mouth to her ears. "He's telling us to mind our business."

"Sorry sir," Athena calls nervously. When the monkey harrumphs and disappears, she ducks her head into Ibrahim's shoulder, laughing. "I don't think scared is the right word… I am in awe."

"I thought the kids were noisy." Other creatures join their cries as cicadas set the rhythm. At the head of the group, Catarina sighs, rubbing her forehead with the back of her arm. She glares at a spiderweb stretched taut by the trees.

"I know we agreed to leave the forest as it is," Cat begins, her lip curling. She squeezes herself between two trees and stumbles into the brush with a grunt. "But if a spider lands on me, someone better squish it."

"Gladly," Paisley whispers. She shakes out her hands at the very sight of the spiderweb and follows Catarina through the safe trees. A cry sounds above, joined by a cacophony of fluttering wings. Light flashes ahead and a loud *knock* comes from their left. "El, you made flash cards, right? You'll warn us if any of these sounds mean we need to go wolfy?"

"We're the predators here," Athena says, though she doesn't know if she believes that. With creatures flying overhead, and the forest seeming to expand before them, it's impossible to feel powerful. The forest speaks in cries and groans. "There aren't trails here. If any of them come close, it'll be curiosity not maliciousness... probably. Make scary noises, like we do for bears on the trail, and they'll go away."

"I kind of want to fight a jaguar. It's always been a fantasy of mine." Paisley bounces on her feet and cracks her knuckles in preparation. A sound like laughter rattles in the deep, and Athena's arm hairs shoot to attention, her heartbeat increasing. She reaches for her knife. "Concerning?"

"The last time something laughed at us, we were attacked."

This laugh sounds sillier than the leprechaun's, but Athena trusts her instincts enough to recognize the signs of danger. Spells protected the Crown. A hex and leprechaun watched the Sword. The Uterus, the true source of the forest's luscious life, is the most desired Sacrament, and the one that poses the most danger to the Imperium and their hypocritical laws.

"I wasn't scared," Athena repeats to Ibrahim, swallowing past the lump in her throat. There's something near them. Hard feet brush the forest floor. The light peeking through the canopies disappears as if afraid. "It was reverence. I walk the trails at home and meditate on the beauty of our Creator and the wonder of His mind, but I think after living in the mountains for so long, I've taken their magnificence for granted."

Smiling, her husband pulls her closer. "And now we're here."

"And I see once again how incredible He is."

How the trees stretch so high their tops vanish from sight, how the vines and leaves drape over their branches in every shape, size, and colour. So many creatures call this jungle home that the constant background noise changes every moment yet never ceases. She used to be obsessed with Eden as a child. Little did she think about how a piece of it exists in every wild. No wonder her mother loved to paint landscapes more than people.

Athena loses herself in His magnificence long enough to slam into Paisley. Before she can apologize, a skinny hand slaps over her mouth. Killian and Ibrahim come to a complete stop behind her.

The forest is silent.

Darkness crawls through the brush like the shadows grew arms. Paisley lowers her hand from Athena's mouth. She and the wolves crouch low at Catarina's feet, their eyes darting from tree-to-tree.

A quiet *whoosh* sounds from in front of them. Catarina throws her hands into the air, calling to her fairie blood, and pushes apart the heavy canopy above them.

Sunlight competes with the darkness below.

Yellow eyes reflect the light back at them.

"Run." Only when all eyes snap to her does Athena realize she's the one speaking. She drops her backpack onto the ground, ripping a bracelet from within, and kicks the bag out of their way. Now is not the time for weight. "RUN!"

Grabbing Ibrahim's hand, she takes off into the trees. Branches snap behind them. The ground shakes beneath their feet. Darkness closes in.

Paisley shifts and twists in one motion, planting her feet into the forest floor, and unleashing what she must think is a terrifying growl. The warning morphs into a whimper when heat cloaks them like a weighted blanket. She doesn't know what she's up against.

"What are you—El, no!"

Ignoring Ibrahim's call, Athena sprints towards the russet wolf and prays her strength will be enough. They slam into the forest floor together, bruising flesh and ripping fur, as a whistle interrupts the lethal silence. In the blink of an eye, a bullet of fire collides with a tree, and splits it into two.

Flame explodes up and across the canopies like a flashover. Wood chips rain over their heads. The forest comes alive with cries of warning mixed with the sound of animals fleeing the blaze. Athena tries to stand and fails, wincing from the pain in her knee.

Paisley whimpers, all human at her side. "You're bleeding."

The flames, burning bright a moment ago, disappear in a puff of smoke.

"Go!" Athena commands, pushing Paisley to her feet. They run together, away from the others, *thwacks* and *snaps* following behind them. Silence cloaks the forest once again. Athena tracks the anticipation as it climbs her spine like a ladder. Every hair on her body stands to attention. The air gathers in a cloud behind them, stealing the oxygen from her lungs. "Down!"

She jumps to one side, forcing Paisley to the other, and watches the streak of fire slam into another grouping of trees. With a great yawn, one tree falls. The other bursts into ash. She clips the bracelet onto her wrist with numb fingers.

"What is this?"

Athena lays her head against the ground and closes her eyes. She listens for the fourth *thud* before getting to her feet—just in time to see the shadow gaining on Ibrahim and Catarina. Fire consumes the forest in an arc, forcing them all to the same choke point.

Paisley grabs Ibrahim's shirt, pulling him back. "It's blocking us in."

"Killian, stop!" Athena screams.

It's too late.

Branches slap and carve at her skin, gravity working to keep her from reaching Killian's wolf in time. He launches off his hind legs, teeth bared and claws extended. Air gathers around the shadowy creature like a tornado. It rips the breath from her lungs, swallowing Ibrahim's cry for her.

With a prayer, she slams into the creature. It flies into a tree, its back *cracking* like a glow stick. The forest comes back to life. Creatures gather overhead, cheering, taunting, screaming, an audience thirsty for blood.

Athena groans. Cradling her shattered shoulder in one hand, she reaches for the Alpha with the other. He crawls across the grass, his once furry stomach bare to the skin. "They absorb oxygen to fuel their fire. In the moments before unleashing, they create a five-foot radius in front of them hot enough to melt bone. If you begin to feel like you can't breathe, you need to run away from it, not towards it."

"Bloody hell." Paisley jogs to Athena's side, flipping her onto her good side when she heaves. "Did you kill it?"

Catarina sprints towards them with knives in both hands. "Get her up! We do not have time for first aid!"

A monkey stands ten feet away and screeches at Athena with the full might of its breath. While the others argue about what to do, she follows the monkey's vision to the creature she felled.

A now moving creature.

"Get behind me," Athena whispers, fighting back the vomit. Despite their warnings, she pushes onto her elbow for a closer look. The creature looks like it walked out of a little girl's dream. Red, orange, yellow, blue, and green swirl in a spiral behind translucent bone. Thick, long white hair grows along its neck. Underneath the slivers of sunlight provided by the shattered trees, its white coat glimmers. "Get behind me."

Ibrahim silences Paisley with the wave of his hand, the tendons in his neck hardening. "She's saying something. Shush! I know it hurts El—

"

Leaves on the ground roll towards it. Sunlight fades away. Its yellow eyes expand into black voids as the light gathers at the tip of its horn. When Paisley turns, her jaw drops. "Is that a unicorn?"

Catarina pulls them both to the ground, trying to cover all three of them, but it's not enough. The unicorn cleared all the trees in their path. It's them, fifteen feet away from the deadly monster, with nowhere to run.

Killian starts to rise.

Someone chokes on the lack of air.

Athena launches forward, slamming her chin against the button on her bracelet.

A flock of birds implode into plumes of ash, not fast enough to escape.

The trees and vines closest to the unicorn burst into flames and shatter when it releases the fire bow from its horn.

Athena raises her arm, sends out a desperate prayer, and tucks her chin into her neck.

The grass, inches from her face, wilts.

With the cry of metal against metal, the shield expands. Fire bursts from either side of it, licking against the rubber soles of her boots and catching the hairs too close to the metal edge. Catarina ducks to avoid the flames curling over the top of the leaf-shaped buckler.

"I know how to kill you!" Athena shouts, hissing when the back of her hand grazes the heated metal. The unicorn drags its black hooves against the mud and glowers at Athena from where she peers around the shield. Can it sense her deception? "I don't want to, though."

"Now is not the time for negotiating," Catarina hisses, slinking into the forest. Charred branches drop from the trees above. Ash and smoke form a shield between them and the creature.

"How do we kill it?" Paisley leans around the shield, teeth elongating. The opaque air swirls and funnels towards the horse. "I can provide a distraction again."

"I think you have to rip the horn off. Your skin will melt when you get too close, though, so you need to be fast." Athena frowns at Catarina crawling through the brush. The unicorn releases a half-pent firebow and stomps its foot when the shield stands against it. "It's made to withstand a thousand blasts!"

It must be the wrong thing to say, for the creature plants its feet deeper into the forest floor and huffs again. Killian's wolf steps away from them, a growl rattling his throat. His fur shortens, his muzzle lengths, and the wolf morphs into something greater. "Wait! Everyone, just hold your horses."

Her command holds power for only a second.

Pinning its ears, the unicorn takes off at a gallop, right towards Killian, who runs at the same speed on two humanoid feet, roaring with the full might of his Alpha. Somewhere in the middle of flame and ruin, they collide.

Killian wraps one clawed hand around the unicorn's neck and lifts it off the ground. He uses the other hand to rip the horn from the creature's skull.

"It would've killed us," Ibrahim whispers, resting his hand on Athena's good shoulder. "Or destroyed the entire forest."

A tree falls somewhere behind them. Vines catch it, but fire crawls around them, breaking their hold. Killian throws the carcass to the ground and crushes the horn, and part of Athena's heart, under his foot.

Catarina marches over to a hot spot and grinds her heel into it. “Albert is not going to believe this.”

“I don’t feel so good,” Athena whispers, answering the call of the earth as it beckons her into the charred grass. Heat presses into her back, but ice chases it away, claiming half her body. She lost feeling in her arm thirty seconds ago. “I think I’m in shock.”

Ibrahim pats her face, speaking, but his voice disappears in the soundlessness of oblivion.

CHAPTER 11

Hurt, Lots of Comfort

"How does she look like a goddess while sleeping?" A disgruntled sound comes from Athena's right. Red dances across her eyelids, occasionally fading and then bursting back to life. Something warm and wet runs down her bare arm. "I've been in their house multiple times. She doesn't have *any* skincare products."

"God plays favourites." Someone else, Catarina, responds. "Delilah used to say she shone, but I thought she was being metaphorical."

"No. She's constantly glowing. Sunlight, moonlight—peak summer? Tan? Forget it. She's a bronzed goddess. I swear she doesn't even have pores!" Paisley comes into clear focus, an inch from Athena's face. They stare at one another, equally shocked, before simultaneously dissolving into giggles. "She's awake!"

Catarina helps Athena sit up on the pile of sleeping bags. The warm, wet thing that stirred her awake? It belongs to her husband… well, kind of. Ibrahim's wolf retracts his tongue, relief flashing in his delicate red eyes, and crawls over her legs. The weight, combined with the roaring campfire, chases out the remaining fogginess in her head. "Who are you talking about?"

"And humble too," Catarina jokes. Flushing, Athena drops her hands onto the beast's head. He nuzzles closer and takes a deep breath. His sigh shakes her entire body. "How are you feeling?"

"Good." She lifts her previously shattered arm and swings it back and forth. "Sorry for scaring you."

"I think Iba was the only scared one," Paisley confesses, patting his head. She stands and stretches, basking in the moonlight streaming from the leftover canopies. The smell of char and ash brings Athena back to the confrontation with the unicorn. Brushing her hands through the scorched grass, she searches for its body. "Killian threw it in the river. We don't know what else might be out here."

Unicorn blood attracts dragons. The creatures share an affinity for fire and territorialism, two shared interests that used to result in entire towns being razed to the ground. Selective breeding nerfed the dragons, reducing their size to that of elephants and limiting their fire reserves, but it didn't quench their thirst for unicorn blood.

"If there are other rare magical creatures in this forest, they'll know where we are," Athena remarks, rubbing the char from her fingers. It looks like a missile struck, flattening the closest trees, and peeling the bark off the ones further back. "I can walk for a bit—"

"Let them come," Paisley suggests, bouncing on her heels. "I'll show them some—"

A snap from behind sends Paisley sprawling. Killian lifts his arms apologetically and smiles at Athena. "Good to see you up. You were amazing."

"He's scared Delilah is going to kick his butt for putting you in harm's way," Paisley whispers, flashing a cheeky grin at Killian when he fake-snarls. He feeds more wood to the fire and peers into the pot hanging over it. "I like her a little less for sending us into this swamp."

"No one sent us. We chose to follow," Killian says before Athena can. None of this is Delilah's fault. She probably knew how to handle the unicorn without trouble, seeing as they didn't encounter any pockets of mass destruction during their short hike here. "I believe you volunteered. Insisted even."

"Semantics," Paisley mutters, scrunching her nose. She glances down at Athena and winks when their eyes meet. "Imagine how crabbed Graham is going to be. We got to face down a unicorn."

"Why does Graham want to fight a unicorn?" Athena runs her nails under the ridge of Ibrahim's fuzzy ears. He flips around to offer his belly, drawing instant laughter from her. "Okay, okay."

Athena scratches his stomach, trying to ignore Catarina's expression. Her sister reacted the same way the first time she did it. They were sitting in the backyard, after the proposal and graduation party, when Athena asked Iba to show her his wolf. He warned her that his wolf and him were not the same.

Wolves lack the complicated thought process involved in being human. They know base emotion, but more importantly, they run on instinct. A wolf likes or does not like. A wolf doesn't consider whether it hungers or needs rest or who its family is. It sees, it does, it lives.

Everyone, Delilah especially, suggested they wait a day or two for the reveal. Del thought it was his human form that prevented the hunter bloodthirst, but Athena knew better. Ibrahim, wolf and all, is hers. He shifted in front of everyone and peered at her with wary red eyes. They thought she'd be scared. Maybe he had, too.

It did scare her, but not in the way they expected. To look into completely unfamiliar eyes and see the soul of the man she loved… it was, and still is, an odd sensation. She fell in love with Ibrahim at first sight, and though her love for his wolf is different, it took one look and she adored him.

Her first thought when she dragged her hands through his wolf's fur was, 'I wonder if he'll sleep in wolf form'. Werewolf fur is softer than anything she's felt before. Like each hair was crafted by God from the fluff of angel wings and threaded together with clouds.

Athena's second thought was, 'is this weird?' The wolf lowered his head into her lap and showed more of his belly. Even though Delilah made little grossed-out comments, Athena decided there was nothing weird about it. She loved running her hands through Ibrahim's hair, holding him, and touching him in every way. That desire to connect with him extended to his wolf.

Sometimes, she sees the wolf slip out when Ibrahim feels cornered or concerned. In those moments, she moves closer and rests her hand right over his belly button. It's not just him protecting or defending Ibrahim anymore. She's got both of them, and they've got her.

"Thank you for healing me," Athena whispers to him, pressing a kiss on the crown of his head. His tail smacks against her ankles and, like times before, she momentarily thinks of how odd this would be for anyone who wasn't her. She might not have a wolf to growl 'mine' like Ibrahim does, but she's got a soul that chants the word all the same.

"May I have my husband?"

She averts her eyes—she cannot stomach watching the shift—and catches Paisley's gaze, finding envy there. Not for Ibrahim, but for a Mate. Every wolf, from the cynics like Mona, to the hopefuls like Graham, craves their Mate. Paisley's the kind to wait and search for her Mate in every man, to dream of him and what he's like. Graham prepares for his Mate but curbs the loneliness with Mona. Mona… she claims Mates are made, but Ibrahim told Athena she's as likely to crane her head at Rallies as anyone else.

They're the lucky ones. Ibrahim and Athena practically grew up together. One look in high school, and he knew what she was. It took her time to understand her draw to him… but they started their lives in the infancy of adulthood.

People like Graham, who turns twenty-five in a month, are considered in their prime. The closer wolves get to thirty without a Mate, the more likely they are to be without one for the rest of their lives. Athena's professors at Requisite didn't seem to know that Mates can fade. She's not sure about the science, since Ibrahim briefly explained it during one of their late-night talks, but reproductive systems play a key role in the Mating Call.

Some wolves who reach thirty without finding a Mate start trying to reproduce with anyone who is viable, especially if they're from an Alpha line. Men maintain their fertility until the last years of their life, but she-wolves lose their reproductive capabilities as early as forty.

For many wolves, finding their Mate when it's too late is their biggest fear—at least according to Paisley and Ibrahim. It occurs when their wolves stop calling to one another and the Mating bond unravels. Ibrahim said Graham will likely ask for time off in the next few years to search the packs. The Garitys, Iba's aunt and uncle, started sending Killian to Alpha gatherings as young as eighteen.

However, an Alpha's reproductive capabilities, whether male or female, last longer than the average wolf's. Iba said most Alphas do not find their Mates until their early to mid-thirties. Wolves crave stability and order, Alphas more than others. It's only after an Alpha senses the happiness and strength of their pack that they seek an heir.

"Husband reporting for duty," Ibrahim jokes, grabbing her hand and pressing a kiss to it. "I think when we get home, we should stay there. Permanently."

She hums noncommittally in response, too preoccupied with observing Killian. He shoulders too much—a devoted son, a father figure to his cousins and their partners, Alpha to hundreds, and now, apparently, a future king to others. A Mate would undoubtedly take on some of the burden, but she's not surprised Killian remains single despite his parents' efforts.

Mona… has concerns about their future Luna and makes them known. She doesn't like the idea of a she-wolf coming in to try to change everything. Some wolves believe in the Wolfmother, who was created to bring love to the moon; they think she matches souls based on the level of praise and adoration given to her by their ancestors. Others, like Mona, think it's part of their DNA, based on pheromones and attraction.

Given the past few months, Athena questioned her beliefs, but her conclusions lead back to God every time. He created all things—whether in His original design or as a result of the Fall and creation's punishment. Souls are God-given. Only God, who is Love, could create creatures imbedded with the unconditional, fierce love integral to Him.

As such, Athena knows the Luna waiting for Killian will be

amazing, equipped to shoulder his burdens with ferocity. Where Killian offers boundless grace and mercy, she'll be swifter with punishment and consequence. Where he brings light and laughter, she'll bring dark and solemnity.

They will balance each other out.

Complement one another.

Together, they will raise a pack stronger than the Hielanders. Strong enough to demolish the legacy of the evil king. Athena knows it. She knows it like she knows Ibrahim is her Mate, like she knows Delilah needs her.

"Where are you?" Ibrahim's voice draws her out of the darkening reverie. In the firelight, his eyes run orange, filled to the brim with concern and adoration. "Am I hurting you?"

She spreads her hands over his thickening chest to keep him in place. He's been getting wider since their wedding. People make jokes about how married couples should expect to gain fifteen pounds, but it's not just weight. He's growing into the man he'll be for the better part of their lives. "No. I was thinking about how lucky I am to have you."

"Because I licked you?" Ibrahim teases, grabbing her face. He pulls her down for a sloppy kiss that tastes oddly like dog. Someone groans by the fire—probably Paisley because she likes making those kind of jokes—but Athena kisses him right back. "I didn't recognize the look on your face."

"I was thinking our Luna will be a warrior. She and Killian are going to change the world." The stars wink at her as if in agreement. Mona may not like the she-wolf at first, but she'll be the kind of woman who wins people over without trying. A woman like Delilah. "And I was thinking I miss Delilah. I know she's okay… but I have this feeling in my gut."

"A bad feeling?"

"No… just a feeling." Like they're all standing on the edge of a cliff, waiting... to be pushed? To jump? To leave it all behind? Hard to say. It might be the foreign noises coming from the forest, or the smoke inhalation, but she prays about it, nonetheless. Praying about Delilah makes her feel more connected to her. In the dark nights, after Mom and Dad's death, she prayed and imagined God hooking her up telepathically to Delilah's prayer line, like a pack link but for sisters. "Do you want to hear what I just remembered?"

"Always."

"I used to think Delilah and I were soulmates," Athena whispers, brushing his twists off his forehead. She runs her knuckle down the slope of his nose and grins at the flutter of his eyelids. They grew up on fairytales and princesses—the romantic in her always believed in soulmates. "Do you think you can have more than one?"

"Wolves can't have more than one Mate. We can imprint thou—"

Her stomach rumbles loud enough to interrupt him. It gurgles right under his head and sets off their shared fit of laughter.

Eventually, Ibrahim stands, unfurling his large frame in front of her appreciative eyes. With none of their party looking, Athena drags her eyes from the top of his head to his feet. He flushes when she shakes her head and clicks her tongue. "Enough of that. That feeling in your gut is what we wolves like to call 'hunger'."

It's also what Delilah would call 'foreboding'.

CHAPTER 12

Just a Girl

"You ever think about dying?" Paisley's question draws a shuddering laugh out of Athena. Killian woke them up before dawn saying he caught Delilah's scent on the air. For the first three hours of the hike, they were rather zealous, spurred by the chase of Delilah and Nattalius and the fulfilment of their little quest. Then they hit the first plateau where Athena couldn't see anything but trees and mountains. "I think this is what it would be like. Moist. Suffocating."

Athena nods, hinging at the waist to rub her knee. She didn't have time to find the witch poultice Daniel suggested, and she needs it now, after their fourth plateau, more than ever. Pain shoots up her leg every time she puts weight on it. Killian already slowed to accommodate her old snowboarding injury, and she knows it's killing him to be a gentleman. He wants Delilah. He wants to run to her.

"I know we said no splitting up—" Athena begins, blinking the burning sweat from her eyes. Her husband, a gentleman like his cousin, jogs to her side and offers her the last dredges of their water. "—but I can't keep going with my knee."

Killian squints at the sun and then back at her, pushing his hair back. The curls don't move, held hostage by sweat, when he closes the gap between them. "We can take an hour or two to rest, eat something, and hydrate."

"What if you, Iba, and Cat keep going?" Athena suggests. Paisley, already on the ground, hides herself beneath a cluster of bushes. "Do you think we're close?"

"Yes…." He wets his lips and glances at the path ahead. "I can go myself. You four stay here."

"You can't go alone." She looks at Ibrahim, trying to wordlessly communicate with him. He won't want to leave her, but Killian cannot go into the forest alone. Dragons, or worse, could be lurking in its depths.

"I will go with you." Catarina drops her backpack onto the ground, the straps leaving wet marks along her shirt. She rearranges her hair and pulls on a bucket hat. "If we are close, Delilah will sense it… Athena, give me something smelly."

"Uh, okay."

Athena pulls the shirt she wore yesterday out of her backpack and offers it with a frown. Catarina shrugs before taking it. "She might run if she thinks it's just the two of us."

They run down the path together, twice as fast as with the group. Athena waits until they disappear into the foliage to take a seat. Little gaps pocket the forest, and she imagines Delilah there, watching them. She must know they're here. She must smell Killian the same way Killian smells her.

"I'm sure she's okay," Paisley whispers from the brush. Ibrahim, torn between staying and going, watches the trail. His jumbled thoughts stop when he notices Athena watching him. "Delilah's strong."

"I'm not worried." She *wasn't* when they first entered. God knows what creatures wait in this forest. To distract herself, Athena drains the canteen, and pictures herself back at home in her housecoat after a long shower with an iced cola in hand. "She's got Nattalius."

"Uh, yeah—yes, he's got her back."

"I meant as bait. Del's a survivor. She'd feed him to the dragon before she let it touch her."

Paisley laughs, the sound a rare comfort amidst the swirling anxiety in Athena's stomach. She tries to drink more water and finds it empty. "Here."

"Thank you." Trading her empty water bottle for Paisley's canteen, she leans back on her rock. Clouds gather above, blocking out the sun, and carrying a gentle breeze across the rockface. Water ripples below, between the canopies and the cliff. "We should replenish our water. Killian's probably running low, too."

Ibrahim stares down at the closest body of water and shakes his head. "Let me. You two should rest up."

"You shouldn't go alone—"

"We can see him from here." Paisley points out, rolling onto her side. She makes a visor with her hand. "If anything goes wrong, I'm a jump away."

"You heard her," Ibrahim jokes, leaning down to kiss Athena. She thanks him with a kiss as enthusiastic as she can muster. "Maybe I'll take a bath while I'm at it. I feel disgusting."

"You smell it too," Paisley teases, smirking from her shaded throne. He stands close enough to tower over her, resting his hands on his hips.

"Rich coming from you. You should—"

He runs before she can fling sand at him. For a human, the steep incline would be dangerous, but Ibrahim practically surfs down the cliff. His feet move like the cartoons until he reaches the basin below.

Athena shuffles to the edge of her rock, swinging her legs, and contemplates following him. A nice cold bath sounds luxurious right now. It'd be a bit unfair though, with Catarina and Killian trekking through the humid forest.

Hopefully, Delilah is right over the next hilltop, ready to come home. Athena wants to cuddle with her husband in their bed. She wants to start planning their first Christmas as a married couple. Last year, she spent it with the pack after another holiday without a text from her sister. This year, Delilah will be home, leaving Athena with two families to think about.

She likes Killian and Ibrahim well enough… and Paisley said they connected. Maybe she'd be willing to spend Christmas Eve at the guesthouse.

Or the packhouse.

Lips twitching, Athena glances at Paisley. "Can I ask you something?"

"Yes, I do want to sneak up on Iba and push him into the water with you." She grins, opening her eyes a pinch to look at Athena. The man in question crouches over the edge of the water, filling the canteens; he swishes them about to kick-start the purifier. "Do I really smell?"

Athena opens and shuts her mouth in the same breath. Eyes widening, eyebrows shooting up, Paisley gasps. "No-no—werewolves smell unpleasant to me, no matter what. You don't smell… worse than normal."

"Ask your question before I throw myself off the edge."

"It's weird Killian volunteered to come, right?"

Alphas do not leave their packs unless required to, whether by other Alphas or the king. In fact, her combat professor even *suggested* separating Alphas from their packs before conducting a raid. A pack without an Alpha to unify them surrenders sooner and prevents hunters and wolves from losing their lives.

Most Gatherings have a time limit for that reason. Alphas leave their Betas behind to lead for a day or two, never longer for fear of jeopardizing their pack's wellbeing… they left a week ago. Who knows how much longer it will be before they return?

"Kind of," Paisley confesses, propping herself up on her elbows. She avoids Athena's eye by focusing on the small pebble she juggles between her feet. A breeze snakes through the tallest trees and blows over them with a hiss. "There's no beating around the bush here, El. It doesn't take a genius to guess why he's here."

"An Alpha would only leave his pack this long for his Mate."

Paisley doesn't verbally respond, but her body—which buzzes like the Energizer bunny at times—stills. Her chest is the one thing moving below the leaves. One breath in, a short one out, and then she blows a raspberry. "Pretty much."

"Has he said anything about it?" She shakes her head, confirming what Athena already suspected: Killian and Delilah are the only two who know for sure what they are to one another. "What are the chances? That sisters would bond with cousins?"

"I think the better question is why Delilah?" There's nothing wrong with Delilah. Athena used to think Del hung the moon until their parents died. After that, her rose-coloured glasses shattered. Each of Delilah's faults have a strength to contend with though. She's charismatic. She's brilliant. She's fiercely loyal. Why not her? Frowning, Athena checks back on Ibrahim. "I don't mean that to be rude—Killian's meant to be king," Paisley continues. "He can argue with Mona all he wants, but there's not been a wolf as powerful as him in centuries. Sean thinks it's his destiny to defeat Hozeir. Half the bloody Alphas already defer to him. Graham's said the only reason his Luna hasn't shown up is because she's waiting for him to be king. He'll need a Luna to take care of the Garitys so he can establish order again."

"And you don't think the pack will trust Delilah?"

"That's not it either." She grabs Athena's shoulder and squeezes until their eyes meet again. All Athena sees within Paisley's turquoise eyes is warmth.

"Sorry. I've been defending her for so long… I don't know how to stop."

"You're not the only one defending her anymore. She's a piece of work—come on, turn that frown upside down, I mean it lovingly—and it would take a lot for the pack to respect her and submit to her, but I think if anyone could make it work, it'd be Killian and Delilah." Paisley rubs her sweaty knees, trying to rid them of dirt. The more she rubs, the more it turns to mud. "I mean, why a hunter? It seems like a cruel trick. I love you, you know I do, but you also know what hunters did to us."

Paisley's parents were nomads, who didn't want to adhere to pack laws or exist under the hunters. Getting pregnant changed everything for them. Alistair and Bonnie decided to try out a pack lifestyle because they wanted Paisley to experience community and fellowship.

When the raids began, and the Imperium started combing packs for loyalists, her parents tried to flee. Her mom died before Paisley figured out that was their plan. She still doesn't know whether they intended to bring her with them. She says she doesn't care, she says she only cares that her father disappeared. Life without a Mate drove him from the pack. He might still be alive, roaming the forests of the UK, half-wild without a purpose.

"Maybe that's what God is trying to do. Maybe He's trying to connect the hunters and werewolves." Athena nods at her own suggestion. Burned bridges need to be rebuilt eventually. Otherworlders, hunters included, need one another to survive. Imagine the beautiful world they could build together.

"And you think Delilah will do that? Delilah. The one who calls werewolves mutts and vampires leeches."

Athena sighs, crossing her arms over her knees. They don't get it. Nobody gets her. "Delilah's… she wants to believe in righteousness and justice. She wants to believe in a world where people take care of each other and are mostly good."

She's terrified. People see Delilah and they assume she's callous and bitter and cynical. They see her strength and stubbornness and take it at face value. Ingrid used to mutter that Delilah had a god complex and thought herself invincible.

No one sees the terror. No one notices the way Delilah worries, or the hope hidden behind her sarcasm. Del wants to believe in a world of good and evil, where the good get rewarded and the evil get their punishment. She wants to believe in fate and destiny and the happily-ever-after they read about as children, but she's terrified of it. She stopped believing in it a long time ago.

Athena watched it happen. She watched her bubbly, happy, energetic sister become an inverted mirror of herself. Like the castle she once lived in crumbled, and from its broken pieces and rubble, she erected a fortress.

And it was from that fortress she waged her wars. Fighting with Mom and Dad. Partying. Disappearing. Going on 'runs'. Making snarky comments on romance movies and rolling her eyes when their parents were affectionate.

She stopped believing in happy endings. She stopped believing in a fair and just world. To this day, Athena can't figure out what happened. One moment she was Delilah before, and the next she was Delilah after. Maybe it was being Awakened—although Athena suspects she was Awakened by their parents' deaths or right before it—or maybe it was the cruelty with which Ingrid and others treated her. In the end, it doesn't matter.

What matters is that the ruins Delilah built her fortress on still belong to that optimistic girl. They may be buried, but the right person, the right situation, the right calling, could unearth them. Delilah Philipa Anne Christos can change the world, and that belief is one Athena never questions.

"Yes."

"Yes what?"

"Yes, I believe Delilah can bridge the gap. I think if she stopped caring so much about what others thought about her and stopped believing the lies people tell her of what and who she is, and what and who Otherworlders are, she will be exactly the kind of person we need."

The wind swirls around them, invisible fingers toying with Athena's drying hair. She opens her mouth and shuts it, trying to figure out how to dispel the tension. She didn't mean to snap. Paisley's the kind of person who likes keeping everything light and airy.

"Sor—"

"You better not be apologizing. You've convinced me."

"I have?"

"Oh yeah. Next time I see Delilah, I'll call her milady," Paisley jokes. Leaving her by the brush, Athena peers over the edge of the cliff. Ibrahim must've finished with the water and found a different path up. "Who knows? Maybe Mona's theory is right."

Athena hums and lifts her hand to surf the wind. "Theory?"

"I'm just joking. You said your parents were together for years before you and Delilah came along, so there's no way—"

"Does the wind seem odd to you?" Athena feels bad enough about interrupting to wince, but not enough to hold her tongue. Wind dances around her wrists, tugging her closer to the edge. As a tendril touches her ear, she hears the beginning of a howl.

Paisley leans her head into the breeze, eyebrows drawing together. "Is someone singing? We're supposed to be stealthy to avoid dragons, not singing!"

Athena's on her feet before she finishes her sentence. "Ibrahim!"

There's only one thing that explains her foolish decision to cannonball off the edge.

Love.

CHAPTER 13

Exchanging Bodily Fluids

The water bottle and canteen lie forgotten on the basin's shore, claimed by the sand and bugs. Footsteps lead to the water's edge and disappear where the pool deepens and where Ibrahim stands with his back to Athena. She cannot see his expression, but she can see the algae crawling across his body. She can imagine his blank expression: the glazed eyes, the gaping mouth, the short, stuttered breaths.

"Iba! Ibrahim Finn Salama! *Mon loup! Mon loup!*" She crashes into the water and fights the unnatural current to reach him. The more she fights, the more the wind grows. "Ibrahim, listen to my voice. Listen to your wife!"

Paisley soars past in wolf form. She almost reaches him, but the wind bests her. It throws the pair of them back into the water, where the algae wait with stunning ferocity. The plants forms shackles around their limbs, rendering Athena useless, and drawing a whimper from Paisley's wolf. She thrashes and fights while Athena quiets her mind.

Instinct. Hunter instinct. There must be something—

"Killian! Catarina!" Athena shouts desperately, trying to free her knife. It doesn't matter. Her knife might cut through the blades of algae, but it won't do anything to the creature commanding them. They shouldn't have gone into the water. "We need to get out of the water!"

Water bubbles at the centre of the basin. Ibrahim lumbers towards it, up to his waist in the water, completely unaware of Athena and Paisley struggling with the algae. Athena's fingertips brush the hilt of her dagger when Paisley shifts and uses her smaller form to slip out of the water's grip.

"My knife!" Athena yells.

Paisley grabs it from her sheath and swings the blade, hacking at algae and the fabric of Athena's clothes, close enough to her skin to draw out a worried gasp. Freed, Athena grabs Paisley and throws herself onto the bank.

"Get Catarina's backpack!" Athena commands, scrambling for her knife. "NOW!"

Paisley shifts midair, tearing up the side of the ridge. Rock and mud fly from beneath her paws.

"Lord, let there be light," Athena whispers underneath her breath, circling the pool. A gust of wind pushes the canopies apart, allowing the sun to shine for a breath. In that breath, Athena finds them.

Mermaids.

She swallows, torn between tracking their movements and Ibrahim's. The water is up to his shoulders and if he gets fully immersed, it might be too late. "Paisley!"

It's going to be too late. With a final prayer, she dives into the water.

The algae slaps her skin, and the water burns her eyes, but she focuses on the family of mermaids swimming in a spherical pattern. At its centre, a siren sings. Her voice, deceptively sweet and angelic, draws Ibrahim in as much as the current. If Athena can cover his ears, or stop their singing, they might make it out of this alive.

The flashcards won't help her. They say **the only way to get close enough to kill a mermaid is to get it out of the water. If you're in the water, it's too late**. If she gets too close to them, they could swipe at her with their venomous talons and end the fight before it starts.

Ibrahim's head dips under the water, fifteen feet away. The mermaids swarm him like locusts and ready their teeth for a bite. Athena screams for him, and it isn't until the water floods her mouth and nostrils that she remembers hunters breathe underwater.

Hunters have mermaid blood in them. She is a hunter. Brandishing her tiny dagger, Athena's scream becomes a roar. She kicks and kicks and kicks; the more she does, the further she drifts from him.

The mermaids laugh. A cold, dead sound.

Something splashes into the water above her head.

Catarina's backpack sinks towards her as the singing siren wraps her hand around Ibrahim's throat. Athena lets the current take her to the bottom of the basin and launches from it towards the backpack. She pulls it apart until she wraps her hands around something smooth. Crushing the glass in her hands, she utters another prayer and blessing over the holy water.

One isn't enough. She crushes two more, even as her palms bleed and the glass severs her nerves.

Then a shriek sounds.

A dozen more follow.

The song ends with a guttural choke.

The mermaid's flesh melts, torn away by the current they created, and strips them to bone. Gone are their scales and hair. Some of the creatures closest to Athena fall to the sand below. Some try to reach the surface. Most swim as far as possible from the holy water and leave Ibrahim to drown.

Athena wraps her arms around him and uses the last of her energy to break the surface. Spluttering and gagging, she shouts for Paisley. Hair hangs in her eyes. Alga covers Ibrahim's bare skin. He slips from her hold more than once as she struggles to swim to shore.

Something, or someone, gets into the water. Splashes and curses follow. Athena cannot help but laugh and tear up at the same time. "What did you do?"

"Holy water. It won't last long." Paisley's pale skin erupts into hives. "I am so sorry."

"It'll heal. We need to get him out of here."

Objects from Catarina's abandoned backpack start floating to the surface. Flipflops, bamboo hairbrush, the map—the map! "I need to get the map."

"Leave it. I'm sure one of us remembers—"

Athena pushes Ibrahim towards the shore and swims back to the centre of the pool. She dives underneath the water to collect as many of Catarina's belongings as she can. The backpack drags her back towards the water, filled with the water-logged clothes and toiletries, but Athena manages to break the surface a second time. She spits rust-coloured water out of her mouth and holds up the map in triumph to Paisley. The she-wolf claps from her spot on the bank beside a stirring Ibrahim.

"You're lucky El is so chill," Paisley groans, pulling her shirt off. A pink slash mars her typically pale torso. "You were being seduced. That's kind of cheating."

"I didn't have a choice."

"You could've pulled out your eardrums," Paisley counters, cracking a grin. Ibrahim vomits onto the bank and offers a half-smile to Athena. "That was Hell. That is where we all came from."

They survived but at what cost? The blood of women, the same blood that helped her to survive, muddies the water. Bits of flesh and scale float around her head, settling into her hair and soul. "I'm sorry."

"Remind me to borrow those silly little flashcards."

Close enough to the shore to stop swimming, Athena starts crawling. Exhaustion bleeds from her bones. She uses the last of her power to swing Catarina's wet backpack into the forest. "Did she scratch you, Iba?"

"I-I don't know. I don't think so."

"Athena, run!"

She glances over her shoulder to find Catarina bounding through the forest. At first, she thinks something must be following her. God forbid a dragon comes now. Then she sees the dark figure moving through the water.

It's too late to run.

Unable to get her feet under her, she flops onto her stomach and tries to fight against the sloshing water. If she can get close enough to shore, Paisley and Ibrahim might be able to drag her onto dry land.

A hand wraps around her kicking ankle, dragging her away from the green. She screams. Ibrahim tries to run forward, but Paisley and Catarina hold him back.

A shadow descends on Athena.

For a breath, between the blood and algae, Delilah's scent strikes her.

The mermaid screeches.

A large black wolf sinks its teeth into the siren's torso. Rivulets of water run off her sallow skin, revealing her veins beneath, but she doesn't let go.

"Let go! Now!" Catarina screams at the mermaid, holding a bottle of holy water in her hand. The creature hisses and let's go of Athena, but the wolf doesn't release her. "Killian, spit it out. We need to get out of the water!"

They pull Athena out and away from the mermaids surging towards the shore. With the creature still in its muzzle, Killian's wolf follows them out of the water. It shrieks and claws at him, but the wolf makes no sound. He spits her onto the ground, too far from the bank to reach her sisters.

Without the water contorting her appearance, she looks human. Black chases the white from her hair; her fingers and nails shrink. Scales fall off her tail. Gills fade into the indents of her ribs. The white glowing parts of her slanted eyes shrink, leaving a startling blue behind. Her vicious glower, however, promises the very worst of hell's evil.

"Killian!" Ibrahim dives to catch his cousin and Alpha. He reaches for the deep wounds in his face but, once again, Catarina holds him back. "What did she do?! What's wrong with him?"

"Mermaid nails are tipped with venomous algae. It works like pufferfish toxin. He'll begin to seize as the paralysis moves through his bloodstream." Athena kneels beside the mermaid, who hisses and tries to army-crawl away. She gets an inch before Catarina drags her right back. "You have seconds on dry land before you shrivel. Save his life and I'll put you back in the water."

"We need blood, spit, tears—their bodily fluids are the antidote." Catarina says, running to the shallowest part of the water and collecting some of it in her hands. She runs back to Killian and throws it on his face. "It's diluted, but it'll slow the progression."

"You look like a woman who came this way," the mermaid hisses, lips peeling back to reveal non-human teeth. Athena fists the grass underneath her. The others gather water in their hands, narrowly avoiding the pawing mermaids, to help Killian. What would Delilah do? "She was smart enough not to get into the water."

"I do not want to kill you to get your blood, but I will. Cat?" It takes the woman a moment to realize what Athena means. Once she does though, Catarina easily moves the canopies apart, inviting the sun to fall across the mermaid's skin. It's hard to choose what's worse: the smell of rotting fish or the creature's awful scream. "Shed a tear for me. Please."

"Blood in teeth," Killian growls, shifting. Paisley leans over him, dragging her fingers through his mouth. She spreads his spit over the wounds on his face as Killian's muscles shiver and cramp. "Let her bake."

The mermaid hisses and spits. Right onto his face.

He relaxes onto the forest floor, heaving in a deep breath. Athena grabs Ibrahim's cupped hands and drops the water over the mermaid's flaking skin. "Can you get me more?"

"He's pretty," the mermaid murmurs, flashing her teeth. "Not as pretty as the other one. He would've tasted so sweet."

"He's bitter," Catarina promises, tossing water on the woman's face. She runs her forked tongue over her plush lips and glances at Athena.

"You said you'd put me back in the water."

"She smells like Delilah," Killian mutters, glaring at the mermaid. His eyes fall to the beads around her waist, which sparkle even without the sun. "Why did she give that to you?"

"What makes you think she did?"

"Don't lie to us," Killian suggests, stopping Ibrahim and Paisley from bringing water to her. He leans close enough to be within reach of the mermaid, but she's only getting weaker out of the water. Shivering. Lips cracking. Eyes withering. "If you got close enough to touch her, we wouldn't be having this conversation. You'd be dust under our feet."

The mermaid licks her lips and opens her mouth. She waits until Catarina pours the water into her mouth to speak. "She wanted to know if any of my family went missing."

"And have they?"

Her eyes bleed black. It's such a shift that the hairs on Athena's arms stand to attention. "A wizard. He trapped a *guppy.*"

"A wizard?" Athena questions, glancing at Catarina and then Killian. Neither offer more than a shrug. "King Hozeir might need a magic wielder for the Uterus."

"It's been gone for years," the mermaid states, gasping for the water Ibrahim brings. "You are too late. All too late."

"Replenish the water before we return her," Killian suggests, nodding at his backpack. The wolves jump to his command while Catarina carts water back and forth for their… captive? "How long has it been since you saw her?"

"We do not count the days—" Killian's hand, gripping her throat, stifles her next words. He loosens his grip when she gasps and cries. "We do not count the days. You say you can smell her on me? Tell me how long it has been."

Killian leans close enough to run his nose over the beads. She offers a salacious smirk over his shoulder and drags her human nails down his back. Wrong sister. Athena smiles back and waits for Killian to finish sniffing. "It cannot be more than a week. We were walking in circles when we heard your cries. It's most potent here."

The mermaid reaches desperately for Catarina. "Her Companion said he couldn't wait to get back to civilization. Give me that."

"Sounds like him," Catarina remarks, dumping the water on her head. A whistle from Paisley announces the completion of their task. "Let me handle her."

Catarina grabs the mermaid's legs and swings her. The woman flies for a moment before crashing into the mud. As soon as her hand brushes the water, she comes back to life. The flick of her tail is the last Athena sees of their captive or her family.

"Let's get out of here," Paisley demands, pushing their shoulders. They run far enough from the water to avoid the reach of the siren's song and, with the battle over, Athena's adrenaline tanks. She drops to the ground, dragging Ibrahim with her, and sighs into his rapidly healing chest. "The Uterus is gone."

"King Hozeir has all he needs to raise his army," Catarina confirms.

The mermaid said the Uterus has been gone for a long time. Then she said they do not count the days. What if King Hozeir's army was here when Delilah and Nattalius came?

Paisley runs her hands over her bleeding knees and voices the question swirling through Athena's mind. "Where is Delilah?"

CHAPTER 14

Their Badder Half

Everything hurts. Her bones. Her muscles. Her head. Her heart. She cannot take any more of this. No more 'rare' creatures hidden in this inescapable jungle. No more running. No more climbing. No more fighting. Athena burrows into Ibrahim's chest like an ostrich in the dirt and prays the sound of his beating heart will drown out her anxious thoughts.

"Worst camping trip ever," Paisley mutters, lifting her canteen to the fire. The campfire paints the small clearing gold but howls and screams sound beyond the darkness. It'd be easy enough to close their eyes and imagine being home without that noise. "Where do we go from here?"

"Back home," Killian states. He raises his hand to cut off their protests before resting it against Athena's muddy shoe. "Delilah's not here. She either picked up the wizard's trail, or she and Nattalius are recouping, like we need to."

"We could find the wizard's tracks too."

"Thea." Catarina's soft voice silences the fight building in Athena's mind. Neither of them are particularly talented trackers, but it's what they're made to do. They hunt. It cannot be that hard to find out where the wizard went! "Delilah might've bitten off more than she can chew. We have no idea what or who she might find if she catches up with the wizard. We can't fight an army by ourselves."

They could barely fight a mermaid. Each of them has their own battle wounds—bruises or rashes or lacerations—and it's been two hours since the fight. Athena subconsciously rubs her ankle and only stops when Ibrahim pulls her hand away and presses a kiss to her temple. "You guys go back. The pack needs you, but it can spare us for a little while longer."

Athena squeezes her husband's hand and brings the back of it to her lips. "Are you sure?"

"If they're staying, so am I," Paisley mutters, throwing her arms up. She lies back on her sleeping bag and crosses her bare ankles. "I'm not dealing with Mona losing her newfound power without you two there to talk her off the ledge."

"Do you actually think Delilah would pursue the wizard into King Hozeir's territory?" Killian directs the question at Catarina, but Athena's the one who whispers, "God forbid."

"No. Her badder half wouldn't allow it."

Most of Delilah's 'reckless' decisions boil down to her own logic. Sometimes it's hard to think like her, but they've traced her steps almost exactly and exhausted their options. If they're frustrated and confused, Delilah was too. What would she do with that?

"She's going somewhere to think," Athena declares, crossing her arms over her stomach. She's returning to the drawing board, as it were. Would she and Nattalius go back to his house? If they left the forest a week ago and caught a flight to Imperio, they all would've been in the city at the same time. Killian would've smelled Delilah. "If Chancellor Montgomery wasn't waiting for them, I would guess they returned to Nattalius', but he would've somehow heard about their return and shown up demanding answers she doesn't have. Delilah hates being pestered."

Catarina nods, tapping her fingernails on her tin bowl. "She'd go somewhere no one could find her."

"Your villa?"

"I have a camera monitoring the yard. I do not have reception out here, but I did in London."

"Somewhere safe," Killian adds, twiddling his thumbs. The fire cracks and pops in the contemplative silence. Delilah's got a house in Rhode Island, but would she bring Nattalius there? Is it safe? "You look like you're thinking something good, Athena."

"I was thinking her place in Rhode Island."

Cat sits up, steepling her hands on her knees. Her mouth opens but no sound comes out. All at once, the other four straighten. "I don't think she'll be far from Europe. If King Hozeir is alive and he has these objects, he's going to be building his army. We all know he wouldn't want to be too far away from the UK or Imperio."

"And you think she's going to hunt him?" Paisley asks, rubbing the bridge of her nose. She looks at the others around the fire before returning to Catarina. "No way. Delilah's not going to fight Imperium's war for them. She's a Bounty Hunter. There's no money in it."

Athena doesn't like the look on Catarina's face. Not one bit. She purposefully trains her eyes on the flames when the deafening silence returns. The secrets are coming out to play again. Rubbing the scar down her neck, she wets her lips. "This has something to do with Delilah's emergency plans for me, doesn't it? For some reason, she thinks she needs to lead the charge into battle."

"It's not that simple."

"Can you make it simple?" Athena counters, dropping her arms. Now is not the time for secrets. If Delilah plans to march against an ancient force, she better wait for her friends and family. She cannot face this alone.

"She won't go after him." When Catarina doesn't offer anything else, Athena faces the horrible notion that maybe he'll go to her. What would a monster like that want with her sister? She brushes away the idea as goosebumps spread over her skin. Ibrahim draws closer and wraps his arms around her like wings, hiding her from the fear and danger beyond them. "But she's going to stay close to see how it plays out. I think she's going to try to figure out what to do with the information they have. How to use it to her advantage with the Imperium and King Hozeir. She and N—the unlikeable side character need to figure out their next move."

Panic strikes like a brand against Athena's spine. If they do not track down Delilah and Nattalius, will the wedding be their last memory together? She may not seek out the evil king but she's not content to sit on the sidelines and watch the action. Delilah's standing on the edge of a metaphorical cliff, practically daring it to claim her.

God made it clear she's playing a big role in this, but not yet. Not without them….

"Where would she hide Athena?" asks Killian.

Cat blinks, dismissing the shadows in her eyes. "What?"

"Delilah had an emergency plan to hide Athena, didn't she?" Killian inquires. If only it were that simple. Catarina's villa, the idea she already shot down, is the emergency plan. Athena shakes her head and lays back down. "Where would Athena be safest?"

"Ingrid was going to bring them both to my house in Imperio. I was going to make it look like we were abducted or possibly killed. From there, we would hitch rides and travel on foot until we reached Ponte de Lima. We all have fake IDs and would change our appearances. There's a spell on the house to hide it from prying eyes." Catarina pauses, staring at the fire.

"Come on, we might not know Delilah as well as you, but she's too resourceful not to have a backup. Portugal is basically the Imperium's backyard, and—" Paisley's voice tapers off. Terrified, Athena sits up, expecting a monster in the dark but instead finds them all staring at Catarina.

Specifically at her twitching lip.

Reaching for Ibrahim's hand, Athena pulls it into her lap. "She had a Plan B, didn't she?"

Catarina whispers something under her breath. She repeats it twice and thrice, too quiet for Athena to hear, but by the fourth time, the word 'blood' drains the warmth from Athena. The fire dances to her chant and, with her final word, it extinguishes into a plume of smoke. In the dark, Catarina speaks, "I know where she is."

CHAPTER

15

Say My Name

Her mouth tastes like sand. There's an endless sea of it, spread out before Athena like the sky above. With the landscape of the Sahara so unvaried, the rocks, mountains, and sand blend into one another.

"*Où est-il*?" the guide, Salah, whispers for the seventh time. He cranks the wheel of their 4x4, sending Athena into Paisley, and Paisley almost out of the back seat. "Hold on!"

"If I hold on any tighter, I'm going to crush the frame of this death machine," Paisley mutters, spitting sand out of her mouth. The driver, as if taking her words as a challenge, veers in the opposite direction. Sand flies out behind them and Killian, clinging desperately to the vehicle's exterior, grunts in displeasure.

An unpleasant whine comes from the engine when Salah drives over a rare patch of greenery that breaks up the monotony of brown, beige, and orange. He slams his hand against the stick shift and beelines for a tall dune. Killian drops off the vehicle halfway up the hill and, in the cloud of dirt and rocks, shifts to keep up with them.

"*Il est là*!" Salah cries, parking at the top of the hill. The 'she' in question is known by most as the Richat Structure, or Eye of the Sahara, and even though it is a geographical phenomenon, they struggled to find a guide. Salah, with crazy hair and crazier eyes, offered to bring them within walking distance of it.

He warned them that it wasn't easy to see in person. The pictures Athena found online made it look like a half-eaten jawbreaker, but those were captured from space. Up close, she cannot see the Eye, only ridges upon ridges of rocks. "This is… underwhelming."

Paisley, glancing at Salah who chats animatedly with Catarina and Killian, speaks out of the side of her mouth. "Five bucks says he got lost."

"He said he's sure this is it," Killian says with a smile, joining them on the ridge. He hikes his backpack higher and consults the watch on his wrist. "We have an hour. If we don't return by then, it'll be a long walk back to the village."

Their guide leans back in his seat, props his sandalled shoes on the steering wheel, and falls asleep underneath the blazing sun. Paisley, covered in linen from head to toe, scoffs. "Do people often not return?"

All three of the fluent French speakers say nothing. More than one local warned them about venturing too far into the circle. Some of them refuse to get closer than the outer rim. Athena listened to a group of older folks tell stories while preparing their communal meal. They talked of a force hidden within the Eye. 'It's not natural,' one warned, wagging a homemade knife around. 'Something created that. Something lives there.'

"Leave it to Delilah to find a *more* dangerous place than the bloody jungle," Paisley mutters, readjusting her veil. They march to the first ring with their heads bowed and linen clothes flapping in the wind. Normally, a breeze would be welcome on a hot day like this, but the Sahara's wind is somehow drier than its sand. "I bet it's a dragon. A lizard-looking dragon with a scorpion tail and pincers."

"It's your turn to take it down," Ibrahim jokes, standing close enough to catch Athena when a rock slips underneath her foot. Her knees threaten to buckle with every step down the steep circle. Fatigue settled in three days ago, and she cannot walk more than a minute without getting winded. Mix it with the dry, sandy air and constant heat… she grabs Ibrahim's arm and wraps it around her waist to keep her steady. "Doing okay?"

She pours some water into her hand and drags it across her forehead. This was not the best week to go on a trip around the world. "It's my period. I'm used to taking it easy."

He nods, glancing up at the 4x4 on the ridge. "Do you think he'll stay asleep?"

"I don't know how he can relax with the sun so bright." Complaining has become her newest vice since returning from the jungle. Swollen feet. Aching knees. The inescapable feeling of being damp—it's the incessant moistness that truly combats her happy disposition. "I want to stop squinting."

Ibrahim shifts and lies in front of her. Gratitude stings the back of her eyes as he allows her to climb onto his muscular back. It cannot be comfortable for him under the sun, with a coat the colour of ink—and yet, the wolf trudges on. His soft fur sticks to her cheek, and each time he takes a step, it jostles her stomach and makes her nauseous, but the exhaustion ultimately wins out.

When her eyes open again, they're settled under a rock. The cool air soothes the heat pulsing along her skin. Paisley offers some trail mix to the group before glaring at the darkening sky. "You remember that kid's show about the bus? Flash floods in the desert?"

"Salah said the weather was perfect for a trip," Killian reminds her, throwing a handful of nuts into his mouth. He chomps on them and stretches his legs across the dark sand. "You're not a worrier, Pais."

"Someone needs to worry—I sound like Mona." She slaps her hands over her mouth and drops. Ibrahim's wolf shakes underneath Athena as she presses her face into the softness of his ears. The momentary tension and exhaustion dissolve into raucous laughter. Four days of travel. Four days of a pressure cooker holding them all together. This is the best way to erupt.

"He said for a trip, meaning the hour to explore and the eight to travel here and back." Catarina's the one who says it. She stares up at the clouds gathering above their heads, matching Paisley's frown. "We're not getting back to Salah on time."

"We can get Delilah and Nattalius and get back to him," Paisley declares, crawling out from under the rock. She brushes herself off and re-wraps the linen over her head. "I'm done channeling my inner Mona. No one needs to be worried; everything will work itself out."

"I like the new attitude," Athena calls, pulling herself out from the shadows. She stretches in the sun and thanks the Lord for it, even though she knows her dry clothes will be wet with sweat again soon. Draining half her canteen in one gulp, she nods at the others. "Let's go guys!"

She leads the charge to catch up with Paisley, regretting the enthusiasm when her knee pulses again. The heat fades, replaced with wind that steals the moisture off her skin. Ibrahim stalks forward in wolf form, side-eyeing Athena as he passes. She pastes a smile on and waves him off towards the desert.

Killian takes off after him in wolf form, leaving his backpack with Athena, and soon enough, Paisley follows. They play on the wind and the hills, bundles of newfound energy.

"I hate to be this person," Cat begins, coming to her side. She holds a torn piece of paper in one hand and a compass in the other. Right after declaring she knew where Delilah must be, Cat started writing on their map of the Amazon. The words make no sense to Athena. Borrowing from Portuguese, German, and English. Something about eyes and palms and blood and Delilah. "But since we are going to be here for hours, I want to see if you can make sense of this."

In the airplane, she tried rewriting some directions on a proper notepad. She labelled it by numbers. Number 1: if war touches them in Ponte de Lima, go to the Sahara Desert. Number 2: find the eye and sit. They discussed what 'the eye' was, but couldn't decide if it was the structure itself, the metaphorical meaning (as in the centre), or a symbol.

"Number three means either the eye or the sky darkens. She said, 'wait for it to get darker than you've seen it'."

"It's going to be awhile until dark…." Athena murmurs, wrapping her arms around herself. It's almost winter. The desert gets cold at night.

"We have the wolves." The wolves in question disappear over a ridge and reappear moments later on the peak. "They'll keep us warm."

Salah permitted them to bring one of their day packs. They don't have what they need to camp, save for each of their canteens and the snacks in Killian's backpack. Athena waves the doom from her mind and forces a smile onto her face. "What did she say to do once it gets that dark?"

"We need to draw something in the sand. I think she said palm… but I don't know who's palm. I know the evil eye is in the center of a palm." Catarina murmurs to herself, drawing her eyebrows together. A palm in the sand and a pitch-black sky. That sounds like a recipe for magic. "And then you need to pour your blood into it."

"What?"

"Into the drawing. There must be more than one drawing." Catarina scratches another question mark onto the rumpled paper. She failed to mention blood. Unable to taste anything but metal now, Athena gags. Cat watches her rifle through Killian's bag, searching for the snack pack. If she doesn't get something in her mouth, she's going to vomit all over the desert. "Then we need to say her name. I remember that part. Spill your blood and say Delilah's name until we can't anymore."

Bile explodes across her tongue. "Please stop saying that."

"You're pale."

"My period." Athena stuffs a granola bar into her mouth, hoping the force of swallowing will take the bile with it. She banishes the word from her mind and instead savours the chocolate chips melting on her tongue.

Except they taste worse than the sand.

"Drink more."

Paisley howl interrupts her sip. After spending so much time with the pack, Athena recognizes their different sounds—like triumph. "They found it!"

She runs to catch up with the wolves and finds them on the other side of the last ridge. Gathered around a short spire, Paisley howls again.

"We're here," Catarina announces, loose pants fluttering in the wind. They bark and chitter between themselves, tails wagging. "I am not going to start running. It's too hot."

Paisley runs around them, a blur of red. She brushes the backs of their legs, forcing them towards what appears to be a bowl inside the spire. Once close enough to touch, Athena leans over the pronged rocks. There's a shape carved into the hollow. If Catarina hadn't mentioned the evil eye, Athena might think it was a botched circle.

"Eye in the eye," Catarina murmurs, brushing her finger over the indent. She steps back to view the base of the structure. Most of the sand is tightly packed, and darker than the rest. "Now we sit."

Discarding her bag, she sits cross-legged at the base. Delilah didn't mention a method; still, Athena instructs them to sit in a circle. Hunters do not—and should not—practice magic, given their history with self-led experimentation. All the cautionary teachings from her professors fade into the background when she takes her seat.

Seminary taught her enough to recognize the beginning of a ritual. Shapes play an important role in them—circles and pentagrams and corners of the room. Ibrahim sits a foot away and Paisley a foot from him. The spire is thin enough to see part of Killian and Paisley from the other side of the circle. An invisible thread connects them all, the spire as their conduit.

Silence lasts for thirty seconds before Paisley blows out a breath. "How long are we sitting here?"

"Until the sky or the eye is darker than we've seen it."

She nods, staring at the hints of blue sky between the clouds. "I need to pee first."

"Wake up, *ya amar.*"

Ibrahim's voice sounds close enough that she should see him. Though even when she raises her hands, she cannot feel him. Fingers crawl over her neck to her face, and then his lips touch hers. "It's darker than I've ever seen it," Athena whispers, searching the sky for stars. There are no heavens here. No sounds or songs beyond Ibrahim's breath on her cheek. "Did you sleep?"

"We took turns," he answers, pulling her up to sit. The fabric of his clothes brushes the hard ground. "Everyone in position?"

Five 'ayes' later, and Catarina speaks, "Draw an evil eye in the sand." It's hard to keep track of her lines in the dark. Half-asleep, Athena digs her knife into the sand. "And a palm tree leaf over it."

"I thought of that," Paisley remarks from the other side of the stone tower. Now comes the complicated part. Athena stands, extending one arm, while slipping her blade into the hand of her other. She presses the tip into the fattiest part of her forearm and drags it an inch. When metal tinges the air, and bile surges up her throat, Athena offers her arm to Cat.

She runs the blunt side of her blade over the wound and lets the blood drip into her drawing. Stumbling, Athena finds each of them. Her healing kicks in before she returns to her own drawing and requires a second cut. With gentle fingers, she finds the drawing etched into the sand and holds her arm above it.

"How are we supposed to know when it soaks in?" Athena asks, leaning towards Catarina. No answer comes from the dark. "The bleeding stopped again."

"Delilah Christos," Catarina says to the sand. The others repeat it, but Athena waits. She expects the earth to shake or the moon to appear in the unnaturally pitch sky.

Leaning forward, lips almost to the sand, Athena whispers, "Delilah Phillipa Anne Christos."

Again. The air hangs with rare stillness over their heads. Catarina repeats Delilah's name. They all do, like an incantation over Athena's spilled blood. Paisley says her name as one word. Faster and faster and faster.

They each take a different approach. Slow. Fast. Ibrahim in different voices. Catarina with different accents. Killian at different volumes. Athena sings to the magic, close enough to feel the sand brush the tip of her nose. Wind stirs. The earth rumbles beneath them. Fear twists Athena's stomach as she reaches for Ibrahim in the dark. They cannot see what might be coming or where the quake began.

"That's it, flashlights on." Paisley flicks her phone on, a single beacon in the night. Pale light floods over the spire and reveals it split in two. She's the first one to dive towards it and look through the crack, so when she speaks Athena braces herself for the worst. "It's a staircase."

A quiet hum drifts towards them from within, compelling them to enter. Each step they take down the stairs brings them closer to the song. Soon the light from Paisley's phone is rendered useless.

Glittering shards of light float through a pink sky. Bits and pieces of a life once lived hang suspended over their heads—children's toys, wilted flowers, a broken cottage made of driftwood and sandstone. Spiral staircases swirl on every side of them, offering a different path, but Killian continues down the steps of their own.

Awestruck, Paisley whispers, "I've never seen anything like this." She reaches towards a shattered bust and pokes it with her finger. The woman's eyes are set wide in stone. Moss clings to the broken side of her face and dark liquid bleeds from within. "It's a witch, isn't it?"

No one needs to answer. Magic tastes like bread on the air—and smells like it, too. Athena's stomach rumbles. Suddenly she cannot think of anything but jam and butter on freshly made bread. Warmth chases the chill of the night from her bones.

Two new staircases build on their own. They float, suspended on nothing, and seem to lead to nowhere. The hum builds into something else. Athena listens to the beautiful piano as saliva gathers behind her tongue.

"Do we go towards the creepy music?" Paisley inquires when they pause. More staircases appear, each attaching themselves to their path. Two lead down. One leads up. Another tilts to the side, and the other forks into another staircase. "I vote run away. Far away."

Athena chooses on instinct. The song haunts the cavern, if it can be called that. It rings and grows and consumes the room. Direction means nothing as bits of stone and neglected art brush her skin. Looking back, she catches her reflection on a downward-moving staircase. A woman whispers. Voices dance with the melody, caressing Athena's ears; one sounds enough like Delilah to tempt her.

Her next step ends with her in a room. When she looks back, a hall stretches beyond her. A long, colourful rug slithers like a snake below her feet and winds towards a wide, sweeping staircase. Streaks of sunlight sneak in through cracks in the sandstone mansion. Prisms of light pulse to the rhythm.

A woman sits at an organ. Her back moves from side to side as she plays. Keys hang about her head like an unbound hat might. Neglected from care, parts of her black curly hair mat against the side of her head, while other parts puff like a cloud.

Athena does not speak for fear of interrupting the woman's lament. Brass pipes curl around the stair banister and above, but the organ sounds better than a siren's song. The front doors fling open and reveal a bewildered Paisley. She edges closer, her mouth hanging open. When she tries to speak, Athena tugs on her hand.

The banister runs like silk under Athena's touch. Call it compulsion or curiosity, she cannot stop herself from drawing closer to the woman. She gets to the top of the stairs sooner than expected and stumbles when the floor levels off.

Ibrahim peeks out from behind a pillar. He comes forth as Killian and Catarina lean over the banister above. The music continues without pause, despite Athena's hand brushing the woman's curls. She retracts her hand when the coil smacks her.

"You must be Athena."

She speaks with the richness of languages no longer spoken. The cadence of her voice echoes from the chambers above. Magic coats Athena's skin like sweat. It curls around her neck with the roughness of a rope.

"Yes."

"Am I the one you seek?" A shrill note squeaks out of the closest pipe. Paisley cries out as the stair runner wraps around her legs and pulls her up the stairs to Athena's side. "Have you come for a taste of glory?"

"Delilah," Athena croaks, touching her finger to her neck. There's nothing there. Not physically. Hunters cannot be cursed or enchanted, and most spells do not affect them. Though this witch doesn't seem like the kind to adhere to the laws and rules. She also plays seamlessly without a sheet of music for reference, her thin fingers never missing a key. "My sister. Delilah Christos."

"Look me in the eye when you ask something of me."

Athena steps forward, hands shaking at her sides. Fabric dances around the witch's body and face, revealing her black skin, before concealing it again. A tattered sleeve winds towards her hand and loops around her fingers. Poppies flower in a band around her ring finger. They die and come back to life, never growing more than half an inch.

"That's a beautiful ring."

She looks up at the witch and swallows a horrified gasp. It's impossible to look her in the eye, for where two eyes should be, a pair of hollow sockets stare back at Athena.

Living in the mountains, she's seen all kinds of injuries. Bears, canines, felines, and even birds. The claw marks are not from an animal. Five lines for five human-like fingers. Pink and gnarled where the rest of her skin is uncommonly smooth and dark. Claw after claw after claw. Stacking on top of each other to create a basket-like weave against the hollows of her face.

The witch cackles, throwing her head back. Her teeth shine in the light and stretch the ruined skin in delight. Light flickers around their heads. Broken piano keys quiver, and the organ's pipes cry in fear or protest. After dragging her arm over the keys, she flings it to the right. A door flies open past Ibrahim's head.

"Thank you." Voices filter out of the newly opened room. Catarina and Killian run down the stairs to their level as Athena pauses at the end of the pipes. "This composition is beautiful."

A smile cracks open the scars. The witch tilts her head to the side, revealing more thick lines of barely healed flesh down her throat. One claw split her ear. Ibrahim reaches for Athena, tucking her into his side, and drags her away from the witch.

The voice-filled room expands before them, no longer sandstone, but wood and rugs and a crackling fire in a hearth. When Athena glances back, there's no longer a door behind them. The music ends abruptly when another door *creaks* open.

The voices stop.

Athena wanders closer and wraps her hand around the metal doorknob. She pries it open despite her pounding heart. A table extends the length of the long room. Nattalius, leaning over the nearest chair, watches Athena enter with a dropping jaw. A pale, tattooed hand—Delilah's hand—pushes him back so she can stand.

It's difficult to say which of the sisters whispered the other's name first. "Delilah."

"Athena."

Nattalius pulls the chair back to allow Delilah to rush to her sister.

Before Athena gets within arm's reach, Del stumbles. The joy fades from Delilah's face like light during a sunset. Her eyes jump from Athena to Ibrahim, filled with a rage Athena recognizes all too well. In a guttural voice, unrecognizable as Delilah's, she whispers, "what have you done?"

PART 2: THE BEAST

CHAPTER 16

Do it Yourself

An old adage says, 'If you want things done right, do it yourself'.

Well, I couldn't do anything to prevent two horn dog teenagers from going at it. I couldn't do Ibrahim's vasectomy for him.

I can do an extreme amount of damage to him before anyone gets in the way. Rip his arms off. Tear his throat out. Crush his penis into a pancake. Remove his testicles from his body and sacrifice his sperm to God.

The All-Knowing One must be getting a kick out of this. How many perils did they face? A leprechaun, a unicorn—a godforsaken mermaid had her hands on Athena—and through all their battles and the ensuing First Aid, not one member of the band of travelling idiots heard the heartbeat.

The *second* bloody heartbeat.

A heartbeat that hammers faster than any fully formed being's, hence why I initially assumed they enlisted a pixie to help. Pixies have high heart rates to begin with and Ayizan, with her abnormal face and anti-normal aura, tends to scare guests.

God, why couldn't it have been a pixie?

It took one look at her. ONE LOOK. A single glance at my unassuming little sister, and I knew there was a little monster growing inside of her.

"Del, please stop," Athena whispers, reaching for me. I stare at her hand and her husband at her side and twist on my heel again. Pacing is the only thing keeping me from lunging at Ibrahim and tearing his head off his gangly body. "We don't know y—"

"THEY don't know yet."

It's all I can do to swallow my roar. I've kept my cool. The only thing worse than Athena being pregnant is Nattalius figuring out she is pregnant. If he knows, the Imperium knows, and if the Imperium knows…

I swallowed the monster down when I first saw her and got us out of the Sahara as quickly as possible. It wasn't until we were in the air, with Nattalius passed out in first class, that I berated them. Bloody fools, the lot of them, waltzing around trying to help me stop King Hozeir when they were carrying his most dangerous weapon yet.

Twice the fools, considering they questioned me repeatedly, asking if I was sure. They don't understand. The hunter in me senses there's a demon in her, but the demon in me knows it's there. In my sister. My beautiful, naïve sister, who, from the moment I declared her pregnant, developed a raging case of lovesickness. She won't abort it. She won't do what's necessary.

"No need to get in a tizzy," the doctor murmurs, offering a dopey smile. He's an idiot. A poodle with two legs. There are no thoughts behind his glazed eyes. Being summoned by the Alpha to his home, on a secret mission, is the highlight of this poor sap's life. It'd be easy enough to take a test, but no—Athena wants to see it. "The machine's almost ready."

None of them can hear it, though Ibrahim's been strangely pensive since I pointed it out. He admitted to hearing the occasional heartbeat, but he assumed it was his. *His*.

Snarling, I circle the room again. Killian let Graham and Mona into the secret. He's preparing to protect her, preparing to protect the pack's newest pup. They think this is simple. They think they can escape the Imperium.

Everyone thinks they are the exception. It's the quintessential part of being created by a stubborn male.

"It's almost ready," the idiot repeats, tapping the glitching monitor. Athena reaches for Ibrahim's hand when the man wipes blue gel across her stomach. She's gained mass from pregnancy and Requisite. Muscle adds bulk to her slim frame, but days of less-than-ideal travel conditions have leeched her natural glow. I'm not surprised she didn't notice the creature growing inside of her with all the excitement—or the excessive implantation bleeding hybrids cause. Spotting will last through most of the pregnancy as the little hellion sinks its claws into my sister.

Rage pours into my veins like sparks into a fuse. I cannot sleep. I cannot eat. I cannot protect her from this. I cannot protect her from herself. I cannot protect her from the Imperium. I cannot protect her from my father.

In a theatrical whisper, the doctor says, “She’ll be okay,” like he wants the whole audience to hear. Killian moves, positioning himself as a wall between me and the insufferable wolf. Our eyes meet across the room. He keeps giving me a look, as if I’m supposed to know what it means, as if I don’t want to tear him apart too. He allowed this to happen. He was supposed to protect her. I trusted them. “The Imprint bond can be as strong as the Mate bond. It’s difficult for the Imprinter to see their Bonded going through pain because they do not hear their thoughts or experience feelings like Mates do.”

Pausing, I bite down on my tongue. Tainted blood floods my mouth, but it’s the pain that keeps me from launching across the room. “Are you saying I’ve imprinted on my little sister?”

“It’s common enou—”

I’m inches from his face in seconds. Warm arms wrap around my stomach and pull me away, leaving the doctor with a single scratch on his throat and me thirsting for more. People are shouting. Athena’s shrinking away. It doesn’t matter that Ibrahim dives forward to protect her. It doesn’t matter that the heartbeat in her stomach picks up.

“Let go of me.”

“It has nothing to do with sex or romance,” Killian whispers, breath brushing my ear. I dig my nails into his arm, but he doesn’t let me go. His stubble brushes my cheek, forcing the monster back. “It happens with hunters sometimes. When you spend a lot of time with somebody, when you must protect them, when you care for them—you Imprint. It means you’d do anything for Athena.”

“I would,” I agree, sneering at the doctor. One of Killian’s arms crosses my chest to prevent me from grabbing the dagger at my side. “I am going to kill the imbecile for her.”

He traps my hand in his and opens his mouth to speak when the monitor bursts to life. Paisley and Mona press forward, both holding Ibrahim's shoulders like they're sister wives. They're acting like this is good news.

King Hozeir's building an army. He has all the Sacraments that matter, except the Crown, which I left in the hands of a witch back in the Sahara, because she's the only one who can protect it from greedy hands. If Nattalius had his way, we would've marched into my father's lair with our one bargaining tool and laid the Hielanders to waste once and for all with the legions of Imperio. He forgets, of course, that King Hozeir has at least one powerful magic wielder with him and his own hosts of loyalists. There are thousands of Otherworlders who want to destroy the Imperium.

Even if we found Hozeir and had every kind of Otherworlder's blood in the Crown, we cannot account for the ones we do not know. No one knows how many hybrids King Hozeir has created. No one knows if he is content with those who already walk the earth or if he has the magic wielder opening portals to hell. There are too many things we do not know, and now my sister is pregnant.

She's got a werewolf and hunter hybrid—a werenter—growing in her womb and there's no doubt King Hozeir already knows about its existence, because of me, because he's been watching me for years. In a few months it will be born and then what? King Hozeir has the Uterus. He can make it an adult in one drink. He can control it. Groom it.

He's going to want Athena. He might take Ibrahim too. Force them to breed. Force the 'pup' to breed.

My mother's worst fear come to life.

It's the reason she killed herself.

Killian rests his cheek against my temple and whispers, his voice too quiet for the others to hear, "This is not you protecting her. You are trying to punish us."

No, I will not cry. A burn scorches the back of my tightening throat and spreads to my eyes against my will. Killian's arms flex, but he releases me upon my silent nod. I cannot stop fighting. I cannot stop being angry. If the rage fades, there's going to be nothing but terror left.

I cannot fix terror.

"She shouldn't be here," Mona remarks, leaning over Athena. My Athena. The rage comes back with a vengeance, and I welcome it like an addict. "How do we know she won't tell the Imperium?"

"Mona, you're not helping," Ibrahim states, breaking his silence. He grabs her hand on his shoulder when she tries to speak again. "If the Imperium comes, we'll need Delilah's help. This isn't about your problems with her."

She steps back like he slapped her. The reaction's enough to sate my need for violence. Flashing a self-satisfied smile, I flip her off hoping to draw out her notorious temper. She abides with a menacing growl. Graham pulls her back like Killian does for me, and the sound of Mona cussing echoes through the small room. Killian tries to speak over her, and in the corner of my eye, Paisley runs her hand down Athena's trembling hand.

I know I'm ruining this for her.

I know this is her dream coming to life.

Wolves wear sheepskins. Nightmares wear dreams.

I hear it before they do and slump against Killian's chest. The heartbeat, like a gavel against a block, pounds and silences Mona too. Smiling, the doctor raises the volume even higher on his monitor and uses his other hand to run his wand over Athena's stomach. Her face lights up when a small blob appears on the monitor. It's too early for features, but the shape looks human. Little ears poke out from the sides of its round skull. Handlike things press against its face.

"Even the kid wants you to shut up," Graham growls at Mona, pushing her behind him. She's no longer making a fuss. Her eyes widen on the screen like mine.

Paisley squeezes Athena's hand and squeals exactly like a pig. "Congratulations, momma!"

Tears unbidden roll down my sister's round cheeks. She pulls Ibrahim closer, her lips open, her chest heaving. When his hand touches her belly, inches from the stick the doctor uses, the creature jumps. "I felt that," Athena whispers, glancing at each person in the room. When her eyes meet mine, unadulterated hope pours out. "I felt him."

"Him?" I choke. For a brief moment, I see Dad beside her, except he has Ibrahim's dark skin and Athena's smile. Philip the eleventh. That mental picture goes up in flames. "Congratulations to you both. Excuse me."

My legs move, but I cannot see my steps.

Athena calls my name. Someone else does too, but the edge of my vision blackens. My teeth brush the healing incisions on my tongue and reopens them.

With the taste of my blood in my mouth, I throw the packhouse doors open, which swing right off the hinges and slam to the ground. I sprint towards the forest, on two stumbling feet, and beg the shadows not to take me yet.

CHAPTER 17

Trust a Horndog to Horndog

Exorcizing demons burns calories faster than any workout.

I rip off my soaked shirt and wring it out into the snow. Steam rises from my skin in thin tendrils. Drips of red follow each of my steps. The hard, icy layer under the fresh snow tore through the soles of my feet hours ago. As soon as one cut heals, I take another step.

I am well and truly exhausted. No more running for me. I cannot breathe without a little rattle climbing from my lungs into my throat. The air hurts to breathe. It hurts to stand in.

The packhouse's front porch creaks under my foot. No one thought to replace the door during the snowstorm this afternoon, so a thin layer of powder covers the front entryway. Blood spreads through it like a disease.

"You should've put on shoes."

Ignoring Athena's gentle voice, I beeline to the fridge. They've signed my sister's death warrant. The least they can do is provide something to sate the beast growing inside of me.

"Can you look at me please?" If her voice were any gentler, I'd scream. "Delilah."

Though the others let this happen to her, they also protected her when she insisted on coming after me. For that, I am grateful. For that, I will not blow the entire house down with a roar. For that, I will let the sleeping wolves do so soundly, while my psyche tears itself to pieces.

"Congratulations." Grabbing a beer from the fridge, I rip the lid off. The metal edges dig into my scabbed palm, pouring blood onto Killian's nice hardwood floors. I'm petulant enough not to care. Damn him and his nice floors. "It's a dream come true."

"Stop."

"Stop what? You've wanted to be a mom since we were kids, and now you are."

"Pretending." She crosses her arms, drawing my attention to her stomach. It's been hours since I've seen her, but there's undoubtedly a bump there. Werewolves have pups quicker than humans. Depending on the bloodline and wolf size, they can be pregnant for as little as four months. Athena won't be that lucky. "I can take the ugly too, you know. I won't resent you for having mixed feelings about this. I'm scared too. I want this baby more than anything else, but I know what a dangerous world I'm bringing him into."

Her speech does little more than incite me. I can feel Ibrahim from where he perches on the stairs. The sound of Athena's watery sigh draws my eyes back to her. In the lowlight of the oven range, the edge of her old scar casts a shadow on her face that her fingers rub away.

"I-I-I know—Clearly you don't-t have a lot of t-t-trust-trust in me right now." She pauses, lips quivering around the unsaid words. "We made you a promise... I made you a promise, and I'm so s—"

"Don't you dare finish that sentence." The bottle cracks in my grip. I push it across the island and throw my arms over the hard surface. A tear rolls down her cheek, and she lets it drop onto her satin-clad chest, landing among other drying droplets. "Do not say you are sorry. I am not angry with you, Thea. I am happy for you."

"It's okay to be angry—"

"I am. At them. This is their fault, not yours. I am angry at the laws the Imperium created. I am angry you will live your entire life fearing for its." Tears burn a trail across my icy cheeks. Her sob breaks the last of my restraint. Circling the island, I open my arms to her. "Come here."

Athena collapses into my arms, and in that moment, everything fades away. King Hozeir. The Sacraments. Nattalius. It's just Athena—my baby sister—and me, safe in each other's arms. The thought lasts a moment and vanishes with Ibrahim's arrival in the kitchen.

"He got a vasectomy," Athena whispers, pulling away. She grabs my face, forcing me to look at her, and not at her husband inching into the room. "I picked him up from the hospital. He was in pain the entire flight to Imperio. It reversed Delilah. This is an act of God."

"Yeah, He enjoys playing with firstborns." I stab my finger towards Ibrahim. "You promised."

Just like I promised our parents. I guess life makes liars of us all.

Ibrahim shifts. He meets my eyes, his own wide and apologetic. Inching closer, he drops his head and twists it to the side, so his wolf's throat stretches towards me. It's an obvious offering. A messed-up apology. Neither of them could stop me from severing his carotid. The beer bottle's jagged mouth would suffice.

"We both did," Athena says, resting her hands on my arms. The little creature's heartbeat pulses through her thumbs into my brachial artery. I can feel it. "If you're angry at him, you're angry at me. If you cannot forgive him, you cannot forgive me. We are one and the same, Del."

"He's not my little sister," I mutter, watching him curl onto his side. He exposes his stomach and stays there, despite my murderous glare. "I'm not going to rub your belly and call you good boy. Get to your feet."

Grabbing the beer again, I drain it in one swig. They don't have anything strong enough to curb the chasm cracking my chest wide open. All my plans flew out the window with that heartbeat. I cannot leave her now. Nattalius and I cannot approach the Imperium. She needs me here.

What the hell am I supposed to do with Nattalius?

"The doctor said I'm measuring at eleven weeks," Athena states, nudging a sonogram towards me. Dutifully ignoring the picture, I search for another beer. I need to find a way to dismiss Nattalius. He should be happy to take credit for the search. Chancellor Montgomery might be suspicious of my disappearance, but he knows how much I hate politics. "He doesn't have a lot of experience with hybrid pregnancies, but he said, given Ibrahim's genetics, I might have the baby in the spring."

"Hunter-werewolf hybrids take longer than normal wolves." They watch me drain the bottle with twin expressions of fright. "Expect to get fat and swollen and have the beasty kicking out your abdominal wall at thirty weeks."

"Delilah."

"Athena."

"Call him a baby." My stone mask slips imperviously into place. It's not a baby. The Imperium's laws may be antiquated and prejudiced, but hybrids are dangerous—we are dangerous. "I am having a baby."

"Your hunter genes are already trying to expel it; that's why you've been spotting so much. Some carriers need to take sedatives as early as twenty weeks to avoid premature labour." Mom needed them. As my dad and his small group of staff prepared the house for my arrival, she laid in bed with a drip Ingrid set up. "It will start trying to get out. It could rip through your uterine wall."

"He's a baby. He doesn't know any better."

I swallow my retort. She's got a crazed look in her eye. The thing is changing her. "Give me your phone."

Thrown off, she hands me the phone robotically. "Why?"

"I crushed mine." Working with Nattalius was not a choice I made lightly. On the days we got along, I remembered the first weeks of our acquaintance. Those memories helped my good mood coast along for a minute or two before we circled back to his betrayal. On the bad days, we argued loud enough to scare off the most curious creatures. My phone wasn't the only casualty of my unfulfilled bloodlust.

"Who are you texting?"

"If Nattalius gets within a mile of you now, he'll know." He might figure it out on his own. Companions just know things about one another. Struck-out tattoo and excommunication aside, he reads me like a book. God knows how much he wants to properly meet Athena. I practically shoved her out of the room before he could get a look at her. "Cat might overlook this infraction, but he won't. He'll give dear old gramps a heart attack."

"Did you know we have a cousin named Daniel?" Son of Mom's

cousin, Peter, nephew of Levi who enrolled both Athena and I into Seminary, twin of Diza, who'd shoot herself in the foot to spite everyone. Pulling my eyes off the phone, I nod. "We met! We were in physiotherapy, and he told me about this injection that breaks up scar tissue."

"You're trying to remove your scar?"

"Not this one. My knee injury." She offers an excited smile and lifts her leg. The skin twists weirdly around her kneecap because of the multiple surgeries it underwent. "You didn't tell me about him."

"I prefer not to acknowledge they exist. Returning the favour and all that."

"I don't think Daniel's like that," Athena argues, glancing back at Ibrahim. She sees the best in everyone.

Admittedly, I haven't met Daniel. Once I found out he worked at Seminary, I made sure to avoid the fourth-year's training ground. Nattalius supported my decision and told me more than once what a self-righteous prick my cousin is. He and my Great Uncle Levi were known for it. One being a man who trains killers but refuses to kill, and the other being a man who works for the Requisition's Department, providing care for the orphaned and Unawakened hunters, but not for his literal flesh and blood who suffered from those same two conditions.

I was the one who reached out and asked Levi to enroll me in Seminary. I was the one who reached out and asked him to enroll Athena. Everything I know about them—Peter working in the healthcare department, and Diza stretching out her Mastery courses to avoid getting a real job—I discovered through my classmates and professors.

"You should go to bed," I remark, handing her phone back to her. This day needs to end. This week needs to end. Unpleasant from start to finish, and now I need to think about my mother's family. "Enjoy it while you can. It's going to start getting difficult, but I'll figure out what the safest sedative is."

Ketamine for me. On drip.

If I were any more of a monster, I'd find something to put the pup down too.

CHAPTER 18

Stupid Lamb

There's a ridiculous amount of spiderwebs in the corner of this room, given the number of giants who call this house home. Killian needs to get on top of sweeping these out because I've counted four different egg nests. He's got a full-fledged infestation coming. An army of spiders to contend with.

I can't sleep. Counting spiders is the only thing stopping me from running again. My skin crawls, trying to escape me, and the uncontrollable dread weighing down my stomach. Athena and Ibrahim went back to their home—their little cottage on the outskirts of the pack territory. Far enough for any cries to be muffled by the wind and snow.

King Hozeir may not know.

It's the paranoia telling me he might. King Hozeir's a resourceful man. If he doesn't have spies in the Garity Pack, then he's got wolves searching for me. How much time do I have before it all catches up? My father. The newest mark on the Christos' record. Nattalius. The Sacraments.

Ayizan.

She wouldn't confirm whether she built the Crown, but I left it there in the hopes she would destroy it. If she is 'the' Blind Witch from the stories, there is no love lost between her and the Sacraments. The Hunter Queen and her Sacraments cost the woman her eyes and her heart. A struck-out tattoo marks a hunter who betrayed their legion. Clawed out eyes mark a witch.

What marks a sister?

Tearing off the comforter trapping the heat seething from my wrathful pores, I cross to the window. Snow batters the glass. A coat of white clings to the earth. It sleeps as my mind rages.

The first hair slips out of my scalp without a fight. Dropping it onto the ground, I pace to the other side of the room. A thin line forms behind me, stand after strand. One after the other isn't enough. Blocking out the thoughts, I fist my hair and pull it. Flesh peels with it, exposing my skull. Blood drips into my eyes, but it's not enough.

"That's enough," a voice whispers as golden light floods the room. Killian jogs forward and grabs my hand before I can continue. The softness in his eyes triggers the hardest parts of me. I strike with my free hand, but he catches it and holds it an inch from his face. Beneath the drive to split open my skull, self-consciousness rears her ugly head. The chunk of flesh and hair missing from my scalp is intertwined in our fingers. He's touching it.

Blood runs down my forehead and cheeks. I still need more. The craving steals my breath.

"Let go of me."

"She's safe," he says, prying my fingers open. The piece of scalp *splats* to the ground between us. Killian drops my hands and reaches for my head, his touch ghosting over the open wound. "Take this."

He all but shoves a doll into my hands. Without another word, he ushers me into the guest bathroom across the hall. Unable to stop myself, I pull at the doll's hair. The head pops off instead. Annoyed, I shove it back on and try again. A single blue strand comes out of its head with a satisfying *snap*.

No pain though. I need the pain. My fingers start towards the back of my head, but Killian's fingers intercept me, redirecting them back to the doll's head. He brings a cloth to my ear. The sight of his consternation—guarded eyes, puckered lips, clenched jaw—in the mirror quenches my destructive thirst. "I didn't take you for a doll guy."

"It was Sophie's."

It's too late to stop. The next tug tears off half the doll's head. "Your dead sister?"

"She did worse to them," he promises, lifting my chin with the pad of his finger. Using his knuckles to push my jaw to the side, Killian wipes away the fresh bead of blood rolling down my neck. He continues to move me like that, each time with soft caresses and unspoken promises. He's gentle in ways I didn't think possible for someone like him. To make his job easier, I hop onto the counter. I'm too lost now to walk away. He bends to accommodate the distance between us, his eyebrows softening. The skin between keeps jumping. Like they want to come together but he holds them apart for my sake.

"You lift your brow," I remark, wanting to touch him. I cannot. I cannot touch him. This one thing I can control. "You're getting wrinkles."

"I don't mind wrinkles." His brow drops, heavy over his gaze. I see why he might lift them now. His thick eyebrows act like curtains over his honey eyes. "Skin is meant to be worn."

"You couldn't say that in a less creepy way?"

Smile lines ripple on both sides of his luscious lips. He's got a dark beauty mark on his stubbled chin and it taunts me, practically asking me to nip it. Averting my eyes, I stare into the lit hall.

I'd devour him. All 6'6 inches. Every bit of his cushy muscle.

"It's a crime to wear those pajamas on sheets with a thousand plus thread count." They're a bit ratty. A hole stretches across the bottom left side of the shirt, flashing a bulge of muscle over his hip. "Is that a paint stain?"

"I could feel your thoughts from down the hall," he murmurs, gathering water in his hands. It slides down my scalp and back, washing away the last of the blood. The antiseptic he uses stings in the best way. As the bubbles fade, he pulls out an ointment. "I grabbed the first thing I could find when I heard you get up."

"Did you think I was going to attack someone?"

"I thought you'd leave." He rubs the tingly cream into my head and opens a random drawer with a hum. It smells a little minty and stings my eyes worse than the blood or tears. "You push yourself too hard. Eventually you'll break, and I do not want that to happen on top of a mountain during a blizzard."

"What makes you think I'm not already broken?"

He ignores the self-deprecating comment and winds his hands behind my head. With deft fingers, he brings a silk scarf around my forehead, gathering all my hair under the fabric before securing it with a knot. "If you had broken, we wouldn't be having this conversation right now."

Oh. We're talking about that, are we? Sniffing, I hop off the counter and leave the wrecked doll beside the sink. He follows me out of the bathroom and into the bedroom without another word.

"I cannot *break.*" I don't know where I'm going or what I'm doing. The walls are closing in. My skin's crawling again. I want to scream and shout and beat my head into the wall. I want to run until the oxygen scars my lungs trying to claw its way back in. "If I break, everything falls apart. Athena needs me. Her *kid* needs me. My parents need me. The humans need me."

Is that a scream or vomit climbing up my throat? More mortifying, it sounds like a sob. I slam my hands into the edge of my mattress and try not to collapse against it. Like my shadow, Killian waits behind me, not touching me physically, but encompassing me in his strength.

Tears fall against my will. My mother's disappointed expression is one I'm familiar with, but it's Dad whose voice haunts me—his harsh whisper demanding me to keep Athena safe, moments after I gave her the scars on her face. I don't remember the snap, but I remember the feeling of her blood on my hands. I remember her scream.

"I promised to protect her."

"You don't have to do that alone."

I need to make a plan. I need to find a way to protect Athena from the Imperium and King Hozeir while preventing King Hozeir from bringing hell to earth and the Imperium from slaughtering the people Athena's told me are our family. Doesn't he know I have to protect them too?

Killian tries to speak louder than the panic. “We are not going to let anything happen to her.”

“It’s not that easy.”

“Nothing’s easy. It’s hard. Sometimes it’s borderline excruciating.” He steps closer. I know he wants to touch me as badly as I want to touch him. I want to reach for him. His heat presses against my back from a foot away. Nothing calms me like his smell. “We weren’t made to take on any of this alone.”

“I wasn’t made. I was inflicted.”

“You were made to be Athena’s sister. You were made for such a time as this.”

“Don’t quote Esther at me.”

“You were made for m—” Holding my breath, I glance under my arm at him. Killian stares out the window, his throat bobbing. When our eyes meet, he puts his hands on his hips. “More. You were made for more than what you have sentenced yourself to.”

“You have no idea.”

“The pain is not your own.” Throwing my words back in my face. I glare at him, clenching the comforter in my hands. “You are punishing yourself. You think it is the price you must pay for being alive. Martyring yourself like you’re nothing more than a sacrificial lamb.”

“I just have trust issues. People cannot be depended on.”

“You said my mother was sick for putting the burden of my sister’s death on me.”

“Don’t compare our parents. My parents did their best.” Mom tried. Dad tried too. He did what he could with a child who wasn’t his own. He loved me as best he could. Killian stands his ground as I step towards him, pointing my finger at his chest. “No, actually you’re right. They are sick. They chose not to put me out of my misery when they had the chance."

"They're sick because they let you believe you're anything less than a blessing."

The sincerity in his gaze knocks down my defenses. Stumbling back, I find the spiderweb over his shoulder and begin counting. Anything to avoid the emotions written clearly across his face.

"I was not wanted," I whisper before he can continue. I press my hands between my breasts, like a twisted prayer. He needs a reality check. I am not Queen Esther destined to deliver the Jews. I am Isaac. My father will come with his knife on the mountaintop and offer me up. Unlike Isaac, I'll have my own blade. Father Abraham and I are going down together. "My mother didn't want kids. Ever. I am more than a mistake—I am a curse. The only thing that redeems me is Athena. That's my purpose. Keep her safe. Offer myself up on a platter when the time is right. I scare the monsters off because I am one."

"Okay."

I shake my head, reaching towards the wound in my head. "I can't keep her safe. I can't stop the Imperium. I can't lose her too."

"*We* can. We will."

When he speaks like that, it's easy to believe him. Unshakeable strength. Unmoving mountain. Vulnerability shines through the hole in my chest. I try to nurture it and keep it as far from him as possible, but the question pours out in the silence. "Do you promise?"

"On my life."

I'm on him in the blink of an eye. My arms wrap around his waist like they don't know where to go. One fist gathers all the fabric of his shirt while the other presses between his shoulder blades. The muscle and bone in his back move beneath my palms when he returns the embrace.

Killian holds me tight enough to stop the shaking. A sob gathers in my stomach, climbing my ribcage with greedy hands. When it comes out, he rocks me. He doesn't try to shush me or tell me everything is okay. He absorbs every sob into his broad chest.

In a couple minutes, when the sobs recede and the tears dry, I know I will regret this. I already know it as I melt at his feet in a miserable presentation of the little strength I have left. Right now, I cannot rein myself in. Every piece of my damaged heart wants its time in the limelight. I want to talk about being near Nattalius again. Trying to kill Athena before I knew what murder was. Kelsey Dyck. My parents. The rejection of Christos' and Blau's I pretend not to care about. My fear of death and desire to disappear and become someone else. He probably never wishes not to be Alpha. He's honourable like that and that's what convinces me.

"I believe you," I whisper to his heart.

CHAPTER 19

Welcome to the Club

"You look how I feel," Paisley remarks, squinting in the sunlight. She offers her tumbler that smells so strongly of vodka it saps the moisture from my mouth. It tastes even worse than it smells, but I take another drag. I need it this morning.

"I prefer Baileys in the winter," I mutter. Unfortunately, my dark mood doesn't affect the weather. I woke in a bed, alone, to a pale blue sky and a sun too bright for December. Every ray of light reflects off the thousands of prisms trapped in the snow and enacts God's personal vendetta against me as it pierces through my eyes into my addled brain. I flop into the plastic seat beside Paisley and hand the drink back to her. "With a dash of coffee."

The wolves take full advantage of the sunlight. Pups band together to build an igloo; a group of teenagers wage a snowball war in the forest, and the older males play a rigorous game of hockey on the ice. That's where I find Killian, gliding on a thin piece of metal with the grace of a dancer, coated in the perfect amount of sweat.

"We were all out. Of both."

I woke up to find him gone, and the sheets rumpled from where he slept behind me all night. Despite showering and scrubbing my skin raw, I still feel the weight of his arms around me. I asked him to stay—I, a hunter, a Christos, asked a werewolf, an Alpha, to stay the night with me. Clearly, he knew it was a lapse of judgement because he snuck out. Hell, if he didn't, I would've.

"I'm going to kill Grady," Mona snaps, marching through the snow to reach us. She offers me a half-hearted middle finger before dropping into the seat on Paisley's other side. "Your days are numbered, Byrne!"

One of the hockey players, with a messy mop of blond hair, stumbles on the ice. I recognize Graham well enough to know he's the one who slams the guy into a snowbank. Paisley hisses for his sake and offers her cup to Mona. "What'd Grady do?"

"He's the one who finished off the coffee and didn't buy more." Growling, she takes a swig of the vodka cran. I hold my hand out for it when Athena and Ibrahim venture out, heading towards a tree decorated with Christmas lights. She's wearing a long, tight sweater dress that emphasizes her tiny bump, and it takes filling my throat with the drink to keep from yelling at her to change. "Why did you come back? You don't want to be here. We don't want you here."

"You two are not doing this with me here," Paisley sighs, pulling the drink out of my hand before I can throw it at Mona. She slurps loud enough to interrupt my retort. "Where's Cat? It feels wrong having a meeting without her."

Mona's golden eyes take on a slight red hue. She glowers at me as I shrug. "No phone. No line of communication."

"You sure?" Paisley questions, jerking her head towards the road. A familiar truck rounds the bend of the main road leading to the packhouse. Catarina cuts the engine and climbs out, wrapped in what can only be described as a Pillsbury Doughboy outfit. Between layers and layers of fabric, her covered eyes find me. "Speak o' the devil."

"What is she wearing?" Mona sounds more curious than catty, a miracle given our cantankerous circumstances. Watching Catarina try to wade through the snow puts a smile on both my face and the she-wolf's. My Companion extends a hand, cussing me out, when she comes to a bank too tall to lift her leg over.

"Why not use the path?" I ask, standing to help her. The wolves strategically flattened the snow to create a network of walking paths across their entire territory. Under the sun, many of the paths have melted, revealing the trampled grass underneath. "Can you even see?"

"I couldn't last one more moment in that house. He hasn't gotten lighter with that cologne." She coughs pointedly, taking her hand away to wrap herself in a hug. "How are you not wearing a coat? I can feel my nipples falling off."

"Claustrophobia."

She nods, mouth opening and shutting when she sees Athena. "She really is?"

"Yeah."

Cussing, she throws the hood off. She looks more ridiculous without it. A tiny head in a sea of bubbled fabric. Pushing up her sunglasses, she sighs. "The prince is arguing about art history with your chef, Mathéo."

"That'll hold him for a couple days."

"God willing."

Paisley offers her cup to Catarina with a pained smile. She accepts and sips daintily as we watch two males argue. One of them throws off his gloves and then they're throwing punches. No one, not even Killian in his delectable jersey, tries to interfere. They let them hammer on each other until blood splatters the ice.

"Do you watch them play a lot?" Catarina inquires, handing the tumbler back to Paisley. Both she-wolves nod. Crossing one leg over the other, she leans her head on my shoulder. "I see the appeal."

Paisley snickers and points at Graham, who rams another guy into the snowbank. "The tall one with a scar is Mona's."

She growls her assent, daring us both with a glint in her eye. I'd take the challenge. Not for Graham, but because I'm feeling keyed up. I'm craving recklessness. Killian struck too close to home. It cannot be a coincidence that the first meeting of the daddy issues club falls on the morning after he reduced me back to a quivering child.

"Anyone else want to stake a claim?" she asks it conversationally, but Paisley's knowing eyes fall on me. "Anyone at all?"

"You're getting too comfortable."

Catarina straightens, turning her shoulder to the hockey rink. The men resume their game despite the blood dripping all over the ice. Killian requires the two brawlers to smack fists and then he looks at us. At me. Reaching for the cup, I drain the rest. "You don't have anyone special, Pais?"

"Nah, I like to leave them guessing," she teases. When Mona scoffs, she flips her off. The vodka stings my throat, but now that Killian's seen me, he keeps glancing over. I need to scratch my skin off and leave my muscle to fry in the sun. "I've loved the same man my entire life."

A hundred bucks says it is Ibrahim.

Sure enough, when I take my eyes off Killian to follow Paisley's eyeline, I find Ibrahim instructing Athena on how to pose for a photo. She juts out her stomach and laughs at something he says. The smile transforms her face, making it glow brighter than the snow. It drives Paisley to pitifully suck the last drops from the tumbler.

"I'm not in love with him. Not really. I'd never hurt her like that." She's looking at me for condemnation, but she won't find it from me today. I'm too tired. Besides, who am I to question what the heart wants? Mine led me to Nattalius and now a man I cannot have. He's got a Mate somewhere. He's a werewolf. He's too good for me.

I'm on borrowed time.

"He's unavailable. Has been since we were kids. I wanted him to be my Mate so badly I *begged* for it, but we knew from the first time he shifted we weren't meant for one another." There's a hint of sadness in her voice, but not the sorrow I know as heartbreak. "Didn't stop me from trying to get him to kiss me at thirteen. I wanted him to be my first kiss, and I thought it'd be like the fairytales… 'True Love's Kiss' is shite."

"You and Graham should be Mates," Mona mutters, clenching snow into her fists. The man in question makes a sudden stop at the end of the ice and sprays snow scraps towards a group of young she-wolfs who eagerly squeal and giggle. "He was planning to go to a Mate Rally before all this happened. He's acting like turning twenty-five without a Mate on his arm is a personal slight to his wolfiness."

"He wants to find his Mate. I want—no one compares to Iba."

"You Imprinted. Once you Mate, you won't remember him. At least that's what Graham believes." This meeting needs more booze. Catarina nods her head, half-listening to them, half-watching one guy peel off his jersey. It's cold enough to freeze the ends of my fingers, but he's bathed in sweat. Normally, there'd be some appeal to his muscular body. My eyes find Killian instead, mussing the hair of one of the playing teenagers. *Damn it.* "Delilah knows all about Imprinting."

"What does Imprinting mean?"

"A strong emotional connection werewolves form, but it's based on choice and circumstance, not fate," I say, throwing a handful of snow at Mona's smirking face. She avoids it easily with a smug laugh. "I've Imprinted on Athena."

"Oh." Catarina cocks her head to the side, watching my sister flip through the pictures her husband took. "Your parents didn't leave you much choice."

"Which begs the question, who qualifies the two of you to be here?" Mona stares pointedly at me. God knows how much Athena's boasted about our dad. He was a good man when he had the chance to be. The older we got, the less he and Mom were around, but childhood pedestals tend to weigh more than teenage angst. "You had a great dad. Athena said he took you to car shows and went hiking with you all the time. He didn't even die that long ag—"

"I looked at Killian last night and wished he was my father."

Mona's lips press together in a thin line, her eyes drifting towards him. Paisley breaks the awful silence with a whistle. "I'd offer you a drink, but we're all out."

"And I still want to devour him."

"My sperm donor was investigating crime between my mother's gaggle and a gang of faeries. He thought she should be 'grateful' for his help." Catarina lifts her gloved hand, summoning a long blade of grass through the snow. It wraps around her thumb for a moment before withering to dust. "That's the extent of my abilities. Do you shake in fear of my hybrid wiles?"

We definitely need more alcohol for this. I glance sidelong at Mona, who follows Graham's every move with hunger in her eyes. "What are your qualifications, bigfoot?"

"Proud member of the Dead Dad club since 2006."

"I wish my dad was dead," Paisley sighs, hanging her head back. Catarina mutters her agreement and they high-five over my head. What a sorry lot we make. "He's probably chasing a rabbit somewhere in Antarctica right now."

"Is that a euphemism?"

Catarina pronounces it 'oo-fin-ism', but I don't have the heart to correct her. Paisley launches into an explanation about the 'lone wolf' behaviour triggered by Mate loss, but her voice fades when Killian glides off the ice. I watch him methodically untie his skates and hold back the urge to tell him to do it slower. There's something about big, calloused man hands doing delicate tasks. Like tying a hair scarf around my head.

He was covering the ugly bald spot.

Cynical blight aside, I know he did it to protect me. He took care of me. Without judgement or condescension. He looks at me no differently now as he swaggers up to our group gathered in the snow than he did yesterday. Paisley shuts up and offers a cheesy smile, but his eyes are on me. Always on me.

"Can I get you anything?"

A snarl escapes my throat when the beast slams two fists against my chest. One day he'll see me, and when he does, his kindness and compassion will shrivel up and die. "Baileys and out of my sun."

He cocks his head to the side and drags his eyes from my head to my toes.

Then he runs.

It's not surprising, but the beast withdraws, placated against the cage of my ribs. My gut twists at the sight of his back turned to me. He speaks to the group of hockey players and then leaves them, too. There's nothing casual or hidden about how I watch him now. When he stops beside Ibrahim and Athena, my stomach plummets. What is he saying?

"You may be the worst flirter I've seen," Paisley points out. She laughs at my sneer. "Don't worry, girls. We'll have each other to rot with."

Mona and I stare at one another over her head. Peeling my lip back, I search for Killian, who disappears into the packhouse without another glance. For the first time in my life, I consider following the person I've pushed away, begging him not to give up on me yet. He's the one who peeled back my walls with his big, manly fingers and unleashed the chaos inside.

I tried to warn him.

"You did a number on him," Mona says as Killian comes out of the house dressed in proper clothing. He catches us watching and gives me a look. I'm not sure what the look is supposed to mean. The beast infers it as 'get off my property', but I understand it as a promise.

"Where's he going?"

Catarina sighs, patting my hand. "To get Bailey."

"*Baileys*," Paisley corrects quietly as Killian climbs into his vehicle. The engine roars to life, but then he's back out to scrape ice and snow off the windshield. "Booze."

"Oh."

Oh. He's going to the store. I glance at Ibrahim and Athena, walking towards the frozen lake hand-in-hand. If he checked to see if Athena needs anything…. "You have a tattooing setup in the house?"

Paisley drops her eyes to me and nods. "Yeah. Killer let me have an entire room; it's kind of sick—"

"Show me."

"Right now?"

"I need the tattoo," I argue, standing. If I cannot run, I need to do something. Something reckless. Something harmlessly irresponsible. "Have you done a lot of tramp stamps?"

She laughs and springs to her feet with the excitement of a leprechaun. I risk one last glance and regret it when I watch Killian move around the hood of the truck, his eyes on me. He holds my gaze as he walks backwards to the driver's side. "No, but I'm down for anything."

Cat inhales shakily, winding her arm through mine. "I am going to need Bailey or something stronger before mine."

CHAPTER 20

Damnsel in Distress

Distracting a self-important man 101: give him a damsel in distress—or two. If damsels are in short supply, a she-wolf will do.

Paisley glowers at me, hands on her bare hips. "You promised this would be fun."

She drops to the ground when Nattalius swings his blade. Rolling like a barrel, she springs to my side and shifts. "You cannot depend solely on your wolf!" he yells.

"I'm having fun." This is the highlight of my week. Nattalius follows Paisley as she skirts around the training arena to where the males stand. He steps to the side when Mona launches at him from behind and watches both of them crash into the snow.

"Have you taught them anything?" Nattalius cannot help being a prick. He directs the question at the small crowd gathered around the makeshift training arena. The wolves covered their hockey rink in a dark tarp to make it less slippery and weighed the edges down with ice to prepare for his 'combat training'. He made the arena smaller to prepare them for a close quarter fight and, in doing so, exposed the werewolves' greatest weakness. "You're too big and clumsy. If you're trapped in close combat, you need to have some knowledge of hand-to-hand."

"Shut him up," Mona snaps at me, mid-shift. I hoped they would humble Nattalius but watching her break a sweat gives me as much enjoyment. If not more.

"I can't touch him." They know that. There's a reason I needed two damsels. Athena wanted to tell Ingrid the 'good' news, and he couldn't be within hearing range. It took less convincing than I thought to get him into pack territory. "I can help him demonstrate if you need a break."

She snarls, all human, and steps back into the circle. They regard each other from either side of it, measuring each other up. I miss the days of sparring enough to lick my lips in anticipation.

Mona's got an inch on Nattalius. They both have lean, slim muscle stacked on their arms and legs. People, even in Seminary, underestimated Nattalius, who's small enough to give them a false sense of security. Most rely on our enhanced strength, but he knows how to take advantage of our agility and wield his body like a weapon. It was one of the first things I admired about him.

"Who do you think will win?" Paisley breathes, dropping beside me. She stretches out in the snow with a satisfied sigh. "My money's on M."

Cat shakes her head, standing close enough for our shoulders to brush. We're in tune enough with him to know the thorough inspection of his blade is all for show. Any good fighter recognizes Mona for what she is—a brute. There's no poise or sophistication to her moves. She depends entirely on her size and strength as a wolf.

I noticed the sheen in Nattalius' eye when he saw her up close. She's fierce. Intimidating. The first time they fought, he kept his guard up. Now he knows how to take her down without trying. A specialty of his.

"He'll let her think it for a moment," I predict, barely speaking. Nattalius hears me. His head turns towards me enough to make it clear. Our three hearts beat to the same rhythm. He might be the only one sparring, but I taste every spike of his adrenaline and anticipation. It's never enough to satisfy the hunger carving out my stomach. "Play on her ego."

Mona launches, still in human form. He pretends to be surprised and twists his shoulder the wrong way. The hit she lands makes no sound in the silence. One step forward, and he's got a leg behind her. Nattalius spins. He plants his foot on Mona's back and sends her sprawling at our feet.

"I'm going to kill him."

"Please do," I murmur, rolling my eyes when Nattalius pulls off his shirt. He'd never reduce himself to think twice about a werewolf, but he's superficial. There are a few beautiful women surrounding the circle, and one is bold enough to clap for him. "The prince returns."

Paisley speaks out the side of her mouth when she asks, "Why do you call him the prince?"

Nattalius strikes before Mona can blink. He flips her over his shoulder, an incredible feat given how much I think she weighs, and smiles at us. "Because I am a descendant of the Hunter Queen."

Mona grabs his foot and yanks hard enough to drop him. Both

Catarina and I cheer louder than anyone else watching. Wrestling him into her arms, Mona locks her legs around his waist. For a brief, beautiful moment, I think she may win. He strikes with his elbow hard enough for a *snap* to sound.

Someone swears.

Nattalius gets to his feet.

Graham starts forward.

"Enough," I demand. Shedding my coat, I pass it to Catarina. One of the guys behind Killian starts hollering like an owl. I step into the arena and usher Mona out of it. "I invited you here to show the wolves what tactics hunters will use against them, not to show off."

"Why would I help the enemy?"

"They're not criminals," I counter passively, meeting Nattalius in the middle of the mat. We cannot hurt each other, but we can 'fight'. "King Hozeir is. He could have hunters with him."

"Any hunters working with him will be executed on sight. Dirty traitors," Nattalius scoffs, backing away.

Behind me, Catarina mutters, "We don't call him that to his face. If his ego gets bigger, it'll crack the ice."

"Hunters are Otherworlders." We were sitting in a pub with Nattalius' friends the first time we had this argument. One of them started talking about how he'd personally find every pixie and crush them under his foot like a bug. None of them liked it when I pointed out their blood binds ours. That comment led to our first real fight. I wonder if he started questioning my heritage then. "Just because your family chooses not to acknowledge those people doesn't mean they don't exist. I'm sure people thought Elke was a traitor when she suggested the coup against your great grandma and look at them now, sitting in seats paid for by her blood."

"I knew you'd go soft." He throws his head back with a laugh. Taking advantage of his distraction, I throw my knife. It cruises beside his ear, close enough for the handle to graze the tip. The males behind him scatter when the blade continues towards them. "Now you're down a weapon."

"I'll live."

He drives forward, giving me nowhere to go but back. His feigned nonchalance from earlier with Mona disappears beneath his white-knuckled frustration. My hair bounces with every unlanded hit. We used to spar once a day. Nattalius convinced Catarina and I that, given enough research, we could find a loophole in our Companion genetics. Back then, we were curious and meticulous.

He's unhinged now. The whites of his eyes expand when he pretends to kick me and, at the last second, redirects his momentum into a punch. Nothing touches me.

I raise my arm in front of my face to interrupt his backhand. I feel each of the hairs on his bare arm touch my covered skin. The wolves watch in fascination as I begin my counterattack. Without being able to touch him, we look more like we're dancing. His body anticipates mine, moving away, or my hand glides around his face instead of into it.

He stops, forcing me to stop. Despite our time apart, this is a familiar dance for both of us. I recognize the beat of his heart beneath mine. Feel the sweat rolling down his brow. All those years ago, I'd revel in this connectedness. I'd been foolish enough to believe the oneness between us was Biblical.

"It's not a coincidence that your sister isn't here." I shut him out as fast as I can. Closing the proverbial doors to my mind and my heart. He's there, though. He never left. We cannot hurt each other with our bodies or our weapons. It won't stop him from wielding his words like an axe. "Like mother like daughter?"

Rage replaces the euphoria of the *vitazeil.* The beast rattles against its cage, prying my chest open with claws of ice. He's inside my mind, but I'm in his. I feel the moment he understands how badly he messed up.

"Enough of this foreplay," Mona snaps, trying to push me back. I vibrate against her palm as everything, but the sound of his carotid artery fades away. It jumps against the thin skin of his neck. Begging to escape. "I'm tapping in."

She shoves me this time, and I concede, trying to tether my consciousness before it explodes in front of so many witnesses. I faintly hear Killian dismissing the wolves. He knows how to tuck and run. Nattalius is too stubborn. I taste his fear cowering behind a thin shield of bravado.

"I will start singing," Catarina warns into my ear. She places a cool hand on the burning skin of my wrist. "Really loud. Kicking back at shadows, no need for the light. You're sorry now, old gezer, what is your lifeeeee?"

"Is that supposed to soothe me?"

She grins and pulls me back towards the bank, a safe distance from my ex-boyfriend, who is still smirking at me. I got those botched lyrics tattooed on my left thigh in a previous reckless spiral. Blasting that song and driving with my eyes closed at a hundred-and-fifty clicks used to be my therapy. After my parents died, I changed tactics.

It's not enough anymore. My demons are waiting with bated breath backstage, ready for the final curtain. Nattalius knows how to draw them out.

"It must kill you," Mona murmurs, circling Nattalius. I wait for her to continue, but she leaves the hook hanging and focuses on picking her nails. A smirk plays on her lips when Nattalius reaches to fix his non-existent sleeves. Glancing at Cat, I raise my eyebrows. "I personally wouldn't be able to show my face, but I applaud you for your bravery. Who needs the approval of others? Vanity is outdated."

"You are trying to bait me, mutt." It's working. His nose twitches when she doesn't react; he has nothing to work with. Instead, Mona stretches and pauses in the centre of their arena, inches from him. "I am not one of your simple-minded pups."

"Simple-minded but pure."

A bomb explodes behind Nattalius' cold eyes. "There's nothing *pure* about any of you hellions."

"And yet our blood courses through your veins. Not only are you a thief, but you're a cheap knock-off." She pins him with a smile so cold it soothes the burn in the back of my throat. "Is that why you ended up with a hybrid for a Companion?"

Catarina sucks in a breath, waiting for my reaction. I cannot move anything more than my eyes. Killian and Graham remain where they are, watching Nattalius with a murderous expression, but they are the only spectators left other than Catarina, Paisley, and I. The others joined the teenagers in the forest and their laughter drowns out the sound of Mona's condescension.

"God's got a great sense of humour."

"He didn't end up with her. She ended up with him," Catarina interjects, glaring at the back of Nattalius' head. He ignores her entirely until she adds, "By your laws, she's our Alpha."

"She is nothing to me. I am no longer part of their legion."

"Bummer." Mona pops her lip into a pout. The patronization in her voice ruffles even *my* feathers. Nattalius' hand twists around his blade. "What shame that must've brought upon your royal line. A hybrid as your leader, another as the third member of your pathetic trio, and still, neither wants you. What must your queen think?"

He strikes silently, like a snake. The knife tears her shirt when she tries to dodge him, but it's a distraction tactic. Before she gets into position, he's there.

Nattalius grabs her throat and slams her to the ground with the entirety of his strength. A crack sounds underneath the thick black mat. He starts to say something, but the sound of her booted foot making contact with the back of his skull drowns it out.

Blood sprays his back.

Mona uses his distraction to twist and snap his arm.

He drops as Mona sweeps his legs out from under him and presses one knee into his lumbar spine. She's got him flattened. In a flash, she has his good arm and one leg in an unbreakable hold.

"It means something," Paisley whispers below me. She shrugs when both Cat and I glance at her. "Someone who shares blood with the original war wager is soully connected to two hybrids, the rarest Otherworlders on earth... in any realm for that matter. A person like *that* is self-important because they've got power and sway, right?"

Crushed beneath Mona, Nattalius meets my eyes. For a split second, I see how much that prospect terrifies him. There's no throne to claim in Imperio. Elke established the Imperium in such a way that one person could not hold all the power against both humans and Otherworlders. And yet, a Kartal is the highest-ranking member of the Five.

Eren Kartal's word is as good as law. The other four follow him because to do anything else would ostracize them from the legacy families. I know how the Kartal mind works. All offspring have a path carved in blood before they're born. Some hold prominent positions in the human world. Others pursue the route of influence by joining the church or serving the community.

From his infancy, Nattalius has been intended for the Five. For the Imperium. He works in the Senate's office now, because Ayça and Safet gave him no other choice. Being in my legion threw off their plans. I am the dark stain on what should've been a pristine record.

The strike cost him influence and respect, but if earth is known for anything, it's absolving men's sins and pinning them onto women. One day, he'll work his way into the Senate of Legionnaires. Once in the Fifteen, he'll schmooze and fight and bribe his way into the Five. It never occurred to me how advantageous having him as a Companion would be for me.

I don't think like a Christos.

"Enough!" Nattalius shouts, wiggling underneath Mona. She waits two seconds before releasing him and wisely steps away to give him a wide berth. Long, wet strands of hair sag over his face. Blood soaks his bare back. Shoulders around his ears, he glares at me. "What?"

I walk forward, peeling off my coat. He tries to refuse me, but there's a bone protruding through the skin of one arm and he needs the other to stem the bleeding. "If you fuelled your body properly, she wouldn't have won that."

Nattalius storms away with half his bloody body covered by my coat. Despite the blood soaking into my boot, I'm no more sated than I was before all this. Now there's just another mess to clean. "He's petty enough to report you to the Imperium."

Mona scoffs, pulling off her shirt. Wiping his blood from her forehead, she spits. "She's my sister now too."

CHAPTER

21

Return of the Momster

"To our victor," Paisley sings, raising her beer bottle. A cheer follows her command and steals all colour from Mona except for red. When our eyes meet, I clap for her. It was a battle of wills, and she won fair and square. Nattalius is off skulking in the woods. Part of me hopes he gets stuck waist-deep in a drift and comes out with a new attitude. The other part knows it'll make pacifying him more difficult. Mona's not the only one he might tattle on. "And to the perks of being a fighter, not a lover."

Mona wraps her lips around the rim of her bottle, her eyes on Graham. "I'm both."

The list of people endangering my sister grows every day, it seems: the wolves who see my sister's growing body, Nattalius, the Imperium and, of course, King Hozeir.

It's not a question of if—it's when.

When will he come for her?

When will he come for me?

I'd go to him if I could stomach the world he wants to build on the rubble of Imperio. I'd take the Crown back from the witch and give it to him in return for Athena's protection. The Imperium wouldn't touch her, and neither would he. King Hozeir could use me as he likes and establish his new world without a war.

One problem: he has sex with actual wolves. Another problem: he's a rapist. If I think about it, a few others come to mind—his clear lack of compassion for anyone but himself, his willingness to commit all manners of evil for the sake of power. To name a few.

But I could stomach that.

Athena couldn't. I doubt I'd be able to hide our benefactor's identity from her husband and, in turn, her. Taking her from Ibrahim is a no-go. Chances of her aborting are zero to none. Turning myself over on my own leaves Athena too vulnerable, but she cannot come with me…

I don't have enough chips for this age-old game.

"What are we celebrating?" Ibrahim asks from the front door, greeted by another round of cheers. Only Catarina and I take a second look at Athena's little bump. Wolves celebrate babies like Jews do our weddings. Most of them don't care that it's a hybrid growing inside her. They don't care that Athena's a hunter. She's a Mate and now a female carrying a pup.

Mona offers him a beer with a smirk on her face. "Humbling a hunter."

"Nattalius," Catarina clarifies for Athena's sake, whose fear and worry melts away when she finds me woundless and nursing a bottle.

She cannot even take two steps into the living room before the Mated she-wolves flock her with their pregnant bellies and crotch gremlins. "They love her."

"What's not to love?" I mutter, glancing at Paisley slithering to my side. I half-expect to find my disgust mirrored in her eyes, but there's only longing. "You'd think they'd stop popping out pups after seeing the number of orphans in their pack. War is coming."

"It's a sign of the health and strength of our pack," Paisley argues, smiling. She puffs out her stomach and holds the bottom of it. "I would look cute pregnant, wouldn't I?"

"You'd be fat, swollen, sweaty, and half-bald." Getting pregnant right now should be the least of her concerns. It should be the least of anyone's concerns. "Your teeth can fall out."

"I don't buy it. You love kids." Paisley steals my beer bottle and drinks from it before stretching out across the chair. My feet barely touch the ground in these seats. Spending time with the wolves is bad for my ego. Most of them are tall, gorgeous, *and* mentally stable. "I saw you with Sloane. You're a turtle, Delilah. Or a burnt marshmallow. Take your pick… I bet you'll find a nice guy and have a whole busload of kids. We'll laugh about this one day and trade tips on how to ensure our kids never see the club tat."

"I can't have children."

Monsters can't have children. My mother didn't phrase it that way, but her meaning couldn't have been clearer. Love doesn't matter. Desire doesn't matter. Biology and law govern choice. Paisley ducks her head and extends the bottle back to me.

"You're sitting with two hybrids," Catarina whispers, staring into her glass of wine. The law is a kindness. Neither of us knows how to be a mother. Cat's mother chose to keep her to spite her father. She saddled an abuser with a child and flittered about the countryside, visiting whenever it suited her fancy. Leonie and Benedict saved her life when they took her off the street. They're good parents, but biology cannot be changed outside of a miracle or magic. "I'd like to have children."

The lip of my beer bottle *clunks* against my teeth. "You would?"

"Yes. I have a lot of knowledge to share." She avoids my gaze and takes a huge gulp of her wine. During our three years of friendship, she never mentioned her desire once—Booze, Books, and Brunches included. "Leonie suggested I start taking nightly walks."

"Sloane would love to be adopted," says Paisley.

"Aren't you supposed to be babysitting?" I question, moving my bottle out of Paisley's reach. The wolves do Twelve Days of Booze and Fast Food instead of Christmas, and everything I know about their routine and schedule has been thrown out for the season. "You and Ibrahim are both here."

"They're at school." She happily accepts Catarina's extended wine glass. "I'm enjoying my freedom."

"Doing nothing all day?"

"I'm hanging with my besties." She moves away before I can say anything to that. A gust of cold air steals the growing heat from the room when Killian and Grady bring boxes of pizza into the kitchen. "Pregnant ladies first!"

"I like her," Catarina murmurs, leaning back. We're the outcasts here as they laugh and joke. Standing on the outside, looking in, isn't a foreign experience for me, but this is the first time an undercurrent of grief slides down my throat. "What are we doing?"

"I am drinking a lukewarm beer covered in dog drool."

"Athena's pregnant."

"Thank you for the reminder."

"King Hozeir has all the Sacraments but the Horn and Crown, which we no longer have because it was given to a witch." She stares pointedly into the side of my head. I knew she was going to force the issue, but I hoped to have something more concrete to offer. God knows Killian will want answers too when he stops giving me the cold shoulder. "Bootleg Dracula knows Athena's pregnant. He knows where the witch and Crown is. He knows King Hozeir is alive and has all the Sacraments."

"Are we stating random facts now? I am drinking my first beer. I need more alcohol to deal with this conversation. Ergo, I need anoth—"

"If he goes to the Imperium, we have nothing. We need to go now."

"I am not leaving Athena."

"Delilah." She sighs around my name and drags her chair over the hardwood floor, effectively cutting me off from my sister, who laughs at something Paisley says. Unable to look anywhere but into my Companion's longsuffering eyes, I am confronted by my reflection. I look like a rabid animal forced into a corner. I *feel* like a rabid animal forced into a corner. "You have no choice but to trust this pack to take care of your sister. You intended to leave her with them before all of this went down. Nothing has changed."

"She's pregnant," I hiss, crushing the bottle in my hand. Blood drips from my fingers onto Killian's perfectly carved table. The smell of blood draws all eyes to me. "That changed everything."

I thought dying would be easy: leave Athena to the wolves and lead my father on a wild goose chase. Eventually he would trap me, and I'd take down as many as his devotees as I could on my way back to hell. A piece of cake.

The Imperium coming after my sister was never part of the equation.

Ignoring the concerned expression on Athena's face, I head towards one of the many bathrooms in the oversized packhouse. Glass sticks out of the bleeding wound. The smell of rotten apples centres me as I crank the faucet.

It's not enough to keep her alive. Losing Ibrahim could destroy her. Losing her 'child' *will* destroy her. There's so little goodness and joy left in my world—I cannot bear the thought of her light going out too.

"We have to stop meeting like this." Killian's joke, which I suspect is for my sake, falls flat. Laughter's the last thing on my mind. He pulls out a first aid kit from the medicine cabinet tucked behind the mirror and sets it onto the counter beside me.

"Do all your bathrooms have first aid kits?" I demand, trying to muster some kind of anger. My chin's starting to tremble, but I refuse to cry in front of him again. He hasn't spoken to me since I snapped at him and yet I see him everywhere I look. He's never far, just silent, and somehow that's worse than abandoning me. All I can think about is the weight of his arms holding me together. "Can't you just lick each other? Like a weird, smelly, canine org—"

He gently pulls my hand out of the water. The concentrated expression on his face takes the cake as my favourite. Brows crinkled. Lips scrunched to one side. *Daddy issues*. "It's healing already. We have cool band-aids for the pups, though. Sloane says the princess ones are magic."

"And here I thought I finally scared you off."

The intensity in his gaze pierces my thinly veiled insecurity.

Dropping his gaze to the rapidly healing marks, he leans forward. Lips, soft as velvet, press into the deepest gash. "I thought you might be feeling raw."

Like an exposed nerve.

Like I'm feeling now.

He holds my hand close enough to brush his flannel shirt. The air tastes like nutmeg on a fall day seated on a porch, snuggled up with a good book. Killian's long hair tickles my inner wrist. I cannot help but brush it back. Goosebumps spread across his neck as I drag my hand behind his head. "What are you doing to me?"

Did he ask that or did I?

Blood rushes to my cheeks.

Blushing is meant for brides. For little girls. Not for fully grown, jaded women.

"I'm going to make sure Nattalius didn't succumb to his injuries." He wordlessly watches me flee like the coward I not-so-secretly am. Skulking in the woods sounds pretty good right about now.

"I am not a petulant child." I would have believed Nattalius if he didn't kick a snowman over when he said it. One of the orphans put it together for their after-school activity. Fortunately, Ibrahim, Paisley, and Athena have the kids gathered around a pot of hot chocolate across the yard, so they don't see the carnage. I dutifully ignore Sloane when she waves. The devil at my side doesn't need more ammunition. "I do not need a mother."

"I can't be a mother."

"Things that cannot be have a habit of being around you," he spits, swearing in Turkish. Using our long trek through the forest to convince him not to say anything would have been wise. Lately, my wisdom is in short supply. The cold air did not chase away the fear and doubts clouding my mind. Catarina's looking to me as the Head to have a plan.

I didn't have the chance in Seminary to lead a hunt. Our raids were organized by the Professors and Senate Administration. As a first year, and never the only legion there, I left most of the 'leading' to the more experienced hunters. My loner tendencies are imbedded in my DNA.

"Why must you complicate everything?"

"I'm no happier that I'm alive than you are."

"If you were smart, you would've sent one of them to finish the job and bury my body in the forest. My parents do not know where I am. The Chancellor knows we were last seen together, but he won't risk losing their support by admitting that." He marches towards Curtis' truck with the attitude of a tantruming toddler. "They will come to your door eventually, but you're a good liar. You were born into secrets."

"A good liar but not smart." Cat was right. The wolves can keep Athena safe while we make a plan. Nattalius might run and tattle or he might stay and fight. God has sent people and circumstances to surprise me all week. "I should get that as my next tattoo."

"This is not a joke. Your sister's broken the most absolute law. At worst, it's punishable by death; at best, it's forced sterilization." I do not need the reminder. Do I look stupid? Forgetful? What is with my Companions stating facts like I have the liberty to forget them? "You cannot survive this world looking for the best in people."

"I never intended to survive," I mutter, pushing him towards the truck. Right on time, Catarina walks through the front door, scowling.

"We're leaving."

They race for shotgun. Nattalius is pompous enough to disguise his hastened steps, but Cat goes for it. She closes her hand over the door handle when he does. "Let go."

"I am second. You are third."

"You are excommunicated," she whispers into his face. She opens the door with a hum, and when he tries to dive in past her, they both start cursing. I briefly contemplate driving over myself with the truck. Orphans gawk from the hot chocolate stand when Catarina jumps on Nattalius' back.

"King Hozeir might be marching on Imperio right now." I say it more for my sake than theirs. Leaning against the truck, I drop my head back against the glass. On special occasions, I think about Mom and Dad watching me from Heaven. Eating grapes and sipping Jesus-wine with a host of angels while sharing quips or criticisms on my choices. Gabriel, cheeky himbo he is, must be laughing his feathers off. "Back seat. Both of you. Now."

"But—"

"NOW!"

Before either of them let go, an unfamiliar vehicle starts *crunching* down the driveway. Another follows it. It blocks our exit and parks alongside my truck. The smell of unfamiliar wet dog pours out of the vehicle when the doors open.

Cat circles the hood, leaning up against me. "Who are they?"

"Mom?"

Mona walks out of the packhouse with the closest thing to human emotion I've seen on her face. She flies down the stairs and pulls the woman in for an uncomfortable hug. Tabitha Salama, the woman who refused to attend her only son's wedding, holds her daughter like she doesn't know how her arms work.

"Amma?" Killian greets his mother with equal wonderment, but there's trepidation too. He glances at me like they've spoiled some secret. Neither of his parents deigned to attend the wedding either. I'd say something, if Sean and Layla Garity weren't staring at me like *I* impregnated their child. "You cannot be here."

"I'm having a good week," she offers weakly, raising a weathered hand to his face. "And I didn't want to ship your Christmas presents again."

A man and woman step out of the other vehicle and suddenly I understand Killian's wary expression.

I look at Ibrahim across the yard, praying for him to see me. He's staring at his mother, shell-shocked. Disappointment bubbles in his doe eyes and Athena rests her hand against his stomach to soothe him. I cannot catch their attention without drawing the others'.

Reaching backwards, I grab Catarina's hand and squeeze as hard as I can without hurting her. She understands immediately.

A blade of grass peeks out of the snow under Athena's foot, slipping between the fabric of her snowpants and skin. Another slithers up Paisley's ankle and draws her eyes right to us.

"Go," I mouth to Paisley. Her eyebrows knit together as she mouths, "What?"

"GO." This time I see the blade of grass pulling on her pant leg. She stares down at it, back at me, and finally at Deirdre. Understanding dawns too late.

Deirdre's bright beady eyes land on my sister at Ibrahim's side.

Disgust flares first. She's a King Hozeir loyalist after all.

Otherworlders are the superior race. Hunters are the enemy. I see the exact moment her eyes fall to Athena's stomach.

She steps back, shielding her face with a neutral expression. Gregory bends to ask her what's wrong, but I'm already moving. Gregory calls her name as Athena calls mine.

Deirdre shifts.

That's not the reaction of an innocent woman.

Let me out.

Charcoal hair spreads like goosebumps across her skin. Her muscles and bones twist through the air. Four feet hit the ground moving as I reach for her. Prickly hair slips through my palm. She's fast, but not faster than me.

Let me out.

"Delilah!"

The wolves don't know what to do. Gregory, a hulking gold wolf, darts towards Athena. Indecision wars on Ibrahim's face. He's slower than Paisley, who throws herself in front of my sister. My split attention affords Deirdre enough time to spin on her heel. The ends of her claws drag across my face, puncturing my eyes and ripping off half my nose.

Blood pours down my face as I fall to the side. Catarina went for Athena. Her footsteps crunch through the snow in their direction. Pulling a knife from my hip, I swipe at the she-wolf. The blade gives her a flank a nice haircut. Little hairs float down over my finger as I fist the snow.

Let me out!

"It's nice to finally meet you, Delilah." She licks each syllable of my name with a smoky Irish accent. When I try to swipe at her again, I fall face first into the snow. Pain chips at my remaining senses. I cannot smell anything. Humor streams out of my eye sockets. No wonder

Ayizan lost her mind. "I would give your best wishes to the king, but you'll soon be seeing him."

She lands a brutal kick to the side of my head. My ears ring, stealing the last of my hunting senses. One breath in. One breath out.

I slide the blade through the cold air and, with all the force I can muster, throw it. The knife sails across my head but I can't tell if I hit her or anything else before the darkness closes in.

Let me out, it pleads.

*

CHAPTER 22

Who's Your Daddy?

There's blood in my mouth.

Unfamiliar blood.

The curves of Catarina's face fade into one big blob. She presses her wrist into my teeth hard enough to hurt and more of that unfamiliar blood floods my throat. Though my stomach rebels against it, the pain in my cracked jaw fades with each pump of her heart.

"You looked very creepy without eyes," Catarina says. She dabs the sinew knitting the severed tip of my nose back to the rest of it. Wind wrestles with her hair, and for a moment, I think we might be flying. "We're safe."

Gargling on blood, I scan the familiar truck bed. I don't have time to ask Cat where Athena is because I hear her. Her worried blabber carries easily through the thin window separating us. I push up onto one arm and yank the window open with the little strength I have.

"Oh, thank God," Athena cries, twisting to look at me. She, Ibrahim, and Paisley take up the entire small back seat. There's blood everywhere. On the roof. On the windows. On *her*. "It's not mine!"

Catarina taps her fingers between my eyebrows. I swat her hands away when they flutter like bird wings against my temples. "What are you doing?"

"Calming your nervous system." She flutters her hands against my face again. We're speeding down an icy highway; blood stains Curtis' truck, and she's treating my face like a piano. "Nattalius ripped Gregory's head off."

"Clean," Paisley adds, leaning out of the window. The wind flattens her against the window as we pass the town's residential limit. "We are all impressed."

"Killian stayed to deal with the parents!" Cat shouts, competing with the wind. We jolt forward when Nattalius slams on the breaks to comply with the new speed limit. She curses at him in Portuguese and then grimaces at me. "Deirdre got away."

I slam my foot against the bed's side panel, hard enough to dent it. Catarina doesn't bat an eye at the slew of curses sliding off my tongue. One week. One day. A moment of peace. It's all I crave. I took for granted the uncomplicated days of tracking errant Otherworlders and sleeping in hotel beds. Making out with strangers. Sleeping in late. Forgetting my name and fate in the bubbles of a jacuzzi bath big enough to fit four.

"I thought you'd want me to get Athena out," Catarina whispers, fluttering her fingers against my hairline. I messed up. Nattalius and Cat did their jobs. He got Gregory. She got Athena.

If I kick the panel again, my foot will go through it. Sustaining another injury will sap too much of my strength and Cat's. "Damn it."

Deirdre could come back. She could be waiting for us at the Alcove with an army. Pushing myself up, I reach for the icepick tucked underneath a tarp. The iron-wrought gates of my parents' house swings open.

Ingrid stands on the front porch with a shotgun in hand and dusty old armour strapped to her body. When the engine cuts out, she surges forward and grabs Athena by the wrist. Paisley and Ibrahim follow them hastily into the house, but I take time to scan the yard. My senses are still weak, but my instincts aren't.

"She's gone," Nattalius states, closing the truck door with a sigh. Blood covers the jacket I lent him. He flicks it off in one move and fixes his hair with another. "Two people alive who should be dead."

"Ingrid sent the staff away." Something I should make permanent. I rush into the house, blade in hand. Paisley hurries to grab Athena something to drink while her husband settles her onto one of the couches. My Companion continues with a heavy sigh, "Are you ready for me to ask what the plan is?"

"The expedited plan. You take her back to the wit—"

"I am not leaving," Athena declares, twisting to watch me in the front hall. When no one comes to her aid, she stands. "The plan i-is someone t-tells me what just-t-t-t happened. I-I don—what happened?"

"Deirdre is one of King Hozeir's loyalists. Right now, she's heading west to cut across the ocean to Euroasia, where his lair is located. She will tell him there's a werenter child waiting to be plucked and the rest of his bloody pack will be on their way here before you can say baby." I tilt my head back, holding the tears at bay. *Be strong for Athena. Be strong for Athena.* Swallowing my panic and fear, I march into the living room. Ibrahim pulls Athena back onto the couch when I drag a chair towards them, bunching the rug up around the legs so it rocks when I sit. I don't care. Right now, I'm trying to hold on to the reins of a horse carting away at a speed the light fears. "That is, if he doesn't have a pocket of loyalists lying in wait outside this godforsaken town."

"Why would they be here?" She wraps her arms around her stomach, leaning into Ibrahim. It's the thing inside of her she's scared for. Athena won't even think to fear for her own life. God forbid she values being alive. "You said pack's respect each other's territory. Loyalists should respect that. They respect each other's—"

I sigh. "They've been waiting for me."

"You?" She smacks her lips together and glances at Ibrahim. When he doesn't meet her eyes, she looks at Ingrid. The old bat won't look at her either. Paisley's the only one brave enough to offer a fortifying smile as she lowers the cup of tea into Athena's shaking fingers. "This is about the emergency plan. Why you didn't include yourself?"

Running a hand down my face, I lean back. "Cat and Nat, you're on patrol. Watch the perimeter. Ingrid and Paisley take the yard."

To my surprise, they listen. One after the other, they leave me and Athena with the elephant in the room. How do you look your sister in the face and tell her your father isn't the man you both grew up with? Memories of him whizz through my mind like a filmstrip.

If she looked hard enough, she'd see the absence of Dad's qualities—no golden skin, no Greek nose, no heart-shaped face. My brown hair is a shade too light. As a kid, I wanted to undergo facial reconstruction surgery, so I would look like either of my 'real' parents'.

There's more to it though—like my mannerisms. Mom was reserved: permanently petrified but obstinately good-natured. Dad was a ray of sunshine. A natural born leader with the ability to make everyone and anyone smile.

The darkness inside of me is hereditary. I *know* it.

"Did Daniel tell you about Mom's brother?"

Athena nods, rubbing her thumb over her stomach. I grit my teeth against the glare bleeding across my face. "Isaac? The one who died?"

"Mom was twenty-six and on her first solo mission, apart from Dad and their legion, when she got the call. It was considered a low-risk op—scale the side of a mountain, get a headcount of King Hozeir's pack, and get out." She was supposed to make an example of someone the king cared about if she could, to remind him of the Senate's watchful eye. The Imperium made it her qualifier to join the Fifteen. Having a member of the Senate, who descended from Unawakened parents, was unheard of. If her brother didn't die, if Dad didn't call to tell her, she might've been the first Jewish woman with a seat at the table. "Isaac was her best friend. She cried herself to sleep on the side of that mountain and when she woke up, she was in a cell.

"The rumours of King Hozeir's treason were whispers between Administrators at this point. Underpaid interns were filing reports by Otherworlders into the system while the Five and Fifteen were arguing about whom to add to the fountain in front of the library." Shaking like a leaf, I stare at the wall over Athena's shoulder. She watches me earnestly, her eyes softening. When Mom told me this story, she didn't include the extra details. Dad did. His rage made a safe place for mine. "When Dad finally found her, and got her out of there, she was twenty-nine."

**

"Wha—"

She smothers the question behind one hand. Ibrahim wraps an arm around her back, pulls her to his chest, and softly kisses her head. It's not hard to imagine the things that might've happened. Athena knows what King Hozeir stands for. She knows the things he did to others. "Werewolf sperm is selective."

Nice one.

"It's not compatible with every womb, but that didn't stop him from trying." There were other women in those cells. Men too. King Hozeir spent most of his days breeding hybrids in the dungeon while the Imperium searched his palace grounds. Mom said she couldn't decide what was worse, the cries of others or the terror of hearing a key in the lock of her cell. I don't think she meant to say it aloud, but once the story started, she couldn't hold back. "At first, he tried to woo her by buying her gifts. But then he resorted to magic. Compulsion. When none of that worked, he resorted to force. She'd been too weak to fight after months of being underfed and locked in a cell."

I swallow back the finer details. Being chained to one place, legs open, unclothed on the coldest nights. How she felt some relief when he visited during the winter and hated herself for it. Dad reached for her then. Held her hand. I hated them a little for planning to die. For taking the easy route to escape King Hozeir… but I cannot blame my mom for doing anything to avoid going back there.

**

"She knew she couldn't take much more, so when one of the guards came to deliver her food, she struck. The guards were not allowed to touch them, especially the ones who could be pregnant, but that didn't stop the guy from refusing to give her food for two days. She got a knife from him, though.

"The Christos' tried to convince Dad that she ran away. After losing her parents, and being separated from David, her Unawakened brother, Isaac was the last of her first family… Dad thought the wolves killed Mom and buried her somewhere in the Hielander Territory, so he started digging. He was at the base of the cliff where Mom was caught when she cut herself."

She never intended to kill herself. Drugged, malnourished, and drained, she tugged on their *vitazeil.* Her blood called to him. "Dad said he felt his shoes melting because of how fast he climbed. He tore wolves apart with his bare hands reach her. He found her chained on the ground, covered in blood, and quivering. Dad carried her for thirty-four hours straight. Highlands to Imperio.

"When they returned to the castle, it was with Dad's legion and the support of the Imperium. You know the result of that."

"But they didn't kill him."

"Dad said it was his greatest failure." My sandpaper tongue leaves a trail of fire on my bottom lip. Here comes the truth. Before I can speak, Athena gasps.

"That's why Mom hated *Beauty and the Beast.*" Clapping a hand against her mouth, Athena lets the tears fall. A stream of grief for our dead mother. Ibrahim whispers to her and rubs her knee in soothing circles. I force myself back into my corner. "I am—I can't believe I made her relive that moment over and over again."

"You weren't the reason she relived it daily." When she meets my eyes, understanding flashes beneath the tears. Athena starts shaking her head. At first, it's gentle enough not to hurt, but then her hair starts flying, and her lips begin moving without making a sound. "Mom thought she lost her period because of the trauma and malnourishment. When she took a test, just in case, she saw two lines."

"No."

"She didn't want kids. She was focused on her career, but it felt 'wrong' to perpetuate the king's violence." A pill. A procedure. Something stream-lined and relatively painless. *Humane.* I wonder how much of her insistence on keeping me alive was merely the refusal to have anyone near her vulva after everything that happened. "D-Philip and her approached the Imperium. They pled her case—my case."

Athena drops her face into her hands. I withdraw and scour the house for a tissue box. When I return, she's frozen. Staring at a picture of all four of us on the fireplace mantle. Ibrahim takes a tissue when she doesn't. "Do you need me to go?"

"No." She shakes her head again, wiping away her tears. "You're my Delilah. Always have been. Always will be."

Using the tissue to wipe her face, she meets my eyes. I know how often peers and authority figures mistake her gentleness for weakness. Catarina falls victim to the stereotype too. Pretty girls with nice smiles and kind hearts are underestimated—treated with kid's gloves and patronizing pats on the head.

Athena's not a silly kid. She's known her mind as long as I've known mine. We get our mettle from our fathers.

"Hold onto that thought."

She leans back, clutching her tissue against her heart. "Del, I can't take much more."

"King Hozeir will stop at nothing to see his vision of earth come to life." Calling him my father aloud burns worse than fireball. She might know the truth now, but Philip's my dad. He's the man who raised me.

Who kissed my scraped knees. Who teased me about boys in school even when I rolled my eyes at him and slammed the car door in his face. King Hozeir's nothing to me. "Now Deirdre is telling him there's a woman with a viable hybrid in her womb. A womb which will be more receptive and fertile after expelling the thing. You were in Mom's body when she had me. Your ability to carry his offspring is almost guaranteed."

"You think he's going to come for my baby?" She clutches her stomach, her eyes threatening to fall from their sockets. Of course, it's the creature she worries about first. "Come for me?"

"Nattalius knows you're pregnant. He will report you to the Imperium. They will come for you, the creature, *and* Ibrahim." A race. Otherworlders vs the hunters. Who can get to my sister and her monster-baby first? "You need to get rid of it."

"Delilah."

"You *need* to. If you don't, they will." She's shaking her head again, but this time she rises to her feet. Pacing the living room, she lifts a fist to her mouth. Anger hardens her jaw. I watch the fight waging behind her eyes. "And they will take much more than your fetus."

"Calling my baby a fetus doesn't make him any less of a child—a blessing." Athena rubs her hands on the underside of her tiny bump. Pinching the bridge of my nose, I drop my head back. Stubborn. So stubborn. "I can't. I won't."

"Then they'll sterilize you! The Imperium will take the child and your uterus. At least that should deter Hozeir. Hopefully, they'll let Ibrahim live." Ibrahim shoots me an exasperated look as he reaches for Athena, who's muttering to herself. This whole mess wouldn't have happened if he kept to himself. Abstinence. One hundred percent effective. Priests go their entire lives without sex. "I will try my best to protect you. Give it a week or two. Deirdre tells Hozeir, Nattalius the Imperium, and, if we're lucky, they will take each other out and solve the problem for us."

I warned them.

"You can command him not to." She nods, her eyebrows drawing together. She kneels before me, sliding her clammy hands into mine and holding tightly. "You can tell Nattalius not to say anything."

"And Deirdre?"

She drops her head onto my knees. Wrapping my hands around the nape of her neck, I let my head fall forward. I roll my thumbs into both sides of her neck. "So, we run."

"You run." I press a kiss on the crown of her head and lift her chin up. Her tears stop coming after I brush them away, but I know her heartbreak will remain. "The witch likes you. She cannot be trusted, but she wants nothing to do with politics, and she hates most hunters. The world will not touch you or it there."

"You keep saying you."

I press my lips together, dropping my hands into hers. "Hozeir has been tracking me since I was born. I can buy you enough time to get to safet—"

"No."

"Athena, be reasonable."

"You do not get to sacrifice yourself. You do not get to kill yourself—Mom and Dad killed themselves, didn't they?" Her eyes widen again as she looks at me for confirmation. She drops, and Ibrahim surges forward, catching her and bringing her to the couch. "You can't. Delilah, you can't-t-t-t. If you do, I will—I'll—"

Lips quivering, Athena stands again. Ibrahim hesitates to move, stuck between standing and holding out his arms in case she falls. I avoided this conversation for this exact reason. She's staring at me with baby eyes: big, watery, and uncertain. Reducing me to the monster who clawed her face and vomited when she sobbed.

"I will die with you. A piece of me." She presses both hands into her chest and steps closer. Tears bubble over again as she sits on the coffee table in front of me. "We might reunite with Mom and Dad one day, but that's too many days away. I need you now."

"I won't be there, Thea."

"What?"

"I am soulless. A demon." She sits back, the colour draining from her face. I've had years to come to terms with it. Knowing Jesus didn't come for the likes of me. The wages of sin is death, but what is the wage of evil incarnate? An uncreated *thing*. "There is no place for me."

"Are you implying that my child, my unborn baby, is *tō'ēḇā*?"

Silence blankets the room.

She searches for redemption in my eyes. A hint of remorse or doubt. I have no intention of instilling false hope. "I know you'd never try to hurt me. I know this is coming from your own pain, but that *hurt*s *me*, Delilah. You are—my baby is… I need to go home."

Ibrahim rushes forward at her shaky request and scoops her up from that coffee table. He brushes the hair back from her tear-stained cheeks as he escorts her out of the room If I run now, I might catch up with Deirdre for round two.

Athena returns on her own feet; splotches of red mark her pale face. Stealing the tissue box, she points at me. "If you leave, I will not forgive you and damn my own soul in doing so."

"Athe—"

"No. *My* Saviour died and rose again. I am not willing to test the power of God a second time." She breathes past a sob, snot dripping down her nose. "We are going to figure this out together. I'm hormonal. I'm angry at the world and God—and yes, you—and I need some time and space to process everything. But then we're going to sit down and figure this out together. That's what sisters do. Say it."

"I will not leave without saying goodbye." The air cools with her red-rimmed glare. Leaning back, I rub my palms down my blood-crusted leggings. "I will not leave without saying goodbye."

"You are my sister," she breathes, blinking to try and hold back the tears. Her face colours all over again as she stumbles out of the living room, leaving me to the ghosts that haunt this godforsaken house.

CHAPTER 23

Wolf It Down

Other people's booze tastes better, a 'grass is greener' kind of thing. Or maybe it's being extra miserable that makes the whiskey tickle the back of my nose.

No running. No fighting. Just me trapped in the low-lit kitchen of the packhouse with an open decanter of whiskey. Everyone's asleep. Including Ibrahima and Athena, who, realizing they are targets, took back the Gamma's old room.

Killian may have sent his parents and aunt back to the island after the 'incident', but they've knocked the next domino down and I don't know what it'll topple. If Layla Garity comes within ten feet of me, I'll punch a hole into her chest. First, for placing the burden of killing Sophie onto Killian, and second, for bringing Gregory and Deirdre back onto territory.

Killian's parents brought two loyalists within fifty feet of Athena. Sean made Deirdre and Gregory his Betas. He stood there with his wife, gobsmacked, when all hell broke loose. He may not be a loyalist like his two closest advisors… or maybe he's better at hiding it.

With thoughts of secret loyalists fresh on my mind, I watch Ibrahim pad his way into the kitchen. He greets me with a pained smile and beelines for the cupboard. A lot of the pack grew up with Deirdre and Gregory as their Betas. When Sean left, Home Sickness drove half of the older wolves to follow him and leave behind their children. Children who might've been raised by the Betas to agree with my father.

"Do you need anything?" Ibrahim pulls a pot out from a cabinet and slides it onto the stove. It's two in the morning and he's making a snack… the life of a teenage boy. Through the whiskey-induced haze, I know he asked me a question. I cannot think about answering because I'm imagining him running away with my sister over his shoulder. Would she go to Hozeir if he asked her to?

Few people I know have met the Werewolf King before, but from their reports, I imagine him as charismatic.

He must be, to an extent. Brute force and fearmongering only get a tyrant so far. They need to be inspirational. Attractive. Believable.

In the past, I avoided thinking about my father. My features do not fit a male face. Trying to imagine the man who made me brings my gaze back to the whiskey. Ibrahim offers me a glass when he pulls his own out. Drinking straight from the bottle has been working fine so far. It's a bit messy, leaving trails of liquid down both sides of my chin, so when he brings me a glass of water, I drag my finger across my lips to collect the leftovers and suck it down.

"Very subtle."

He doesn't respond to my quip. Using the fridge door as a shield from my stare, he starts rifling. A house full of creatures with enhanced hearing requires some grace, but he clinks and clacks like they're all deaf. Ibrahim grabs a carton of milk and pours it into the warming pot. It starts steaming before long and then he adds some seasoning. Cinnamon. Nutmeg. A hint of cloves.

Warm milk before bed. Either he and Athena are more 'one' than I thought, or he's preparing her comfort drink because she cannot sleep. All it takes is one thought of my sister, and suddenly all I can hear is two hearts safely beating upstairs. "What's it like in your head?"

He grabs a whisk and swirls the liquid into a reverse tornado. It's not like Ibrahim to ignore someone, but everyone reaches their limit, eventually. I know what I would think of someone who hurt Athena. Time to go. "Do you mean with my wolf? The Pack Link?"

"Being perfect," I murmur, tilting the glass to the side. Water pours out onto the handmade table. There's a constant cry in my head—words spinning, fighting for freedom, shredding my brain. Sometimes the right words make it out to allow me a moment of peace. The cliché of ditzy beauty pageant queens naming 'world peace' as the change they want to see in the world cheapens the necessity for it.

I need peace.

It's what I look forward to most in death.

Blissful silence.

"I'm not perfect."

"I thought it was the Mate bond that made Athena think you walked on water." He and his cousin. *Good* guys. People who take care of others without expecting anything back. The kind of people who brighten up a room when walking into it. Golden hearts and kind eyes. Like Athena. They deserve each other. "You're basically Jesus. You'll take care of her."

"I am not Jesus." He giggles like a kid and toys nervously with the hem of his shirt. He sighs and, after one last swirl of the whisk, shuts off the oven and drops into the chair beside me. "No one is."

"Right."

"I'm serious." Fingers shaking, he reaches for my empty glass. Ibrahim pours himself a full glass of whiskey and chugs half of it. I fight back a smile when he starts coughing. "That was a mistake."

"Trying to prove a point?"

"Killian told you about his sister, Sophie?"

"Everyone wrapped around her finger? Precocious, funny, fierce... the reason Mona is the way she is." Mona lost her father and best friend in the same year. In the throes of 'celebrating' her win against Nattalius, she told the Daddy Issues Club about how Sophie handled people like him. We took a momentary pause and declared our subgroup—the Dead Family Club—in session. "Let me guess, she was an inspirat—"

"I hated her."

The word 'hate' comes out soft and affectionate, closer to a whisper than a declaration.

My lips make an audible sound as I shut them. *Hate* didn't make the list of things I expected him to say. I thought he'd say she was an angel, or a second sister, or a gift to humanity... this is better. His knee bounces when I don't say anything. At first, he limits the energy to one part of his body. The entire table shakes by the time he finishes the whiskey.

"Sorry, I shouldn't say something like that about someone. What I mean—"

"She sounds like the kind of person who sucked the oxygen out of the room. Egomaniacal. Only child syndrome. Everyone was wrapped around her finger, but she used those strings like a puppeteer."

He deflates—shoulders flying back against the chair, chin dipping, air whistling out of his lips. "She used to bribe me with chocolate bars to leave her and Mona alone."

"Chocolate's bad for dogs."

"It makes us sick." His lips open and close enough to make him resemble a fish. His shaking legs suggest the return of his nervous energy, though he keeps his hands clasped on the tabletop. "She knew that—obviously—but, uh, if I was sick, I couldn't follow them around."

"Why did you keep eating it?"

Rubbing a hand over his neck, Ibrahim shrugs. "I dunno. I'm—I was a dumb kid."

"Whiskey gives me heartburn." Drinking isn't something I enjoy most of the time. I'm too cheap to buy the good stuff and too broken to stop hurting myself. My darkness loves finding gloom in others. The roar in my head softens to a cry. "Were you happy when she died?"

"Kind of." He winces, spreading his hands. "I know that makes me bad."

"I was relieved when my parents died." Relived and furious. Athena wouldn't leave bed for a day. She tried to rally the staff and me, but I think she knew there was something wrong with my grief. I didn't cry at the funeral or when lighting the candle. My tears came later, and they tasted bitter. "For the first time in my life, I felt like no one was waiting for me to screw up."

That feeling didn't last long. Ingrid made her opinions on my conduct clear. One last bender before leaving for Seminary. Like I wasn't seventeen. Like I hadn't lost my parents. Like I hadn't been given guardianship of my fifteen-year-old sister before I could vote. "Exactly."

He releases another one of those clarifying breaths and relaxes into the chair again. This time, he drops his head and hooks it over the wooden back. I do the same, searching the ceiling for spiderwebs. One. Two. Three. A nest. The comfortable silence stretches on.

"I didn't have someone my age. Paisley came a year later, but Mona was all I had before her. The other kids... they thought I was annoying. Too 'bouncy'. I had a bad habit of interrupting and talking too fast. Sophie said I was shadow, and I should stay in the back with the rest of them." I twist my head to the side, watching him swallow. Nothing matters after 1 AM. Etiquette and expectation go out the window. Skeletons use the dark to sneak out of their closets. "I wanted to hang out with Killian, especially as I got older and girls got grosser—"

I snort before I can stop myself. Boys are the gross ones. Girls get their periods and create complex hygiene routines to circumvent their newfound insecurity. Pubescent boys stink up the place and think it's funny. The longer it takes for them to start wearing deodorant, the more their brain cells die.

"But Uncle Sean kept him busy. He wasn't allowed to hang out or play tag in the forest." He jumps and rushes over to the stove. Flailing his gangly arms, he breaks up the thin crust on top of the milk and pours it into a mug. "I'll be right back."

He's got long enough legs to move steadily but darts like a bullet. Straining myself, I listen to the tail end of a conversation between him and my sister. Ibrahim returns with a huff and takes a seat. "Where was I?"

"Killian wasn't allowed to play tag."

"My dad died a year before Sophie. We knew his death was coming—Home Sickness—but it was inevitable. The disease hits fast and leaves no survivors. I was laying on his chest when he died. I heard his breath stop."

"Wow."

He nods, licking his lips. "Mona was there too. Death is a communal thing with werewolves. The moon cycles, and we do too."

"Circle of life."

I keep nodding for his sake when he pauses. If he expects me to run, he's sorely mistaken. This is the first time in weeks I don't want to go anywhere. I fill the glass again and nudge it towards him. He abstains this time, so I drain it for him. "We weren't expecting Sophie's death. She was exuberant."

He means dramatic.

"When she started shifting, and said her pain was different than others, Aunt Layla didn't listen."

"I hate that woman."

Hate is a strong word. A rare one for even me to use, but mothers are a sore spot.

"She was sweating and screaming and then all the adults started panicking. I went to grab her hand, but my mother told me to stop getting in everyone's way. Before I could leave, Killian came, and I tried to follow him, but he was too fast. Mona was screaming for Sophie…." I recognize the haunted look in his eye. Tears gather around his waterline. "I knew where Sophie kept the chocolate, so I went to her room, while my family was screaming and mourning the loss of a child, a sister, a best friend, I stole from her. I stole from my dead cousin."

"She bought the chocolate to bribe you. It was yours."

He giggles but tries to cover it with the back of his hand. My own chuckles work their way up. When we quiet, he shakes his head. "I threw up so much it was dripping out of my nose. I fell asleep on the bathroom floor covered in puke, and when I woke up, my mother said I was being selfish and stupid—she didn't mean it to hurt. I was being stupid and selfish."

"How old were you?"

"Nine."

"I'll throw her and Layla into the ring. See how strong and mighty they feel when they're facing me."

"I guess the point I'm trying to prove is that everyone has a capacity for evil. We all make decisions that hurt others or hurt ourselves. Sometimes, we walk on water. Sometimes, we drown and need someone to pull us out." He shrugs, peering into my eyes. There's a wisdom within his giggles. "It isn't a death sentence; it's being—sentient?"

"Sapient."

"One of the s words."

"Go take care of my sister." He smiles and reaches for my hand. The brief touch brings tears to my eyes. I never thought to want a little brother, but it's not too bad. Walking away with a little pep in his step, Ibrahim starts humming. "Hey, Iba?"

He trips on his foot when he tries to spin. A lamp falls off the living room end table, but he catches it with one hand and braces himself against the couch with the other. "Yes?"

"You're not stupid."

"Thank you, Del."

He maintains a semblance of composure until he gets to the darkest part under the loft. I think he forgets I have better night vision than wolves. His victory dance is adorably teenage boy and draws a laugh up my throat. My amusement fades with the laughter.

Athena was wrong—she doesn't need me anymore.

CHAPTER 24

Kiss the Girl

"You claim to have a changed heart, call him daddy, and start crying." Catarina lifts her hands and flaps them like a bird to fan away my retort.

Drinking bleach. Injecting myself with battery acid. Shaving my head, tattooing Mr. Clean on my brow, and scrubbing the Kartal family manor top to bottom with a toothbrush. Every single option preferable to throwing myself at the feet of King Hozeir and calling him 'daddy'. "And I present myself, another hybrid, as an addition to his collection. We can take him down from the inside."

"You can make flowers turn towards the sun."

Catarina licks her lips and mutters a curse under her breath. Ignoring the lecture, seeing as I cannot understand half of it, I spin in Killian's leather office chair. I don't know why he keeps an office when he doesn't use it.

Werewolves play in the snow-covered fields below. Some in human form, some in wolf. A group of Deltas spar on the ice. Kids work on a neighbourhood of igloos with my sister and the Gammas. Paisley leads a line of five girls in a circle around the biggest ice dome as they launch handfuls of food dye at the frozen bricks.

Sitting above them, able to see the mountains, river, and forest stretching out like a canvas, gives me a new appreciation for Witchhill. The pack's territory works like a fishbowl. If Killian knew more about war, he'd plant more trees or erect stone walls to protect them. At the very least, he'd hide traps in the forest.

But no. He has the Deltas patrol the forest to 'keep an eye out' when they are not on shift as rangers or loggers.

That's it. A dozen scouts snaking through the brush….

No one monitors the river, not even in the winter, because they assume the current will take them under. Worse yet, the pack assumes no one will come for them. Killian trusts the fishbowl. So far from other packs, he's become complacent. Pack wars happen all the time in Europe, especially around Russia and the Slavic countries.

Before I go, I should talk to him about bettering their defenses. They need to add some traps on the perimeter, or at least a barbed wire fence to make it clear where their property begins and ends. Nattalius and Catarina studied war techniques in Seminary; they'd know how to turn this fishbowl into a fortress.

"I am *trying*, Delilah. For Athena." My attention snaps to her. Tensions are running thick in Witchhill. I dismissed the staff, except for Ingrid, for the Christmas season. She and Nattalius keep my new phone busy all day with complaints about each another, and Athena keeps my mind busy all night with her loaded silences and brief glances. I should've left before it got hard. "We don't have time for good manners."

"Good heavens. What would Lady Kartal say? Manners are what separate us from the *animals*." Catarina watches me as I throw one hand back. Thinking about Athena is my full-time job. Not a day goes by where I do not try for her. "You want to take King Hozeir down from the inside? Play the spy? Say we trick him and get in. Then what? Is Athena staying with the witch or is she here? Do we hope the Garitys hold off the Imperium from finding her long enough for us to prevent the war from coming to them? *If* we manage to kill him and dissolve the Hielanders and live, do we try the same tactic with the Imperium?

"Should I pick up my father's torch? Gather the hybrids and march on Imperio with our banner raised? It'd take a couple years, but we could raise a tenth of their forces." By then, Athena would be the proud mother of a tiny terrorist. The witch would be a sorry substitute for me as a godmother, but the kid was never supposed to exist so they cannot be picky. "We keep them from getting the Horn. Use the Sacraments to wipe out the Five and the Fifteen. All we need to do is maintain our rule through violence and brainwashing—"

"What is that phrase? Going out on a swing?"

"Alone. I wanted to go out swinging *alone*." I am no ruler. For goodness sakes, look at what happened when I received actual responsibility for the first time. I've been Athena's guardian for three years, and in that time, she started dating a werewolf, got kidnapped by my ex-boyfriend, married said werewolf one month after reaching legal age, and did the *one* thing I told her not to do. Eighteen years of being her older sister. Three years of being her guardian. One command and she couldn't even follow that. What kind of destruction would I bring with hundreds of werewolves?

Then again, with the Crown, they wouldn't have a choice. If I managed to invade the Hielanders, kill Hozeir, and live long enough to use the Sacraments, I'd hide in his castle with his army at my beck and call. The Sword and Breastplate would never leave my side, even in sleep, and there would be a drip welded into my veins for the Crown. After every battle, I would use the Uterus to resurrect them. Eventually, the hunters might stop trying to get me, but they were sired by pride and raised by violence.

They speak no other language.

I pinch the bridge of my nose and use the pain to dismiss the scheme. These thoughts are not my own. "It wasn't supposed to be a big deal. It wasn't supposed to affect anyone other than myself—"

"Delilah. Your death was going to affect someone before Athena got pregnant." She stares down at the thick fabric of her long-sleeved, black top. We sleep in our combat gear. I've slept with a knife under my pillow long before I was Awakened, but now the slightest brush of fabric when one of the wolves shifts in bed wakes me. I know I need to make a move before the Imperium or Hozeir do, but those who 'care' about me are standing in my way. "Have you thought about the kid?"

"I've thought of nothing else since she told me about it."

"He will need his Auntie Delilah."

"We're not doing this."

She huffs and sits forward as I spin my seat away from her. I am not 'Auntie Delilah'. It is not a 'he'. *Don't you want to see the next Philip?* "You were chosen for this—I can feel you rolling your eyes. Who else is qualified to help Athena and Ibrahim raise this child? You know what it feels like Delilah. You know how scary his little mind will be—"

"How large do you think King Hozeir's army of hybrids is?"

"You are not giving yourself over as breeding stock either."

Spinning back around, I slam my palms on Killian's desk. The force sends vibrations up my arms and into my skull. Metal coats my tongue with each deep breath I take to stave off the monster. "You insist I keep everyone alive. This will keep me alive."

"You want me to believe you'd let him use a child? *Your* child?"

"The Imperium will not take me. They have no use for me." I pull a loose strand out of my bun, ignoring the wary look on Catarina's face. She reaches and grabs my hand when I start twisting nine or ten strands around my finger. "You want me to live? I must make myself valuable enough to guarantee Athena's safety... no matter who that protection comes from."

"Not Hozeir. He's the worse of two evils."

"Is he? What is forced sterilization if not a form of rape? What has he done that the Imperium didn't start first?"

She sits back, raising her eyebrows. "Where is this coming from?"

"Forget it."

I need to kill King Hozeir, wipe the minds of every person who knows Athena is pregnant (whether by magic or the Crown), take her to the Sahara and convince the witch to let her raise her hellion in the fortress. If I return the Sacraments to the Imperium, I might have enough leverage to guarantee my family's protection, assuming a rogue legion doesn't decide to hunt hybrids, as some are prone to do, and come for us.

This also assumes there is no one—such as Nattalius' relatives—in Imperio who would use the collective Sacraments against the Otherworlders. Radicals exist in every organization on both sides of the spectrum. There are hunters who believe the Imperium needs to relax their laws and integrate with the Otherworlders. There are hunters, some of whom I've had the misfortune of meeting at Nattalius' side, who believe we've strayed from our original mission: to rid the earth of Otherworlders.

I know some high-powered members in Imperio believe the Hunter Queen still walks the earth. Drinking from the Uterus can supposedly grant immortality, and many believe she was the one who discovered that… all it would take is one of her doppelgängers to pretend. One good actress and hundreds of foolish hunters would ride into a new war. War no matter who starts it will bring unspeakable loss. To Otherworlders. To hunters. To humans.

Lesser evil does not exist in this world.

"We need a bargaining chip."

"I am the—"

"For the Imperium. We know they win this war, Delilah. Otherworlders may believe in King Hozeir's mission, but they would rather face the Imperium than be subject to his rule." Catarina shakes her head, a dark expression on her face. Sunlight shines into the room, directly beaming on her; a result of the fairie blood woven into her genetics. Her freckles twist and bend when she reaches for me. "You know there is no love lost between me and the Imperium, but they are our best option… we have the Crown! That must count for something."

"Yes, and they're already displeased with me because of that."

The Senate summoned me a week before Athena's wedding. I couldn't put it off for long, but I needed time to decide my next move. Athena would say God led me to hide the Crown with the witch. She'd say He knew I would need it in my possession.

After leaving the Crown with Ayizan, I went to Imperio. My

father's father and Nattalius' mother practically interrogated me, and it took a lifetime of self-restraint not to comment about the Senate being no more important than a small claims court. The Imperium, the Five, those who make the actual decisions for the hunters, didn't care enough about my possession of the Crown to call me in. Me having the Crown didn't garner their attention.

Most of the Fifteen believed my story about using the Crown on myself. Not much is known about hybrids; the pompous pencil pushers spend more time sipping expensive booze in an exclusive speak-easy type bar located on the main strip than investing in learning more about them. The concept of me separating my wolf blood from my hunter blood sounded reasonable enough for them to dismiss me.

It helped that the two Antes sitting on the Fifteen spoke in my favour, especially after my grandfather and Ayça joined forces. Ingrid's cousins claimed she witnessed me command myself to hide the Crown where no one would find it and forget where I put it. Even without her interference, they wouldn't have done anything to me.

God forbid anyone finds out Delilah Christos, the black stain on her family name, ended up in a disciplinary hearing.

"We use the Crown, get blood from the gnat, return to Imperio, gather the Senate and Imperium into one room and command they protect Athena... and raid the Hielanders. Again." She doesn't have the stomach for it. Catarina's bold suggestion softens with her crinkled brows.

After all, she's a scholar. The perfect world in her mind has a person of every nation, race, class, language, and religious group gathered around a table to share their stories over dinner. In her mind, conversation, understanding, and compassion should run the world. She's smart—too smart to believe it—but naïve enough to have hope.

Earth's crust is comprised of the decomposed bodies of innocents and intellectuals. Pacifists. The ones who refuse to do horrible things like control the minds of others or kill children. She'd stay by my side as I marched into Imperio with the Crown on my head.

And she'd spend the rest of eternity hating herself for it.

Cat wasn't raised religiously, but she was raised questioning. Leonie and Benedict believe in some kind of god or supernatural force, because religion must exist for a greater reason than people simply making up answers. They believe in the importance of 'good', whatever that means.

My parents raised me on God, on Jesus, and tried to tell me He wasn't responsible for hunters. Hunters were created by the Catholics, though. Religious men and women who wanted to rid the world of evil. Maybe that's why I know good cannot win. Purity gets tainted. Gravity naturally pulls us down.

The hunters 'holy' quest led to the imprisonment and abuse of a child. What experiments did they perform that the Imperium refuses to speak about? What horrors of man might one find in the Book of Other? People say two wrongs don't make a right, but what is right?

God Himself unleashed plagues. He killed children. Wrath came from God as much as love did. He takes pride in revenge.

Where does that leave His Creation?

"This gives a whole new meaning to that whole 'heavy is the head that wears the crown' thing."

"Are you willing to do that, Del? Would you exploit this object created in murder?"

"You forget I don't have a soul," I whisper, drumming my hands on the desk. Damned if I do, damned if I don't. "I will let you in on a little secret. Athena? She makes me human. She worries over kindness and compassion and empathy. Jesus is her light but she's mine. Threaten her? Take her away? There's nothing but darkness left."

"Very intimidating," Catarina drawls, her expression blank. "I know you. Athena knows you. She said herself you are too scared to believe in righteousness and equality—"

"Excuse me?"

Blood drains from Cat's face, stripping away the warm bronze of her skin. Before she can cover her sorry butt, Killian walks in. He pauses behind the long table in the middle of the room, gaze flitting from me to her and her to me. "Am I interrupting?"

"Not at all," I respond through my teeth. Scouring my nails up his leather armrests, I spin. "I might steal this chair. Someone should actually use it."

"What's mine is yours." He rounds the C-shaped desk in three strides. I try to give him a wide berth to access the computer, but he's close enough to brush my arm. Catarina raises her eyebrows as my cheeks puff. With Christmas alive and well in the packhouse, he smells of pine and ginger. I cannot get too close to him anymore. It's unbearable.

To make matters worse, Athena insisted on hanging mistletoe all over the house. If I were a paranoid person, I might think she's been moving the plant to the places I frequent.

"I need my planner." My brain, the little traitor, vacated the premise at first whiff of him. I know his planner is on the desk behind me. The chair and I are directly in his path. "Delilah."

"Yes?"

His lips twitch. The whole of his beard moves with them. I love how he says my name. In my twitterpated state, I don't notice him drawing closer until his breath becomes mine. "Would you like to hand me my planner?"

"Such a typical man, expecting a woman to do the work for him."

He hums and drops his hands onto the armrests. Inches from my fingers. Drawing his thumb up the side of my wrist, he leans in just a tad more, close enough for his beard to graze my lips. "Am I typical?"

"Do you want me to call you special?" I whisper, a lump in my throat. Flirtation comes naturally to me. The more confident and coy a girl appears to be, the more men fall over themselves—humans and hunters alike. Killian is my only exception. My fake confidence waves a white flag when he comes near. Tongue twisting, I lower my chin and curl my lips into a knock-off of my demure smile.

"I'd do all the work," he promises, dropping his eyes to my lips. Catarina murmurs something about needing to use the restroom and escapes in a pitter-patter of heels. "And you can call me whatever you want as long as I can call you mine."

A laugh bubbles up underneath the layers of tension and want. When his smile breaks, I do too. "Does that line normally work?"

"I haven't used it before."

"I must be the special one then."

He nods once, decisively. A lop-sided smile tugs up one side of his face. Athena loved *Beauty and the Beast* growing up, but the *Little Mermaid* was the one I insisted on watching until I could quote every line. Somewhere, a demented bird and crustacean orders him to kiss me. I hear the song as if it were playing in earnest.

Kiss him.

Dropping my hands onto my lap, I play with the bottom of his shirt.

I don't know if I tug him closer or if a magnetic force draws us together.

Our gaze collides.

Eyes holding.

Nerves firing.

Throat drying.

Killian brushes a strand of hair behind my ear and keeps his hand there. Want gives way to need. All-consuming. I'm tugging in earnest now, one hand fisted in his shirt, the other winding into the back of his hair.

His eyes start to close, his thick eyelashes fluttering. I twist the hand in his hair too, smirking at the purr in his throat.

In a blink, he stiffens.

"We're under attack."

"What?"

"From the mounta—"

"Catarina!" I shove past Killian and skid to a stop to avoid colliding with her. Howls sound across the territory. Her eyes widen as Killian shifts and jumps off the loft to the living room below. "Protect Athena."

Sprinting after him, I dive over the wooden railings. Killian's halfway across the yard by the time I get outside. The Gammas coral the kids, pushing them towards the packhouse. I meet Athena's eyes briefly before taking off into the forest. Snow crunches underfoot. Deltas pour out from their houses. Far off, on the highway, I hear a logger honking.

I heard from Nattalius this morning. Ingrid said he used up all the hot water. He could've talked to his parents. Sent a message to the Imperium. There could be a thousand hunters in the forest, and I wouldn't know.

Werewolf heartbeats bounce off the trees.

Their scent plugs my nose.

Killian barks. His voice echoes through the trees. Moments later, the smell of blood hits me.

One of the heartbeats stop.

Killian pauses—a momentary hesitation. I overtake him, launching off a rock with a dagger in hand. There's nothing but a dead werewolf lying in the snow.

"This isn't a hunter's doing." Two-inch lacerations circle the wolf's throat. Blood inches through the snow towards me. Killian leaps over me, his hackles rising, and growls at the empty forest. I take a breath and force myself to focus only on the heartbeats closest to me. Mine, steady now. Killian's, fast but stabilizing. A third, to the north, rapid and only getting higher. I point a finger in that direction and grin when the snow crunches beneath our enemy's retreating paws. "Get him."

With a snarl, Killian takes off. Snow flies behind his paws as he sprints through the trees. A moment later, the entire pack descends. Graham cracks through a smaller tree to cut-off the rogue.

"They'll get him," I tell the werewolf, kneeling beside his throat. Yelps sound at the back of the forest. "He's dead."

I should've told them to keep him alive. The Imperium wouldn't send a wolf.

Blood pools around my bare hands as I sift through the snow. King Hozeir must've known they would kill him. He sent one wolf because he wanted to send a message—

Something white sticks out of the bitemarks. I chance a look at the group of mourning wolves who howl and whimper in a circle around the dead invader. They seem occupied for the time being.

Prying the wolf's jaw open, I slide my hand down his throat. The slip of parchment comes out, covered in spit and blood. **Blood of my blood, we are weakest with the new, and I charge with the full.**

The letters are choppy. Ink bleeds from one letter into the other. Rubbing my thumb over the paper, I rip it. Once. Twice. Three times.

I keep ripping until there's nothing left.

Killian drags the intruder towards me, eyes on his dead Delta. I step back a respectful distance, hands covered in the deceased's blood and saliva, and wait. The entire pack will be here soon to lay them to rest. In the waiting, two Deltas lick their fallen fighter clean.

Dropping the corpse at my feet, Killian sits back on his haunches and shifts. His despair-filled eyes stay on his lost follower; blood covers his mouth. "Why send one?"

"To leave us a message," I answer, rubbing my hands into the back of my shirt. Death has become a good friend to me in the last three years. Death—not grief. Grief chokes and cuts and twists my stomach into knots. "He knows about Athena."

"That's the message?"

"An eye for an eye. A wolf for a wolf. A hybrid for a hybrid." I point to myself and step back. The smell of wolf saliva clings to the back of my shirt. Killian's too busy tearing up to notice. "Take care of your pack. I'll hold the perimeter."

He nods, his chest heaving. "I'm sorry. I lost control. We needed him alive."

Soulless.

Shifting, Killian directs the wolves without words. Graham and Mona drop their heads and lift the lost Garity onto their backs. As they organize in mourning, I try to distinguish the scents on the intruder's torn-apart body.

Killian apologized. He trusts me.

Cold.

Nothing else matters but keeping Athena and her spawn safe.

Dark.

CHAPTER 25

Last Christmas

Blood of my blood: me.

We are weakest with the new: the new moon rises tonight.

I charge with the full: werewolves are the strongest on the full moon. Two weeks from today. January 2.

Committing the note's words to memory, I repeat it in my mind for the thirtieth time. They appear like fire against the back of my eyelids. Blood of my blood. We are weakest with the new. I charge with the full. *I* charge with the full.

Bright eyes, not unlike my own, flash in the dark. A man stands before me. He wears the body of a bear and teeth line his forehead like a crown. I force my eyes open to rid his image. King Hozeir's coming to the pack in two weeks.

"We've doubled the sentries. Pups are sleeping in the packhouse." One of the pups in question scream down the hall. A *thud* shakes the books on Killian's bookshelves, followed by rushed shushing and giggles. Paisley and Ibrahim make a face at each other. "Everyone living in individual cabins have been moved to the central area."

After the lead Delta finishes, Graham moves all the figurines on the to scale diagram of the pack territory into the centre. The diagram is sorely lacking in fortifications, despite my warning to them. I point at the forest and ask, "Where is the pack at with bettering the defenses?"

He glances at me, his throat flexing. Graham and the dead wolf, James, were good friends. The two of them narrowly escaped King Hozeir the first time his reign was threatened. He can distrust and dislike me if he wants, but we all know the king would've come for the Garity Pack eventually, whether or not Athena and I were here.

If Killian is the strongest, he's either a threat or an asset.

"We set up bear traps and trip wires per your suggestion," Graham murmurs, staring at Killian across the table, who nods his encouragement. "Trail cameras are on their way."

"Some of the pack hunt like humans, yes?"

"A handful," Killian confirms, stretching his arm over his stomach. He leans his elbow on it and plays with his beard when Graham points to hunting trails carved into the Styrofoam trees. "Why?"

"Set predator platforms here, here, here, and here," I instruct, pointing at various places on the map. During sleepless nights, which has been (almost) every one I've spent in the packhouse, I walk their grounds. Growing up in Witchhill comes with perks. Knowing where King Hozeir's forces might gather, or how hunters will move in, gives me an idea of where the pack is most vulnerable. "There are speciality stores in Banff and Crowsnest, but you'll want the one in Banff. Ask for silver bullets compatible with your rifles. If you tell them you're trying to keep hunters out, they might open the backroom for you."

"Backroom?"

"Every store pretends they don't exist, but faeries share their tips on how to hurt and mess with the Imperium." Cheeky buggers. "Do you have a good relationship with the coven?"

"Good enough." Killian nods, spreading his hands across the table. His lips twitch like the last time he leaned towards me. Taking a deep breath, I focus back on the map. Sister in peril. Dead wolf. Estranged father coming. "I was thinking of purchasing a Shield."

"King Hozeir has a magic wielder, but it will give you time to organize the troops." The Imperium would blast right through a Shield. I glance at Athena, cuddled up with a tea, and dig my nails into the table's lacquered surface. She cannot stay here. "You should see if either of your parents remember the specifics of what King Hozeir did to move his troops without the hunters tracking them."

Killian has been considerate in letting me give orders and suggestions. But even he will put his foot down if I suggest moving the entire pack and going off the map. The Imperium's hands are full with the mainland, they won't care about a random pack going missing… until Nattalius reports the hybrid in my sister's uterus.

I glance at *it* this time.

Covered in a thick cable-knit sweater, her bump doesn't exist. She looks like any teenage girl in the height of winter, save for the dark bags under her eyes, the permanent red lines around her irises, and the patches of raw skin at the peaks of her cheekbones. I couldn't hear her crying, but she refused to leave her room for two days straight after our last family bonding session.

It ruined everything.

"Hozeir will try to get Athena," Killian states, rubbing a hand over his jaw. They created a custom figurine of her. A little owl, like the tattoo I got for her. "Can you stay close to the packhouse? Graham will assign you two Deltas. One for the night and one for the morning."

"I need to take a patrol shift," Ibrahim whispers, reaching for her. She nods, nuzzling his hand, and rests the cup of tea against her stomach. "Mona offered to take nights."

Mona plays with her acrylic nails, grunting when all eyes fall on her. "I'm not a cuddler."

"Thank you, Mo." Everyone goes quiet when Athena stands and walks over to the table. She meets my eyes across it. "What about you?"

"What about me?"

"Hozeir wants you too," she argues as her hand inches towards her stomach. The creature's heartbeat picks up at her touch. "I want Christmas, Del."

Mona's head snaps towards me, her eyebrows curled up against her edges. Silence falls as I clench and stretch my hand. I expected Ibrahim to tell his sister and Killian, though neither of them appear to have any idea. Graham glowers at me. "Why does Hozeir want her?"

"I'm a hybrid."

Paisley gasps, too theatrical to mean it. "You *are*?"

"You smell," Mona remarks, crossing her arms. She leans over the table and scrutinizes the expressions of those around it. "Is anyone surprised?"

"I was."

She ignores Athena's mumble and cocks her head. "How does *he* know you're a hybrid?"

"My mother was responsible for the raid." The Ninth Christos Legion killed more wolves than any other. Hielanders first. Related packs second. "Revenge."

Athena's mouth pops open and she makes a face at me—a distinct, eye-bulging 'tell them' face. "Delilah."

"He wants to breed you," Paisley gasps, her eyes widening in horror. She glances at the others to see if they've come to the same conclusion. Their expressions range from distress to anger. "He's so old. He's probably got an ancient STI."

The colour drains from both Athena and Ibrahim's faces. I doubt King Hozeir intends to breed *with* me. Nonetheless, bile claws up my throat. "I don't think he wants me for himself."

"He considers himself one of the original Lycanthropes. The originals think they're better than the rest of us who evolved." Mona's tone brims with boredom. She stops chewing on the edge of her thumb when she notices everyone looking. Propping one hip onto the table, she forcibly crosses her arms. "My point is: he's going to want her little eggies and his pure sp—"

"He's my father."

A bomb could drop, and it would be quieter than the expression on Paisley's face. She jerks back, the ends of her eyebrows lifting. Bubbles of spit pop at the corners of her mouth. "He's your—Jesus, Mary, and Joseph. You're the president of the club; all in favour say—"

"And you had the audacity to act like we were the monsters?!" Mona smacks her hands on the table, sending little figurines diving for the hardwood floor. Her jaw cracks and grinds as her muzzle lengthens. "Do you have sex with wolves?" She points at Athena's swollen torso with gleaming eyes. "Like mother, like daughter?" I already know where she's going with this when she points her finger at my chest. We're halfway across the room from one another, with a table between us, but I know I can rip out her tongue before she says it. "Like father, like daughter?"

"Mona Feme Salama!"

I don't know who's more surprised to hear Ibrahim shout. His wife, his cousin, his best friend, his sister, or me. Jaws drop all across the room.

Ibrahim drops his hands to his hips, shoulders heaving, and pins her with a great impression of a glare. "The Imperium knows about Delilah. She's alive, standing here, trying to protect my wife and child. You know why that is… think about things before you say them for once."

His voice cracks when he adds something in Arabic. They stare at one another as silence tries to mend the crumbling bridge between them. Mona and I understand each other in a way others might not. Anger shines in her eyes, shielding her vulnerability with steel. Her clenching jaw a weapon against tears. "I'm not even supposed to be here, right? I will wait instruction with the rest of the Deltas."

She pushes off the table and stomps away, her shoulders straight back. When she slams the door, the rest of the figurines fall. Ibrahim sighs her name and squeezes Athena's arm before moving to follow his sister.

"Leave her," Killian demands, his voice soft, though not soft enough to extinguish the sparks flying across the room. His Beta glares at me like he might claw out my throat. "I know it doesn't feel good, Iba, but you're not in the wrong. Let her take some time to reflect while we figure out what this means for the pack."

"It means nothing for the pack," I state, avoiding eye contact with him. Seeing condemnation or anger or—God forbid—hurt in his eyes will be more than I can handle. He doesn't know about the note either. None of them do. It's a secret I plan to take to my grave. "King Hozeir believes he has a claim on me. He's been trying to find me for over a decade and has stopped at nothing to reach me. My mother made it clear he would catch up to me one day, and it was my choice what to do about it. I would rather die than let him use me, and I will be taking as many of his followers with me as possible."

"That's a stupid plan," Paisley snaps when no one else responds. She swears underneath her breath. "We can come up with something better than that."

"Not with Athena carrying another hybrid. When it's born, he won't need me anymore." I lose all value. All leverage. "Assuming he hasn't found another werenter in the last twenty years."

"Maybe he wants to play father."

"It's not up for debate."

Killian's eyes bore into the side of my head. Could I come up with a viable plan given the chance? Perhaps. With the most powerful werewolf in however many generations, his advisory team, my Companions, Ingrid, and a blind witch, I might find the perfect Hail Mary. There might be a solution where everything works out perfectly.

One scenario in a sea of a thousand bad ones.

No one knows how many wolves in the Garity Pack subscribe to their king's opinions. As war begins and progresses, alliances change. I trust Catarina and Killian, both begrudgingly and irrevocably. I trust Ingrid to take care of Athena. I trust the witch to stay out of the war and maintain a space untouched by it. If I went there with Athena, and my father followed, Ayizan would toss us both out.

If we stay here and try to weather the storm, King Hozeir and the Imperium have two clear places to make camp outside the pack's territory. They could come from both sides and crush us. Stupid fishbowl.

The Imperium, its governing body especially, does not like me. They know who and what I am. My presence amongst the pack might set them off after King Hozeir reveals himself. It puts everyone here in danger.

My death. Athena in hiding. It works.

"You want to die." Killian stares at me in a way that makes it seem like a question, but there's a finality in his words. Want isn't the right word.

I want silence.

I want rest.

I want the pain to be gone.

I want the voices to fade.

I want one day without a storm on the horizon. One day where I'm not afraid to turn my back or round corners without looking. One day where I lower my guard and don't need to protect myself. One day where I can be anyone but me.

Death is the answer. Oblivion. The end of my miserable existence on this earth. I hope God's gracious enough to give me a couple hundred years of nothing, a prolonged sleep, before throwing me into the fire. He doesn't feel the effects of time and He must have kindness in his heart to give me Athena, so it won't cost Him much.

"Can we have the room?"

I've been staring at the table too long, but I rip my eyes off it to meet my sister's stare. She doesn't even glance at the others, not at the Alpha she's dismissing from his own table, or her husband who defended our honour, just at me. "That's not ne—"

"You've said enough," Athena states, holding her hand up to halt my protest. She looks at Killian, her eyelids drooping and lower lip trembling. "Please."

"Everyone out."

He glances back at me as they start filing out, a promise in his eyes. I'd like to hide in his arms. Let the world burn around us and hole up here, but the world's coming. The cosmos. Heaven and Hell. Fate weaves her fabric under God's watchful eye, and she knows we're not meant to be. She's pulling at the seams. Trying to separate the monster from her hero.

"Christmas," Paisley chuffs, closing the door behind her. The thick wood does little to muffle her next comment. "Happiest time of the year, eh?"

Athena spends fifteen minutes straightening out the room. She bends to grab the figurines Mona sent crashing to the floor and returns them to their places. When I offer corrections, or try to move them somewhere else, she shakes her head.

This goes on until I purposefully take her figurine and put it on Killian's desk. "That's not funny."

"I'm not used to you being angry," I confess, leaning against his desk. She plucks her figurine and marches it over to the diagram of the pack territory. "I don't know what to do with myself."

"Protect yourself! Fight for yourself!" She throws her hands up, a breath rushing out. Running her hands through her messy hair, she leans onto the table. With her head dropped, her shoulders caving, she looks a lot like our mother. Sounds like Dad though. "I want Christmas."

"It's coming. The décor looks nice."

"One last Christmas with all of us together." She's stalling. Trying to find a solution I haven't thought of. One to prevent me from running.

I'm selfish enough to let her.

"Okay."

"Okay?"

"I might give you New Years," I murmur, crossing my arms. If I leave on January 1, I can get to Europe within the day. He didn't leave instructions on how to find him, but Nattalius and I came up with a few ideas and his wolf helped me narrow them down. Besides, he'll be watching. I don't know how many loyalists he'll send to get me. Keeping one alive should be easy. A little silver, a lot of blood, and a single drip of holy water to the forehead every thirty seconds should get the location of his lair out of any self-respecting Delta. "But once I'm gone, so are you. You and Ibrahim will go to the witch with Catarina."

"We won't leave the pack."

"Then I guess this is goodbye."

She gapes, hurt flashing across her face. "Seriously?"

"Yes."

"Okay," she relents, hiding one behind her back. I have a sneaking suspicion her fingers are crossed, but she knows yes is yes and no is no. "Two weeks."

"Twelve days."

"Twelve days of Christmas."

"Keep the mistletoe away from me," I warn, pushing off the desk. Once I get to King Hozeir's hiding place, I'm going to start burning everything and everyone in my way. He's going to be drowning in blood by the time I get to him. If I get to him. "I know you're moving it."

"One last thing," Athena whispers, wringing her hands over her stomach. She takes a deep breath when I twist on my heel to face her. "I was upset—"

"Rightfully so."

"I couldn't think of the right words." She pulls out a scrap of paper. For a moment, I think maybe she found my father's warning and the panic steals yet another year off my life. "I wrote a letter. 'Delilah, you have been my idol since we were kids. I used to feel so guilty for calling you that because of the Commandments and so I'd come up with different words, but it's the closest one. I've looked up to you my entire life. Your fierce strength. Your sense of humour. The way people gravitate towards you'."

"They tend to run in the other dire—"

"Stop interrupting." I raise my hands in surrender and step back. Hearing her talk about me in a reverential tone feels like sandpaper to the sternum. "'You used to read me fairytales and tell me all about happily ever after. We used to pray about having that together. Then I saw you stop believing in it.

"'I saw you start to believe what others said about you. I heard what the parents and kids at school used to say. How you were dangerous. How you belonged at a boarding school or military camp. I know they convinced you to agree with them, but I never did.

"'You've never stopped being my big sister. My protector. My best friend. My role model. I never had to be afraid of the dark, because I knew you'd scare it away. I was never insecure, because you told me how capable, smart, and beautiful I was every morning before practice. I rarely doubted myself, because I knew you believed in me. On my loneliest nights, I knew I could call you and you'd be there. Over the phone, getting a plane ticket, coming back to me.

"'I realize now I have been a bad sister." She raises her hand to stop me from speaking. I swallow back a sob with another dry laugh. "'Because I haven't told you all this. I gave you space when Mom and Dad died because I thought you were running from the pain of losing them. Now I realize you were running from me. You were trying to save me from you. You thought I'd be better off without you."

She licks her lips; tears brim on her waterline. There are four spiderwebs in one corner. I focus on each individual strand to avoid the ache blooming at the base of my skull. "'But I'd be nothing without you. You loved me in such a way that I didn't let any guy other than Ibrahim take me out because I knew they wouldn't treat me the way you made me believe I deserved. When I got into my accident and thought my world was ending because I couldn't compete at the Olympics anymore, you nursed me back to health. You told me my purpose and worth were a matter of fact. Unchangeable. Unshakeable. And I believed you, because I knew my older sister knows best."

Ugly crocodile tears roll down her face. The crack of her voice punches me in the gut. I do not remember a time, save for confirming the pregnancy, that I was so scared. One wrong move on her snowboard shattered her leg. The helmet she wore cracked in one place. It took getting loaded into the ambulance for her to rouse. I thought she was dead. I thought I was alone.

"'But in this, you don't. In the way that you know me better than I know myself, I know you better than you know yourself. I see now that you don't know you, but I do. I know you are kind—scoff as much as you want at that—but I see it every day in the way you care for me. I know you are thoughtful. I know you are funny. I know you have a beautiful heart that's been broken and bleeding and you're trying to protect it because that's what you do. You protect. You resource guard'."

"I'm not a dog."

"'You protect my baby even though you pretend to hate him. And I know you're pretending to hate him because you were led to believe that hybrids are monsters. That you are a monster'." The paper flutters in her pale hands, covered in ink and scribbles. She meets my eyes for the first time with splotches of pink across her cheeks. I'm sure mine look no better. "And as the person who knows you best, I am telling you that you are not a monster. You have more soul than most of the people I meet. You are a delight to the eyes of our Father and He calls you His. If my child ends up being even half of who you are, I will consider myself doubly blessed.'"

"Is that it?"

"I didn't write this down, but I know you won't believe me. Not now. But I'm going to wear you down. I'm going to have the time to do so, because purpose is permanent and He decides, not us." Athena walks over and grabs me. She tucks her chin into the place that has always belonged to her between my neck and shoulder. "I will read this letter out every single day if I have to. I will put up cheesy affirmations you'll hate. I will fill a jar with three-hundred and sixty-five notes about how much I love you. I will send you flowers every day with a list of words that describe you because I know how much you love gifts."

"Excessive."

"Not enough," she corrects, cupping my face. I search for the spiderwebs again, but she stays there. Inches away. "In the words of our father, you are *χαρά μου*. Both of you."

Grabbing one hand, she brings it towards her stomach. I don't fight her when she places my palm to her sweater. For her sake, I apply a little pressure, like a squeeze. Hearing Dad's pet name for us from her lips brings me back to the last time I felt a pregnant stomach. With the woman who gave Athena her face and gentle spirit.

Like then, there's an imperceptible connection. The creature's heartbeat jumps. Something deep within me comes alive as I *feel* its beat. Hidden under human flesh. A split mind.

"He loves his Auntie."

"You probably have heartburn."

Stepping away, I rub my hand down my leg.

She's right.

It's not enough to only protect Athena.

I need to find a way to keep them both safe. Permanently.

CHAPTER

26

An Eye for An Eye

"What does this do?"

Athena grabs the compact metal box and tries to wedge her nail under the indent on the side. Snatching it from her hand, I push it back onto the shelf. "Unless you want to put your husband in the hospital, I suggest not playing with any of these things."

"What does it do?" Paisley parrots, looping her arm through my sister's. The wolves weren't aware of the witch-owned utility shop a short four-hour drive out of town. Sunlight streams into the large, stain glass windows, bathing the cluttered store in a rainbow of colour. It appears to be a wooden, derelict camper parked in a semi-abandoned, overgrown lot from the outside. Once inside, however, five different tidy box-shaped rooms offer specialized weapons and tools against various kinds of Otherworlders.

The witch running the store, with her oversized spectacles and feathers braided into her hair, plays the flute as she sits cross-legged on the counter. She doesn't seem concerned about the teenagers playing with the dangerous objects lining her shop.

"It's a silver bomb. Lethal to vampires and werewolves." Leaving them in that section, I wander up to the counter. The flute music continues, but the witch is no longer holding the instrument or blowing into it. She eyes me warily, fingers twitching in her lap. "They need to see the back room."

"Back room? The rooms you see are the extent of our versatile shop." She hops off the counter and pulls out a brochure. It expands when she opens it, doubling in size. Flipping chunk after chunk, she drops a dictionary-sized book onto the block between us. "We do not keep some items on hand for safety reasons, but if you provide your Imperium number—"

"Let me speak to the owner."

She rubs her lips together, glancing up. Either she's looking to God for help (unlikely) or there's a room above us I cannot see. "The owner isn't in today."

"You sure about that?"

She pauses and glances over her shoulder at Killian. After spotting the faerie-provided prank section, the boys hustled over to it with unencumbered delight. Preparing for a raid is apparently overshadowed by stinky body wash and milk that tastes curdled to the first person that tries it but no one else.

"Yes."

Nodding, I walk over to the shelves lining the walls beside the front door. Potions and pre-cast spells make up the bulk of the stock. She squeaks when I pull the topper off an unveiling spell and blow it towards the ceiling. The wooden ceiling glistens and warps, revealing an open circle above the desk.

Pieces of wood slither down from the hole, attaching to one another, forming a spiral staircase between the first floor and second. I bypass the gawking witch to mount the stairs. Defensive weapons take up the first wall, I see. Nets, traps, and mines fill the rest of the circular room, save for a small booth behind a transparent shelf filled with herbs.

"No guns?" Most utility shops carry anything from handguns to rifles. Hunters heal fast, but a machine gun tears apart faster. "Or is this the 'extent' of your back room?"

"We do not believe in guns," announces a witch, presumably the owner, who steps out of a small office to the left. Skunk-scented smoke pours out in plumes behind her. "What are you looking for, hunter?"

"I am not looking for anything. They need to prepare their pack for a raid." Athena and Paisley clamber up the stairs first, followed by the male wolves who shake the shelves with every step. The witch's bong falls off her desk and clatters against the hardwood floor. "Show her the map and list."

Athena produces the crumpled list with a shaky smile, handing it to the witch. Her obnoxiously bushy eyebrows raise with every item I suggested. She plays with the tendrils of smoke pouring from her mouth before sucking it back in through her nostrils. "You are not with the Imperium I see. Follow me."

I leave them with her and jog down the spiral staircase to the bottom level. The flute witch shoots me a dirty look over the book she's folding back into a small brochure. "How much to use your looking glass?"

The brochure drops, forcing her to step back. Bewildered eyes flit to the staircase and back to me. "We do not sell looking glasses."

"I didn't ask to buy a looking glass. I asked how much I need to pay you for the use of yours."

"How—looking glasses are…." She shakes her head. Pulling out my wallet, I offer a hundred dollars. "You can't be serious."

I add an extra fifty and slide it across the counter. Steps creak above our heads. Muffled voices discuss a maze of mines and how to have an auto-detonator detect hunters versus werewolves. "I'm on limited time here."

She adjusts her glasses. Not a surprise. Most witches keep their looking glasses somewhere accessible and nearby. Incorporating her looking glass into the lens of her prescription glasses is ingenious.

"Are you going to return it to me?"

"What use do I have for your looking glass?"

Her eyebrows knit together, and her fingers freeze an inch from the arm of her glasses. "Wait, what use do you have?"

"You'll have it back before you can blink those near-sighted eyes."

She's young, perhaps young enough not to know why she should never give her looking glass away. All witches receive a looking glass upon their first menstruation. Ayizan explained it works as a private telephone line. Every witch who has a looking glass can be reached through it. She didn't explain any other magical principles, but I suspect it helps them to focus and develop their magic.

"You may be a… whatever you are, but Polaris is a Mother." Polaris must be the shop owner. Mothers tend to stay close to their coven. As the eldest members of the coven, and often the experts on one branch of magic, they raise the witchlings. It's their duty. The Matriarch and Mothers provide for and raise the witchlings to the point of specialty in any given branch of magic. A Mother, so removed from her coven and running a utility shop, speaks to a level of disunity back home. "Mind your manners."

Saluting her, I step into the snow-littered yard surrounding the camper. It's impossible to see the upper level from outside. Pine trees, frosted from the cold December air, stand as an immovable wall behind the camper. Mountains spread out beyond that.

Maneuvering around pillars of refrozen snow, I reach the forest. As light as I am on my feet, I still sink to my knees. Bits of ice catch on my fleece leggings. The moment I stop hearing their heartbeats, and the one of my sister's child, I kneel in the snow. A streak of sunlight might be hard to find with the grey sky, but Ayizan said a flashlight should be good enough.

With my phone face down, its flashlight blinding me, I slip the lenses out. One allows the light through. The other consumes it.

"Ayizan." Witches do not use last names. When filling out citizenship information, they supply descriptions of the landscape surrounding their coven or a specific attribute of their magic. No witch name is ever the same. Given at birth, used for life.

I hold snow in my hand and watch it melt into the concave shape of the glass. It pools there; the light gathers in liquid like melted silver, reflecting my appearance. "Show me Ayizan."

Silver swirls, disrupting my image. As she answers, the looking glass rises. The silver and glass meld into one and expand. Ayizan's face appears in full colour from her own looking glass. "I knew I should not have explained the glass to you."

"It's good to see you, too."

She cackles, throwing her head back. The thick patchwork of scars spread down the column of her neck and the curve of her jaw. Betrayal comes with a heavy cost, and yet they are not cruel enough to strip her of her name. Instead, she's been cut off from her coven and exiled from her sisters. Never again will she see them.

I lower my voice, though no one is near enough to hear me. "You have kept it safe?"

"Who would come for it? Who wishes to see the one who cannot see?"

"I need it."

She smiles, her teeth morphing from white to gold to rotted and back to white. As the scars were inflicted and cursed by another witch, she cannot change them, but I suspect changing appearances is easy for her. When we first met, I didn't have time to ask all the questions I wanted to.

I was dying.

"You said I was to keep it hidden from everyone."

"Do not be difficult." The goofy smile on her face shakes. She distrusts hunters. It went against her better judgement when she stumbled upon me, bleeding out and covered in dirt, and saved my life. Witches, by nature, nurture, evidently at great cost to themselves.

Hunters see them as the worst kind of Otherworlders. Humans who choose to use demonic forces to give themselves power at the expense of their fellow 'man'.

Witches consider themselves inherently maternal. According to Killian, Otherworlders view the witches as their mothers. Long ago, witches were midwives and apothecaries. The craft began with a desire to alleviate pain and treat injuries. However, the road to hell is paved with good intentions and soon the desire to experiment led the witches to the devil's doorstep.

Nevertheless, many witches still consider it their responsibility to care for the weak. To heal. To feed. To clothe.

Ayizan brought me somewhere safe. Warmed me by the fire. Treated my wounds and made me a potion to increase my healing. By morning, I had enough strength to be appalled with myself for getting captured by a witch. She laughed when I labelled myself a captive. Even at reduced strength, I would've been able to kill her.

I knew what the scars on her eyes meant. I knew she'd betrayed her coven. Most witches who lose their eyes kill themselves. Being apart from the coven is too hard. I suspect others, like Ayizan, wait in hopes of redeeming themselves. It's difficult to know the mind of a woman gone mad in isolation and rejection. Without the window-view into her soul, I cannot understand the thoughts whirring through what I suspect is a brilliant brain.

Especially if she is the Blind Witch. The one who fell in love with a hunter and lost everything for him.

The Imperium's history of their relationship leaves a lot to be desired. After returning to Imperio, and removing Nattalius from my legion, I went to the library. Catarina thought my sudden interest in witchcraft came from a desire to find a workaround of the hunter's protection against curses, so I could hurt Nattalius the way he hurt me.

I wanted to know if the witch who saved my life was the one who created the Sacraments. Every entry about the witch who created the Sacraments called her 'The Queen's Witch'. Her name rarely appeared alone, because they needed to include the hunter who 'converted' her. All told, there are seven records about 'The Hunter and The Queen's Witch' and six of them offered little to no actual insight into the events surrounding the Sacraments, much less the minute details of the couple. One story, written by the youngest member of the Hunter Queen's legion, told the full truth—the hunter used their relationship to further the Imperium, and she loved the man enough to let him.

With the fall of the Hunter Queen, the witch lost the protection of both the Sacraments and hunters. The coven came for The Queen's Witch and her hunter. Him bleeding out on the ground, with the light draining from his eyes, was the last thing she saw before they stole her sight. If Ayizan is the Blind Witch, she had—*has* every reason to distrust me.

"Hunters never do what they say," she sings, fingers playing on the air. Piano music drifts from thin air through the looking glass. "They take and take and take."

"What would you have me do?" I ask genuinely, elbows on my knees. She tuts and continues her mindless melody. "I need a bargaining chip."

"It's all power and politics and pain. Who can give the most pain, take the most power, make the most politics." The witch picks at her scalp, disrupting the matted sections of curls. Some might find it difficult to look upon her face when first meeting her, but I don't mind it. Having a person without eyes takes away the burden of their perception. "Power, politics, pain. Pain, power, politics. It is a man's world."

"My sister is pregnant."

She howls, cocking her head to one side. "I know."

"I need to protect her."

"Politics, power, pain, protect. You can protect her without the other three."

"Not permanently."

"Hmm." Her lips split across her teeth. The flicker of joy melts away as she moves within the looking glass. So much of my ability to read others comes from their eyes. Without them, I'm left to watch the way her head moves, how her lips twist or flatten or split. "No, no, no, no. Not another child. No one cares about the children."

"Another child?"

"I cannot get involved," she states. The madness creates interesting pictures across the canvas of her face. I catch rare glimpses of her previous self—all the passions and beliefs held by a once vivacious young woman. The woman she was before witchcraft changed her, granting her a long life, and then taking her eyes. A woman who believes in love and equality and protecting the innocents. "Power, pain, politics, protect, passion, pregnant, permanent, pressure."

"Do you mean the witchling who made us?"

"Hunters take and take and take. You give, give, give."

Witches do not share the Imperium's concerns about hybrids. They value the lives of all creatures and view each rarity as an opportunity to expand their craft. I wondered whether she would continue to extend kindness to me when I returned to Ethiopia after finishing Seminary. Two months passed between her nursing the wounds Nattalius caused and returning to the cave.

She wasn't there.

I asked every native near to the cave about a Witch Doctor in the highlands. None knew of the tales pertaining to a woman with her eyes clawed out. Many told me about the 'werehyenas' who made their homes in the depths, but I killed the wolves. Every single one of them. Male, female, old, and young.

I found a witch in Logia who said many magic-users travel to the Horn of Africa, particularly Ethiopia, for herbs and plants because they are more varied than other regions. Knowing that, I asked every herbologist in the area about a woman matching Ayizan's description. Changing the scars inflicted by other witches is impossible, and it's hardly a trait that goes unnoticed, especially among the superstitious.

One of the herbologists knew of her, though they tried to hide it. Eventually, they confessed she made the trek to his store once a year. I assumed she employed a portal or spell, but finding her footprints was relatively easy after purchasing a trace. It would've taken a month straight of jogging to find her.

"The scales are uneven again, but I need a favour." Purchasing a motorcycle from a young guy, I made the trip from Ethiopia to Mauritania. After a week, because of the weather and the necessity of rest and food, I arrived at the Richat Structure. She made me wait another two days, sitting there in silence, before she opened her world to me. "I have a plan—"

"Plans, politics, power, pain, protect, passion, pregnant, permanent, pressure, premonition."

"Keep your premonitions away from me. I do not want to know."

"Scorekeeping is for men," Ayizan murmurs, waving her hand from one side to the other. When I first said I didn't want to be indebted to her for saving my life, she said the same thing. She changed her tune soon enough. They always do. "Tell me your plan for power."

CHAPTER 27

Left Behind

"Glad to see you're making the most of this purgatory."

One downside of hunter hearing is the inability to feign sleep. Even if I slow my heartbeat enough to match the rhythm of a pulse at rest, Nattalius can feel my working mind. Peeling my eyes open, I offer my mug, which is filled with more Baileys than coffee. "That's the Catholics. You'll get it right, eventually."

"It was a metaphor." He takes the drink from my hand and takes a hearty sip while his eyes crawl over the mountains. I discovered this spot and the thick, cozy hammock during one of my mandatory walks. My sister, and her child, have turned me into a walker. Gallivanting through the forest at all hours of the day when I cannot bear sitting alone in the dark. It's never silent then. The voices get louder. My mother's. My dad's. My monster's. My own. "This is genuinely awful."

"Snob."

"I'm only here because I'm waiting to hear what decision you've made regarding your father." After drinking my blood to save his life, Nattalius looked up every raid/case my parents took. It didn't take long for him to find a werewolf who spent enough time with my mother to impregnate her. "Something you know. Something I suspect you are enjoying."

Scoffing, I drain half the mug. "You know, if you try to leave Ingrid will lock you in the basement."

"You think I am going to tell the Imperium about your sister's indiscretion."

"If anyone found out you withheld that information, it would hurt your future career in the Imperium. I may not be willing to play the game your way, but I understand the rules."

"There will be nothing left of the Imperium if we continue to follow your schedule." He stares down at me and plants his hands on his hips. Nattalius says schedule in the worst way. Shed-jew-ull. Two days until Christmas and he's worried about my timetable. "Your sister is nothing special—"

"A wise man would walk away about now."

"There are hundreds of thousands of other hunters. Billions of humans. All put at risk by the agenda of your f—" I throw the mug close enough to his head to distract him. With a twist and flip, I end up on my feet. My patience for Nattalius is thin on the best of days. Constantly waxing poetry about duty and loyalty as if he didn't lure me into my worst nightmare and leave me there to die. "The Imperium is strong, but the Sacraments are stronger."

"I guess your ancestors should've thought of that."

"King Hozeir will burn the Imperium down and claim the world as his own. Innocent humans will be treated as game. The Gates of Hell will be opened for all manner of creature to escape. He will be the ruin of earth."

"And you know this how?" King Hozeir's goals have never been publicized. It was all rumours, whispered about at bars and spread like STI's on college campuses. He, like many white men before him, thinks his kin must be superior to others. That much is clear from his actions, but what he wishes to do beyond breed hybrids and unleash them on Imperio is uncertain. "You don't spend time near humans, so expect this news to shock you, but they are far from innocent. Humans cause more damage to each other and this world for sport than demonic creatures do out of necessity. King Hozeir may travel with a wizard, but it is the witches who first accessed the portal. Without the help of a Mother—all of whom removed themselves from society—there will be no new Otherworlders for you to whine about. How will you pass the time?"

"I should know better than to think I can depend on you."

"Excuse me?" I exclaim, turning around. He slips past me, stomping like the petulant child he claims not to be, and stuffs the hands in the pockets of his wool coat. Where is Mona when I need her? She'll hit him for me again. "You cannot depend on me? Where were you when I was bleeding out, begging for help?"

"You lied to me."

I hasten my steps to overtake him and soon we are practically running out of the forest in a competition with no winners. "I'm not doing this again."

"You deceived me. You tricked me into favouring you."

"Say love Nattalius. For once, say the word."

"I could not love something like you."

Some*thing*.

He loved me. Enough to tell me about the changes 'we' would make to Herzog's Manor when we moved into it, starting with the awful landscaping in the front and ending with the portrait our family would have on the walls. A family I told him couldn't happen.

I waited for him to say it. I opened myself up to the possibility of marriage after years of denying myself a happy ending. I didn't lie, and he never said I love you—we deceived one another, over and over again.

"This is the best show I've seen in a long time," Grady whispers, his voice shattering the eye contact between me and my ex-boyfriend. We glance at the packhouse porch at the same time to find rows of blinking eyes watching us. "I'm team Delilah."

"No one is team Nattalius," Paisley whispers, wincing when his eyes narrow on her. Raising her glass, she leans over to Athena. "Why did they break up?"

"Why did we date?" I counter, hands on my hips. Kartals do not share their secrets but may as well drag the court of public opinion into this argument. We keep having the same debate, tossing out the same insults. Condemn me. Absolve me. It might fix me. "Let's start off there. I walked into Seminary, a newly Awakened hunter—about to become an adult—and someone said my name like it meant something. Who said 'she's a Christos' first, Nat? Camille Laurent? One of your friends made a little comment about how I must be a baby; she said I was a Christos, and then you repeated it. 'She's a Christos?' You couldn't believe it. Why?"

"I am not discussing this in front of a kennel."

"You knew from the first day you saw me that there was something wrong with me. You put that aside because I was a single, naïve girl, with a big name, who would look good on your arm." Someone emits a low 'oooh'. It sounds a lot like Grady again. More wolves join him until a ring of them forms in the yard. Nattalius starts walking away, so I shrug and face Paisley. "I tried to resist. I knew if I told him what I was I'd be endangering my life and Athena's. I told him to stay away from me. I gave non-answers to date invitations. I avoided your touch!"

"You are one of the most stubborn people I know!" His lips quiver, losing the fight to contain his volume. Mommy and daddy would be very disappointed. With that, all his refined manners go out the window. He messes up his hair, disrupting the flat pattern enforced by gel, and leaves it to flap in the wind. Sweat gathers on his upper lip when he chokes on a bitter laugh. "That was you fighting me? No. The moment you found out you were my Head, you took that as permission to do whatever you wanted. You and Catarina invaded every part of my life—"

"I wanted to be loved. Okay? I was desperate for it. You were Prince Charming and, for once, I wanted to be the princess. Do you want me to say that, Nattalius? My parents died and threw me into a world I didn't have a clue about. You were kind, and smart, and you knew what you were doing, and I was desperately hoping that would rub off on me… I have apologized. I have left you alone. I stopped talking to everyone after coming back because I knew if anyone found out it would look bad for you."

"We're skipping a chapter." Athena tries to stop Paisley, but she waves her hand at me. "You tried to avoid dating him. You failed. What happened from there?"

"Seven months of Nat, Cat, and I against the world. We spent every day and almost every night together. Dreaming up a future—"

"I spoke of a future. You knew we didn't have one."

A chorus of 'oohs' this time.

"I wanted to believe in it. I did. I prayed and hoped and dreamed you would be willing to forgive me for what I am." Companions date. It's inevitable. They love each other because biology forces them to. Biology made me a monster. Biology should've made him accepting of that. "Then came the eighth month of my first year in Seminary. We were assigned a vampire raid."

Vampires terrify him. He suggested I ask the Senate to reassign us, given the size of our legion.

But they wanted a small legion who could proceed undetected. Get in. Kill the Vampire Queen. Get out.

Over the course of the four-year Seminary program, hunters learn to imitate Otherworlders. They gain access to Otherworlder scents and attend a boot camp to learn the movements and mannerisms of the most common, dangerous creatures. We had a two-hour lesson from a fourth-year student and a limited supply of musk. The odds were against us from the beginning, but we were doing well. A door stood between us and the queen. One last step before we could return to Imperio with a completed assignment, and I could join the second-year class with Catarina and Nattalius permanently.

"We were pretending to be fledglings looking for a new clan. They accepted us instantly and set up an audience with their queen to make us permanent members." I wait for Nattalius to interrupt, to make some comment about how I set us up for failure. When we gave our debrief to the Senate, he had a list. A list breaking down every mistake he witnessed. "Catarina's nose began to bleed. She wasn't used to the dryness of the Chilean desert."

"Seriously?" Paisley whispers; her eyes widen as she sits forward. A running commentary plays behind my back about how 'that's what hunters get when they go after innocents'. If people stopped using that word so much, it might regain some of its value. "A nosebleed?"

"The vampires knew what we were. I told Nattalius and Catarina to watch the doors so I could get the queen. As the Head, I was the strongest. Vampire monarchs are heavily guard—"

Mona snorts and crosses her arms, staring Nattalius down. "You ran in there, didn't you?"

"Defending the door was a job for one. Any longstanding clan has spells at the ready to protect their monarch and even the great Delilah Christos couldn't withstand hundreds of vampires and magic." He unbuttons his coat when he turns to glare at her. Graham sneers at him over Mona's shoulder. "I was right. Even with me, they still outnumbered us sixty to one."

"You distracted me."

"I protected you."

"You ran after the queen!" I shout, my adrenaline pumping now. Being in that dark labyrinth of rock reminded me too much of my parents' grave. Once blood started spilling, and my beast started thirsting for a bite, I lost myself. I don't know how many of them I killed. I tore apart enough bloodsuckers with my bare hands to stain them black. "Cat called for help. I said leave the queen. You chased her."

"It was the assignment—"

"IT WAS YOUR PRIDE!" The voice shouting isn't mine. It's guttural, rattling with claws and fangs. Darkness invades my vision as I step towards him. When he cowers, so do I. "I forgot I wasn't the first one you betrayed. You left her. You knew she was a hybrid—everyone in the class did—and that's as good as a death sentence to you."

"You two could handle it."

"Or maybe we were chosen for this high-level assignment because your mother convinced her fellow senators to give us—to give you—a chance. A first year and two second years handling a covert op against an ancient clan? It's unheard of. If we succeeded, I'm sure it would have nicely padded your resume for Senate elections and the Imperium."

"It was our duty to kill her."

"It was your duty to defend and fight with your Companions. To prioritize their needs above your own. Above any other. That is vitazeil."

Arguments erupt around us. Right versus wrong. A group of older women argue about whether the Imperium would be Alpha or me. Mona remarks she'd go after the queen, which sparks an argument between her and Graham. The others start weighing in.

Nattalius and I stand, isolated, in a sea of barking werewolves. It brings me back to his ultimate betrayal in the Ethiopian Highlands.

"Enough!" Killian's voice draws me out of the dark and casts me naked under a microscope. I knew he was gone. My seventh sense, my Killiandar, tracked him driving off the territory this morning. He's not supposed to be back yet. Supposed to or not, he climbs out of the ranger truck and silences the pack with a single quirk of his eyebrow. "What is going on out here?"

"They're airing out their dirty laundry. We're getting all the Delius lore."

More than one person mouths the couple name Paisley gave us with a perplexed expression. Killian scans his pack as they keep repeating it. A teenager tries to explain to the group of older ladies why couples combine their names. "You have assignments. Battlements to prepare.

Patrol duties to complete."

"Please Killian," Paisley begs, eyes widening when he glares at her. She hops to her feet and scuttles over to him. "We know Nattalius went after the Vampire Queen against Delilah's orders. I think they're about to break up."

"Catarina and I followed him. We were fighting off vamps from every direction, but I knew… I knew Nattalius couldn't handle her on his own." I first discovered Nattalius' blood-doping addiction when I went to wish him luck before a Seminary Tournament. On top of his strict diet and fitness regime, he regularly withdrew his own blood and injected it back in before physical tests or raids. He appeared stronger. Faster. Deadlier.

Catarina didn't get a nosebleed.

He took out too much blood and pumped too much back in. Nattalius thought the injection site and ensuing bruise would heal before we reached the throne room.

He was wrong.

"We found her. Dispatched her. I smelled Nattalius' blood on her, so I told Catarina to call the medevac." Had Nattalius been at full strength, had he properly fueled his body, he might've been able to kill her on his own. "I found him on the ground, his throat torn open, seconds from dying."

Nattalius stares at his hands, rubbing his lifeline with one thumb. I was terrified. Assignments and raids begin month six for First Years. I'd seen blood and gore and worn them like clothes. It was never us, though. Never one of my Companions.

"Hunters inherited the ability to drink blood and reap its benefits from vampires. Nattalius told me about how the Hunter Queen used to let her legion drink from her and send them back out to battle. He was reaching for my wrist." I pause, wetting my lips. With Killian closing in, and the crowd staring daggers at Nattalius, this no longer seems like a great idea. "I told you there would be a cost."

Nattalius' jaw clicks. "I didn't expect damnation."

"You do not believe in—"

"You would've known by then," Athena whispers, wrapping her arms around herself. Others nod with her. "The scent of her blood would've told you everything you needed to know."

I cut a vertical line into my arm and waited for him to refuse. He didn't hesitate; he latched onto my arm and refused to let go. My blood filled his mouth. Hatred filled his eyes. "I had no choice."

"Die," Mona suggests, her smile sickly sweet. "Take your pride to the grave."

"Medevac arrived. You didn't speak a word the entire flight. It wasn't until we stood in front of the Fifteen and their Legionnaire that you opened your mouth. You humiliated me. You blamed me for everything."

"You should learn to control your Companions."

"I didn't ask for this. Any of this! I didn't ask to be created. I didn't ask to be born. I didn't ask to be Head."

He ignores me, playing to our audience with a sigh. "I broke up with her in front of them. My mother thought it was a disgusting display of adolescent emotion."

"You needed to separate yourself from me. You knew you would find proof and you wanted to be able to take me down without threatening your status."

"Eliana meticulously followed policy. I found her case in the

Administration Building." Nattalius scrunches his nose at that. He would have preferred for me to be a dirty secret. If I was, he could have presented me to them as a prize greater than the Vampire Queen. "The Imperium knew about you. They knew where Eliana and Philip 'ran away' to."

The Imperium can be selective with their sterilization. Hunter hybrids occasionally find themselves lucky enough to conceive and be left alone, so long as their children swear fealty to the Imperium. However, the threat hangs like a blade from above. Catarina could be dragged into Imperio's hospital at any moment. "You couldn't report me. You couldn't stay away from me because I finished the assignmen—"

"You refused to leave me alone."

"I gave you space."

"And yet I could smell you in my veins!"

"You chose to drink, dude," Grady mutters with a smack of his lips. The rest of the wolves murmur their assent—even Killian, who hasn't stopped staring at me. Is he disgusted? Is he seeing what I am?

"Two months later—"

Paisley gapes, dwarfed by Killian behind her. "There's more?"

"We were assigned to raid a pack in Ethiopia. It wasn't our first assignment after Chile, but you were acting differently. You kept making small talk with the other Heads. You were avoiding us. You wouldn't look me in the eye."

"I am a gentleman and a Kartal." He shrugs, still so blasé about the moment that ruined us. That ruined me. "The legions revere me."

"The raid went sideways. The pack secretly took in another and merged into one. Their numbers were twice what we thought. Our legion was told to watch the flank. When another wave of wolves came, you stood in my way."

"My mistake."

"You kept forcing me to step back because I couldn't shove you out of the way. When I tried to use my weapons, you moved into me, so I would stumble and lose my footing." It was a clever trick. By the time I realized what was happening, my foot went over the edge of a steep drop. "I fell off a ledge. I don't know how long the fall was, but I hit the floor hard enough to black out.

"When I regained consciousness, I could see that we lost. The raid was being called off. I heard footsteps and looked up. There you were. Standing over me from the top of that cliff."

"I was hoping you died in the fall."

"I was healing, so you howled."

He smiles, flashing the top row of his teeth. "I am a talented howler."

"You left me there. You knew what happened to my mother. You knew how much I hated werewolves." That earns a couple of exclamations. My eyes zero in on Nattalius'. To this day, I protect him. I've always protected him, keeping others from finding out his 'shameful' secrets, and still he left me there. Bleeding. Broken. Whimpering for him to help me. "I blacked out again. I don't know how I got out, but I know the hunters were long gone when I woke up. I was bleeding out on a hilltop in a foreign land, covered in flesh, guts, and blood. Alone."

"What is the expression? You made the bed; lie in it."

"I walked to Imperio from that hilltop. When I arrived at my dorm, you and Catarina were packing away my stuff. You told her a werewolf took me over the edge with him, and you tried to get my body, but they were already cleaning my bones."

"She didn't come for y—"

"I declared him a traitor and struck out his tattoo that evening," I declare, addressing the crowd. Walking into class the next day was worse than rotting on that hilltop. With his arm on display, Nattalius sat with his friends and stared at us with cold indifference. I don't know what stories he told them, and I don't care to. "Catarina and I minded our own for the next two months. I considered finishing the four years, but he made sure it was a hostile environment."

"You humiliated me." He shirks off his coat, throwing it into the snow. Red colours his tanned cheeks as he pulls off his pressed sweater. The button-down follows. "My mother cursed the day I was born. My father did not speak to me for weeks."

"My mother was raped and killed herself to avoid meeting that fate again. One of my fathers was her rapist and the other joined her in death. Are we finished now? Will you let this go?"

Anger's an ugly emotion on anyone, but it pulls the skin taut around Nattalius' gaunt face. His skull remains in one place as his muscle and cartilage shifts. "You should've laid down and taken it like a bi—"

Crack.

The rest of his sentence flies with his body. Werewolves scramble to avoid his flailing form.

His body hits the snowbank with an awful crunch. Tiny snow crystals hungrily consume the crimson blood pouring out of him. It smells a hint like me.

Pressing a hand to his snapped jaw, Nattalius glares at me.

No, not at me—behind me.

Killian's bloodied hand drops onto my shoulder. He pulls me behind him when my ex stands. Blood dribbles out of his mouth and nose where

Killian's punch landed. I've appreciated the Alpha's large hands for braiding girls' hair and cutting wood, but never for punching. Half of Nattalius' face morphs with the growing welt.

"Get off my territory," Killian snaps, his eyes flashing gold. Muscles bunch at his shoulders as each vertebrae begins to expand. Every wolf within the circumference of the sharing circle drops their heads and flash their necks to him. I fight the urge to start purring. "Now."

"I am going back to Imperio."

"Wish a Merry Christmas to my grandfather for me."

Nattalius holds his jaw in place, eyes falling on me. Killian growls. A true, menacing growl that sends delightful skitters down my spine. Pressing a hand between Killian's shoulders, against his heart, I commit the image of Nattalius scrambling towards his car to memory. The vehicle shakes with the force of his entry, and he doesn't even take the time to brush the snow off his windshield.

The car fishtails out of the makeshift parking lot, spitting snow and dirt at us. Killian's body vibrates underneath my palm. Bloody fist clenched at his side, he takes a deep breath. "Get back to your assignments."

I've never seen a crowd disperse so quickly. Some of the wolves shift to get away faster. Paisley whistles from where he left her and scrambles when he twists abruptly around. Eye to eye with his chest, I squeak. Like a mouse.

Words won't come out. They tease my mind with the promise of forming a coherent sentence and run scared when I try to latch onto them.

"Excuse me."

At first, I think I said it.

Then I watch him walk away. Briskly. Without a second glance. He dives into the forest with a whine, half-man and half-wolf, disappearing from view and hearing in the blink of my disbelieving eyes.

CHAPTER 28

Elbows Deep in Bird Anus

I half-hoped Killian left to finish the job.

Unfortunately, Catarina was on the phone with me when Nattalius arrived at the Alcove, healed and fuming. He left ten minutes later with his luggage, Cat, and a scowl.

I had to tell her about the new moon to convince her to leave. If Cat thinks I'm safe until the New Year, she won't interfere with my plans. Besides, Leonie and Benedict love holidays. That family's traditions have traditions. She cannot miss out on them for me.

Before she left, Cat promised to watch Nattalius, and she meant it. In the last twenty-nine hours since they left Witchhill, I've received dozens of pictures and texts. They arrived at the airport to find the Chancellor's assistant waiting expectantly. Montgomery didn't care enough to detain Catarina, but Nattalius got into the limo and left Catarina to find a ride to Imperio.

I have been dutifully ignoring the Chancellor's email with my summons. Christmas Eve is meant for turkey, Christmas movies, hot chocolate, ugly flannel pajamas, and staying up until midnight. Politics and play can wait.

I have more important things to worry about.

Killian walks into the kitchen at the same moment I shove my hand into a carcass. With half my arm trapped in the bird's cavity, and the other one covered in garlic oil, I freeze. He's been avoiding me. Or I've been avoiding him. As soon as Nattalius and Catarina left yesterday, I went home. After a day of sitting with Ingrid in silence, I returned to the packhouse with all my Christmas dinner supplies and have been hiding in the kitchen ever since.

Dismissing the staff was the right thing to do, but now that my arm is lodged into what I believe is a bird's anus, I'm beginning to regret sending Chef back to France.

"Are you making turkey dinner by yourself?"

"Chef insisted on teaching us the basics."

"Turkey dinner is a basic?"

"For him? Yes. I also hand-rolled croissants and know how to prepare a perfect beef wellington." With raised eyebrows, he scans the array of food clustered on his island—notably, the wall of onion and garlic stacked between me and him. "Macaroni and cheese is where I shine. He even confessed mine is better than his."

"Athena—"

"Sick. Little monster doesn't like the smell of raw meat and garlic."

Neither of us suspected Athena's sudden aversion to dead animals and potent vegetables until I crushed the first garlic clove. She almost vomited in the stuffing. After ten minutes of throwing up in the bathroom down the hall, she came out with a nose plug on. I banished her to the hammock with a sleeve of crackers and a thermos of fresh hot chocolate.

I knew vampires were sensitive to the smell of garlic, but it never occurred to me that werewolves might have an aversion too. The distinct scent of onions clings to the air, feasting on the moisture in my eyes, and seeming to burn Killian's, if the way he is rubbing his eyes is any indication. I thought the scent of freshly cut aromatics would keep him away from me.

He's everywhere. Always at the corner of my vision, even when I'm avoiding him. I dreamed of him last night. My father was trying to take me away, but Killian kept pulling me back. He punched King Hozeir right in his unimaginable face and scooped me into his arms. I watched the world around us blur when he whisked me away.

I can fight my own battles. My insistence on doing so has created rifts throughout my life. Having someone else willing and strong enough to fight them for me? An aphrodisiac. His proximity, an island of onions and garlic away, kicks my heart rate up a notch. Removing my hand from the turkey, I step over to the sink.

With my back turned to him, I lift both hands. Does smelling like a dead animal repulse him or trigger a primitive desire to hunt? The garlic oil is losing potency. I can smell him. I can hear his heartbeat. I can feel his warmth.

"I'm sorry."

"What?"

"I was out of line," Killian states, hands clasped behind his back. He sounds sincere, but he doesn't look sorry. "I know you have a past with werewolves—"

"I have wanted to punch Nattalius in the face for years. That was the best Christmas present you could've given me."

One side of his mouth hikes up, giving me a glimpse of his rare masculine arrogance. Desire twists my stomach into knots as we eye each other across the island. Forget the turkey dinner. This is my feast. "I am not apologizing because of that. He deserved far worse. No one speaks to my—friends like that."

"That was convincing."

His playful dirty look curls my toes. Everything this man does elicits a reaction from my body. Athena, Paisley, and Ibrahim convinced the wolves to wear ugly Christmas sweaters until the movie marathon tonight. I don't even know what the thing on his sweater is supposed to be, but it's endearing. My mind goes to laying my head against the soft fabric while watching the movie. "I am not your Alpha. I had no right to manhandle you."

You can manhandle me anytime.

"You don't owe me an apology, Killian." God knows what I would've done if he stayed. Thoughts warred in my head. Scathing, sarcastic quips. Embarrassing, gratitude-laden hiccups. If he stayed, I would've thrown myself at him—damn the consequences. I've known longing and want for my entire life, but this is something else. "Shouldn't you be more upset that I lied to you like I lied to him?"

I am not good enough for Killian.

Nattalius and I deserved each other. We used one another in our different ways and ended up hurting each other—and Cat—when it all fell apart. Neither of us were faultless in the messes we left behind. In a messed-up way, we were and are perfect for each other.

One day, Killian will find his Mate. A she-wolf who rivals Mona in size and strength. With a gentle spirit like Athena, who knows how to welcome people and bring them together. Entertaining any thoughts of romance between the two of us is cruel. Our stars aligned for a moment, but he's going to shoot ahead, and I am going to fall.

"You were protecting yourself. Someone had to." He rounds the island and twists, so his back faces me. Some people have butterflies in their stomach, and some people have bats. My bats come with teeth and tiny little pincers. They climb their way up my sternum, trying to feast on my stone-covered heart. "Put me to work."

He's supposed to be put off by the onion and garlic. Not rolling up his sleeves and meticulously washing his hands. "I don't need help. I've finished all the prep."

"Do you want to mash the potatoes or stuff the turkey?"

Us having a staring contest, alone in the kitchen, with his hair pulled back and sleeves up to his elbows, only enthuses the bats. Snow falls outside the window like it does in a dream. Romantic yellow lights wound around green garlands cast shadows over his lips. Lips I cannot stop staring at. "Don't touch my turkey."

The sounds of the electric beater and skin on oiled flesh compete with the rushing blood in my head. Our backs brush when I reach for the bowl of stuffing. "I knew what you were that first day in the store."

"I think you got a whole flavour profile with the amount of sniffing you were doing."

"Then I saw your tattoo, and you said it wasn't for you."

"It's not."

"My mother recognized your parents' names—I told her about you when they visited. She said they led the march against King Hozeir.

Dierdre might have tried to take revenge, even if Athena wasn't pregnant." He throws multiple sticks of butter and four cups of cream into the giant pot of potatoes. Murmuring, Killian opens the fridge to collect green onions. I watch, transfixed, as he cuts with a precision Chef would be proud of. "I'm not upset with you. I do wish you were the one who told me about your past; I could've held you during the hard parts."

"I don't need holding."

"Everyone needs holding." Inhaling slowly, he shuts off the beater. With a hand full of stuffing lodged inside the turkey, I watch his shoulders drop. "I needed to walk away to stop myself from doing that."

"I, too, find it difficult not to throttle—"

He spins. Strands of dark hair coast his forehead, begging for my fingers to comb them back. When he speaks, it's with the gentleness one uses for an injured toddler. "I want to hold you. All day, every day. I want to fall asleep holding you and wake up with your head right here." He chops a line across his heart. My favourite place. "It's been killing me not to say this from the first second I saw you. I knew who you were to me in that grocery st—"

"You're wrong."

Pushing the heels of his palms into his eyes, he leans against the counter. "I don't understand how you keep resisting this."

"You're right. You don't understand." I thought Nattalius would be the last person to break my heart. What he did to me cannot compare to what I've done to myself for even entertaining the idea of Killian. I should've pushed him away and let myself bleed out on Witches Hill in June. "I am not a wolf. I have no Mate."

"I've seen—"

"You haven't!" I swallow the end of my shout. Blood wells up around my nails, where they dig into the scarred flesh of my hands. Glancing over my shoulder, I listen to see if I woke my sister on her hammock. After a moment of silence, I sigh. "If you saw what I am, truly, you would not be here."

"I know who you are, Delilah."

"No, you don't. You don't know me. We know next to nothing about one another." The bats finally reach my heart. It starts bleeding, pouring acid over my ribs, burning the muscle of my lungs. A muted cry rises from the tips of my toes and unleashes against my skull with a reckoning force. "I am not who you think I am."

I'm leaving in less than a week. Never seeing me again is the best thing I can offer him for all of his kindness. Eight months together, an eternity apart. His infatuation should fade with the distance. Mona said when wolves find their Mates, they forget about everyone else. The heartbreak. The attraction. In a few years, I will be nothing but a fragment of once upon a time.

Holding his gaze, I spread my arms out. He knows I'm not his Mate. If I were, there would be more signs. Save for the Heat I entered when first arriving in Witchhill, I haven't shown signs of Mating. My periods are shorter. Ovulation is less painful. I'm sleeping the same as I used to. It doesn't hurt to be apart from him.

I can count on one hand how many times I thought of him during my world tour.

"What is your dream car?" He crosses his arms and rests his hip against the island. Rolling my eyes, I pull the turkey pan over. Amusement flashes in his eyes when he realizes I'm using the dishes to form a barricade between us. He won't protect himself, so I need to do it for us both.

"Cars are the things with wheels, right?"

"Is Darla it?"

My beautiful convertible. Dark red, like my nails, like blood, and smooth as sin. I didn't get as many chances to joyride this summer with wedding prep and hiding the Crown. Not to mention the ridiculous amounts of packages I was sending, covered in my scent, to distract my father's henchmen. "She's one of them."

"Top three. Darla is number one?"

"It's hard to choose. She's competing with a '65 El Camino. They're impractical, but pretty. I'd want the Powerglide upgrade and one of the four-barrel, two-hundred-and-thirty horsepower three forty eights. Archie and I talked about finding one and restoring it, but parts are difficult to find and fixing any bed damage would take hours because of its reinforcements." I know he has no idea what I'm talking about. Killian isn't a car guy. He sends Graham to the dealership every few years with instructions to find a vehicle that 'hauls good'. No one in the pack owns their own vehicle. They have an entire schedule hung up in the garage and a library-card-like system to track who has what.

I cannot contain myself, though. Cars were my first love. Hours in the garage, covered in grease, were my medicine. Had my parents not signed me up for martyr duty, I'd be a mechanic or a car designer. "Third would have to be a '70 Camaro Z/28. Change out the cam—camshaft, not camera—and add a double pump, and it might compete for second place."

"Those are all Chevy's."

"I'm a Chevy kind of girl. I have a Tahoe on the island."

"If you need my strength for the bed, let me know." He returns to the potatoes, acting like that sentence wasn't double-sided. The turkey starts cracking from the force of my fists plunging into it. With stuffing bursting at the seams, I step back and wash my hands. How dare he make me think of making out in the back of a new car underneath a moonlit sky? "It's your turn to ask a question."

"I don't remember agreeing to twenty questions."

"Make it a good one."

Scoffing, I hold my wet hands away from me. Where did he put the towel? "What's your favourite colour?"

He laughs. I do look comical, flapping my hands to dry them. The question is ridiculous too. Classic, but childish. Uninteresting enough to keep him away from me. "Dark red."

The flapping ceases. Hands on my hips, I twist to face him. He's closer than I expect. With a towel pinched between two fingers, Killian gives me an award-winning smile. "Try again."

"It is."

"Do you think you have game? You tell a girl your favourite colour is the same as hers and she thinks, 'Wow, we must be fated for each other'?"

"It's not a game."

Darla's dark red. Every time I get my nails done, I ask for coffin shaped and the tech's deepest cherry red. The colour of blood. Athena painted my ring fingers with some red glitter for a touch of Christmas cheer. Snatching the towel out of his hand, I snort. "Right."

"I didn't have one until I met you. You poked my chest at the store, and I noticed that your lips were starting to match your nail polish. Right then, I thought to myself, 'I finally found my favourite colour'."

I intended to prod him again before he dropped that bomb. Now he's too close, and I'm terrified to touch him with those same-coloured nails.

His eyes drop to my lips and mine drop to his. Slightly brown. Glistening with the unscented lip balm he applies every morning and night. Like he's been preparing for this.

"It's mistletoe." Standing an inch from him, I can see the shape of it on his ugly sweater. A sweater I'm certain my meddlesome little sister bought for him when she purchased one for her husband. "Traitor."

Killian, the mischievous mastermind he is, sucks his smile back. "Is it?"

"I think the stuffing needs more onions."

I crush an unpeeled onion in one hand, letting its juice run down my arms. My eyes begin to burn. Killian watches, lips popping open, thick eyelashes flying up against his eyebrows. "Are you using garlic and onion to deter me?"

"You can never add too many vegetables."

"Delilah." Picking the peels out of the lump of onion, I flick them into the garbage. He steps closer; his stomach presses against my arm with his every breath. "If you wanted me to kiss you, there's no force in Heaven or Hell strong enough to stop me from doing so. Onion, garlic, stale coffee, fish, morning breath—nothing would prevent me from claiming you as mine."

"That's because you are a dog, and you have no taste. One kiss isn't a—"

"If I taste you, you are mine. No more running. No more pushing." His touch ghosts my bottom lip. My knees buckle, drawing me closer like an offering.

Kiss me.

I don't know who says it, but for once, my entire body hums in agreement. When I drop my cheek into his hand, the world goes silent.

His eyes light me on fire. "Do you want me?"

Am I nodding? Am I shaking?

"Use your words, *cara m'anama*." I have no idea what that means, but all the bones in my body liquidate. He winds an arm around my back to hold me against the island. "You try my patience, but I've spent twenty-five years waiting for you. I can wait until you're begging for it."

He reaches past me to pluck a whole onion off the counter. Wordlessly, he bites into it like an apple and saunters out of the kitchen.

CHAPTER

29

You Filthy Animal

I'm awake.

Darkness crowds my vision. One of my sleepover partners pulls our shared blanket off my legs. Staying up until two AM—after consuming twice my weight in turkey and an entire carton of spiked eggnog—severely impaired my decision making. We should've gotten a blanket for each of us. I should've gone up to my guest room instead of crashing in Paisley's room, but Killian's t-shirt was tight, and my tongue was loose.

None of that matters now. There's something wrong.

My heartbeat picks up, though I cannot see or hear anything. I feel it though: a deep sense of wrongness, something out of place. I strain to find where it's coming from and search the dark for a sign of movement.

Bodies move on sheets. Snores sound from above. Boots crunch somewhere in the distance. Sentries march through the forest, taking calculated footsteps and even breaths. Snow whispers to the ground in greeting.

It's a silent night, worthy of the song, and still, something is watching me.

Mona and Paisley sleep soundly beside me, undisturbed. Flesh meets metal under my pillow. Sliding the pad of my finger over the blade, I focus on my breathing. I match each breath with Paisley. Breathe in. Breathe out.

He's here.

Awareness pours through my veins like the gas before the flame. One of Paisley's many hanging plants sways. Head against my pillow, I stare at the rug underneath her bed. The fibers flatten into the perfect shape of a foot.

Launching, I slash the dagger in an arc towards the creature I cannot see. A hand shoots out of thin air, dissolving the knife into dust. The wizard slaps a hand over my mouth, muffling my warning call, and pulls me underneath the heaviness of a cloak now all too easy to see. Green chains slither from his neck to mine, binding me to his body, cutting off my fight.

Let me out.

"Hunters are immune to many kinds of magic," the man whispers, tightening the chains to the point of asphyxiation. I'm inside the Cloak. No one can hear him. No one can hear me. "But you're not a hunter, are you?"

Let me in!

"Go to sleep, little hybrid."

My head bounces with every step. The spell rolls off my body with every breath of cold air. A werewolf, who smells worse than most, grips my calves with jagged nails. A thin layer of hair covers his bare skin. In the groggy haze, I wonder whether it's my father. I expected him to be larger. Scarier. Mightier than words.

Casting me off his shoulder, the werewolf grunts. He shifts and takes off, back to where he came from. The ice cutting into my bare arms awakens my senses. The sentries no longer move through the forest. I cannot see Graham, but I know he's sleeping twenty feet away from me in the snow.

The wizard must still be wearing the Cloak. I cannot sense him in the forest or the house. Part of me hopes he left me here with werewolves who will be all too easy to dispatch.

The greater part of me knows he probably went back for my sister.

Snowflakes melt against my forehead as I lay there. The liquid runs in rivulets from the bridge of my nose to the curve of my jaw. I want to move, but I don't know where the spellcaster or his fighters are. They might be close enough to hear my steadily beating heart.

A portal forms behind me. Sparking. Popping. Sizzling. I've imagined what King Hozeir's prison cells would look like. Nightmares plagued me for months after my mother explained what happened to her. I dreamed of the cell she was chained in and lost sleep, questioning whether he used old shackles or thick metal cables. I see them now.

Shackles hanging from short chains.

One set looped to the rough stone walls.

Another in the ground.

Shutting my eyes, I listen to the sound of crunching snow. The wizard must be close enough to cast the spell. He's coming towards me with two dozen werewolves. I cannot hear or smell him, but I know he's there. A missing number in the equation. Obvious when searching for him. My sister's with him. I know it deep in my bones.

Weaponless.

Against a wizard who could put me under with a single word.

And an open portal, inches away, that leads to who even knows how many more reinforcements.

Let me in.

I could let them take us. I could let my father have me if he promises to keep Athena safe and leave her child alone. The wizard put a spell on me, so she wouldn't blame me for being captured and doing what I needed to. I could leave her in the forest and use the portal to invade my father's lair. With the element of surprise, I wouldn't need to waste the energy to find and get to him.

I promised her Christmas, though.

One werewolf comes close enough to kick snow onto my bare foot.

I cannot trust King Hozeir. He said the full moon, and here we are, with me in my pajamas, hungover, left on the freezing forest floor, while his minions drag my pregnant sister out of bed. They're trying to steal us across the globe before the pack realizes it. I'd have four months, max, before the king would steal Athena's kid and weaponize him. Four months to kick the throne out from underneath the Werewolf King.

Let me out.

A familiar darkness grows behind my eyelids. I remember this. Silence seeps across my mind like fog off a lake at nightfall. It chills my blood. Claims my bones. Soothes my mind.

I know it's there.

My monster.

Save Athena.

Or die trying, she responds.

My nails grow. Mind searching for the absence. Seeking it in between the bodies of the wolves.

Mine.

I launch off the snow with a growl, diving between the front line of wolves. My body collides with nothing.

The wizard goes flying with my sister caught in his chains.

With a roar mighty enough to shake snow off the trees, I rip the wizard off the ground and off my sister. He yelps, his eyes whiter than brown. Magic gathers around his body. It burns my nostrils.

His hands raise.

I bite one off.

Blood pours out from the tattered skin. His bones crunch between my sharpening teeth. Spitting out the pieces, I throw him into the open portal.

"What are you?" he shouts, holding his hand to his chest. Two wolves launch at me. One misses, and I catch the other by the throat, slamming them into the ground. It yelps underneath me when the weight of my knees shatters its spine.

Muscle climbs over my arms and across the widening expanse of my back. The weight of me crushes my first victim. Its eyes burst, spewing blood over the snow and splashing my thinning lips. The taste of it coats my tongue.

Draws my muzzle forward.

Curves my spine around the werewolf and its exploding heart.

The wizard desperately circles his remaining hand towards me. Light floods from the tips of his fingers as he snatches the portal out of the air.

One wolf launches for it. I grab the scruff of her neck and throw her over my shoulder. Another sneaks behind me, diving towards the rapidly closing gateway. It closes before he gets through.

The smell of blood distracts me. Not my victims or the wizards, but my sister's. A head wound oozes and soaks the snow below her.

Lips peeling back, I snarl at what's left of the king's measly forces. "Run."

Most listen. Those left join their friend, crushed, torn, and bleeding from every possible opening. Long gone is the white snow. Rivers of milky crimson blood wind through the trees and taint the crisp night air.

Reaching forward with sharpened talons, I brush the hair away from Athena's closed eyes. Her breath curls in white clouds against my grizzled face. One of my legs is too long, the other two short. I grunt as I throw her over my shoulder.

My fists bleed from the cutting bite of sharp snow. Wolves move with grace. Lithe bodies in tune with four feet, tail a rudder, ears the guide. I am more gorilla than canine. Back matted with muscle and short fur. Legs bent.

Slow.

Too slow.

She's fighting. Pain hammers into the base of my spine with each step. An ice chip working away at my bone and marrow.

My sister's baby moves against my shoulder, protesting the way I carry her and the cold snow falling against her bare skin as the trees thin.

It's not comfortable for any of us. I hold her feet in one hand and her torso with the other to keep them warm.

A single person stands on the deck of the packhouse. Magic coats his hair. He leans against the pillar, one hand clawed, the other clutching his stomach.

I stop, staring at him across the yard.

Ibrahim steps down into the snow. He whispers his wife's name and then looks at me. Rock-hard sinew. Misplaced bones. Overgrown nails. Jagged teeth cutting into my own lips. "Delilah?"

"She's here," I grunt, sliding Athena off my shoulder and into my arms. Her dark hair fans out across the snow when I lay her down in the safety of the moon and man. "They are still out there."

"I will wake—"

"No. Protect her." Lust bursts across my brow, colouring the night red. "I'll handle this."

My neck stretches when I tilt my head back. The smell of blood and fear complements the fresh mountain air. It's intoxicating. A growl swells in the pit of my stomach. Vibrating within my chest. Shaking loose every invisible chain left from my captor.

I let it loose.

Roaring, I slam my fists into the snow. The sound bounces off the trees, weaving a net for my prey.

Legs snapping, I launch into the forest. The first two wolves yelp when I catch their tails and crack their backs across the trees. Blood and fur cling to the bark as I leave them there to die.

The forest quiets. Bated breath teases my ears.

Clambering up a tree, I smile. "I see you."

The werewolf dies with her plea on a human tongue.

One by one, they die. Blood freezing before it leaves their bodies. Some climb the trees to escape. Another tries to dive through the ice into the river. I punch a hole through the ice and pull them out by their eye sockets. The wolf yelps and whimpers with every agonizing second I spend ripping them from jaw to crown.

"I know you are there," I whisper, throwing the corpse back into the water. Their footsteps head north. Cracking my neck from one side to the other, I embrace the ice's burn. "Ready or not, here I come."

Two feet, two hands thump against the snow and ice. Soon they morph into one fluid movement. Galloping across the forest, winding through the trees, I find my rhythm. The closest thing to freedom I know.

My body collides with the wolf's. It tries to twist beneath me, but I move with it. With one hand on his pulse, the other pressing two fingers under his ears, I snarl at him. "Let me speak to him."

The wolf shifts. Morphing into flesh and blood before my eyes. Human eyes filled with horror mean nothing more to me than an animal's. "I-I don't—"

"Your Pack Link," I hiss, squeezing his throat. The human gasps and pleads as I drag them towards the water's edge. Covering his face with my hand, I slam his head through the ice.

He struggles. Bubbles spiral out of the water.

Rounded nails pull at my flesh.

I growl at him when he comes back up. The skin of his pack members wiggle between my teeth. Their fur coats my tongue.

"Let him see through your eyes. Let him hear with your ears."

The whites of his eyes darken. My whimpering catch freezes. "You're magnificent."

"The moon is not full."

"You dismissed your hunters," the king responds through his servant. His shoulders lift and drop as if on strings. "Is it wrong for me to want to spend Christmas with my family?"

"You come near what's mine, and I will tear you in two." It's not my voice speaking. Delilah's voice twines with mine and pours out as I tighten my hold on the man. "We charge with the full."

This is what we are.

Claws on his chest, and my jaw clamped around his head, I tug. Muscle and bone snap. The king recedes as I chew on his servant's flesh and bone.

CHAPTER 30

Piles of Heads, Piles of Bodies

The whispers quiet when I shut off the shower. The packhouse guest bathrooms have locks on the door, but I was desperate enough to use the communal one on the main floor. I needed to get the pieces of flesh and fur off me before the entire pack saw… somehow, I don't think it matters.

Eyes follow my every move, cautious and curious, from the shower to the mirror. My hair needs to be cut. It's been months since I trimmed it and it shows. I'd like to believe that's what they're talking about. The first swig of mouthwash burns my eyes, but not the taste of death from my tongue.

"Fitz, you're on cleanup," Paisley announces, poking her head into the bathroom. She sucks her lips in when she sees me there, aggressively brushing my teeth. "Don't you all have somewhere to be?"

"Gamma's orders," 'Fitz' states, smacking one of the other she-wolfs on the back. They all file out of the room past a humming Paisley, but the Delta pauses at the door to cast a backward glance at me. A flush of red washes out her freckles. "Call if you need help."

"You're the one who fell asleep on duty." Mona shoves the tall woman aside with her shoulder when she enters the bathroom. Dutifully ignoring Fitz's dirty look, she jumps onto the counter beside me. "Killian's got a shower spa with multiple heads."

"Good for him."

'Cleanup'. The wolves woke up to a bloodbath. One of the sentries said they came face-to-face with a decapitated wolf. Body parts litter their beloved forest. Piles of heads. Piles of bodies.

My monster's messed-up Christmas gift.

I woke up wrapped in bloody fur. The beast deposited me into the body of a wolf it eviscerated. Half-dressed, wrapped in intestines, I made my way back to the packhouse. Whatever happened. Whatever it did. It took my everything.

I walked into a house brimming with concerned werewolves. The sentries pulled back. Ibrahim tried to keep everyone calm, but they were ready for a full invasion. My arrival, dramatized with the blood of a foreign wolf soaking every inch of my skin, caused enough outcry to hurt my head.

Mona offers me a paper towel, narrowing her eyes. "You really don't remember?"

Gagging, I lean over the sink. A ball of fur *splats* out of my mouth into the basin. Paisley inches closer and peers at it, her jaw dropping. "That's disgusting."

"I don't remember anything after the wizard cast a spell on me."

Details wait for me, accompanied by a blinding headache. I was outnumbered, unarmed, in front of an open portal, and Athena's life was at risk. I have no idea if it stripped the Cloak and left the Sacrament forgotten and undetectable in the forest. The one thing I remember with perfect clarity is speaking to my father. He sounded proud. *Pleased.*

"You're raging."

"He tried to ruin *Christmas*," I whine, rolling my eyes. Mona scoffs while Paisley grabs a cleaning bucket and enters the shower stall I tried my best to rinse out. "Did Killian tell you to watch me?"

"Athena. Like you said, it's Christmas."

"We haven't opened presents yet."

"And we won't until tomorrow. Alpha's orders." Mona leans back, assessing my reaction with amused eyes. Winding floss around my middle finger, I offer her a smile and ferociously attack my teeth. Another day lost to this ridiculous promise. I should've gone into the portal and used the monster to wreak havoc in their territory. Last time, I had the magic of the witch and my rage to replenish my strength. Now, I am a husk filled with blood and fur. "Would you like to see what you did?"

Paisley's head pops out of the shower. "Mona!"

She pulls out her phone and brings up the footage from the trail cameras. A creature swings from one tree to another with a roar. It crawls up towards a person cowering between a coupling of branches. The human opens her mouth to scream but she cannot make a noise when the beast mangles her larynx.

"I've never seen anything like it," Mona muses, eyebrows raised. She flips to another video; in this one, the hulking figure cracks a werewolf's head into two pieces. "I don't know what that is."

"Bigfoot's white cousin."

"She's deleting it," Paisley says from the stall. She appears when Mona doesn't say anything. The way they stare at one another annoys me more than the slippery flesh evading my floss. "Now."

"I *was.* You might be Gamma, but don't start thinking you can—"

I snatch the phone from her hand, snap it over the counter, and throw the two pieces into the garbage. My hands shake around the zipper of my toiletries bag. "Would you like to see it?"

Mona cocks her head to the side, eyes sparking. The fire snaps and cracks when I lunge forward with a dramatized snarl. "Yes."

"Keep talking; it likes to play," I mutter, marching out of the bathroom in my towel. Still bickering, they follow me. Deltas gawk at me as I run up the very public staircase. Worse yet, Athena waits beside my guest room with a frown. "Send them away."

"She's overwhelmed," Athena whispers to them. Sighing, I search my bag for something comfortable to sleep in. I spent an hour in the shower scrubbing my skin raw. The drain clogged with all the hair I pulled out. "Iba said you saved me again."

He's seen the monster before, but Killian… he must've seen the footage. I wonder if he's thanking God for my restraint now. *Beg me for it.* I want to be angry, but I only feel exhausted. Desperate for the smell of him and the softness of his sheets and the safety of his arms.

"I don't know."

She follows me into my room with dumb and dumber right on her heels. "You cannot shift on demand?"

"Bad things happen when I do," I snap, jerking my head back at her shocked expression. The door is open. I am naked. Scabs cover my bare body, healing slower than normal because I have nothing left. Athena tries not to look, but her eyes drop to my hands where I scrubbed them to the bone. "Leave please."

"That must be really scary," she whispers, removing her long cardigan. The fabric rubs all wrong against my bare skin. "You need food. Then a nap. It's Biblical."

"Elijah napped first."

"If you go out like that, Killian's going to lose his mind," Mona warns, staring pointedly at my legs. The cardigan might be long, but it's clear I have nothing on underneath. "You can borrow one of my satin sets, but if you get blood on—"

"Keep it."

I flee the room and my sister's suffocatingly kind eyes. I single-handedly tore two dozen wolves apart and she's acting like I'm a valiant knight. Whispers follow me down the hall. For an Alpha, Killian doesn't take security seriously. Isn't the Alpha's wing supposed to be mysterious and forbidden?

I close his door behind me and drop my head against it. Blood drives against my brain in quick thrusts. Eyes fall on me. Two thin pieces of glass separates me from the full power of his stare.

"Are you okay?"

"Do I look okay?"

Killian closes his laptop without a word. In one graceful move, he puts the laptop onto his desk and rises from the chaise. I walk over to his bed as he disappears into another room. When he comes back out, there's a t-shirt in his hands. Gratitude wells up in my eyes. Slipping the scratchy fabric of Athena's cardigan off my raw arms, I face him.

Killian stares at my face the entire time he bunches the t-shirt around his wrists. "Arms up."

I follow wordlessly, a tear falling when the soft fabric coasts down my skin. Brushing past him, I climb into the impeccably made bed. Killian removes the decorative throw pillows and stacks them at the foot of his bed. Darkness waits for me, beckoning me in, but I'm too scared to go.

"I don't want this," I whisper it to the abyss. Another tear burns down my cheek when Killian crowds my vision. He slides into the bed, barefoot but fully clothed, and draws my head onto his upper thigh. "I don't want this responsibility. I want to be selfish."

I had the upper hand in that battle. Those wolves didn't know what to do with something like me. They were running. Hiding. Now King Hozeir knows what I am. He knows I am coming. He's waiting for me.

"He won't come here again. He's not searching for me anymore," I reassure him. Killian brushes his fingers through my wet hair, arranging it across his pillow. He whispers something too quiet for me to hear, but it's tender enough for me to understand the meaning.

Outside, the cleaning crew whispers and speculates, but in here, in his arms, I choose silence. It lasts for only a moment before the noise in my head becomes louder than what's outside. Too many options, too few choices, and never enough time. I know what the wolves will say; I know what Mona's thinking… Killian can't think it too.

"I cannot control it. I cannot use it to help us."

"I wouldn't ask you to."

"Others will, others do." On paper, having a hybrid on the hunter's side of the war is an advantage. Fight fire with fire. The problem is: fire doesn't discriminate. It burns everything in its path, the old, dead brush, and the new, growing saplings. My monster didn't kill Athena, but it might not know the difference between a Garity and a Hielander. "Nattalius tried to imply *I* owed something to the humans. For someone who hates me, he really overestimates my strength. I cannot protect them. I cannot protect myself."

"He knows you are worth two of him."

"I want a future."

"Fight for one."

"Did you miss the part where I said I'm not strong enough?"

"You won the first battle. You need to rest up for the next." He squeezes the back of my neck and drags his fingers, applying the perfect pressure across my exposed temple. Goosebumps spread across my arms and pull me closer. I throw a leg over his calves and wrap an arm around his thigh. "You forget the Lord of Hosts clears the way for his warriors."

"I—"

"Save your fight, *a chuisle*." Before I can ask what that means, Killian, the biggest baddest Alpha born in centuries, opens his mouth and sings. The song reminds me of something I heard in church a long time ago, but I cannot wade through my exhausted mind to reach the memories. They fade into the dark as I do.

"Paisley says I have to ask if I can sit on your lap," Sloane declares with the enthusiasm of a prisoner on death row. Pale, freckle-covered hands present me with an oddly shaped blob covered in homemade wrapping paper. Considering I drove the Gammas (of whom my sister is now an honourary member) to the craft store to buy the orphans Christmas crafts, I know there's a miniature Christmas tree made of popsicle sticks, covered in clay ornaments, within. "I made you something."

"This is incredible."

She flushes with pleasure when I gush and closely inspect the tree. The ornaments range from egg to pear-shaped, though none of them are quite circular enough. Cracks line the brittle surfaces, but she filled them with glue and gold glitter. Glitter that falls onto the fleece leggings I forced on after waking up from my twenty-two-hour nap.

"Athena said you didn't have a tree at your house. Now you do."

"That's very considerate." I've spent the entire holiday season at the packhouse. Sleeping among the wolves… something I thought I'd die before doing. "It's the perfect size to put on the dash of my car. Then I can keep it with me all the time."

"I like that idea."

"I was going to give you a gift, but this is so amazing! How am I supposed to compete?"

With wide eyes and a cheery smile, she snatches the tree back. Killian watches from the other side of the large living room with a smile meant for my eyes only. My heart lurches painfully as he hands the orphans one gift each. Some of the wolves celebrate with their own family before coming to the packhouse. The single ones, without close families, join the Alpha and his family for all holidays.

I can hardly hear Sloane who stands less than a foot from me, because the chatter, laughter, and gleeful screams threaten to blow the roof off the house. Athena reads one of the orphan's new books with them, her eyes meeting mine when Sloane dives into my lap.

"I want my gift—please."

"It's under the tree," I whisper, pointing to the pink peeking out from behind the branches of the huge Christmas tree. She springs to her feet and climbs over the people strewn across the floor. Enthusiasm bleeds out of her, and she waits a moment before tugging desperately on Ibrahim's sleeve. He searches the tree for the present before meeting my eyes with an expression I am beginning to recognize as exasperation. "The pink one, Iba."

Sloane's friends crawl closer with wide eyes as he struggles to unearth the forty-pound box. A couple of them offer to help her unwrap it when he finally gets it out and plants the box in the middle of the room. Pink ribbons meet in a perfect bow on the top, and Sloane pulls them away with reverence.

The haste returns in full, empowering her to tear the wrapping paper apart. A finger brushes the back of my neck, tickling the hairs gathered there. Leaning into Killian's touch, I smirk at Mona who fends off the crowd with an empty cardboard box.

"Is there a pony in there?"

"Are you jealous?" His lips twitch at my response, distracting me from my girl. When she unearths a face painting kit the size of her body, everyone goes silent. Colouring books and markers follow. When she reaches the canvas and water colours, she starts tearing up. "They can all share."

He snorts when Sloane ditches the gift to grin at me. The light in her eyes, her fuzzy Christmas pjs, the way she fights against mounds of wrapping paper to get back to me—she's the cutest kid I've ever seen. "You'll bite anyone who tries to touch her stuff."

"Thank you, Delilah!"

Sloane wraps her arms around my neck with surprising strength. The smell of synthetic strawberries and oatmeal clings to her ratty blond hair. Next gift: a new hairbrush and leave-in conditioner. Paisley will have to pick it up for me. "Go play with your gifts."

"We will take care of her until you come back."

Adding Sloane to the emergency plan will add all kinds of complications but they might be worth it. I can't save everyone, but maybe I can save her. *And leave her friends to die? So, she can carry that guilt for the rest of her life without you there to blame?*

Her friends compete to share their requests the fastest: a couple want to be winter fairies, another wants a snowman, and a toddler points to his nose and keeps saying 'red'. Some of the older kids come closer and ask to see her new gifts, including the mean older girl who I threatened to kill this summer. Our eyes meet, and she continues forward when I nod my head.

I cannot protect Sloane any more than I can protect myself. I can't even bring myself to look at Killian when I speak. "You're setting yourself up for disappointment."

A small box invades my vision. His eyes crinkle in the way I love most when I gape at him. "It's not a ring."

Ignoring my drumming heart, I pull the box out of his hand. Eight months, two nights in his bed, a hundred conversations, charged eye contact, fleeting touches and he mentions a ring.

It doesn't scare me like it should.

"Am I supposed to know what this is?"

Smiling, he unearths the small vial from a swath of silk. Red liquid swishes within, opaque enough to appear black in the dark, but see-through when I hold it up to the light. "Paisley said you want a red tattoo."

"A big red tattoo." Emotion gathers in the back of my throat like a cough. When I mentioned wanting a red piece to Paisley during our daddy issues session, I didn't expect her to pass on that information. The snake on my Companion band has roses for eyes, and there are bloody footprints behind the puma. A rose winds around one of my middle fingers and others blossom between the shattered glass and grandfather clock on my thigh. There's a bit of red everywhere, but not one dedicated to my favourite colour. "I have been debating the style. It's between realism or a Japanese style, but I don't want a dragon or snake."

He slips out a folded piece of paper, revealing the sketch Paisley must've drawn. I knew she was talented after seeing Mona's spine piece, but this is a different style than what I've seen. Line work and shading work to mesh the styles together. "You have an owl for Athena and a puma for your Companions."

"And a wolf… for Sloane?"

Lips twitching, he stands. "Exactly."

"I didn't get you a gift."

"You getting this tattoo is my gift."

"Because she told you I want a sternum piece?" At his furrowed brows, I run a finger along the band of my bralette beneath my shirt. Killian looks anywhere but at me when he clicks his tongue. "I might let you—"

"Stop."

He walks away at my snicker, shaking his head like he doesn't know what to do with me. A little voice tells me he knows *exactly* what he'd do with me.

CHAPTER 31

It's not You, It's Me

I'm a coward.

Always have been, always will be. The dark scared me until I realized I was the scariest thing in it. On my hike back to Imperio, I considered letting Nattalius off the hook and pretending nothing ever happened. I used to get drunk and/or high between nursing Athena back to health after her career-ending injury. How many jobs did I take to avoid going back to Witchhill and the heartache waiting for me here?

The prime example of my cowardice? Sneaking out of the packhouse at three in the morning after the final heartbeat slowed.

I slip out of bed with a burning chest. Paisley took half the day to finish my newest tattoo. The tight band of my sports bra presses against the second skin. Getting a tattoo before marching into my last fight might've been a poor idea.

Dead is dead. New tattoo or not.

The door to my guest room silently swings open. I made sure to tape the latch down last night. Hooking my thumbs into the straps of my backpack, I glance at Killian's door. He breathes deeply on the other side, his arm stretched over the space I should be taking up. We're in tune with each other. More now than ever.

Heartburn sends acid up the back of my throat and pounds against the cage of my ribs. I rub it away and force myself down the stairs, away from him. The front door opens with a quiet hiss, allowing wind and snow to invade the warmth of the packhouse. I slide through the small crack and close it in the same movement.

Killian leaves the porchlight on all hours of the day in case anyone needs him. It's the one light shining in the dark and ceaseless snowy night. My boots scuff too loudly on the shoveled porch. Ice crystals crunch when I put too much weight onto one foot. Sneaking out was once a skill I could put on my resume.

"This is your idea of a proper goodbye?"

Clenching my fists, I glance at Athena. A piece of paper flutters in the wind between her index and middle finger. I promised a goodbye. She didn't stipulate it needed to be in person. Writing 'there is only one solution, αντίο' on a napkin and slipping it under her door when they both fell asleep fulfilled my obligation.

The guilt wells back up with the tears in her eyes. "Did you leave a note for Killian too? Pais? Sloane? What about their goodbyes?"

"I promised you, Thea. No one else."

"You are marching to your death and thought a note would be enough?"

"You think I'm braver than I am." She rolls her eyes, banishing the tears, and stands. The little monster has given her an attitude. "I do not want to look you in the eyes and say goodbye. I can't."

"Then don't."

I throw my hands out, fingers soaked by the snow and wind. Everyone wants something from me. It's not enough for any of them. I'm not enough. "It's me or the baby. And I'm the one old enough to understand that sacrifice."

"There doesn't need to be a sacrifice!"

"It's not your choice, Athena."

"No, you've made that clear. Why don't I get a choice? Why do you get to protect me, but I don't get to protect you? I'm an adult, Delilah. I'm strong too—"

"I gave you those scars," I snap, gesturing at her face. Warm yellow light chases the shadows away from the thin white lines. "You were two years old and, just like every other two-year-old, you thought the world and everyone in it lived to serve you. I was enraptured with you until I realized that, as an older sister, I was expected to share—and you didn't even know what sharing meant. Mom and Dad kept telling me 'she's too young to get it, you have to show her'. They kept drilling it into my head that 'a good big sister sets a good example', but it was my first time being a sister, and I didn't know how to do that. All I knew was nothing was mine—it was ours, and Dad wasn't really ours anyway."

"Del."

"We went out on a hike. Dad and Mom argued about which route to take, and they got a little lost. You started complaining about your feet hurting and mine were hurting too, so I complained. I asked to sit on Dad's shoulders, and he refused. He said you were younger and maybe we could take turns, but I didn't want to take turns—"

"You were five."

"I attacked you."

"Was it the first time?"

Mouth flapping, I throw my hands up again. "That's not an excuse."

"Mom and Dad should've taught you how to handle your emotions." She cups my face in her clammy hands, eyebrows knitting in the middle. "You think because you hurt me as a kid that you need to sacrifice yourself for me? You think because your emotions sometimes come with claws and fangs that you're a monster?"

"That's the definition of a monster."

"There is no definition of a monster. It's a word created by humans to characterize things that scare them, that they don't understand. The future is a monster. Death is a monster. You are not." Warmth explodes across my chest when she pulls me in. Rubbing the space between my shoulder blades, Athena forces me to rock with her. Being held still feels foreign. After shifting for the first time, I kept everyone at a distance. Mom and Dad told everyone, including Athena, that a wild animal on the trail attacked her.

That same week at the grocery store, I heard one of the neighbours discussing what vets do to animals who attack people. For a month straight, I dreamt of being put down. I imagined Ingrid would do it because she never liked me. Every night, I begged God for forgiveness, and every day, I tried to be 'good'.

"If you're doing this because you think you need to atone, stop. Please. Jesus paid the price for our sins already. I want you."

Fifteen years of compounded guilt pulls my stomach into my toes. She loves me in ways I have never deserved, now more than ever. How dare she? How dare they? The burn in my chest explodes, melting skin into muscle and muscle into bone. Tattoos. Hugs. Laughter. Stories. Strawberries. Coffee. Baileys.

"I know it's not fair to ask you to stay, but please."

"It's not about atonement." Her head shakes against mine. Tightening my hold, I press my nose into her neck. This is what I cannot do. My heart's going to give out. "You trust me?"

"With my life."

"If I don't do this, someone else will."

"Let them do it. Leave them to their wars and let's all hide."

"It's our war." I hesitantly place a hand over her bulging stomach. The child within jumps in response, as if ready to pick up his arms. "I'm the only one who can fight it."

She sobs and traps one of my hands against him. "Please."

"You'll forgive me." Her arms tighten to the point of choking me. Whispering it again underneath my breath, I squeeze her one last time. "You have to forgive me if we are going to see each other again."

"*Στο καλό.*"

I was never one for goodbyes. I cannot remember if I ever said that word to my parents. "*Αντίο, χαρά μου.*"

Leaving her on the porch, with her tears freezing my shoulders, and mine freezing my heart, I run into the woods. There's only one way to protect them.

CHAPTER 32

So You Want to Start a War

"Can I get you anything?"

I doubt the flight attendant would know what to do with himself if I said, 'World peace and the erasure of racism', so I stay silent. The miniature bottles of whiskey from in-flight bars give me an irreplaceable kind of glee, but I need to be sober for what I'm about to do.

Unfortunately.

He moves on, and I manage not to growl at my seat companion for drinking without me. The rest of the fourteen-hour flight pulls me in and out of consciousness. Our rocky landing chases off the last of my stupor.

An angry woman cusses me out for taking too long to grab my bag. One foul look has her slinking back into her seat. I've yet to hurt a human with my supernatural abilities, but I have four days—including today—before I'm supposed to be making resolutions to be a better person.

The airport savours strongly of tears and heartache. Unlike back home, people mind their business. No forced smiles. No well-wishing. I trudge out of the dim hall and into the hallways surrounded by sleek glass and silver frames. Sunlight bathes the tarmac as it crawls over the horizon. With my bag on my back, I head towards the back of the airport.

A terminal hides between two bathrooms, marked by hands cradling an anatomically correct heart. Fishing through my favourite leather jacket, I remove the card inside. Shaped like a vertical doorhandle, a light begins to flash. I scan the halls for the last time before swiping the card through the groove.

"Welcome, Mr. Kartal. Distinction SA847."

The door swings open, revealing a network of cubicles and the half-dead interns who man them. I step through the portal and right into Nattalius' eyeline. Halfway through a sentence, he stands and throws a thick file onto his desk. His co-workers gape when he chases me across the office. "I knew it."

"Thank you." Flicking the card at his head, I slip out of the building and into the next. He calls my name, his hastened steps eating up the distance between us until he reaches my side. "Go back to your desk."

"What are you doing?"

"None of your business."

"You used my badge to get into Imperio without passing through customs," he seethes, trying to grab my shoulder. Ducking out of his grip, I rush into the public area of the Senate building. He slicks his hair back, but it flies in different directions when he sprints to cut me off. "You cannot touch it."

"Touch what?" I question, glancing over his shoulder. The Horn, encased in glass, sits safely behind his back. Rolling my eyes, I adjust the strap on my shoulder. "I'm not declaring war. Calm down."

"Why are you here?"

"It's not your problem anymore, Nat. You made sure about that. Go back to your office and keep schmoozing. I know how much you want to be the Imperium's Assistant—"

"I lost out to Joslyn because I was too busy trying to save our world from destruction."

"Your world," I whisper, pointing at the hunters dressed like him, watching us. They gossip and leer, shocked at the way I poke his chest with my gaudy nails. "Stop drawing attention to me."

"Tell me what you're doing."

"What I have to." I wish I could shove past him, so I do the next best thing by shoving into two others. Nattalius watches with his hands on his hips as I run to the second level of the Senate building. Imperium Hunters stand guard on both sides of every door on this level. They watch me with wary eyes when I bypass the public sector.

My phone starts ringing with Catarina's ringtone. What a tattletale. Declining her phone call, I open my chat with Ingrid. **It's time.**

Thick marble pillars give way to a large chamber. Joslyn Gonzalez, Nattalius' long-time rival and former boss, sits behind a computer with a bored expression on her face. When she glances up at me, her entire face transforms. "Delilah. What are you doing back in Imperio?"

"I need to report a Hybrid."

CHAPTER 33

Bet You Didn't See That Coming

I took a gamble choosing the Five, but I wanted less of an audience. However, cutting out the middleman of the Legionnaires and Nattalius' mother, who would tell him everything just to complain about me, may not have been my brightest idea.

The guards eye me where I stand unnaturally still. It's taking all my restraint not to pace or rub my clammy hands on my pants. A camera whirs behind my back, zooming in on me for the umpteenth time. Either they are going to accept an audience with me in the next ten minutes, or I'm going to leave. Too many people have seen me already.

Joslyn comes out of the court room shaking her head. Without a word, she scurries past the guards and disappears around the corner. One of the guards and I make eye contact between watching her hasty exit and the aimless swinging of the chamber's double doors. She raises one immaculate eyebrow and adjusts her grip on the AR strapped across her chest.

"Enter."

Rolling my eyes, I step into the domed room. The Imperium's court doesn't have a place for a jury or record-keeper. Five average-looking men sit on the grand wooden bench and watch me kick the door closed with my muddy boots. Call me petulant or suicidal but looking into Philip Christos the seventh's face makes my blood boil.

He looks like Dad. All golden skin, bright eyes, and shiny hair. Despite being well over one-hundred, he's wrinkle-free and ninety percent muscle. A vein pulses in his jaw when I refuse to back down from his baleful stare.

"What are you doing here, girl?" Nattalius' grandfather has a habit of calling every woman 'girl'. He manages to make the statement sound like a slight. Peeling my eyes off my great-grandfather, I offer a pained smile.

"Did Joslyn not tell you?"

Philip's the first one to crack. "Report your hybrid and be done with it."

"As you already know from your records, and have likely guessed, my sister is mated to a werewolf. They're expecting."

After hours spent on a cramped plane, I'm grateful to finally stand, but they should have chairs in here. Something other than the monstrosity of a bench and their gold-backed seats. In my search for one, I find the mural painted onto the rounded walls. The Hunter Queen stands on a mountain of dead Otherworlders with her flaming Sword in one hand, the Horn in the other at her side, and the Crown on her head, bathing her in multi-coloured blood.

What a safe place this must be for the Otherworlders who come to report real crimes.

"You came to report your own kin?" Stefan Antes, Ingrid's second cousin, stares down at me with his lip curled. Across from him, Laurent and Hauser whisper to each other. While there is no head to the Imperium, Eren Kartal sits an inch or two higher from the others, smack dab in the middle. When he raises his hand, they all go quiet.

"I underestimated you. My daughter told me you were softened by the humans." Eren leans back into his seat, sparing at glance at Philip. He's too busy glaring at me to notice. For a man who wishes to pretend I don't exist, he's got a lot of feeling in my dad's eyes. "Has she come in with you? We are lenient to those who turn themselves in."

"It's quicker for them to get rid of it themselves. If they send proof of the cleanse and preventative surgery, we do not inflict penalty," Louis Laurent offers, waving a hand. The door opens behind me without a sound. "Joslyn will show you the process—"

"She's keeping the baby."

The door *slams* right back into place, creating a breeze that flutters my flyaways and interrupts the staring contest I'm having with my grandfather. One of his eyes begins to twitch, just like my dad's used to, and despite the gravity of the situation, I smile. Kristof Hauser clears his throat, stands to his feet, and clasps his hands behind his back. "Under the law—"

"Save your spiel. I'm fully aware of what the law says. You guys hammer that into our brains in Seminary." When he tries to continue, I reach one hand out to mimic shutting his mouth for him. Philip's face purples more and more as I toss my backpack onto the ground. "Just as you knew it was my sister I came to report, you know I have the Crown in my possession."

"Are you trying to threaten the Imperium?" Stefan questions, blinking incredulously. He leans across Philip to stare at Kristof on the other end. "When was the last time we were threatened?"

"Guards!" Eren Kartal shouts, standing. He presses his hands over his ears, which is comical enough to widen the smirk on my face. "Seize that bag."

"I don't have it here, old man. I gave clear instructions to a trusted individual to deliver the Crown to King Hozeir if you do not agree to my terms."

He rocks back, the chair squeaking when it slides over the wood. Two guards surge inside—the first grabs me, and the second takes the bag. I don't fight the woman pinning back my arms. "Send for my grandson and Catarina Guererro."

"Did you miss the part where I said *trusted*? Nattalius is a snake, much like the rest of your family. Cat… she doesn't need to be part of this. If you would stop with the dramatics and calm down, we might be able to get somewhere without blowing my cover."

"Your cover?"

He chokes on the words. Ripping my arms out of the guard's, I walk back to the door and force it shut. The guards are two too many, but it's too late now. "King Hozeir wants to unite the Otherworlders, including hunters, who believe in his mission. You know as well as I do there are those in Imperio who agree with Otherworlder rights."

Laurent, red-faced and spluttering, pipes in. "None of which we would allow into this building."

"Are you sure?" I question, raising an eyebrow. I glance pointedly at the guards who glare at me in turn. "That's beside the point. King Hozeir has been building an army for the last twenty years with one goal: to take the five of you off your cushy seats and put himself in them."

"What is your point?" Laurent demands.

"My father's been searching for me since my infancy. He wants to trust me. He wants me to help him take over the world." The guard inspecting my bag throws it back onto the floor, the clothes and weapons spilling out of it. He shakes his head when Eren raises an eyebrow. "If I present myself to him and say I've had a change of heart, he'll let his guard down. I could kill him properly this time."

Eren inches forward, his hands crawling over the end of the bench. "You know where he is?"

Nattalius either didn't show them the map we put together in November, or our guesses were completely off… and it can't be the latter, so it must be the former.

"How?"

Glancing at Laurent, I shrug. "He made a mistake."

I got a good whiff when the wizard opened a portal right into the heart of my father's dungeon. Hunters, hybrids, Otherworlders of every race. Ash and orchids clung to the dusty footprints on the stone corridor. The wizard's breath still travelled in white swirls inside the well-lit dungeon. The metal bars, confining my father's captives, were shoved into crudely carved rock.

"You want us to pardon your sister and her hybrid for services rendered?" Eren says each word like he cannot believe he's hearing them.

"I want the Imperium to pardon and protect her from the moment I leave this room to its end."

"The Imperium will never die."

"Precisely." I smile at Eren the way my monster does. He takes a seat again and drums his fingers on the armrest. The others on his flank inch closer to discuss the offer among themselves privately, but there's no privacy in this room.

"If we allow this girl, we open the door for others," Louis whispers, shaking his head. "A *hybrid* is trying to force us to grant leniency to another one of its kind. This creature has been hiding from us for how long? Hiding under her great uncle's name and learning the Imperium's weaknesses from our own teachers? How do we know she is not already allied to Hozeir? How do we know she hasn't created hundreds more like her?"

"You know the legitimacy of my life. You may not have been the one to grant my mother pardon, but my birth was registered in your books."

"And yet she did not stay long enough to fulfill her obligations," Kristof counters, one eyebrow raised. He steps away from the others and unearths a file from his side of the bench. "She was required to bring you in for preven—"

"Call it sterilization. You and I both know that's what it is"

"She broke our laws."

"Technically, the baby will only be a werewolf when it is born," I argue.

"Werenters do not have the same liberty as winters or vanters, they are Awakened as soon as their family shifts. It's an inevitability with those wild beasts."

It was worth a shot.

"If you are awarded an exception, nothing stops other hybrids from asking the same," Louis continues, steepling his hands. They give up on their little huddle and go back to their places spread over the bench. My great-grandfather stares above my head at the bloodied queen painted onto the wall like he's begging for her to return and rid them of me. "Your sister knew the consequences."

"As do you if you turn me away. You revealed your hand already—you do not know where King Hozeir is. He's got every Sacrament except for the Crown and Horn. Maybe he's already here, in this room, creeping up behind you."

Kristof falls for it, twisting around with a knife in hand. The guards surge forward to protect the Imperium as I laugh.

"And if you fail to kill your father?" Eren demands, a storm raging across his face. He cuts a glance to my great-grandfather, but Philip's squeezing the life out of a crystal glass. "You expect us to protect her and her little Otherworlder then?"

"If I fail to kill my father, you will have more important things to focus on than punishing my sister for not using birth control."

"No. I think we will find your sister and her husband, remove the parasite, and put down the dog. You'll be more than willing to supply us with your father's location and the Crown after a round—"

"I am a Christos. They have a proud legacy in these halls, in the fight against evil, and I will continue it whether I have your permission or not. Your protection of my sister and her offspring is not a necessity; it is a gift to yo—"

Philip slaps both palms on the bench, standing in all his giant glory. He points a meaty finger at my head with a face so red a tomato would be jealous. "You are not a Christos! Our blood does not run in your veins."

"And yet here I am. Delilah Christos at your service."

"How dare you—"

"You interrupted her threat," Eren states, his shoulders heaving. Though I cannot see the collar around Philip's neck, I know Nattalius' grandfather holds the leash. "Your desperate plea is a gift to us?"

"You've mistaken me, Eren. This is neither desperation nor a plea. I come here to offer an olive branch." By now, Ingrid should have used a portal and Catarina's keycard to get into Imperio. They *should* be halfway to Ponte de Lima. If Nattalius hasn't told the Imperium about the places my father might be hiding, he might not tell them about Catarina's second home. Shoving my hands into my pockets, I flash my best Christos smile. "I am going to my father. I am going to kill him. Your response either guarantees my participation in the raid to dispel his forces or the passing of his throne to me."

"And you dare call yourself a C—"

"Fight against *evil,* papa. If you think sitting on this bench, demanding others to do your dirty work and playing God, makes you good, you've got another thing coming."

"You want the throne—"

"No. I want my sister, her husband, and her baby to be safe. I want to cruise with the top down along country roads, only checking over my shoulder for other vehicles. I want to be left alone. I want them to be left alone." Resentment comes naturally to me and my monster, but it's going to require a lot more than grandparental neglect to make me take my father's crown. To be the King of Wolves, you need to be a werewolf. "If the only way I can make that happen is by becoming your worst nightmare and tearing Imperio down, brick by brick, I will."

"The 'baby' is in danger with or without us. Your father collects hybrids."

"Let me worry about him."

"You kill the king, we pardon and protect your sister Athena, her husband Ibrahim, and the child currently in her womb."

"Meaning you will eliminate any*one* or any*thing* who tries to hurt them." The Imperium's always been more lenient on hunter hybrids anyway. I don't know whether Athena's little one will be more monster or man, but they'll have the chance to find out. I swear it on my grave. "As long as the Imperium reigns."

"What makes you so sure Hozeir will trust you?" Louis scoffs, his eyes boring into the side of Eren's head. He commands one of the guards to go fetch 'Miss Gonzalez' and clasps his hands in his lap. "You have evaded him for fifteen years. You were seen coming in here. You'll be killed as soon as you show your face."

"You'll have to give him a reason."

EPILOGUE

Every muscle in my body cries as I try to haul myself up onto another ledge. Wind whips around me, adding to the burn in my eyes and throat. The fabric wrapped around my wrist makes a loud *splat* when I slap it against the rock. Pain chases off the vertigo. *Almost there, almost there, almost there.*

Rolling onto the ledge, I drop my head. Darkness steals me away from the Alps. Stars dot my vision.

Of all the stupid plans and schemes.

I don't see you coming up with something better.

The beast crawls back into its corner when I force my knees underneath me. My kneecap is already healing. Enough to let me put some weight on my leg. I use the wall to prop myself up, lungs aching, teeth chattering. Blood soaks me from head to toe, marking my entrance into the network of caves.

Cheap cologne propels me forward, leading me to my first torch. I grip it with the hand I still have, trying not to fall over.

A man speaks to me in a language I vaguely recognize. He rushes forward when my knees buckle. Strong arms wrap around my body, and in the haze of blood and pain, I briefly wonder if Killian found me.

"Leave me."

"You are safe now," the man promises, lifting me off my broken foot. He hoists me up and into his arms like a princess, protecting me from the growing crowd of onlookers. "Call the king."

"She's not one of ou—"

"Shut it," a she-wolf snaps, touching either side of my swollen cheeks with her hands. Her face blurs in and out of focus as I am laid down on the cold floor. "We help our kind."

"She's a hunter."

"She's a wolf."

"She's both," the man growls, sweeping my hair out of my face. A finger prods the place where my great-grandfather severed my hand. Nauseated, I push the werewolf's face out of mine and vomit onto the stone. "Where's Jacob?"

"What is all this commotion?"

Goosebumps skitter up my arms at his voice. A shadow spreads across my vision, replacing the wolves who eagerly back away. I expected him to be larger than life, but he's shorter than the men I've spent time with over these last few months. Muscle climbs on top of other muscle along his compact frame. The tartan slung over one shoulder reveals two sides of his thick chest and a blanket of dark hair. Long golden-brown hair flows over his shoulders, identical to mine.

The similarities end with his eyes. Bright green. Distinctly unhuman.

King Hozeir's all monster, no man.

"Hi daddy."

New year, new me.

Acknowledgments

Firstly, I want to acknowledge Mrs. Plaum who this book is dedicated to. As mentioned, she was my fourth-grade teacher and the one who first suggested I become an author. What I didn't mention is her terminal diagnosis and that 50% of the proceeds on all sales of this book will go towards a cause of her choosing: the Stollery Children's Hospital in Edmonton, Alberta, Canada. It didn't surprise me when Mrs. Plaum chose the Stollery as her cause, because she has dedicated her life to bettering those of the children in her care. I am a better woman for knowing her, and I pray that the donations made in her name will offer opportunities to thousands more children.

Secondly, I want to acknowledge you, dear reader. Mrs. Plaum gave me this dream, but it is only made possible by you. Your buying the books. Your reading the books. Your reviews. Your recommendations. If it wasn't for you, and for her, I wouldn't be who I am. Thank you for letting me live this dream as long as I have.

Thirdly, I need to acknowledge my family. Mom for pestering me to get book 2 into your hands (it should be in them tomorrow, July 15th). Dad for being proud of me from the first word written to my book being on shelves beside your favourite authors. My siblings for always checking in and seeing how I'm doing and encouraging me. Especially to Un for supporting me in literally every way. K for keeping me grounded.

Fourthly, a huge thank you to my editor Eden, for your encouragement, enjoyment, and engagement. Your comments, whether you thought they were professional or not, made editing—which is sometimes painful—a breeze. One more masterpiece to go!

Fifthly (is this even a word? It doesn't look like a word), to Jessica who designed the beautiful cover for this novel. There were a handful of designers who refused to touch a second book, but you were willing and more than that you exceeded my every expectation. Thank you for this work of art!

Sixthly (I hate this 'word' too), and what should perhaps have been firstly, I want to acknowledge my Heavenly Father who created my mind and my capacity for imagination and who fills my dreams with worlds I probably would never think to create on my own. You are the og dad and I pray your unconditional love, and delight would be clear to all those who touch this book. Thank you for being χαρά μου.

About the Author

Ashley Godschild began telling stories when she was three years old to anyone who would listen. Her family, Soccer Moms, poor, unsuspecting cashiers at Superstore so she could get free suckers… she finished her first actual novel at twelve years old and then proceeded to erase it all and start again. By the age of sixteen, she'd finished over thirty novels and had an agent actively pursuing her and that original story she'd gotten down on paper. Instead of publishing and going down the traditional route with the novel that made her an author, she deleted everything she'd ever written and started all over again. Now, she has over 200 books planned (87 different series') and the list continues to grow.

Ashley enjoys rewatching the same three shows (Gossip Girl, House, Criminal Minds), spending time with her family, and can be lured out of her home in Canada with the promise of either a sweet treat or a good book. *The Predator and The Prey* is her sixth published book, and it would not be possible without the grace of God and support of her loved ones.

ASHLEYGODSCHILD.INK | @AUTHORASHLEYGODSCHILD

Want a free-eBook?

If you purchased the physical book, you might be eligible to receive a free digital copy. Check out my website or socials to find out more.

www.ingramcontent.com/pod-product-compliance
Lightning Source LLC
LaVergne TN
LVHW030000070825
818052LV00018B/241

* 9 7 8 1 0 6 8 9 3 4 5 4 4 *